P9-DCY-100

33,227

Dailey, Janet.

This Calder sky.

"I'm Glad You Saw Me In This."

Her voice was low—lower than a whisper, yet steady and direct. "I wanted you to see that I really could be a lady someday."

His gaze made a raking sweep of her and the dress.

"You'll never make it," he said, his dryness rustling through his voice. "I've never met a lady yet who went around in bare feet."

A green-eyed fury shattered the picture of composure as Maggie reached around for the first thing she could lay her hands on. He laughed softly because this kind of lady he could handle. He pulled her toward him and forced her hands to flatten themselves on his chest.

"I *will* be a lady," she hissed, and tried to strain free of his steel hold.

"It doesn't matter." Lazy with satisfaction, he ran his eyes over her animated features. "What man wants a tame, dull lady when he can enjoy the excitement of someone who is all woman? You don't need to change to satisfy me."

The need to impose his will on her ran through him. The rashness of it made him catch her shoulders and pull her against him. His mouth silenced her faint outcry with the domination of his hard kiss.

THIS CALDER SKY

Janet Dailey

PUBLISHED BY POCKET BOOKS NEW YORK

This novel is a work of fiction. Names, characters, places and
incidents are either the product of the author's imagination or are
used fictitiously, and any resemblance to actual persons, living or
dead, events or locales is entirely coincidental.

Another *Original* publication of POCKET BOOKS

POCKET BOOKS, a Simon & Schuster division of
GULF & WESTERN CORPORATION
1230 Avenue of the Americas, New York, N.Y. 10020

Copyright © 1981 by Janet Dailey

ISBN: 0-671-83606-4

First Pocket Books printing August, 1981

10 9 8 7 6 5 4 3 2 1

POCKET and colophon are trademarks of Simon & Schuster.

Printed in the U.S.A.

PART I

A sky of sunshine;
A sky of change;
This sky that covers
The Calder range.

Chapter I

Beneath a clear sky, the Montana plains rolled to the far horizon in an undulating sea of grass. This great, sprawling rangeland was broken by lonely buttes and wandering ravines. It was a huge, almost empty, always challenging land. Its vastness made the small man smaller and the big man king.

Where once the shaggy-maned buffalo had grazed, a herd of six hundred red-coated Hereford cattle was gathered in a pocket of the plains. Held in place by an encircling group of riders, they bawled their discontent. Into this milling confusion, cowboys working in pairs walked their horses into the herd to slowly and methodically cut out the crippled cattle—dry cows, the cows with poor spring calves, and the odd steer that had escaped the previous autumn's roundup.

Webb Calder pointed the nose of his claybank stud at the cow to be separated from the herd, then sat deep and easy in the saddle to let the horse do its work. The stallion was the color of the yellow mountain cat from which it took its name, Cougar. The instant the cow was isolated, the claybank frustrated its every attempt to rejoin the herd—getting low, coming around on a dime, and springing forward with the swiftness of a cat.

To the big-boned man in the saddle, the rangy stallion was a source of pride. He'd picked the horse out of a range-wild group of yearlings and earmarked it for his personal remuda. The breaking and training he'd done himself, turning the animal into the best cow horse on the spread. It was never something Webb Calder

3

bragged about, and any compliment was met with the casually indifferent reply, "The claybank is good."

He had a philosophy that if you were the best, you didn't have to tell anybody—and if you weren't, then you'd damned well better keep your mouth shut. He lived by it, and expected the others around him to live by it, too.

When he and the yellow horse had the cow separated from the herd, the cowboys moved in from the flanks to push the animal over the lip of the ground's pocket to where the cut of injured or inferior cattle were being held. Two more riders took his place to work the herd.

Riding back to the gather, Webb was joined by Nate Moore, who had worked the cut with him. The lank, weatherbeaten rider was one of a small corps of cowboys who had their roots dug as deep into this Montana range as Webb Calder had. Yet, some invisible quality stamped Webb Calder as the cattle owner.

For this was Calder land as far to the south as the eye could see, and beyond. All the livestock, except strays from the bordering small ranches to the north, carried the Triple C brand of the Calder Cattle Company. It was the heritage left by the first Calder who pulled up stakes in Texas and drove his herd north in 1878 to find free grass. That ancestor, Chase Benteen Calder, had carved out an empire that was measured in square miles numbering nearly six hundred. He'd held it against warring bands of renegade Indians, homesteaders, and jealously ambitious neighboring ranchers. He'd paid for it with Calder blood, nourished it with his sweat and the bones of drought-stricken cattle, and buried the Calder dead under the Montana grass.

Of the score of cowboys who had made the drive with Chase Benteen Calder, most had drifted, but a few had stayed to build a new life in this raw land. These men formed the nucleus of the group of forerunners to Nate Moore, Virg Haskell's wife, Ruth, Slim Trumbo, Ike Willis, and a handful of others, born and raised on the Calder ranch, like Webb. Their loyalty was a deep-seeded thing, ingrained into their souls as surely as if they carried the Triple C brand.

This thread of continuity ran through each generation, tying them together. The old ones eventually gave way to young blood, bringing change without ever changing.

Cresting the rise of the untamed plain, Webb reined in his horse.

Satisfaction ran easy through him as he surveyed the scene before him, the teamwork of all the riders working the herd with efficient, well-oiled precision. He liked it best when he could get out among them. Although he was there out of necessity, since his decision determined which was the poorer stock to be culled from this herd, the sheer pleasure of the work made him take part in the actual cutting of the cattle.

The pressures and responsibilities were enormous and endless for the man who owned a ranch as vast as this. New salesmen or cattle buyers often commented on its size, and Webb was fond of quipping dryly, "It takes a big chunk of ground to fit under a Calder sky." He didn't know how it ranked against other big ranches in the country, whether it was first, second, third, or far down on the list. If anyone asked him, he couldn't have answered and he didn't care enough to check. His only interests lay in making it prosper and keeping it intact for his son.

The responsibilities were heavy, but so was the power he wielded. Webb Calder believed himself to be a fair man. There were some who would say he was exacting. And still others would claim that he ruled with an iron hand. Resentment born out of envy and jealousy made him the object of hatred from a silent few. As far as Webb Calder was concerned, he had never raised his hand against a man without cause. When he acted, it was swift and with purpose. Indecision could eventually spell disaster for an outfit the size of the Triple C.

It was one of the things he'd tried to teach his son, Chase Calder, named after their Texan ancester. There was more to running a ranch than keeping books, raising cattle, and going to the bank. But how do you teach a man to be a leader, to handle men?

Before Chase had taken his first step, Webb had set the baby boy on a saddle atop an old bellmare and wrapped the tiny fists around the saddle horn to take him on his first ride. By the time Chase was two, he was given the reins. When he was five, he went on his first roundup, tied to the saddle so he wouldn't fall off if he fell asleep.

Horses and cattle were part of living. Those things Chase learned by osmosis, unconsciously absorbing the knowledge into his system until it was second nature.

But it was the subtleties of command that Webb wanted him to learn. From the time the boy had understood his first sentence,

Webb had tried to drum these things into his head, shaping and molding Chase to take over the ranch someday. He'd warned Chase that as his son, he would have to work longer, be smarter, and fight rougher than any man-jack out there. No favor would ever be granted him by Webb—no concession would ever be made because Chase was a Calder. There would be no special privileges because he was the rancher's son. In fact, the reverse would be true. In his teens, Chase had the hardest jobs, the rankest horses, and the longest hours of any man on the place. Any problems were his to solve. If there was trouble, he had to be man enough to fight his way out of it, either with his fists or his wits. Chase couldn't come to his father and expect help. Webb pushed him as hard as he dared without breaking the boy's spirit.

Even as Webb Calder watched the two dozen horsemen at work, he unconsciously and instinctively kept an eye on his son. Chase was taller than the average cowboy, wide in the shoulders and solid in the chest, yet youthfully lean and supple with a rider's looseness about him. The sun had burned a layer of tan over hard and angular Calder features. Dark-haired and dark-eyed, he seemed older than twenty-two—except when he smiled. Then he seemed careless and guileless. His son was still an unknown quantity to Webb. Maybe some might think he demanded too much, but he was firmly convinced it was the tough things that were good for a man.

The horse beside the claybank blew out a relaxed snort, making Webb shift his glance to Nate Moore. He was building a smoke and licked the paper with a stingy tongue. Without looking up, he spoke. "He's a good boy." He guessed the object of Webb's thoughts.

"Lil would be proud of him." Webb uttered his late wife's name and broke a silence that had lasted more than twenty years since her death. Time had erased the grief of his loss. Now the memory of her was another tradition.

It was something an outsider couldn't understand—this lack of expression the true Western man showed when he lost a comrade or a loved one—the failure to reveal keen sorrow. What a man felt was kept inside. The face an outsider saw looked cold and unemotional. Yet beneath the hard exteriors of these men, there was all the delicate sensitivity of a woman, hidden from view.

Revealing it displayed weakness. This was a land where only the strong survived.

"Yes, she would," Nate spoke with the cigarette in his mouth and squinted his eyes at the pungent smoke curling from it. The expression deepened the sun-creased lines splaying from the corners of his eyes. Without turning his head, his attention shifted to the young cowboy, Buck Haskell, riding on the same side of the herd where Chase was. For apparently no reason, Buck had spun his sorrel horse to face the opposite direction and spurred it toward a slight gap between riders, reaching an invisible point the instant a cow attempted to break from the herd. Respect glinted in the older cowhand's eyes. "That Buckie has more cow sense than some cowboys three times his age," Nate declared. "And how he loves those rank broncs. The more contrary they are, the better he likes 'em."

Webb's mouth tightened. "Yeah, and he's always got his rope down. I've never caught him at it, but I know he does."

"Hell!" Nate chuckled. "Every young cowboy is going to sneak off and rope something now and then."

Webb conceded that with a lift of his heavy brows. "Buck is a likable boy, but I worry about that wild streak in him."

With curly blond hair, blue eyes, and a perpetual grin, Buck was Virg and Ruth Haskell's son, born two days before Chase. When Webb's wife, Lillian, didn't have enough milk to breast-feed Chase, Ruth had taken over as wet-nurse. A year and a half later, after Lil had died, Ruth cooked and kept house for Webb. So Buck and Chase had been raised practically as brothers. It was natural that Webb took extra interest in Buck.

The hand-rolled cigarette never left Nate's mouth, but he managed to pull the corners into a dry smile. "You're forgettin', Webb. We were wilder than that when we were twenty-two."

He exchanged a wry glance with the cowboy. "Maybe so."

From the broken land to the north, a trio of riders approached the herd's gathering point. Webb centered his gaze on the short, wiry rider a half-stride in the lead. His face lost its expression, becoming heavy-boned and hard.

"Who's that with O'Rourke?" He didn't take his eyes from the owner of the small, two-bit spread on a north strip of the Calder boundary.

Nate looked, his eyes narrowing less from the smoke and more from recognition. "His boy. The skinny one must be his girl." He had pulled the warmth from his voice, making it flat.

As he skimmed the pair riding with Angus O'Rourke, Webb inspected first the gangling eighteen-year-old boy with lank black hair sticking out from beneath his hat. The boy kept looking at his father, seeking some form of guidance. The girl was a small slip of a thing, looking more like a young boy than a girl. There was a glimpse of the slick, black sides of her hair beneath the hat, but Webb couldn't tell whether it was cut that short or pushed under the crown. Both the shirt and the Levi's appeared to be cast-offs of her brother's. Both were too large, making her look all the more skinny and shapeless. Except for the heavy fringe of lashes around her green eyes, there was nothing about the set of her features to distinguish her from an immature boy. There were spurs on the heels of her rundown boots, an old and cracked pair of leather gloves on her hands, and an ill-fitting jacket dwarfing her small frame. The sight of her rankled Webb.

"A girl shouldn't be doing a man's work," he muttered and turned his head to thrust his hard gaze at Nate. "You ride down there and tell the men to watch their language. If I hear so much as a 'goddamn' out of them with that girl around, there's going to be hell to pay when she leaves."

Nate pinched the fire off the end of his cigarette, letting the ember fall into the cuff of his denims, where it was crushed dead. The unsmoked portion of the cigarette was tucked away in his pocket as he reined his mount toward the cowboys working the herd.

Webb watched him leave. The modern world may have advanced into the space age with computers and high technology, but there were sections of the West where time had changed very little. Everything was more mechanized, but most of the work was still done on horseback.

The old codes lingered. Women were scarce and treated with respect until they showed they didn't deserve it. A man settled his own problems; he didn't take them to someone else. It wasn't hard to understand when put in perspective. In the case of the Triple C, there was a thirty-five-mile-long driveway before you reached the front porch of the main house. A respectable-sized town of more than a population of one hundred could be a hundred miles away, and more.

The Calder ranch sat on an area of land larger than the state of Rhode Island. With the kind of power that gave Webb Calder, he was virtually his own law, answerable to almost no one but God Almighty. Wisely, he never tried to ride roughshod over anyone else, only now and then letting his authority be felt. He turned a blind eye to the dirt-farming Andersen family trying to eke out a living on a half-section of ground on his east boundary. Webb knew they butchered a steer or two of his each year, but he wouldn't see women and children go hungry. But God help the man who lifted his hand against the Triple C for his own gain.

His gaze narrowed in silent speculation on Angus O'Rourke, who was riding toward him. The man spent too much time dreaming and found too many excuses for why he couldn't succeed. O'Rourke was a weak man, always wanting the easy way. There wasn't any place for that kind in this country. Sooner or later they were weeded out.

The hard, fixed stare from Calder made Angus uncomfortable. How he'd love to ride up and spit in the man's eye. He licked his dry lips nervously, telling himself that the day would come when he wouldn't have to kowtow to the likes of Webb Calder. But the assurance was old and rang hollow in his mind. He'd been a dark, handsome man once, with glib Irish charm, but lines of dissipation were beginning to take away his looks, and people no longer believed in his grandiose plans for the future, having heard too many in the past that came to naught.

"If he asks us anything, what should we say?" The anxiously whispered question came from his son.

Angus didn't turn his head or look around to answer. "Don't say anything. I'll do the talking."

"I told you we should have hazed those thirty head back across the fence last week, Pa," the girl stated calmly.

"And I told you they needed a few more days of good grass, Maggie!" The argument had already been hashed over several times. "Those cows just strayed, that's all. And we're just here to cut out our strays, like we always do."

He reined his horse down to a walk to cross the last few yards to Webb Calder, stopping at a right angle to him. Flashing the man one of his patented smiles, he respectfully touched a finger to the pointed brim of his Stetson.

"Good morning, Mr. Calder." Angus O'Rourke sounded deliberately cheerful and carefree.

"Angus." The stone-faced man with the hard eyes simply nodded in response to the greeting.

Irritation rippled through Angus. He was angry with himself for not calling Calder by his first name, and putting them on equal terms. The man had a way of making him feel worthless and a failure. Hell, he was a rancher, too, the same as Calder . . . in his mind. But Angus hid his bitterness well.

"It's a fine day, isn't it?" he remarked with a broad, encompassing sweep of the clear sky. "It's mornings like this that make you forget the long winter behind you. The meadowlarks out there singing away. Wildflowers are sprouting up all over, and those little white-faced calves all shiny and new." It was a few seconds before he realized his prattle was making no impression on Webb Calder. Again, Angus checked his angry pride and hid it behind a smile. "You remember my son, Culley, and my daughter, Maggie."

Webb Calder acknowledged the boy's presence with a nod. The black-haired boy paled under the look and mumbled a stiff, "Morning, sir." Then Calder looked at the girl.

"Shouldn't you be in school, Maggie?" It was a question that held disapproval.

Actually, her name wasn't Maggie. It was Mary Frances Elizabeth O'Rourke, the same as that of her mother, who had died four years ago. But having two women in the family with the same name had been too confusing. Somewhere along the line, her father had started calling her Maggie, and it had stuck.

She shrugged a shoulder at the question. "My pa needed me today," she explained.

The truth was she missed more days of school than she attended. In the spring and fall, her father claimed he needed her to help on the ranch. Maggie had grown to realize that he was too lazy to work as long and as hard as he would have to by himself. The ranch was such a shoestring operation that they couldn't afford to hire help, so her father took advantage of her free labor.

During the winter, the tractor was broken down half the time, which meant they didn't have a snow blade to clear the five-mile drive to the road where she could catch the school bus. When her mother was alive, she'd saddled the horses and ridden with Culley and Maggie to the road on those occasions, then met them with the horses when the bus brought them back in the afternoon. But it was always too cold and too much trouble for her father.

Maggie no longer missed going to school. She had outgrown her clothes and had little to wear, except blue jeans and Culley's old shirts. At fifteen, nearly sixteen, she was very conscious of her appearance. She had tried altering some of her mother's clothes to fit her, but the results had been poor at best. None of her classmates had actually ridiculed the way she dressed, but Maggie had seen their looks of pity. With all her pride, that had been enough to prompt her into accepting the excuses her father found for her to stay home.

Her mother had been adamant that both of her children receive an education. It was something Maggie remembered vividly, because it was one of the few issues that the otherwise meek woman wouldn't be swayed from, not by her husband's anger or his winning charm. So Maggie kept her schoolbooks at home and studied on her own, determined not to fail her mother in this, as her father had failed her so often.

The disapproval that was in Webb Calder's look just reinforced her determination to keep studying. Maggie made no excuses for what her father was—a weak-willed man filled with empty promises and empty dreams. All the money in the world wouldn't make her father into the strong man Webb Calder was. It was a hard and bitter thing to recognize about your own father. And Maggie resented Webb Calder for presenting such a stark example of what her father could never be.

Realizing the conversation was going nowhere, Angus O'Rourke turned his gaze to the herd gathered in the hollow of the plains. His face took on the expression of one reluctant to leave good company but had work to be done.

"Well, I see a Shamrock brand or two in the herd." He collected the reins to back his horse before turning it toward the cattle. "I'll just cut out my few strays and head them back to their own side of the fence."

"I'll have one of my boys help you." Webb started to raise a hand to signal one of his men.

"We can manage," Maggie inserted. They may be poor, but she wasn't short on pride. She'd been taught by her mother never to accept favors unless she could return them someday, and it was ludicrous to think a Calder would ever need a favor from them.

Webb Calder's hand remained poised midway in the air while he looked silently at her father for confirmation that they wanted no help. "The three of us can handle it," her father stated to back up her claim, although he would have readily accepted the offer if she hadn't spoken up.

The hand came down to rest on the saddlehorn. "As you wish, Angus."

As he turned his horse, Angus flashed Maggie a black look and rode toward the herd. She and Culley trailed after him. Feeling the Triple C riders looking at them, Maggie sat straighter in the saddle, conscious of their overall shabby appearance, from their clothes to their ragged saddle blankets.

From the far side of the herd, Chase watched the motley trio of riders approach. Nate Moore had already passed the old man's orders around, so he knew one of the three riders was female. Buck let his horse sidle closer to Chase.

"How do you tell which one's the girl?" Buck's low voice was riddled with biting mockery.

"It must be the small one." Chase let a smile drift across his face. "She's supposed to be the youngest."

"She's young, all right," Buck agreed dryly. "I like my women with a little more age on 'em and more meat on their bones. Crenshaw was telling me this morning that Jake Loman has him a new blonde 'niece' working in his bar."

"That right?" Chase murmured, aware, as everyone was, that Jake's "nieces" were prostitutes. "That man does have a big family, doesn't he?"

Buck grinned. "When this roundup is over, you and me are going to have to check her out. She might know some new tricks of the trade."

"Another week of looking at these cattle, and I'll be satisfied if all the new girl knows is the old tricks," Chase replied and turned his horse to head off an errant cow, succeeding in changing its mind about leaving the herd.

By then, Buck had returned to his former position several yards ahead of Chase. And there was no purpose in trying to resume that particular conversation. The O'Rourke family worked the herd to cut out their strays, while Chase and the other riders kept the cattle loosely bunched.

Chapter II

During the noon break, the cowboys switched again to fresh horses from the remuda string held in a rope corral close to the camp. Chase swung his saddle onto a blood bay gelding with a white snip down its nose, and pulled the cinch tight. As he stepped into the stirrup and swung aboard, Buck rode by on a blaze-faced roan.

"Hurry up there, pilgrim. We're burnin' daylight." Buck admonished in a poor imitation of a John Wayne drawl.

Chase held in a sigh. From the day he could remember, Buck had laughed, joked, and grinned his way through each hour. He appeared never to take anything seriously. Reining his horse around, Chase fell in alongside him.

"You're a hopeless case, Buck," he declared with a brief shake of his head.

"I know it, but ain't it fun!" He grinned so often, there were already permanent grooves in his cheeks, and laughter lines fanned into the corners of his eyes. "I've been thinking, Chase," Buck said very sober and straight-faced. "It wouldn't be right for both you and me to visit Jake's niece at the same time."

"Why is that?" Chase gave him a slow sideways look, knowing he was being set up for something.

"Once that little gal gets a look at this face and this body, she's going to forget you're even around. That just wouldn't be fair. We're practically brothers."

"Buck, you have to be the most conceited man I know." There

14

was a rueful lift to one corner of Chase's mouth, slanting it at a mocking angle.

Buck was acquiring a reputation as a ladies' man, not wholly unjustified. There was something about his engaging smile and the laughing wickedness in his eyes that the women went for. Through tall tales, wild flattery, and sheer persistence, Buck eventually wore down any woman's resistance. It wasn't Chase's style, although he usually got what he went after, too.

The remark only drew a laugh from Buck. "I've told you before, Chase, that I'm really you and you're really me. My momma just switched us when we were babies so she could have the handsomest one for her own," he said, repeating his often-told theory with a twinkling look.

"Is that right?" Chase mocked his friend with a challenge. "Then why is it you have curly hair and blue eyes like Miss Ruth, instead of brown hair and eyes like me and my dad?"

"Hell, I ain't figured that out, either!" Laughter peeled from Buck's throat, ringing loud and hearty.

The thunder of running hooves attracted their attention to the herd they were approaching. A cow had been separated from the others, a Shamrock brand on its hip. Now it was bolting for freedom, its tail high in the air. Pursuing it was the young O'Rourke girl. Chase watched her force the cow to turn, then manhandle her horse onto its haunches, and roll it back to keep the cow from taking off again, slapping a coiled rope against her thigh.

"That little gal sure can ride," Buck remarked. "She's making that heavy-headed nag do things it didn't know it could do."

"You spoke too soon," Chase said as the cow made another lunge for freedom. When the girl stopped the horse and tried to haul it around on a pivot, the bay couldn't get its legs under itself and lost its balance. The girl was catapulted from the saddle as it went to its knees. She hit the ground hard and didn't immediately move. "I'll see if she's okay." Chase spurred his horse forward.

Half a dozen other riders had seen the spill, too. If the downed rider had been a man or a boy, they would have waited to let him get up on his own. But the fallen rider was a girl, and that made all the difference.

Chase reached her first, dismounting and walking to where she was sprawled face down in the grass. She had just started to shakily push herself up from the ground. Her hat was knocked askew, but the coiled lariat was still in her hand.

"Are you hurt?" he asked.

"No."

He heard the broken, airy sound to her voice and guessed she'd had the wind knocked out of her. Bending, Chase took hold of her arm. "I'll help you up."

As he began to lift her, he reached with his other hand to catch her under the opposite arm and stand her up. The unbuttoned jacket was hanging open. When his hand slipped inside, it closed around a soft, budding breast. For an instant, he was stunned by the rounded shape hidden under the oversized clothes.

Before he could move his hand, she had found her feet. "Take your dirty, lousy paws off me!" She knocked his arm down. The violence of her action caused her hat to fall off, and a swathe of long black hair spilled free to ripple in black waves nearly to her waist. "What do you think you're doing?"

Chase released her arm. "I'm sorry, Miss."

As he apologized, his dark eyes were taking in the changes in her appearance, the mass of black hair, the embarrassed flush to her cheeks, and the blazing fires in her angry green eyes. Perhaps his apology would have been accepted if his curious gaze hadn't wandered down to her opened jacket, trying to see the jutting roundness his hand had felt.

The coiled lariat was in her right hand. She lifted it to strike at him, a stream of abuse coming from her lips. Chase raised his arm to ward off the blow and backed up. But she came after him, whipping him with the coiled rope. He shielded himself with upraised arms and continued to retreat.

"I told you I was sorry," he reminded her tersely, holding his anger while feeling like a fool for being beaten up in front of all these men by a young girl.

"Oowee! Look at that little gal give Chase hell!" Buck's voice taunted from the sidelines, where the other riders were smiling and chuckling at his predicament. "Go after him, honey!"

That did it. The next time she swung the rope, Chase ducked it and grabbed her wrist, wrenching the lariat from her grip with the other hand. When she tried to hit at him with her free hand, he captured it, too. Her head was thrown back to glare up at him, her breath coming in short, angry spurts.

"You crazy little spitfire, stop it!" Chase shook her hard once. "If you don't start behaving yourself, I'm going to use this rope on your backside."

Her eyes dared him to try. "Give me my rope," she ordered.

The heat of anger—or something equally as violent—was running through his veins. Chase didn't take time to sort it out. All his muscles were coiling into tight bands, a raw tension building inside of him and seeking an outlet.

"Maggie!" Angus O'Rourke came striding up to take the matter out of Chase's hands. "What on earth were you doing, girl?" Chase released her into his custody and took a wary step away. "Now you are going to apologize to Mr. Chase Calder for making him look like a fool in front of all these men," Angus ordered.

Chase didn't feel the last phrase was necessary. It was a little man's dig at the public humiliation of a big rancher's son. His jaw hardened as the girl's eyes swept the onlooking group of riders before returning to him with a taunting gleam. A nerve twitched along his cheekbone, the only visible indication of his inner feelings.

"Tell him you're sorry," her father urged.

Chase knew she wasn't a damned bit sorry, and neither was O'Rourke. He wouldn't accept an apology forced from her. "Let it ride, O'Rourke," he mumbled, and walked to his horse.

Buck was on the ground, holding the reins to both his and Chase's mount. He handed the latter to Chase, his blue eyes dancing with wicked mischief. Buck said nothing, wise to the taut control Chase was exercising over his anger.

While Chase mounted, the girl had turned her back to him and was winding her black hair into a coil to fit under the tall crown of her hat. With that accomplished, she swung into her saddle and rode off with her father, not glancing again in Chase's direction.

"You sure did have your hands full with that wildcat," Buck commented, deciding a safe amount of time had passed. "What set her off, anyway?"

"I rubbed her the wrong way," Chase replied coldly.

"Buck!" There was no mistaking the commanding voice of Webb Calder. He rode his horse into the center of the riders. "You heard my order this morning. No swearing in front of the girl. You are on foot the rest of the day." The punishment was severe for someone like Buck, who thrived on the excitement of horse and rope.

"Hell, it just slipped out!" Buck protested.

"Two days on foot. It slipped out again."

"What?" Buck gave a vivid display of incredulous astonishment, his arms lifted from his sides in a gesture of innocence. "She can't hear me, not from clear over there!"

"Three days. That's for arguing." Webb never backed down. He was harder on those he liked. Lifting the reins, he started to turn his horse.

Buck's hands moved to his hips as he shook his head in disgust. "Shi——"

The word was never finished as Webb Calder turned back. "Do you want me to make it four days, Buck?"

He swept the dusty black Stetson from his hand and threw it to the ground. "Sweet jumpin' jehosaphats!" Buck expelled the words in a rush.

A smile cracked the sternness of Webb Calder's expression. "Now you've got the idea, Buck." Touching a heel to the horse's flank, he started it forward.

"Three days," Buck grumbled.

"I'll take your horse back to the remuda." Nate Moore edged his horse up and reached down to grab the trailing reins.

When Chase started to ride away, Buck caught at his bridle to stop him. "Put a word in with your old man. I didn't do anything to deserve three days."

"Speak to him yourself." Chase knew better than to ask a personal favor from his father. Buck knew the rules, but he always believed there was a way around them.

Returning to the herd, Chase took his place while O'Rourke finished his cut. It was a slow business due to the small rancher's lack of trained horseflesh and the inordinate number of strays in the herd. Any one of a dozen Triple C cowboys could have finished it in a third less time, and all of them were itching to do so, including Chase, but without an order from his father, they sat in their saddles and watched. O'Rourke and his son worked the cows, while the girl held their gather some distance away, beyond the range of Chase's vision, behind another one of those low rises in the deceptively flat-looking plains. Her image kept slipping into his mind, the coiling tightness within him never fully released.

The branding fires were hot when Angus rode through the herd the last time and found no more Shamrock cattle. He signaled to the ramrod Nate Moore that his cut was finished, and rode out from the Triple C herd. The impatient expressions of the riders indicated that his ineptness had caused an unnecessary delay. His mind had a ready excuse because he couldn't afford the high-priced cutting horses they rode. Never once did O'Rourke consider the hours of training that went into making such an animal, hours he wouldn't spend trying to improve the ability of his grade horses.

Angus knew that the delay would work to his advantage, so he convinced himself the slowness had been deliberate. If the Calders were impatient to get on with the work, he would be ignored as an irritating nuisance that was finally out of their way. While he was silently congratulating himself for being so intelligent, he filed away a mental reminder to explain to his son how cleverly he had planned everything.

Angus' pleasure was fleeting, vanishing the instant he saw Webb Calder positioned between himself and the cattle Culley and Maggie were holding. His throat and mouth became dry, and he could feel his palms sweating. There was no choice but to ride up to Calder. Silently, Angus cursed that the man had no right to sit there like some goddamned king expecting everyone to tremble before him.

"Sorry for the delay, Mr. Calder." There, he'd done it again, Angus realized in frustration—humbled himself to the man. "We'll be on our way now."

Webb Calder made no comment. His gaze swept to the Shamrock cattle bunched beyond him to his left, deliberately drawing attention to them. "I count thirty-seven head, plus calves. That's quite a number to *stray* onto Calder grass."

Nervous sweat was forming beads on his upper lip, but Angus forced out a smile and a laugh. "You know how it is, Calder. A cow sees grass on the other side of the fence and finds a way to get to it. They don't respect such things as boundaries." His gaze skittered away from the hard stare to look at the thick grass he stood on. There was enough graze on this range to support half again as many cattle on it than Calder ran. The man should share his plenty with those who had less. "My few head didn't deprive your herd of any graze," he added resentfully.

"I don't graze my pastures to the roots," Calder snapped and carried the statement no further, but Angus understood the implications of it. He bristled at the inferred criticism that he was mismanaging his land, never admitting the observation was justified. "I'll buy your story this time that all those cattle *strayed*. You start riding that fence line, O'Rourke—or my men will do it for you. If you can't keep your cattle on your side of the fence, I will."

He paled at the threatening tone. "Culley and I are going to make that fence tight first thing tomorrow, Mr. Calder. You don't need to have any worry on that score. It's been a hard winter, and being short of help like I am, I had to let some things slide to take care of others, but you can rest assured, Mr. Calder, that you aren't going to have any problems with my fence."

"I know I won't." Webb reined his horse away and urged it into a canter toward his herd.

Angus turned his horse in a quarter-circle to watch Calder leave. The quaking was replaced with anger. He spat onto the ground. "The greedy bastard. So high and mighty." His mouth curled in bitterness. "My day will come. You just wait and see." He slammed his spurs into his mount and sawed roughly on the reins, spreading the horse's mouth to keep it from bolting into a gallop toward the bunched Shamrock cattle.

"What did Mr. Calder say to you?" Culley blurted out the question the instant Angus reached them.

"He was just throwing his weight around." He shifted in the saddle, avoiding his children's eyes. "Let's get these cows drifting home."

Maggie glanced from her father to the disappearing rider and made her own guess about the conversation. Slapping the coiled lariat against her thigh, she started her side of the cattle moving east, while her brother worked the other flank. They would turn them north later, at the river crossing.

Hazing the herd toward home ground required little conscious attention. Maggie's actions were almost automatic, leaving her a lot of free time to ponder the day's events. The incident with Chase Calder stood out sharply in her mind, partly because she had been so embarrassed to have taken that spill in front of so many expert riders, and partly because they'd come to her aid because she was a girl, thus, supposedly less able to take care of herself.

But mostly it was because of those fleeting seconds when Chase Calder's hand had inadvertently closed on her breast. The strangeness of the sensation had tingled through her like an electric shock, exciting in the frightening kind of way that something forbidden usually is. Her initial anger had been a direct result of that rush of panic.

Then, when she'd looked into his face and seen the recognition of her as a woman, she'd been hurt because he hadn't seen it before. Had she been beneath his notice? She'd seen him more than half a dozen times in the last couple years when she'd gone to town for supplies. Hadn't he ever looked at her before?

She would have been less than honest with herself if she hadn't admitted that she had watched him with a certain amount of interest. After all, he was a rich, young, rancher's son, the object of a lot of girls' fantasies. Even discounting who he was, Chase was roughly good looking in the Calder way.

Her glance strayed down to the baggy Levi's she was wearing. She wasn't always going to wear somebody else's clothes. She wasn't going to live the kind of life that her mother had known with her father. She was going to be somebody—the lady her mother had always wanted her to be—someone important. People were going to go out of their way to speak to her on the street and not shake their heads in pity when she went by.

Her mother. She had been such a gentle woman, so slim and fragile, old before her time. Maggie had been only twelve when she died. The cause of death had officially been attributed to pneumonia, but Maggie knew her mother had literally worked herself to death. She could remember her clearly—always working from the dark of morning to the dark of night, always struggling to maintain a decent home for her family, always defending her husband's failures, and never complaining. Maggie had grown up protective of her mother, quick to defend her when her father complained that dinner wasn't on the table the minute he walked in. She didn't condemn her mother for her self-effacing attitude; rather, she considered her mother had been misguided. There was nothing self-effacing about Maggie.

Ambition burned in her. Not the dreamy kind her father had.

Hers was fierce and consuming, driving her to obtain an education even without regular schooling, and to secret away nickels and dimes she had squeezed out of the slim amount her father gave her to buy their food. Someday she'd have the money saved to leave, and no one was going to stop her.

Maybe she would come back someday, wearing one of those elegant dresses like the models in the fashion magazines. She'd love to see the looks on people's faces. She smiled just thinking about it.

The point where they would ford the river was just ahead on their left. Maggie fell back to the rear of the herd as they angled the cattle toward the bank, bunching them closer together. The river was as high as it was ever going to get. Winter run-offs and spring rains made it chest-deep, except where there were deeper pockets. At the ford, the river ran wide and shallow, from ankle-deep most of the year, to thigh-deep in the spring.

The clean, clear sight of it winking at her through the cotton-woods on the banks reminded Maggie how grimy and sweaty she was. They'd been without running water in the house for almost two weeks since the pump to the water well broke down. Her father had been tinkering with it—with no success. She'd been hauling what water they needed from the barn, which was supplied by a different well. The prospect of hauling and heating enough water for a bath seemed daunting in light of the chores to be done and the supper still to be prepared when they reached home.

The riverbank began to slope gently to the water, worn down by years of crossings. They turned the cattle down the slope, bunching them tightly. The leading cows balked at entering the water. Yipping and whistling, they pushed the rear ones forward, forcing the leaders into the water. The crossing was accomplished with little fuss, the sluggish current offering no problems.

Maggie dropped back to ride beside her father. From this point on, it was an easy mile's ride to the fence line. Between her father and Culley, they could handle the cattle with no difficulty. Having risen at daybreak to help with the morning chores and working every hour since, Maggie felt entitled to a half-hour or more of respite and the chance to actually immerse herself in water instead of merely sponging off the day's dirt.

"You and Culley can take them on from here," Maggie said.

"Where do you think you're going?" Her father shot her a challenging look.

"Swimming." She tossed the answer over her shoulder as she reined the horse away from him and back toward the river.

"There's work to be done!" he shouted.

"I'm sure it will be waiting for me when I get home."

"I didn't keep you home from school today so you could swim in the river," he called after her.

As she rode away, Maggie didn't look back or give any sign that she'd heard him. Angus shook his head in frustration. He just didn't understand that girl—always talking back to him, never showing him any respect. She was the image of his dear, sweet Mary Frances, but she had neither her gentleness of spirit, nor her softness.

Lord knows, he'd tried his best to be a good father to her. They had a place to sleep and food on the table. He'd promised to buy her all the clothes and pretty things a young girl should have. Nothing he ever did was enough for that girl. She was a regular hellion; never gave him a minute's peace.

Now, Culley was a good lad. He always listened and understood why things were the way they are. Angus wished Maggie were more like her brother. But Culley was a boy. It was easier to relate to a son. A father had to choose his words so carefully with a daughter. If Mary Frances were alive, she'd explain things to Maggie and make her understand that it wasn't his fault they were poor. It was men like Webb Calder who wouldn't give a man a chance to get ahead in this world.

Chapter III

With a deft flick of his wrist, Chase let the rope sail out and made a quick dally around the saddlehorn as the loop settled around the neck of a calf. In the work-a-day world of the cowboy, calf-roping did not entail the rump-sliding stops of the horse or the calf being jerked to the ground when it hit the end of the rope, as the rodeos depicted. With little theatrics, the calf was roped and dragged on foot to the branding crews to be vaccinated and branded.

Yet the scene held more excitement and confusion than a rodeo, in this arena of wild range land under acres of blue sky. Men were rushing everywhere, on foot and on horseback. There was the running banter of challenges and the bawling of the calves and bellowing cattle, riders dodging ground crews in pursuit of a calf, and men ducking loops. Churning hooves had ground the grass into the dirt, exposing the soil and sending up a thin haze of dust to blur the proceedings.

The scene assaulted the senses, dizzying the eyes that tried to take in all the action, confusing the ears that tried to separate the jumble of sounds, and assailing the nose with the combining odors of sweat, manure, and burning hair.

Through the maze of man and animal, Chase towed his protesting calf. It was Buck who came trotting up to flank his calf and bring it to the ground. Sweat had made streaks of mud on Buck's face. While he stabbed a dose of vaccine into the downed calf, a second cowboy pressed the hot Triple C brand iron to the calf's hip. Then Buck was loosening the noose and casting it free to let the bawling calf race back to its momma.

As Chase began recoiling his lariat, Buck paused for a breath. "I can't take three days of this, Chase. All for one measly little 'hell.' It ain't right. It just ain't right," he insisted.

"The world is tough, Buck." The line of his mouth curved, alleviating some of its natural hardness.

"That's a profound statement coming from the heir to all this," Buck scoffed and took a tired stride after another roped calf.

The comment made no impression on Chase as he started his horse toward the herd. He accepted without question that the Calder empire would be his one day. He'd grown up with the knowledge. There had never been a moment when he'd thought of any other possibility. Someone called his name, and he stopped. Looking around, he spotted his father motioning for Chase to join him on the sidelines of the action. He walked his horse through the branding melee and reined in next to his father's stud, pushing his hat to the back of his head.

"What is it?"

"I want you to come back to the house with me for dinner tonight." At the vague surprise that leaped into Chase's eyes, his father explained, "Senator Bulfert is flying in around five. He's having dinner and spending the night with us before going on to Helena in the morning. It's time you had some firsthand experience with behind-the-scenes politicking."

"More lessons?" A reckless quality entered Chase's smile, revealing an amusement for the endless schooling by his father.

"So far, all you've learned are the basics," Webb answered with total seriousness. "If you expect to successfully run this ranch someday, you have a long way to go."

On this subject, his father had no sense of humor. Straightening in the saddle, Chase pulled his hat down low on his forehead and wiped the smile from his face. "Yes, sir."

"I know you think this ranch practically runs itself." Webb read the thoughts in his son's mind. "But when the time comes for you to take over, you are going to have your hands full, because they are going to try to take it away from you."

"You keep talking about this 'they,' but you never tell me who 'they' are." Chase couldn't imagine anyone threatening to take the ranch from him. How could they?

"That's going to be your problem, discovering which one of your friends or neighbors is making a move against you. This ranch seems secure, but it's vulnerable because it's so big." His features became tainted with a grim sadness. "Nobody really likes you when you're big, son. Sometimes that is the hardest thing to realize . . . and accept."

It seemed to Chase that his father was exaggerating, but he held his silence. He'd learned long ago there was usually a great deal of truth in what his father said, no matter how skeptically he regarded it at the time.

"I left the pickup parked at the pasture's east gate. Nate will ride along with us and bring the horses." Webb gathered his reins. "Let's go. We don't want to keep the senator waiting."

"You have the senator in your pocket, and you know it," Chase remarked dryly.

His father just smiled. "If you have a man in your pocket, he's usually pilfering."

Chuckling softly at his father's wry wit, Chase followed along to meet up with Nate Moore on the near side of the herd. When the experienced ramrod noticed Chase, his gaze swung back to Webb.

"You never said I'd be losing a man. What's the occasion?" he questioned, reining his horse alongside theirs.

"The senator is arriving to spend the night."

A dancing light entered the older cowboy's eyes, although his expression didn't change. "Old Bullfart is coming, huh?"

"Senator Bulfert is coming, yes." Webb stressed the senator's proper name, but there was no censure in his tone.

"I suppose it pays to have friends in high places," Nate conceded, "even when they stink."

"I do my best to stay upwind from him so the smell never reaches me," Webb replied and urged his horse into a reaching canter.

Both Nate and Chase quickly followed suit to keep abreast with him, but never ahead. It was one of the unwritten laws of the range—never ride ahead of the boss.

Five miles from the herd, cottonwoods thrust their greening heads onto the horizon, marking the river's course. Their route was the same one O'Rourke had taken with his cattle. The small rancher's passing was plainly marked by the trampled grass, slowly straightening. As they neared the fording place of the river, Webb

Calder slowed his horse to a canter, then a walk, his gaze running to the opposite bank.

"When the branding's done, I want you to leave a man behind to check O'Rourke's fence line, Nate," he ordered.

"Planned on it," the foreman nodded. "I thought a few too many of his cows had strayed for it to be an accident."

The comment strummed a chord in Chase's memory, taking him back to a time when he'd been twelve or thirteen. He had accompanied his father on a fall roundup. On that occasion, a different rancher had more than a hundred cattle "stray" onto the Calder range. There had been a heated and bitter argument between the rancher and his father, the rancher claiming there was more than enough graze for both of them and that his father should share it. His father had ordered the man and his cattle off Calder land and swore he'd shoot the next animal that strayed onto it.

At the time, it had seemed the man had a valid point. There was enough for all. Later when he'd questioned his father about it, Webb had explained that if he let one small rancher bring his cattle onto the Calder range, he'd set a precedent to admit all the others into his boundaries. Then it wouldn't be his land anymore. Once a line was drawn, never step back from it to draw a new one. A man had to take a stand or forever retreat.

Passing the point where the cattle tracks turned down the gently sloped bank to the river, they continued in a straight line to the east gate. The river made a sweeping bend, curving itself closer to their path. When his horse turned its head toward the river, pricking its ears in interest, Chase looked in the same direction to see what had attracted his mount's attention.

Through a gap in the trees, he saw a saddle horse tied to a log on the opposite bank. A quick eye caught the Shamrock brand on its hip and Chase reined in sharply. A frown creased his forehead as he searched for the horses of the other two riders and the reason why the O'Rourke clan had stopped there. Instead, his gaze found clothes hanging from a dead limb of the fallen log, and a second later, he saw the flash of a white body in the river. The figure surfaced and Chase saw the long black hair, wet and shining sleek in the sunlight. A cold smile touched his mouth, a glint of revenge flaring in his dark eyes.

Nate Moore was the first to notice Chase wasn't behind them.

Checking his horse to a slower walk, he turned in the saddle to look across the several yards that stretched between them. "Boy, you coming?"

"Go on ahead. I'll catch up with you." Chase absently waved them forward as he watched the nude girl in the water.

"Where are you going?" Webb stopped his horse when Chase started to turn back the way they'd come.

Chase paused long enough to answer. "To settle some unfinished business and even the score." The faint smile spread into a reckless grin as he finished turning his horse and spurred it into a canter toward the river crossing.

The sharp-eyed Nate had already spotted the reason. "The O'Rourke girl is skinny-dipping in the river."

Webb sighed in faint disgust. "Stealing somebody's clothes is a boy's prank. I thought he'd outgrown such things by now."

But Nate was less critical. "That girl stung his pride when she made him look silly in front of the boys. If I was him, I might be wanting to get my own back."

By his silence, Webb conceded there was some justification for his son's actions. He pointed his horse toward the east gate again and let it settle into its reaching walk.

Crossing the river at the ford, Chase turned his horse and followed the water course for a quarter of a mile to the spot where he'd seen the girl. He found the cut in the bank that she had used to reach the sandy bar and angled his horse down it, following the tracks of her mount. At his approach, her bay horse whickered an inquiry, but the girl splashing in the water was oblivious to his presence. Chase rode to the log and leaned sideways in the saddle to scoop up the clothes hanging on the stump of a limb.

The water was cold and invigorating. Maggie had discovered that if she kept moving, its chilling temperature was tolerable. It was a minor discomfort when measured against the pleasurable sensation of all that clear, sparkling water flowing over her skin. Along this stretch of the river, the water was only chest-deep. Maggie let her feet sink to the bottom and pushed the heavy wetness of her long hair behind her back, wiping the water from her face.

"Now, who do you suppose these clothes belong to?" The taunting question went through her like an electric shock.

She pivoted in the water, nearly losing her balance, as her rounded eyes sought the intruder. Chase Calder was leaning forward in his saddle, an arm resting on the horn, holding *her* clothes in his hand. The first shock of embarrassment gave way to outrage.

"You put those back where you found them and get out of here!" Maggie faced him, her arms floating atop the water to keep her balance.

"Are these yours?" He feigned surprise, which only angered her more.

"You know they are."

Chase held them up to examine them. "They can't be. They're a man's clothes, too big for a little thing like you," he mocked.

"They're mine—and you know it!" She had stopped moving and the chilling water began to numb her flesh. She had to hold her jaw tight to keep her teeth from chattering.

"But I don't know that," he insisted.

"You put them back, Chase Calder!" Her voice was trembling, from anger and the invading cold. "You put them back and ride out of here!"

"I can't do that." Rolling the clothes into a bundle, Chase half-turned in the saddle to tie them behind the cantle.

Maggie watched him with growing panic. "What are you doing?"

"Taking them with me, of course," he replied, finishing the tie and straightening around to gather up the horse's reins. "There's some poor cowboy walking around out there with no clothes on. We can't have that." He clicked to his horse and reined it away from the river.

Panic filled her when she realized he was actually going to leave with her clothes. "No! They're mine! You bring them back here!" Alarm was in her voice, weakening its anger to fear.

Checking his horse, he turned it in a quarter-pivot so it was standing parallel with the river. Iron hooves clattered on the sandy gravel of the bar as the horse shifted impatiently, waiting for its rider to make up his mind where they were going.

The sunlight striking the crystal-clear water of the river turned its surface to glass. From his vantage point in the saddle, Chase saw the naked white shape of her body beneath the water—slim and high-breasted. He had a young man's appetites, and the spring roundup had meant a long fasting period, so the sight of her easily aroused him.

In the beginning, Chase had intended only to take her clothes and ride off a ways before leaving them where she could find them. Now he was unconsciously changing his plans, wanting to see her without the distortion of the water to interfere with the sight.

"If they are your clothes, why don't you come and get them?" he challenged smoothly.

Maggie drew in a sharp breath, sensing a change in the air. Some new undercurrent was present, vaguely threatening. She sank a little deeper in the freezing water, its coldness lapping into the hollows of her collarbone.

"No."

"If you want them, you'll have to come get them."

"No." Her refusal was more forceful this time, but her teeth had started chattering from the numbing cold. She moved her arms in the water, trying to keep the circulation going. "You leave my clothes where you found them," she insisted in a wavering voice.

"I can't do that." He shook his head briefly and shifted in the saddle, as if making himself more comfortable. "I'll just have to wait until you come out of the water to claim them."

"I'm not coming out while you're there," Maggie retorted.

"I'm not leaving until you do." Chase could see she was shivering, and guessed the water was icy. "You'll freeze in that river. You'd better come out before you turn blue."

"I'll freeze to death before I'll ever set foot on that bank with you there!" An impotent kind of fury raged through her.

"You stupid little fool." Chase saw the mule-stubborn expression on her face, and his jaw hardened. He'd taken a position and couldn't retreat from it. That left him only one recourse—to advance. "In that case, I'll just have to come out there and get you."

Her wide-eyed look held panic. "You wouldn't dare." But there was doubt in her shivering voice.

"Wouldn't I?" He raised an eyebrow and reached for the coiled lariat tied below the saddle pommel.

His horse was instantly alert. The lariat represented the kind of work it understood and enjoyed. When its rider pointed the horse at the figure in the water, it pricked its ears curiously at the girl, then swiveled them back and forth, uncertain that its rider actually intended the human to be the objective.

Shaking out the loop, Chase walked the horse into the water, ignoring its rolling snort at this curious business. The loop of the rope was held low and free of his right side, ready to be swung into action when the time came.

For several long seconds, Maggie watched him come closer, part of her refusing to believe that he would go through with it. Then she tried to swim out of his path. Chase put the spurs to his horse, sending it plunging through the water to turn her back. The river ran past his boot tops, its temperature colder than he had realized.

As she tried to change directions and elude him again, the only sure target his rope had was her head. At this depth, the loop would lay on the surface, catching her around the neck. He had to maneuver her into shallower water, where the rope could settle around her middle. It became a cat-and-mouse game, with the outcome foredestined, because the cat was too quick and the mouse was too sluggish.

The icy temperature of the river had stiffened her muscles, making her reflexes slow and her movements uncoordinated. Maggie floundered in the deep water, going under once before her toes scraped bottom to push her to the surface. The cold had sapped her strength. Weak and quivering, she was frightened by the new danger of drowning.

When it appeared that Chase had followed her too far into the river's channel, his horse snorting nervously at the water rising midway to the point of his withers, Maggie struck out frantically for the solidness of the bank. All her effort was concentrated on trying to run as she reached belly-deep water.

A complacent smile was curving Chase's mouth. His horse had begun its turn to shore a second after the girl had made her break. It was lunging through the water after her while Chase lifted the rope to circle it above his head. While he made the calculations of distance and speed, the other part of his mind was noting the jutting swell of her profiled breast and the snow-white cheeks of her bottom as she ran from him.

The rope made two swings above his head before he let the loop sail to its target. It settled over her shoulders and Chase jerked it tight just above her elbows. The horse stopped as quickly as it could in the water to hold the rope taut.

Maggie struggled wildly, twisting and straining, trying to loosen the binding rope, animal sounds of desperation coming from her throat. Despite her struggling efforts, the tension on the rope wasn't eased. She cast a wild look over her shoulder, a curtain of wet black hair getting in her way.

With his quarry captured, Chase urged his horse forward while his eyes took in the nude beauty of her. The horse was momentarily confused by the command, trained to hold the tautness of the rope until its captive was set free, but at the insistence of its rider, the horse obeyed. Chase kept the rope tight, feeding the excess to his left hand and coiling it up.

He made no attempt to check the horse until it was alongside the stumbling, splashing, still-struggling girl. Close up, the unblemished perfection of her naked flesh was even more beautiful. Chase pulled her backward a step to draw her even with his saddle and bent down to scoop her up. The tight noose pinned her arms to her sides.

When he hooked his arm around the front of her waist, it was like grabbing hold of an icicle. Even through his jacket, he could feel her coldness. What lusting thoughts he'd possessed were overridden by concern for a person exposed too long to the river's frigid waters. He was angry with himself, disgusted by his actions. The girl was nearly frozen, and all because his damned pride had wanted revenge. Chase hauled her kicking, twisting body onto the saddle in front of him.

"Let me go!" Her wet hair draped over her breasts like swathes of black silk, while her pinned arms crossed to hide the lower, triangular patch of black hair from his sight.

A distant part of his mind noted the fury of her order. Even now, when she had to be frightened of his intentions, she didn't plead with him or show fear. There was an absent registering of respect for her indomitable spirit.

Other considerations were uppermost in his thoughts at the moment. "Hold still and I'll take the rope off of you." Chase issued the terse command while trying to hold her straining, wiggling form in the saddle, with the horse sidestepping nervously beneath its unruly burden.

She looked at him warily, not trusting him altogether. She was shivering too violently to be motionless, but she ceased struggling. As Chase relaxed his tight hold on the reins to loosen the rope, the horse started for shore. He let it go and lifted the noose over her head, tossing the lariat onto the gravel. Immediately, she tried to slide off the horse, but Chase stopped her.

"Put my jacket on," he ordered, shrugging out of it and draping it around her shoulders. She was practically engulfed in it. Chase saw the long, black lashes come together in silent appreciation for the body warmth it held.

Holding her around the waist, he stepped out of the saddle. Even dripping wet, she weighed no more than a minute. He could feel the violent tremors shuddering through her body, but she didn't make a sound, remaining rigid in his arms, rejecting his assistance. A broken limb from the dead tree rested on the sunny stretch of the sandbar. Chase set her on the ground next to it and began breaking the dried wood into pieces.

"It'll only take a couple of minutes to get a fire going," he said, but received no response.

The sun-sered wood was like tinder, catching with the first match. Chase fanned it with his hat and let it burn good for a minute, then built a tepee of fatter pieces to keep it going. The girl scooted closer to the warmth it sent out, huddling deep inside his jacket, which came all the way down to her thighs. His gaze swept over the moisture beaded on the raised flesh of her bare legs. As he began unbuttoning his shirt, she slanted him another one of those wary green looks.

Using his shirt as a towel, he began drying her legs, starting with her feet and working his way up the calves of her legs to above the knees. He rubbed hard to stimulate the circulation. His roughness brought a barely stifled sound of protest from her. Chase knew he was causing a thousand nerve ends to tingle painfully.

When he was through, he jabbed a long branch upright in the sandy soil beside the fire and draped his damp shirt over it to dry. It was only then that he became aware of the squishing wetness of his socks and boots. He pulled them off and squeezed the water from the woolen socks, laying them on the outer edge of the fire to steam.

Through all of this, Maggie watched him silently. Feeling began to steal back into her body, the shuddering reduced to occasional shivers, thanks to the warmth of the fire and the heavy, man's jacket around her.

Both her father and her brother, Culley, were small-built men.

Neither had the broad, muscular chest and arms that Chase Calder had, or that thick patch of chestnut hair on his breastbone. She studied the play of those flat, ropy muscles as he worked, all hard flesh and bone. He seemed a mountain of a man to her. A trace of awe surfaced and Maggie fought it down the only way she knew how.

"You look ridiculous in that hat with no shirt or boots," she told him.

"I do, huh?" Taking off his hat, he set it on the ground and ran a hand through the unruly thickness of his umber hair. Then he cast her a wicked glance. "You aren't exactly well dressed, either, kid."

"That's because you took my clothes." The wetness of her long hair against her skin was becoming uncomfortable. Maggie tried to lift it outside the collar, while keeping the jacket securely around her and her arms inside. "And I'm not a kid," she added in protest, still struggling with the heaviness of her hair.

"I noticed," he murmured dryly. Vividly, he remembered what she looked like beneath that jacket and could attest to the fact that she possessed a woman's body. The memory of it stirred him as he watched the trouble she was having. "I'll do that," Chase volunteered and rose to step behind her.

Starting at her cheekbones, his fingers moved down below her ears and tunneled under the heavy weight of her hair, lifting its length from under the jacket and spreading it down the outside of the back. There was a certain sensuality in holding all that hair in his hands. It burned him like a black fire. Chase released it and stepped away to pick up a stick, snapping it in two in an effort to stop the surging rush of his white-hot senses. He crouched beside her to add the broken pieces of wood to the fire.

"How old are you, Maggie?" He used her name unconsciously, riveting his gaze to the dancing flames.

"Sixteen." She bit her lip at the lie and admitted, "I will be in August."

Chase turned his head to study her, a smile slanting his mouth. "Sweet sixteen and never been kissed." There was a harsh quality to his mocking tone that didn't match the way he was looking at her.

His words caused Maggie to huddle deeper in the jacket, drawing her knees to envelop more of her legs in its hugeness.

"Clyde Barnes kissed me once when we were playing in the schoolyard."

"How old were you then?"

Her chin went a little lower and she avoided his gaze to stare at her toes. "Thirteen." There was a defensive crispness to her answer.

"Nobody can say you aren't without experience," he murmured with drawling roughness.

"I never said I was experienced." She flashed him a sideways look of injured pride. "Clyde wasn't even thirteen yet." The intensity of his gaze was more than she could hold. "I know it's different when a man kisses you."

There was a pulsebeat of silence; then his hand was on her neck, turning her head and lifting her chin toward him. "How do you know that?"

The penetrating darkness of his gaze disturbed her in an excitingly curious way that seemed to heighten all her senses. She couldn't answer him, too captured by the wild certainty that he was going to kiss her and she was going to find out for herself if it was true that a man's kiss was different.

Chapter IV

Slowly bending his head toward her, Chase exerted a slight pressure on her neck to pull her forward. She didn't try to draw away or resist him. Before his mouth touched her lips, he inhaled the fresh, clean smell of her—like the air after a summer rain. Its simple earthiness filled him. When his mouth settled onto her unparted lips, they remained motionless with innocence. He moved over their softness, seeking a response, and was dissatisfied when he didn't get it. Her uncertainty about what was expected from her was somehow transmitted to him.

Chase lifted his head a scant inch from her lips. "Don't hold your mouth so stiffly. Relax," he urged in a soothing murmur. "Let your lips move against mine."

"All right." Her sweet breath fanned him, stirring him.

This time Maggie offered a tentative response to the pressure of his mouth. She liked that funny little curling sensation it created inside her. Under his guidance, her confidence grew and was rewarded with pleasure.

His thumb began drawing lazy circles in the sensitive hollow below her ear, arousing more senses. There was so much warmth tingling through her body that Maggie found it hard to believe that only minutes ago she'd been shivering from the cold. She was trembling, but for an entirely different reason.

When Chase ended the second kiss, her lips clung to his for a brief second. She was glad when he stayed close and didn't draw away. She stared at the masculine line of the mouth that had

36

produced those wonderfully new sensations flooding through her. Her gaze wandered over the flaring width of his nose and the angular points of his cheekbones before being caught by the intensity of his eyes. Except for the burning vitality in his eyes, he could have been carved out of stone. Maggie was unaware that his extreme wants were holding him motionless. She became faintly puzzled by the luscious way she was feeling, wondering if it was normal.

The long, shaky breath she released was almost a sigh. "Are you supposed to feel all quivery inside when a man kisses you?" It was an artless question, prompted by a curiosity she couldn't contain.

"Not with every man—just one or two." His voice vibrated from someplace deep within him.

By slow degrees, Maggie began moving her lips closer to the line of his mouth. The hesitation was caused by an inner sense, warning her that this was an experiment that could get out of hand, but her natural boldness carried her past the point of caution. Chase didn't make her come all the way—meeting her at a spot in between.

This time when his mouth closed over hers, she knew exactly what to do. The eagerness of her returning kiss brought an instant, and demanding, response from him. She felt she was being eaten up, consumed whole by the ravishing hunger of his kiss. The subsequent weakness made her sway, but his free arm moved, his hand catching her shoulder to hold her steady.

He shifted his position so she didn't have to lean to reach him. The softness of her seemed boundless. Her lips yielded to the probing intrusion of his hard tongue, but her white teeth presented an irritating barrier. He withdrew. There was no need for force when instruction had already shown she was an apt pupil when properly coached.

"Open your mouth, Maggie," he murmured against the corner of her lips.

This time there was no resistance and his tongue penetrated into the dark, secret recesses of her mouth. At first, she kept her tongue pressed tightly to the bottom of her mouth, avoiding contact with his. Gradually, she relaxed, letting her tongue touch his and curl around it until the two were wildly mating, turning Chase raw with a greater need. His arm was around her, one hand splayed between her shoulder blades, while his other hand remained on the smoothness of her neck.

The bulky jacket kept him from getting as close as he wanted, the jacket and the hands and arms beneath it, holding onto it. Frustrated and unable to control the powerful and primitive desires too long suppressed, Chase untangled his mouth from hers and sought the lobe of her ear, taking it between his teeth and nibbling at it, wanting to eat all of her and feed this insatiable appetite that consumed him. His hand glided down her throat, paving the way for his kisses and pushing aside the dusty collar of his jacket to expose the hollow of her neck and shoulder. He felt her tremble and heard a faint moaning sound. He was pleased to know he was affecting her with his caresses, drawing her into eddying currents of passion with him. Yet the embrace was too one-sided. He was doing all the holding and touching. His body craved the sensation of her caress.

"Give me your hand," his husky voice instructed, and Maggie slipped a hand through the overlapping folds of his jacket.

He guided it to the solidness of his bare chest. Her fingers spread over the heat of his skin, muscles contracting in a quiver beneath her touch. She began a tactile exploration of his manly torso and found it more exciting to touch than to admire at a distance. Curling chest hairs softly brushed her sensitive palms; nerve ends tingled in delighted reaction. Muscles rippled in his shoulder and arm, and Maggie gloried in the contained strength beneath her fingers.

His mouth came back to claim her lips in a driving possession. The raw urgency of his kiss pushed her backward, his arm slowly lowering her to the ground. The jacket cushioned her naked flesh from the gravely bed of sand. His hand traced her arm, using it to insinuate his way inside the jacket. The sure, easy cupping of her breast in his palm made the intimacy seem so natural. Her fingers loosened their hold on the jacket. Somewhere, she lost the reason for keeping it shut. The coolness of the air against her skin only made the warmth of his touch all the more pleasurable; and it left her other hand free to double the amount of territory she could explore. Also, there wasn't anything in the way to stop him.

The firm roundness of her breasts was his undoing. If he had possessed the strength of will to stop before they went too far, Chase lost it at that moment. All he retained was the control to take it slow and make it an experience that would be as gratifying for her as it was going to be for him.

His thumb circled the rosy peak of a breast, feeling it grow hard under his stimulation. Then his mouth began a slow foray to its irresistible lure, but was sidetracked by other attractions on the way—the leaping pulse in her throat, the tantalizing hollow at the base of her neck, and the delectable curve of a shoulder bone. Finally reaching his destination, his tongue encircled the hard button of her breast and she breathed in sharply in reaction, drawing away from him.

Chase kissed the rounded curve. "Don't be frightened," he murmured.

Frightened. Was that what she was feeling? She was nervous, but there wasn't any fear involved. It was a sensual adventure, discovering the untapped depths of her desires. Each new touch introduced her to a whole new realm of sensation. She, who was so clear-headed, practical, and realistic, was being carried away by passion. What was more, she was enjoying every second of the dazzling journey.

Her hands glided over the bulging muscles of his arms to the back of his shoulders, silently assuring him that she wasn't afraid. A slender hand curved itself to thickly corded muscles of his neck, fingers sliding into shaggy dark hair to apply a downward pressure when his mouth opened on her breast and he took the nipple inside it. His erotic suckling caused a peculiar tightening of the muscles low in her stomach, creating a raw ache that begged to be assuaged. She writhed slightly in an attempt to ease the building pressure, tightly clenching her inner thighs together.

Aware of the signaling movement, Chase let his hand roam downward from her breast while his tongue and lips continued to give it their attention. On the slow descent, his hand caressed the curve of her waist and briefly cupped her hipbone, then paused on the quivering flatness of her lower stomach. At the slight arching of her hips against its weight, his fingers slid into the silky patch of hair and rubbed the area with a gentle firmness.

Instinctively, her hips began to move in slow, rhythmic gyrations. Sidetracking her attention, he dragged his mouth from the peak of one breast to let it climb to the crest of the other. While he teethed the pointed crown, his massaging fingers made a more intimate search until he could feel the warm moistness of her. Soft animal sounds of pleasured torment came from her throat as she writhed and arched her hips high to further his entry. She was driven wild by the sensation.

Heat flamed through him at this totally uninhibited response. With a groan, Chase ripped his mouth from her breast to bruise her lips, separating them with the hard thrust of his tongue. His own fevered throbbing was driving him; need was screaming through his system. While one hand continued to work her until she was loose and ready, the other unbuckled his belt and unfastened his Levi's. She moaned in protest when he took his hand away to hunch out of his pants.

Wedging her legs apart with his knee, he slid himself between them, priming her again with his hand before attempting entry. Hot eagerness boiled inside him, but he beat it down, probing into her by slow degrees. When he reached the thin barrier of her virgin veil, his first attempt to pierce it brought a muffled outcry of pain. She twisted away from his mouth, pushing at his chest with her hands as she tightened her legs and hips in an attempt to force him out. Chase held himself still with an effort.

"No." Her head was turned away from him, her eyes tightly shut as her hips continued to strain from him. "Don't." Her voice was husky, disturbed, but not pleading.

He stroked her hair with a trembling hand, brushing his mouth across her jaw and cheek. "It's too late, Maggie. I can't stop now," he muttered thickly. "Don't pull away from me. It will only make it worse. It always hurts the first time, but don't fight me, honey. I swear it won't hurt for long."

After a long second, Chase could feel her forcing her body to relax, but she kept her face turned away from him. He began kissing her neck while his hands slid down to hold her hips still. When he moved against her again, she tensed but didn't struggle. Chase was as gentle as he could be, but he knew it wasn't enough as her fingernails dug into his shoulders and a choked sound of pain ripped through her throat at his penetration. With slow, steady strokes, he carved out the opening. The shuddering tension of near-satisfaction grew hard within him, but he knew it was too soon and forced himself to stop to contain it.

When he ceased his movements, she slowly brought her face around. He concentrated on the ivory smoothness of her features and the vivid contrast of her black hair. He was shaken by the rare combination of pride, beauty, and strength.

"I didn't know anyone could have such beautiful white skin and hair so black—blacker than a midnight sky." His heavy-lidded gaze wandered slowly over her face and hair in loving approval.

"Is it over?" It was a quick, tightly worded question, disillusionment clouding her green eyes.

The look reminded him of a child given a lollipop that promised sweetness and tasted like chalk. A smile gentled the hard angles of his features.

"The pain is over, honey," Chase assured her softly. "Now the pleasure starts."

He brought his lips to hers, kissing them softly while his hand cupped and caressed her breast. The sure, steady stimulation by all parts of his body soon persuaded her hips to move in instinctive rhythm with him. Beads of perspiration formed on his upper lip as he sought the right ways to please her and lift her to the crescendo pitch of satisfaction while holding off his own.

Blood pounded through his veins, pulsing molten hot. He began to lose his grip on reality. There were no longer two heartbeats— one one. There weren't two bodies, but two matching halves coupled in a frenzied reunion. It went on and on for an eternity of minutes until their joy in each other reached a shuddering climax.

Holding her close against him, Chase lay on his back and stared at the dazzling blue sky overhead. Both of them were quivering in a kind of stunned aftershock. His hand was burrowed into the slight dampness of her hair, while she rested her cheek on the hard pillow of his chest. Thoroughly content, he angled his head to see the way she curled against him.

"I was right, wasn't I? I did give you pleasure." He wanted to hear her say it, to know beyond any doubt that it had been a shared experience.

She tipped her head way back to meet his eyes, boldly proud, exhibiting no shyness. "Yes." The simple affirmative answer told him all he needed to know and more.

Chase took a deep breath and forgot to let it out as his eyes ran over this girl who was all woman. In his twenty-two years, he'd known only two kinds of women—the ones you respected, and the ones you didn't. He dated the first kind and bedded the second.

Yet Maggie didn't fit into either category. She was fifteen going on twenty-six. She had been a virgin when he'd taken her, but there were no recriminating tears in her eyes now. As crazy as it sounded, he had more respect for her now than for the women society indicated deserved it. Chase realized that he didn't want it any other way.

His arm tightened around her middle to carry her with him when he sat up. He slipped a hand under her knees to lift her into the cradle of his arms as he pushed to his feet. Automatically, she curved a hand around his neck for support. Her glance was curious, but she asked no questions.

Chase stopped beside the upright stick he'd draped his shirt on. "Grab my shirt."

He waited until she had unhooked it, then carried her to the river, setting her feet down by the water's edge. Taking the shirt from her, he dipped it in the water, then turned back to her to gently wash the dark stain of lost virginity from between her legs. When he had finished, she reached for the shirt. Puzzled, Chase hesitated before releasing it to her. He watched while she rinsed it, then straightened to wash him. He was moved by the pink color in her cheeks, a sign she was slightly embarrassed by her boldness.

Taking the shirt away from her and tossing it aside, he crooked a finger under her chin and lifted it. She looked into his eyes with a natural directness, the top of her head barely reaching his shoulder. The smallness of her made Chase feel massive, the protective male instinct surging strong within him.

"Maggie." All the hundreds of things he didn't know how to say were wrapped up in that one word. His hands framed her face as he bent to kiss her with a gentle fierceness. Her slender hands gripped his wrists, holding onto him. Reluctantly, Chase lifted his head, unaware of the stirring breeze that swept his shirt into the river, where the sluggish current caught it and carried it downstream. "It's getting late." A grim smile touched his mouth as he let her go and walked back to the dying fire.

Pulling on his pants, he didn't bother to zip them yet and reached to pick up his nearly dry socks, standing on one foot to put them on. He was tugging his boots on when he noticed Maggie watching him, his jacket clutched in front of her for warmth, still naked beneath it.

"What's the matter?" Chase straightened, raising a puzzled eyebrow.

"You haven't given me back my clothes," she reminded him.

The sound of his throaty laughter made her smile. The world had never been more perfect than it was at this minute. Maggie wasn't sure what she was feeling, except that it was right. Which was why she didn't examine it too closely, in case its beauty faded like one of her father's elusive dreams.

Chase's horse had wandered under the cottonwoods to graze on the tender young stalks of grass growing at the base of their trunks. The trailing reins had kept it from straying very far. It shied when Chase approached. A softly spoken command had it standing quietly while Chase untied the bundle on the back of the saddle. Returning to the fire circle, he tossed the clothes to her.

While she dressed, he walked to the river's edge for his shirt, not staying to watch her, as she had watched him. Maggie supposed there were some people who would have considered it improper the way she had stared so openly at his physique. But she didn't understand why it should be wrong to admire a man's body. Men stared at women all the time. She was tucking her shirt into her jeans when Chase came back, still shirtless, to pick up his jacket.

As he shrugged his shoulders into it, Maggie asked, "Where's your shirt?"

"It must have been blown into the river and sunk." He didn't sound concerned about it, but she guessed he probably had a closetful of shirts. So what was the loss of one? He kicked gravel onto the fire and scattered the embers. "Are you ready to leave?"

"Sure." She piled her hair under her hat as she walked to the log where she'd left her horse tied.

Chase was in the saddle and waiting for her when she mounted. "I'll ride with you part of the way," he said.

Maggie led the way through the trees and up the shallow ravine to the wide, open plains. Facing the broken ridges to the north, she set her horse at a canter. Chase moved his mount abreast of hers. They cut the trampled trail the Shamrock cattle had left and turned onto it. It was a short mile to the boundary fence where strands of barbed wire forced them to stop.

Dismounting, Maggie walked to a wooden post and kicked out the stone, wedging it in the posthole. Drooping wire permitted the post to sag flat on the ground. Chase stepped on it, holding it down while Maggie led her horse across the downed barbed wire. Together, they set the post in the ground again, Chase steadying it upright while Maggie stomped the wedging rock into place. When it was finished, they stood on either side of the fence, postponing the parting a moment longer.

"I'll be seeing you," Chase stated, dissatisfied with the phrase, but finding none other that he was willing to say.

"Take care." She kept her response casual. Standing on tiptoes, Maggie took the initiative and leaned over the top wire, prompting Chase to kiss her one last time.

She turned away from the fence before Chase did, gathering the reins to her horse and stepping into the saddle in a quick hop. As she reined her horse toward the sloping rise to the ridge top, she waved to him over her shoulder, and received an answering salute. She felt suddenly sad to hear the hoofbeats galloping away from the fence while she started her bay up the slope.

Near the crest of the ridge, Angus O'Rourke sat silently on his horse, shadowed by a clump of pines. He had come back to see what was keeping Maggie and pulled up when he saw her approaching the fence, accompanied by none other than Chase Calder. His first thought was that she was being escorted off Calder land. And he'd been angry—but not angry enough to ride down and confront the man. His muttered abuse of the high-handed and arrogant ways of the Calders had been issued from afar.

But Maggie had kissed him . . . with the ease of a pair of lovers. The sight shook him all the way to the bone. She was just a little girl. He damned the Calders a thousand times over for corrupting innocent children. It was time he was having a talk with her, explain some of the facts of life to her. If only Mary Frances was here, he thought. She would handle it so much better—woman to woman. It was difficult for a man to put it in terms delicate enough for a young girl's ear.

He watched her ride up the slope, unknowingly coming straight toward him. His horse whickered at its stablemate. The serene smile went from her expression when she saw him. She briefly checked her mount, then let it continue on.

The sharp look she gave him made Angus explain his presence.

"I came back to look for you." The ground became rocky, forcing her to bring her horse down to a walk the last couple of yards.

"Sure, Pa."

Something in her attitude irritated him—a vague smugness, as if she knew a glorious secret that she wasn't going to share. "How come the Calder boy was with you? Where'd you meet up with him?"

"At the river." Her gaze never left the land breaking in front of her.

Her answer didn't tell him anything, certainly not what was uppermost in his mind. "He kissed you."

"Yes, he did." She turned her head to give him a cool look.

Suspicion crowded into his mind. There was a swollen softness to her lips and a secretive aura about her. "What else did he do?"

She didn't hold his gaze, but turned her head to stare straight ahead, her chin jutting forward at a defiant angle. "I don't think that's any of your business."

Reaching over, he grabbed the reins to stop her horse. "I'm your father and that makes it my business. Now I demand to know what happened."

"Why?" she challenged, meeting his anger with an unshakable directness, temper flashing in her green eyes. "If something happened, what would you do, Pa? Would you even try to do anything about it? Or would you just walk around making empty threats to the air?"

"So help me, God, if he laid a hand on you, I'll—"

"Yes? What will you do?" She taunted him openly. "Tell me, Pa."

Angus swallowed his rage, needing to know first if he was being goaded without cause. "I want to know if he . . . did anything to you." He stumbled over the words, his voice low and trembling.

Maggie watched the red flush come and go in his face. Her own defensive anger faded at his uncomfortable attempt to ask a question. It was probably harder for fathers to deal with their daughters' sexuality, she supposed. She discovered some pity, an emotion she thought her father had already used up, for the pathetic figure wanting so desperately to uphold her honor and not possessing the guts to carry it through.

"Yes, Pa, he made love to me," she sighed tiredly. It never occurred to Maggie to lie.

There was a long moment of silence while he turned his head from her, his eyes blinking furiously. "These damned Calders!" he cursed in a vibrating voice. "They always gotta have it all."

"Oh, Pa, can't you just once put the blame where it belongs?" she demanded in weary exasperation. "If it's anybody's fault, it's mine. It was what I wanted. I could have stopped Chase, but I didn't want to."

He shook his head, denying that. "A man will always have his way with a woman. Calder deserves the whip for forcing himself on you."

"Pa, you're not listening to me." Her protest seemed hopeless. Why did he always have to twist things to put the blame on others? In a flash of wisdom, Maggie realized that her father couldn't accept the truth that she had been a willing participant, because to him, it would mean that he had somehow failed as a parent. Her father couldn't accept personal failure. It always had to be caused by someone, bigger, stronger, or more powerful. The Calders acted as a natural scapegoat for all his problems.

"Don't worry, girl. No one is going to ruin my daughter and get away with it." There was a malevolent gleam in his eye. Here was another reason to hate the Calders—a reason any man, any father, could understand.

But all Maggie saw was how much he loved the role of the martyr. She didn't. She slapped the horse with her reins, sending it bounding forward.

Chapter V

Leaving Maggie, Chase put his spurs to the blood bay and raced it in a flat-out run. There was going to be hell to pay for keeping his father waiting. The fact that he'd forgotten all about it until a couple of minutes ago said something for his total absorption with Maggie.

Horse and rider splashed across the river's ford at a gallop, and up the sloping bank to the other side. With a rounding turn, they headed for the east gate. A bellowed shout behind him rang above the thunder of his horse's racing hooves. Chase looked back to see Nate Moore waving at him and reluctantly pulled his horse to a plunging, sliding halt. The blood bay danced under him, blowing and snorting while Chase waited for the foreman to catch up with him.

"I've searched half the river for you. Where the hell have you been?" The ramrod glowered his displeasure at being kept away from the herd on a fool's errand.

"Sorry." Chase offered no explanation.

"Your father couldn't wait any longer. He left a half-hour ago or more," Nate informed him. "He said, when I found you, I was to tell you he expected you at the house for dinner tonight. And I'd say you had better have a damned good reason for not coming right away."

"Right," Chase murmured, his mouth tight. Again the spurs jabbed the bay, sending it forward to stretch into a run with the second stride.

Nate let his eyes follow the rider for a minute before turning his mount toward the distant herd. "He's got a hard, punishing ride ahead of him, horse." It was a habit left over from his young fence-riding days when a cowboy's horse was sometimes the only living thing around to listen. "His butt is going to know it when it gets there. If the ride don't make it sore, the chewing it's going to get will finish the job."

As he reached the trail that intersected the river crossing, something in the open stretch of water caught the cowboy's eye. He slowed his horse, trying to identify the colored object. At this distance, it looked like some kind of material caught on a rock, a shirt, maybe. A strong sense of curiosity made Nate turn his horse for a closer investigation.

The piece of clothing was on the far side of the ford. Nate crossed over and dismounted to scoop it out of the water. It was a shirt. Nothing wrong with it either that he could tell. The initials, C. C., penned onto the label made him pause.

"Come to think of it," he murmured again to his horse, "Chase had his jacket buttoned all the way up. The day's cool, but not that cool." He wrung the water out of the shirt and stuffed it in a pocket of his saddlebag before swinging into the saddle. "Now, how do you suppose he lost that shirt in the river?"

It puzzled him. And if there was one thing that drove Nate crazy, it was not having all the pieces to a puzzle. It had happened to him once. He'd been snowed in at a line camp one winter for a month and a half, waiting for a warm chinook wind. There had been a thousand-piece jigsaw puzzle of a sailing ship. He'd spent the whole time trying to put it together, only to discover it was two hundred pieces shy when he'd finally counted them. He was a tenacious man; once he had his mind set on something, he wouldn't let go of it. He still had those eight hundred pieces of that puzzle in a box, figuring that someday he'd find the rest of them and finish that picture.

He turned his horse upstream. When he'd been looking for Chase earlier, he'd only stopped to make a cursory search of the riverbend where the girl had been swimming—and that had been from the opposite bank. Nate decided that a closer inspection might provide him with a few more puzzle pieces.

Following the tracks of two shod horses, he went down the cut in the bank leading to the gravel bar. At the edge of it, he stopped his horse to study the ground. There were horse droppings by the fallen log, which meant one of the horses had probably been tied there. Grass was cropped by a couple of cottonwoods, which meant a second horse had time to graze.

He walked his horse halfway to the blackened fire ring. Branches were poked in the ground around it. About the only reason for them that Nate could come up with had to be to hang clothes on to dry. Studying the man-made indentations on the ground beside the fire and the scuffled gravel, Nate read the story that was written there. Nate took his hat off and put it back on, all in one gesture that indicated his unease at the knowledge.

"Sometimes I get too curious, horse, and find out things that are none of my business." He laid the left rein along the horse's neck to turn it, then checked the swing halfway around when he noticed a partially uncoiled lariat nearly hidden by gravel a horse's hooves had kicked over it.

A good, supple rope was a vital tool of the cowboy, not to be left lying around for the elements to stiffen it. Stepping down, Nate finished rewinding it and tied it to his saddle. He remounted quickly and headed for the gully climbing to the top of the bank, detained long enough from his duties by his obsessive curiosity.

The ranch road running from the east gate was part of an interconnecting web of roads that crisscrossed the vast Triple C range. Some of the roads, like this one, were little more than two parallel ruts worn into the earth by truck tires. The more heavily traveled roads were hard and smooth as cement.

Avoiding the uneven ground of the rutted track, Chase ran his horse on the grassy verge next to it. For five miles, he galloped the blood bay, then slowed it to a trot for two to let it blow, and urged it into a ground-eating lope for the next five. After walking it for a mile, he covered the last six miles to the ranch headquarters at a hard gallop, the lathered horse laboring at the end.

The headquarters of the Triple C resembled a town in miniature. The cluster of structures included the usual ranch buildings of barns, sheds, and a bunkhouse, plus a small warehouse store stocked with all sorts of essential supplies, ranging from hardware and vehicle parts to utility clothing and foodstuffs. The store was also where the mail was collected or distributed, and outside there were gasoline pumps for ranch vehicles. Another building was a first-aid center and semi-dispensary, as well as a kind of animal hospital. A welding shop doubled as a blacksmithy. In addition, there were a half-dozen small homes where the married hands lived, those who weren't camp men living on one of the distant sections. On the northeast side of the collection of buildings, a long grass strip served as a private landing field for the ranch planes hangared in the accompanying metal shed and for those of invited guests.

The massive two-story main house dominated the entry enclave—it was appropriately referred to as "The Homestead" by the cowboys. Its front entrance faced the south, a wide porch running its length to provide an overview of the other buildings gathered at its feet. Stone chimneys punctuated its slanted roof, few of them used since central heating had been installed some years ago.

Riding into the ranch colony, Chase slowed his foaming horse to a canter and guided it straight to the barns. Before the bay came to a complete stop, he was peeling out of the saddle and looping the reins over the horse's head to lead it inside. Abe Garvey, a Triple C native relegated to the ranks of stablehand by advancing age, emerged from the interior shadows. Chase identified him with a brief glance as he led the horse into a stall and hooked a stirrup on the saddle horn to loosen the cinch.

"Has the senator's plane landed?" With both girths freed, he lifted the saddle from the horse's back and draped it over the stall railing for the time being.

"A half-hour ago, give or take." The old cowboy moved on about his business while Chase wiped the sweat from the horse with the wet saddle blanket.

The roping horse was too valuable an animal to be put up hot, no matter how long Chase's father had been waiting for him. No one volunteered to walk the horse down for him, and Chase didn't ask. A man was responsible for the care of his own mount. Until his father handed over some authority to him, Chase was no different from any other cowboy on the place. That's the way they treated him, especially the veterans, because they knew in their own way they were training their future leader. Chase had to measure up to their standards as well as his father's if he wanted to command their respect, as well as their lives.

When the horse was cooled down, Chase turned him into the stall and carried his saddle to the tack room. Abe was sitting on a bench, repairing a broken bridle strap, his arthritically crippled legs tucked under it.

"See that my horse gets an extra measure of grain tonight, Abe," Chase requested, and old man merely nodded, not one to speak unless it was required.

Leaving the barn, Chase set out on the long walk across the ranch yard to The Homestead. He'd walked out some of his own stiffness cooling the horse, but he was still bone-tired from the long, jarring ride—his muscles sore and demanding a rest. There was always activity around the headquarters—ranch hands coming and going. Chase nodded to the ones he passed and waved to those in a distance, a gesture that amounted to little more than an upraised arm.

His unwavering course brought him to The Homestead, where he pushed himself up the steps, his spurs clinking in unison with the heavy tread of his boots on the wood-plank floor of the porch. When he crossed the threshold of the front door, he heard the booming voice of the senator coming from the den, to his left. Chase paused in the entry hall, which was an extension of the sprawling living room, sectioned off by the arrangement of the furniture. His glance strayed to the polished oak banister of the staircase emptying into the living room, but he resisted its invitation.

Brushing the worst of the dust from his clothes, he walked to the open doors of the den and removed his hat as he entered the room. Besides the florid-faced and seemingly jovial senator and his father, there were three other men in the room. Two of them Chase recognized from previous visits as aides of the senator, and the third was an influential government official from the state house, George Bidwell.

His arrival naturally made him the focal point of attention, his tardiness earning him a sharp-eyed look of reproval from his father. A sense of protocol directed Chase to the guest of honor.

"Welcome to the Triple C, Senator." He greeted the politician and submitted to the man's pumping handshake. "Glad to have you back. I'm sorry I wasn't on hand to meet your plane when it landed."

"Your father told us you were detained. Out helping with the roundup, I understand?" The lilting inflection of his stentorian voice made it a question.

"That's right."

"Busy time of year." The senator spoke in short, clipped sentences. He slapped Chase on the shoulder in a comradely fashion. "You remind me more of your father every day. Doesn't he, George?"

"Yes, he does. He's more handsome, though." George Bidwell rose from the leather armchair to greet him. "Hello, Chase."

After shaking hands with the sparrow-faced man, Chase made the rounds, renewing his acquaintance with the senator's assistants. When that was accomplished, Chase found himself standing next to the senator once more.

"Have a cigar. My own special brand." The politician placed it in Chase's hands, not bothering to see if he wanted it or not. "Wes, fix me another whiskey." He directed the order to an aide, then raised an interrogating eyebrow at Chase. "You'll join us for a drink? Make it two, Wes."

"If you don't mind, Senator"—Chase raised a hand to veto the drink order—"I'd like to wash off this dirt and cattle smell before I join you in that drink. If you'll excuse me?" The last was a polite request encompassing the entire group.

Leaving the den, he started to cross the living room to the staircase, his spurs jingling with each stride. He'd barely gone halfway across the room when a woman's voice stopped him.

"Chase Calder, don't you dare walk on those beautiful oak floors with those spurs!"

A woman stood at the far end of the room where a hallway led to the kitchen; her blonde hair appeared lighter with the accumulating additions of gray-white strands. The stern expression on Ruth Haskell's face was reminiscent of his childhood days, when she was as quick to scold him for wrongdoing as she was her son, Buck. Chase had never fully understood how she always knew when he was doing something he was not supposed to.

"Sorry." A reckless smile proclaimed his guilt as Chase bent to unbuckle his spurs. She was gone when he straightened, returning to the kitchen to continue the preparation of the evening's meal.

With his hat and the spurs in his hand, he climbed the stairs, divided in the middle by a landing. The top of the stairs faced the south, and his bedroom was in the northwest corner, the only one outside of the master suite that had a private bath. All the guest rooms shared adjoining baths. Entering his room, he tossed the hat and spurs atop the quilted coverlet on his bed and started unbuttoning his jacket.

In the den, Webb had heard the reprimand Ruth Haskell had issued and waited until he heard Chase's footsteps on the stairs before excusing himself from his guests on the pretext of checking on dinner. He climbed the stairs after his son and knocked once on his door before opening it without waiting for permission to enter.

Bare-chested, Chase was standing in the center of the room just taking his arm out of his jacket sleeve. The incongruity of wearing a jacket without a shirt unconsciously registered in Webb's mind, but his thoughts were concentrated elsewhere at the moment.

"What kept you?" Webb didn't bother with the preliminaries, but went straight to the point.

"I have no excuse, sir." Chase walked to the closet to hang his coat on the knob.

"I'm glad we agree on that point." Webb followed him with his eyes, watching him closely. "Do you realize how long I waited for you at the gate? What took you so long?"

There was an expressive lift of naked shoulders. "I just lost track of the time." He crossed in front of Webb and stopped at the chest of drawers.

"You were just having so much fun that you didn't pay any attention to what time it was getting to be," Webb concluded with a lack of patience. He noted the grimming set of his son's mouth.

"Something like that," Chase murmured stiffly and opened a drawer to take out a clean pair of shorts and socks.

Muscles flexed along his shoulders. The movement drew Webb's attention to the small, half-moon marks on his son's shoulder, four in a row. His gaze narrowed on them in sharp curiosity. The only thing he could visualize leaving such an imprint were fingernails. His mind clicked with the memory that Chase hadn't been wearing a shirt under his jacket. There was no indication that the finger-nails had attempted to scratch. It was as if they had dug into Chase's skin to hold onto him.

Then Webb put together the ingredients of the scene—a teen-aged girl swimming naked in a river, and a virile young man with almost three weeks of enforced celibacy behind him, the two of them alone on an empty stretch of river. He could guess the result of that situation. He stared at the marks on Chase's back, not wanting to jump to the obvious conclusion.

Shutting the drawer, Chase glanced at his father to see why he had become so silent. The frowning concentration being paid to his shoulder caused Chase to twist his head around in an effort to see what his father was studying so intently.

"Is something wrong?" he asked, reaching back and breaking his father's concentration.

Webb's gaze lifted sharply. "I was trying to remember how old the O'Rourke girl is." The slight jerking of Chase's head told Webb his question had struck a nerve, but his son recovered quickly.

"Sixteen." Chase fell into the same trap Maggie had, trying to add those few months to make her seem older than she was. "Why?" He was uncomfortable with his father's probing questions, but he didn't let it show—uncomfortable because of his strong need to protect Maggie, to shield from eyes that might judge her by accepted standards—wrong standards.

Examining his son's closed expression, Webb kept his suspicions to himself for the time being. "No reason." He turned to leave. "Hurry up with your shower. Ruth is serving dinner in forty-five minutes."

"I'll be down directly," Chase promised, but didn't move until his father had left the room.

At the sound of footsteps retreating from his door, Chase entered the bathroom and paused in front of the mirror. Twisting to one side, he was able to make out the red marks on his shoulders where Maggie had dug her nails into him. Obviously, his father had noticed them, too. Had he guessed what had caused them? A heavy sigh broke from Chase as he turned to the shower.

Throughout dinner and the serving of coffee and brandy in the den afterward, Chase tried to appear to be paying attention to the various discussions, but most of the time his mind was wandering.

The senator had passed out more of his cigars. This time Chase smoked his, the richly fragrant tobacco smoke rising like a cloud above his head. He rolled the butt between his teeth and watched the white smoke.

The whiteness of the smoke made him think of the milk-white perfection of Maggie's skin. He was aware how much she had awakened his protective instincts. A sudden smile broke across his features as he realized he wanted to protect a girl who had whipped him with a rope in front of a dozen riders.

"Look, Chase appreciates my joke even if no one else does," Senator Bulfert declared. Hearing his name brought Chase sharply back to the present. He joined in with the laughter of the other men and hoped to hell no one asked him about the story the senator had just told. He encountered his father's steady gaze and knew that was one man he hadn't fooled.

Removing the pan of water from the stove, Maggie rinsed the soapsuds off the dishes stacked in the sink. Both her father and brother were sitting at the kitchen table, whose white enameled paint was turning yellow with age. She didn't bother to suggest that since she had cooked the meal and washed the dishes, one of them could help her by drying them. Neither of them did women's work. She took a towel off the rack and started drying them herself.

There was a brooding quality to the atmosphere. Maggie could feel its heaviness. Her brother had said nothing to her, but she knew her father had told him his version of what had transpired between her and Chase Calder. Culley had avoided meeting her gaze all evening, but kept stealing glances at her when he thought she wasn't looking.

"How I miss your mother," her father murmured in a melancholy voice and took another sip from his whiskey glass. A gentleman always had a shot of whiskey after a meal, or so he had always said to their mother in defense of the practice.

"I can still remember that day my ship docked in San Diego and I had a three-day pass. Our cruiser had been out to sea for nearly three months." He leaned on the table, directing his words to Culley. "Me and a buddy of mine went out on the town. I mean, we really painted it red. I was drunk one whole day and don't remember anything we did. Finally, I passed out and my buddy left me to sleep it off in the car."

"And when you came to, you heard the church bells ringing." Culley had heard the story before, but his comment was a prompting for his father to continue.

"That's right." Her father refilled his whiskey glass without letting it get empty first. "The way I was feeling, I knew I had done some sinning that needed forgiving, so I followed the sound of those bells for a couple of blocks before I found the church. I was wearing my dress whites, so I brushed myself off good before I went inside. Mass was about to start when I walked in, so I took a seat in one of the rear pews."

"That's when you saw Mom for the first time." It was an old story to Maggie, too, but this was the part of it she liked.

Looking objectively at her father, she could see how very handsome he had once been. She remembered the snapshots she'd seen of him in his navy uniform. It wasn't any wonder that he'd swept her mother off her feet.

"I was looking around at all the beautiful stained-glass windows when I noticed your mother sitting in the next pew with her parents and her sister, Cathleen. I smiled at her and she smiled back. With that white scarf over her head, she reminded me of paintings I'd seen of the Madonna. She was so beautiful I couldn't take my eyes off her." Some of the vivid roughish charm he'd once possessed was captured once more in his smile. "You can bet that after church, I made a special point of meeting her."

"And you invited her to come out to your ship and promised you'd personally show her around," Culley said.

"She came, too, but she brought her sister, Cathleen, along. I had an awful time convincing Mary Frances that I wasn't like some of the other sailors in port. I had more trouble convincing her parents and her sister. But I knew the moment I saw her that she was the girl for me. We were married four weeks later. I thought I had the world by the tail," he sighed.

Her father didn't carry the story beyond that point, but her mother had told Maggie the rest of it—how her father hadn't been able to find a decent-paying job in California after he'd been discharged from the navy. Since he'd always dreamed about owning a cattle ranch, he'd taken the money her mother had inherited from her grandparents and bought this ranch in Montana without ever seeing it first. Maggie remembered how her mother used to talk about their plans to remodel the house, plans that were never realized. The additions were tacked onto the main structure in a helter-skelter fashion. During the last two years before her mother died, she rarely mentioned the plans to remodel their home, as if she knew it was another one of her husband's dreams that wouldn't come true.

Much of what Maggie knew about the early years, she had gleaned from reading between the lines. When her father had first arrived, he had believed ranching was a snap. All a man had to do—so he thought—was turn a bunch of cows loose on the range with a bull and the next year sell the calves for a huge profit. He didn't realize how much work went along with it, from constantly checking and repairing fences to bailing hay for winter feed, not to mention wet-nursing a bunch of dumb cows and calves.

The land on which the Shamrock Ranch was located looked ideal for raising cattle, but the rough terrain supported little grass. Each year there were cows that had to be destroyed because of broken legs. Rattlesnakes took their toll, too, as well as coyotes preying on calves or crippled cows. And the water supply was insufficient. In bad years, even the house well went dry. But the Calder ranch stretched to the south with its abundance of rich grass and water.

Her father was always dreaming of ways to make it big. One year he tried his hand at panning for gold—certain he would strike a mother lode. But gold-prospecting was hard, back-breaking work, requiring hours of labor with no guarantee of finding color. Lacking persistence, he soon gave it up. Another year, he tried to convince gas and oil companies to drill on his land, but all their surveys were negative. With visions of hitting a gusher, he tried to drill one himself, but he gave up before they had even gone deep enough to hit water. It was too much work. He was always certain there was an easier way to strike it rich—like the Calders.

Not once in all the years they'd lived there had there been enough money for her mother to return to California to visit her family. Her mother's parents had died and there hadn't been enough money to travel all the way there for the funeral. Her mother had cried then. They still received a Christmas card each year from her sister, Cathleen, a widow who lived in Los Angeles.

Angus slammed his fist on the table, startling Maggie out of her reverie with an explosive release of his Irish temper. She turned to look at him and saw the black petulance in his expression.

"Calder isn't going to get away with it!"

"Pa, don't start in on that," Maggie protested stiffly.

But he took another swallow of whiskey and paid no attention to her. "It didn't matter to him that you were a good girl. Did he have any respect for that? No, he's a Calder. He does whatever he damned well pleases, and doesn't care if some innocent person has to suffer."

He had been building up to this outburst all evening, she realized. Nothing she could say or do would silence his tirade, so she clamped her mouth tightly closed.

"Calder isn't going to keep his mouth shut. No, he's going to start bragging around about it, spreading ugly stories about Maggie," he declared.

"If he opens his mouth, I'll shut it for him," Culley threatened.

"You'll do nothing of the kind." In spite of her resolve to stay out of this, her temper flared. "All this is nothing but a lot of boastful talk!"

"I'm going to do more than talk, little girl." Angus O'Rourke stood up, weaving a little, his face white beneath its tan. "I'm going to have myself a talk with old man Calder. He thinks that him and his son can do anything, but I'm going to tell him that they can't. They aren't going to get away with what happened today. You just wait and see. I'll put the fear of God into them."

"Pa, stop saying things that you have no intention of doing." Maggie turned away. She was tired of his empty words.

"I am going to see Calder!" he stated emphatically.

"When, Pa?" She looked at him with mocking skepticism. "When the sky turns green?"

"Don't sass me, girl!" He pointed a threatening finger at her, but she showed her indifference by turning away.

PART II

A sky of justice
A sky so strong
This sky that pays for
A Calder's wrong.

Chapter VI

The senator and his party left at mid-morning the next day. Chase and his father accompanied them to the ranch's grass strip to see them off. As the plane climbed out, it wagged its wings in a final farewell salute, the sunlight winking off the shiny surface of the metal.

Scratching a match over a denim-covered thigh, Chase cupped the resulting flame to the cigar the senator had given him before boarding the plane. He puffed on it, then held it between his teeth while the aromatic smoke curled into his nose. As he turned to walk back to the car with his father, he curved a forefinger around the cigar to hold it away from his mouth.

"If nothing else, the senator knows a good cigar." He slanted a wry glance at his father.

"Your mother never could stand the smell of those things." The softness of fond memory was in Webb Calder's expression. Then dry amusement filtered through it. "I've never understood what there is about a cigar that turns so many women off."

"I don't understand it, either," Chase agreed and opened the passenger's door of the car to tuck his long frame inside. "Drop me off at the Number Two barn so I can collect my saddle. I'll catch a ride with the cookie when he takes the noon meal out to the drive."

"There's no need for that." Webb shifted the car into gear and turned it down the smooth lane. "They'll be through there in another day. There are some things here I want you to do."

"I'll have to ride out there, anyway, to get my gear." His bedroll and everything else were still at the camp.

"No problem," his father replied smoothly. "I'll send word out for Nate to bring it when he comes in."

Chase lost his taste for the cigar and irritably stubbed it out in the car's ashtray. His hard jawline was thrust forward as he gazed out the window, a grimness pulling down the corners of his mouth.

"You don't look too happy. Is something bothering you, son?"

"No." The denial came sharp and quick. Chase tempered it, turning an emotionless face to his father. "What could be wrong?"

"I thought you might tell me."

The astuteness of his father's eyes made Chase turn to the front again. "There's nothing to tell," he shrugged.

"Not even about the O'Rourke girl—Maggie?" The quiétly worded challenge wasn't permitted a response as Webb continued. "When a man needs the satisfaction of bedding a woman, it's understood that he stays away from young girls and those from decent families. There are plenty of whores and experienced women around to satisfy a man's appetite for sex." He paused to run a glance over Chase. "Take some fatherly advice and think on it, son." But something told Webb that his advice had come too late. Immediately, he began considering the options if there were a backlash. Meanwhile, he lined out the tasks he wanted Chase to accomplish that day.

That night, Chase found his bedroll and saddlebags in his room. Among the clothes was the shirt he'd lost. He stared at it, knowing the questions it must have raised, and knowing that none of them would ever be asked. He lay in bed that night and stared at the ceiling for long hours, knowing his father was right. Maggie was a child, not even sixteen yet. He had no business messing around with her.

Leaning on the counter in the commissary section of the warehouse, Webb went down the list of supplies included on the purchase order. "You're ordering a lot of sugar, Bill. Are you sure someone isn't operating a still on the side?" Even as he questioned the amount in a joking manner, he signed the authorization at the bottom, and smiled at the man in the wheelchair behind the counter.

Bill Vernon was fourth-generation at the Triple C Ranch.

Except for five years which he'd spent training and working as a computer programmer, he'd spent all his life here. He'd returned seven years ago, disenchanted with city life despite the higher pay, to cowboy again. Three short months later, a fall from a horse had left him paralyzed.

The Triple C took care of its own. When Bill had recovered, Webb had put him in charge of the commissary, expanding the responsibilities to include the warehouse stock and making Bill into a bookkeeper of sorts. He and his wife, and their two children, lived in one of the houses furnished by the ranch.

There was a sense of family among the descendants of those who had stayed with the first Calder. They were all tied to the land and tied to one another, not like the drifters who worked a month or year and moved on. They were a hardcore band of followers whose first loyalty was to the brand.

"It looks like a lot of sugar, I admit," Bill Vernon replied with a quick smile. "But with summer coming on, the women will be canning, so we'll need more than usual on hand—or so Marlyss tells me." His smile broadened into a grin. Marlyss was his wife, a saucy, freckle-faced girl from the Montana wheat country up north. They'd met and married at computer school. She helped him out in the commissary, working behind the counter and stocking shelves, while he did the paperwork.

"I'm sure Marlyss knows what she's talking about." She was quite the homemaker, from what Webb had heard and seen. "Where is she, by the way?" He glanced around the small shop area.

"Over at the house, checking on Timmy. His tonsils are inflamed again."

"Boss!" One of the hands called to him from the sun-brightened doorway, and Webb turned. "O'Rourke's outside here, askin' to see you."

For a split-second, Webb held himself motionless. These last four days he'd been expecting something without being sure what it would be. Now it had come. He straightened from the counter, accumulating his thoughts and formulating his contingency plans.

"Tell him I'll be right out." He gave the message to the cowboy and glanced at Bill. On the surface, he retained a calm and casual expression. "Was there anything else we needed to go over?"

"No, I don't think so." Bill Vernon shook his head and wheeled his chair at a right angle, taking the purchase order Webb had signed.

With a curt nod, Webb took his leave. "Take care." He turned and walked out the commissary door into the bright sunlight.

After four days of ranting and raving, mostly to himself, and being goaded by Maggie's taunting insistence that he would do nothing more than talk, Angus O'Rourke had worked himself into a fever pitch of hatred that had finally brought him face to face with Webb Calder. He had stayed outside the ranch store deliberately to make Webb Calder come to him, as if this small thing would give him a psychological edge.

If it did, it was taken away when Webb stopped before him, tall and barrel-chested, forcing Angus, who was half a foot shorter, to tip his head back in order to look into Webb's face. Angus detested people looking "down" at him, especially Webb Calder. His mouth curved in smug contempt at the way this mighty man was going to squirm before he was through with him.

"Hello, O'Rourke. You wanted to see me?"

Angus lifted his chin a belligerent inch higher. "Yeah, I want to talk to you."

With a brief nod of willingness to listen, Webb Calder said, "I was just on my way to the house. Why don't we talk there?"

Angus had just taken a deep breath to let fly with his accusations. The offer of hospitality took the wind out of his sails. The rare times that he'd been at the Triple C headquarters, he'd never been invited to the house. It was a grand-looking structure. Just for a minute, he was uncomfortable at the thought of being inside. Then he reassured himself with the knowledge that he was finally being treated as an equal, something he felt he justly deserved.

It was impossible to talk while crossing the yard. The man's long strides forced Angus to walk faster than he usually did. He was puffing slightly when they reached the house and was irritated because Calder didn't appear to be out of breath.

Entering the house, Angus couldn't keep from staring at the huge living room with all its fine, comfortable furnishings—strong, solid furniture built to last. It was a man's house, possessing none of the dainty touches of a woman. His own home seemed a shack in comparison. His dream of living in a place like this seemed further away now that Angus realized how far he had to go. It filled him with a sense of wild desperation.

Calder was opening wide a set of double doors to his left, and Angus realized their discussion was not going to take place in the spacious living room before him. He turned to follow Webb into the library. There was a cavernous fireplace with the wide, sweeping horns of a longhorn steer mounted above the mantelpiece, and furniture covered with genuine leather. Bookshelves held bound volumes of works ranging from the masters to animal husbandry. Behind a huge desk, a framed map hung on the wall, yellowed with age and outlining the boundaries of the Triple C. Angus stared at it as Calder walked behind the desk to sit in the stuffed armchair.

"It's the first map of the ranch," Calder explained, noting Angus' interest in it. "Almost a century old now."

Angus was choked again by the feeling that it was wrong for one person to own so much. It festered inside him, an infected wound that poisoned him. The map, the house, the man—all made him feel small.

"What was it you wanted to speak to me about, Angus?" Calder inquired, so calmly, so authoritatively.

"My daughter, Maggie. Your son forced himself on her. He found her swimming in the river and took advantage of her." He rushed his words, the heat building in his voice. "It's a fact. She told me so herself, so there's no use in you denying it."

"I wouldn't presume to call your daughter a liar," Calder replied smoothly. "My son is a healthy young male, and your Maggie is just coming into womanhood. I wouldn't deny it's conceivable that there might have been a liaison between the two of them."

He'd expected an argument, a flat denial that a Calder would do such a thing. His anger was temporarily without direction until his mind played back Webb's statement in which nothing was admitted and no blame assumed.

"Your son isn't going to get away with ruining my little girl. I'm here to see to that," he stated. "It doesn't matter how you want to twist it. What he did amounts to statutory rape. She's fifteen, under age. He can go to prison for that."

There was the briefest pause, during which Webb Calder

regarded him steadily. "I'm sure you have considered that if you press charges, your daughter would have to appear in court. Her testimony would be public record. It's unfortunate, but only too true, that in cases where rape is charged, it's the girl who suffers the loss of her reputation. No father wants to see his daughter publicly shamed."

The shame would touch all of them. A trial would have this whole part of the state talking. Wherever any of them went, people would whisper behind their backs and point. It was something that Angus had thought about over and over again. His face became mottled with frustration because Calder knew they would suffer more than he and his son.

"Your son took my little girl and used her for his own pleasure. I'm not letting him get away with it," Angus insisted in a tight voice. "I demand that he do the right thing by her."

An eyebrow shot up in challenging surprise, a studied action that seemed to imply Angus wasn't too bright. "I hope you aren't suggesting marriage, Angus, because that would be a bigger mistake than the one they made. Your daughter is much too young to be any man's bride, and my son isn't ready to settle down in married life. I know you are trying to ensure that your daughter doesn't suffer any loss of respect, but for parents to force their children to marry because of a single indiscretion would be wrong. She would be unhappy with my son, and I know that's something that as her father you want to avoid."

Angus hated Webb for being so damned level-headed and practical. He shifted in his chair, aware that he was being made to look like a fool and helpless to know how to change it. He clung to the one thought that burned steadily within him.

"He isn't going to get by with what he did. He's got to pay for it," Angus repeated in steadfast determination.

"If I had a daughter"—Webb Calder leaned forward in his chair and casually rested his arms on the desk to study him—"and if I believed something of this nature had happened to her, I'm sure I would be feeling the same sense of outrage that you are. I would insist on some form of retribution, too. It wouldn't be unreasonable to expect compensation—a settlement for damages, if you will."

"Are you saying that you want to buy me off?" Angus

challenged with narrowed eyes, his pride stung by the offer. "Do you think money can erase my daughter's memory of what happened out there by the river?"

A faint smile touched Calder's mouth, hinting at shrewdness. "I'm certain there is no dollar figure that would be adequate compensation. It's merely a gesture of goodwill. You and I are reasonable men, Angus. It would benefit neither of us to have this story spread around, creating gossip and scandal. The wise thing is to settle the matter as best we can. What other alternative do we have?" He looked across the desk, waiting for a suggestion. Unable to meet the directness of that gaze, Angus wavered. None of his threats had seemed to touch this man. All of them had been brushed aside. He'd not even had the satisfaction of making the man squirm.

Before the silence became awkward, Calder reached for a pen. "Why don't I write out a bill of sale to you for, say, twenty-five head of prime stock—your choice—and mark it paid in full?" He reached for a piece of paper.

Watching Calder, Angus' mind raced. If he left this ranch empty-handed, without even the satisfaction of knowing he'd put Calder in a difficult position, then he'd accomplished nothing but to make a fool of himself. He wasn't even able to truthfully brag that he'd put Calder on the spot. His bluff had been called. Something had to be salvaged from this. It wasn't Calder's place to be dictating the terms of a settlement; it was his. Calder had already started to write.

"Make it fifty head of my choice," Angus demanded.

Lifting his head, Calder gave him a steely glance. "Fifty head it is," he agreed, and Angus wondered if he should have demanded more—a hundred, maybe. He cursed himself for settling too cheaply. Calder owned two hundred times that number, maybe more. But something in that hard, cold stare kept Angus from upping the ante. The palms of his hands felt clammy as Calder reverted his attention to the bill of sale he was writing, the pen scratching across the paper in bold strokes.

When it was written, Calder offered it to him, forcing Angus to rise from his chair to reach for it. Looking at the bill of sale, he was burned again with the knowledge that he'd sold too cheap. It sounded like a lot to him because he had so little, but it didn't even make a dent in Calder's pocket. He hadn't made Calder pay—he'd been bought. He felt puny and sick inside.

Webb reached for the telephone on his desk and picked up the receiver, dialing a number. He glanced once at O'Rourke, observing the bitter regret in the man's expression. It was always that way whenever a buyer met the asking price; the seller always wondered if he couldn't have gotten more.

The ringing line was answered. "This is Calder." Webb identified himself and didn't wait for a response. "Is Nate there?" At the affirmative answer, he said, "Tell him I want to see him at The Homestead."

Hanging up the phone, Webb pushed the chair away from the desk and stood up. O'Rourke continued to stare at the bill of sale, not immediately noticing that he had risen until he walked from behind the desk. Then he pushed quickly to his feet.

"Nate Moore is one of my foremen." Webb walked toward the entry hall. O'Rourke followed him. "He has an excellent eye for cattle—a very experienced man, well qualified. I'm sure you'll find him very helpful. You know him, don't you?" He opened the front door and motioned for O'Rourke to go first.

"I've talked to him a few times . . . in town." It was a terse answer, an enlargement on exchanged greetings and comments about the weather.

"Of course." Webb nodded as he guided the man to the top of the porch steps. Nate's lean shape was just crossing the yard. "Here he is now."

As the ramrod approached the steps, his glance flicked to the shorter man, then darted sharply to his boss, silently speculating. But he merely nodded a greeting to both men.

"You wanted to see me?" The question was put to Webb Calder.

"Yes. I've just sold O'Rourke some cattle—fifty head of his choosing. I thought it would be best if you arranged to show him the herds and set up a delivery time."

"We can look at the herds tomorrow morning around nine, if that suits you?" Nate turned to O'Rourke.

"Nine . . . nine o'clock is fine." He shifted uncomfortably.

"As for delivery, we can truck them over, or you can drive them through to your place—whichever you prefer." The foreman shrugged.

"I'll let you know in the morning," Angus grumbled in ill temper as he folded the bill of sale and tucked it in his pocket.

"I'll meet you at the barns at nine o'clock." Nate named the meeting place.

O'Rourke nodded and flashed a dark look at Calder before descending the steps and striking out for the battered pickup truck parked in the yard. Both Nate and Webb watched Angus go.

"He doesn't look pleased with the bargain," Nate observed in a deliberately low voice.

"Nobody ever is," Webb replied, then turned to enter the house, dismissing the foreman by his action.

Nate lingered, then shoved off to return to the barns. In one way or another, females were always at the heart of a man's troubles. Every man made a fool of himself over one at some time or another. Nate was just glad he'd never been fool enough to marry one. He liked being free to come and go as he pleased, with no one nagging him about where he was going or when he'd be back. The Triple C provided him with all the family he needed.

When dinner was over, Chase and Webb took their coffee into the den, leaving Ruth to clear the table. Chase walked to the ornately carved walnut bar in a corner of the room and unstoppered a decanter of brandy.

"Do you want some in your coffee?" He half-turned to glance at his father.

"Not tonight." Webb refused and studied his tall, broad-shouldered son. "O'Rourke came to see me today." Chase had started to set the decanter down, but the statement stopped the movement in mid-action. After an instant's delay, it was carried through.

"What about?" Chase broke the ensuing silence but didn't turn around.

Silently, Webb admired the way his son kept himself contained. It wasn't good if someone could read a person's thoughts by his expression. An iron hold on the rest of his emotions would come in time. The boy was still young.

"He claimed you forced your attentions on his daughter," Webb replied. "Do you deny it?"

"No." He continued to face the bar, stirring his coffee.

Webb liked the bluntness of the answer, its absence of an excuse and lack of any disrespectful reference to the girl. It showed breeding and the assumption of full responsibility for what transpired.

"Did you make any promises that I should know about?"

Again, it was a straightforward "No." The immobility was broken by a surge of rippling energy that turned Chase around in tight-lipped anger. "O'Rourke had no right to bring you into this. He should have talked to me."

"It's been settled."

"Settled? How?" Chase shot the questions at his father, a sharp ring of demand within them.

"I gave him a bill of sale for fifty head of cattle."

"Fifty head. And he accepted that?"

"Yes."

Chase half-turned his head away, his mouth curling in disgust. "I would have had more respect for the man if he'd tied me to a pole and whipped me. Why didn't he come over here and beat the hell out of me?"

"It's what I would have done in his place. I'm not so sure I shouldn't do it, anyway," Webb stated grimly. "It's natural for a man to sow his wild oats, but he shouldn't do it in young, virgin fields."

"That's occurred to me more than once these last few days," Chase agreed on a breath of self-derision. He set the untouched cup of brandy-laced coffee on a side table. "I'm going for a walk and get some air."

Chapter VII

The closest town to the Triple C headquarters was a wide spot in the road called Blue Moon. It was a standing joke that the town was so named because something exciting happened there only once in a blue moon. The gas station was also the grocery store and post office. There was a café next to what was once a roadside inn with rooms for travelers, but the inn was now a saloon-bar, called "Jake's Place," complete with a private gaming room in the back. The upstairs rooms were where Jake's "nieces" did their business. The café next door did a good trade, mostly because the owner, Bob Tucker, was reputed to be the best damned cook in the state of Montana.

In addition to those commercial buildings, there was a combination dry-goods-and-hardware store, an abandoned grain elevator, and a house that had been converted into a clinic where Doc Barlow came twice a week to see his patients. Beyond that, there were half a dozen houses for the thirty-odd residents of Blue Moon.

A pickup truck marked with the Triple C brand rumbled off the highway and bounced over the rutted ground, churning up a cloud of dust as it was braked to a stop in the parking area between the gasoline-grocery store and the saloon. Buck Haskell swung out of the passenger's side of the cab, his boots hitting the ground before Chase opened the driver's door.

"Tucker better have some blueberry pie left!" Buck declared. "I've been tasting it for the last ten miles."

"You've been telling me that for the last ten miles, too," Chase said, dryness rustling his voice.

"Hey, Chase, you got any cigarettes on you?" Buck slapped the empty breast pocket of his shirt. "I'm out."

"All I have is a pack of cheroots."

"Wait for me. I'm going to run in the store and get some." Buck started toward the grocery store while he forced his hand inside the pocket of his snug-fitting Levi's for the money.

Chase leaned against the tailgate of the pickup to wait for him, tipping his hat to the back of his head, a faint smile showing in his expression. The door to the grocery slammed twice—once when Buck went in, and immediately afterward, when someone came out. Chase glanced around with idle interest.

The sight of Maggie O'Rourke was like a clean, wild wind rushing through him. In these last two weeks, he had managed to push her from his mind, but seeing her again erased those two weeks of forgetting. Her flowing black hair was tied at the nape of her neck with a faded blue scarf. She was wearing blue jeans and boots and a white blouse of sorts. He couldn't see much of it because of the two large grocery sacks she held in her arms. A slight frown marred the smoothness of her forehead as she looked into the sun. Chase realized she hadn't noticed him yet. He straightened from the tailgate, readjusting his hat to sit squarely on his head, and stepped forward.

"Hello, Maggie," he said quietly.

She stopped, her gaze running to him. Some emotion flickered in her eyes before her expression became blank. "Hello, Chase." She didn't falter over his name or appear self-conscious at seeing him again. "How have you been?" It was a polite question and he noticed how her lips lay together, full in the center.

"Busy." He dragged his gaze from her mouth. "Let me carry one of those sacks for you."

She hesitated an instant before surrendering one into his hands. The white blouse she wore was too small. The fullness of her young breasts made the front gape between the buttons. She shifted the other sack in front of her to hide it.

"We've been busy, too." She started walking again and Chase shortened his stride to walk with her, carrying the sack in the crook of his arm. "You'd be surprised how much extra work there is when you acquire an additional fifty head of cattle." Her voice was stiffly proud, like the way she was carrying herself.

"What is that remark supposed to mean?" A faint irritation ran through him at her tone.

She gave him one of those slanting looks that he was beginning to associate with her. "It means I'm not some tramp whose favors can be bought with fifty head of cattle. Maybe what I did was wrong, but it doesn't mean I'm bad."

"Maggie, you weren't wrong. I was." He took the blame. "The gift of the cattle was a way of saying 'I'm sorry.'"

"Well, I'm not." Her lips were pressed firmly together. "I didn't think Pa would make trouble for you. I mean, he talked a lot about it, but I never thought he would actually try it. When I think about him going to your father and telling him what we did, that's what makes me feel like . . ." They were passing the inn when she paused and cast a quick glance at the upstairs windows. ". . . one of Jake's 'nieces.'"

"You're not supposed to know about them." His mouth twitched almost into a smile, amused by her directness.

"You mean I'm not supposed to let anybody *know* that I know about them. Everybody does," she returned dryly, "and only pretend that they don't."

"You shouldn't feel like one of them," he insisted. "I know my father doesn't think of you that way."

She stopped beside the passenger's door of a battered pickup and turned to look at him. "What do you think about me, Chase?"

"I think you are a remarkable and very beautiful young girl." Looking into her candid green eyes, he felt the pull of her presence tugging at him. This time he resisted the urge to take her into his arms.

"Beautiful? In this?" She looked down at her clothes with a glance that was wryly skeptical. Then she sobered. "I guess you're just trying to be polite, but you don't need to. I know what people think about my pa . . . and the rest of the O'Rourkes, too. Pa always blames someone else for his troubles. But I don't want you to think that I blame you for what happened. I knew what I was doing. I know you said you'd see me, but after the trouble Pa caused, I want you to know that I'm not expecting you to come around."

"Why not?" A gentle quality took the roughness out of Chase's craggy features.

A frown briefly wrinkled her forehead. "Because—"

"Chase!" Buck called and came trotting from the direction of the store. "What are you doing? Playing carry-out boy?"

"Meet me tomorrow at the fence line around ten o'clock. Can you make it?" Chase murmured quickly. She nodded uncertainly. Louder, he asked, "Where do you want me to put this sack? In the cab or the back of the truck?"

"In the back is fine."

After setting the sack in the rear bed, he took the one from her arms and put it with the other. He touched a hand to his hat. "I'll see you." Then Chase turned to meet his friend. "Are you ready for that blueberry pie?"

"Sure am." The last time Buck had seen the O'Rourke girl, he had labeled her a wildcat and a tomboy. Now he was picking up a different impression. His curious and dancing blue eyes studied the change.

The boldness of his inspection caused Maggie to become more self-conscious. She slipped the tips of her fingers into the front pockets of her jeans, hunching her shoulders forward to ease the strain on the shirt buttons. Her head was tipped at a proud and challenging angle under the rude stare, but Chase was turning away, prompting Buck to follow a second later.

Buck caught up with him in one stride, casting a half-glance in his direction. "I take back what I said about her the other day," Buck murmured in a low voice. "You sure as hell can tell she's a female." As he opened the door to the café, he looked back at the girl. "Maybe it's time I started calling on my neighbors."

The gleam in his buddy's eyes sent a ripple of unease down Chase's spine. Buck tended to be careless of a girl's feelings, lacking a conscience when it came to sexual conquest. That protective instinct bristled within Chase, arrogantly blind to the possibility that he wasn't in a position to judge.

"Leave her be, Buck." It was a terse reply, his tone bordering on hard authority.

"Why should I?" Buck challenged with a frowning smile and followed him into the café.

Chase attempted to smother the raw irritation with his friend and succeeded in making his voice light. "Let's just say that I saw her first and leave it at that." But there was a look of dark warning in his glance.

"Damn, but you're selfish, Chase," Buck teased. "I always share with you, don't I? We nursed at the same breast, didn't we? I even let you take my rightful place as the Calder heir, and this is the way you repay me." He feigned a wounded look and swung his leg over the back of a chair to sit at one of the café tables. "Just for that, you can buy my pie. Hey, Tucker!" he called to the man behind the counter. "I want two pieces of your blueberry pie, and Chase here is paying for it."

Chase noticed Angus O'Rourke sitting on a stool at the counter, but he let his glance slide past him to the rotund owner of the café. "Just coffee for me, Tucker, since I've been stuck with the bill."

"Old Moneybags is trying to pretend he's broke." Buck laughed, an unlit cigarette dangling from his mouth while he searched his pockets for a match. "Got a light?"

"I've got a friend who's a moocher." Chase tossed a book of matches onto the table in front of Buck. "You get paid more than I do. What do you do with your money?"

"By the time I drink a little whiskey, play a little poker, and keep the ladies happy, it just seems to disappear." Buck grinned and puffed on the cigarette.

Tucker crossed the small café, carrying two plates of pie and two cups of coffee in his pudgy hands, the front of his white apron stained with spattered grease and food. Nearly bald, his head was too small for his solidly round body. He stopped beside Chase's chair to set the order down.

"Tell Webb my freezer is getting low on meat, so I'll be out to see him one of these days to buy me some Calder beef to butcher." His voice was a monotone, as if it required too much effort to alter its flat sound.

"I'll tell him," Chase promised and watched the big man amble back to the counter. He wasn't deceived by the man's slowness or voluminous bulk. That protruding stomach was as solid as iron. A year ago, Chase had seen him move with a swiftness unusual in a man Tucker's size and level an obnoxious customer with a back-handed swing when the man had begun to use foul language in front of some townswomen. And he'd seen Bob Tucker hefting a whole carcass of beef like a sack of potatoes. He wasn't a man to mess around with.

All the cowboys toed the mark in his place, or Tucker bodily threw them out. His food was the best around for miles, and the prices were reasonable, yet there was something about the man that Chase didn't trust, but he didn't know what it was.

At the counter, Angus O'Rourke had overheard the message Tucker had given Chase to pass on to his father. After two weeks, Angus was still brooding over the results of his confrontation with Webb Calder, growing more certain with each passing day that he had been cheated out of his just due. The sight of Chase Calder sitting in the café, virtually unpunished for the wrong he'd done Maggie, awakened the hostility in Angus. Instead of directing the heat of his anger at the one who aroused it, he unleashed it on the café owner.

"How come you're doing business with Calder?" Angus demanded, yet keeping his voice low so he wouldn't be overheard. "Ain't he rich enough without you buying your beef from him? What's wrong with some of us other small ranchers around here? You want our trade, but you're not interested in doing business with us."

Tucker paused in front of Angus, marble-sized eyes regarding him indifferently. "It isn't by choice I deal with Calder. I have no more love for the man than you do. But I serve only quality beef. You other ranchers all have range-tough beef, so I have to buy from him to get decent meat."

But it rankled Tucker because it always seemed to him that Calder acted as if he were doing him a favor selling him Calder beef. Nothing was actually said or even suggested, but Tucker knew other cattle buyers made purchases by the lot, not one steer at a time. If he hadn't been local, it wouldn't have been worth the time or the trouble for an outfit the size of the Triple C to bother with him. They didn't care about his business. It would suit him fine to take it somewhere else, but no one else had the quality he demanded.

"If the only thing that will suit you is Calder beef, then buy it from me," Angus challenged. "I bought fifty head of his stuff a couple of weeks ago."

"Fifty head?" Tucker eyed him with skepticism. "Where'd you get the money to buy prime stock?"

"That isn't any of your damned business." Angus sat up straighter on the stool, offended by the question that implied he was too poor to afford Calder cattle. "Are you interested in buying my beef or not?"

"You probably bought some of his culls, but I'll stop by your place tomorrow and take a look." Tucker didn't put much faith in O'Rourke's claim to owning prime Triple C beef. "I'll be there sometime in the morning."

"Don't forget to bring your money," Angus taunted and pushed his empty cup toward the heavyset man. "Put some coffee in my cup while you're standing there blowing hot air."

"If there's any hot air circulating around here, it's probably coming from you." Tucker picked up the cup and pivoted his massive hulk to hold it under the spigot of the coffee urn.

"Wait until tomorrow morning and we'll see who's full of hot air," Angus replied smugly.

After Chase had left her, Maggie had lingered by the pickup, aware that her father was inside drinking coffee while she and Culley ran his errands. To go into the café while Chase was there would, no doubt, start her father off on another of his tirades against the Calders. Just seeing Chase would probably set him off. Maggie decided the sensible thing to do was find her brother and see if he had completed his errands. As she turned away from the café, she saw Culley trotting across the highway where the hardware store sat. She waited by the truck for him to join her, noting the scowl on his face.

"I saw you with Calder. What did he want?" he demanded, stopping in front of her.

"He helped me carry the groceries." There was a lilt of defiance in her voice that questioned his right to insist on an answer. "Did you get the part for the well pump?"

"It didn't come in yet." His answer was brisk with impatience. "The conversation you had with him—I suppose you expect me to believe that you just talked about groceries."

"We talked about a lot of things . . . that aren't any of your business," she retorted.

His mouth thinned into an angry line. "I suppose he wants to see you again."

"And what if he does?" Maggie challenged.

"I suppose he asked you to meet him somewhere," Culley guessed. And he ordered, "Stay away from him, Maggie. He just wants to get in your pants again. Can't you see that? Haven't you figured it out from the last time?"

"Is it so impossible that he might like me?"

"He might like you, all right," her brother conceded. "But you don't think for one minute that he's going to get serious, do you? You are just the daughter of a small-time rancher to him. He'll never think you're good enough for a Calder."

"Who says I want him to get serious?" she flashed. "A girl likes it when a man pays attention to her, but that doesn't necessarily mean she wants to marry him! You may be content to be the son of a small rancher with dreams that will never come true, but I'm not. I want an education, because I'm not going to live like this for the rest of my life!"

"You are my sister." On occasions, her brother's temper could match Maggie's. This was one of them. "I don't want to see you get hurt. And that's what is going to happen if you see Chase Calder again. One day you're going to find yourself in trouble, and he's going to forget your name."

"I'm not going to get in any trouble." Maggie denied that first. "And Chase has been nice to me."

"That's because he still wants something. But once he's through with you, you'll just be dirt to him. He's a Calder. And if you have an ounce of sense, you won't forget that. You'll never be anything to him except someone to roll in the grass with. Stay away from him, Maggie. Don't prove that I'm right," he warned and brushed past her to enter the café, as if he were afraid if he stayed longer, he would do something violent.

Maggie stared at his retreating back. She was trembling, too, from the force of her anger. She yanked open the door of the pickup and climbed into the cab. She waited in stiff silence for Culley to fetch their father so they could return to the ranch.

But her brother's words preyed on her, clouding her thoughts.

Chase was already at the fence line when she finally rode up the next morning. She had silently debated with herself for almost an hour trying to decide if she would meet him or not. In the end, she came because she had to find out if Culley was right about Chase.

Dismounting, Chase slipped between the barbed-wire strands of the fence to catch her horse's bridle when she stopped it. Her gaze moved warily over his lazy smile of greeting without being able to judge anything from it.

"You're late." He moved to the saddle, reaching up to span her slim waist with his hands and lift her down. "I was beginning to think you couldn't make it."

"I was trying to make up my mind whether I should come or not," Maggie replied honestly.

Her feet were on the ground, but he continued to let his hands rest on her waist. He felt her stiffness and was impatient with it. He had subconsciously been anticipating the melting softness of her. Bending his head, Chase sought to establish his dominion over her lips. There was a corresponding pressure to his kiss, but it was cool. He lifted his head to look at her, but her unwavering gaze was studying him, measuring him.

"I'm glad you came," he stated.

"Why?"

"Because I wanted to talk to you," Chase replied and tried to smile away her seriousness.

Her hands pushed at his arms to casually remove them from her waist so she could drift away from him. "I know that's what you said you wanted." Her voice seemed to imply that he meant something different. Chase followed her and she turned to confront him with her suspicions. "Culley says the only reason you want to see me is to have sex."

For an instant, Chase was stunned by her bluntness before amusement took hold. "Are you always so frank?"

"Is it true?" she persisted. "Is that the reason you want to see me?"

The stubbornness in her expression told him that she meant to have a straight answer. He opened his mouth to assure her that he had decided she was too young and inexperienced, and his seduction of her the last time was a mistake he didn't intend to repeat. But looking into her eyes, Chase realized he was only kidding himself. Given the chance, he'd make love to her again. That particular threshold had been crossed once and would be recrossed anytime the opportunity presented itself. There was no going back to an innocent, hand-holding relationship. The knowledge didn't please him and he tried to avoid acknowledging it.

"I don't know how often the Triple C could afford it, if it costs fifty head of cattle every time I do," he jested.

Anger flashed in her eyes before she turned away. "That isn't funny."

He watched her take a step away and sighed, "No, it isn't. But there isn't a simple answer to your question, either." She gave him a sidelong look, which he held. "I'd be lying if I said I would never want to make love to you again, because I would. But sex isn't the only reason. If it was only physical satisfaction I wanted, I could get that from Jake's girls. So it has to mean I want your company, too. I guess the truth is that I'm a little fascinated by you."

"Why?" But there was less demand in the question.

Chase shook his head because he didn't know. "Maybe because you are so honest and direct about what you think and what you want. Most women try to pretend. You haven't learned how yet."

"Is that bad?" She cocked her head to the side.

"No." He smiled easily. "It makes you special."

There was a profound truth to that statement that Chase was only just beginning to realize. There was satisfaction in possessing her body, but he wanted her more than that. This meeting was a test. If he tried to make love to her today, he'd lose her. But he knew, also, that if he didn't have her this time, he would the next and the next. And she would come to him as willingly as she had the first time. Knowing that, Chase could wait.

"Both your father and your brother must have warned you about seeing me," he guessed and challenged her to make her reasons clear. "So why did you meet me?"

"Because I wanted to." The lift of her shoulders was an expressive statement of her independence, but she let her gaze swing away from him.

"Why?" It was his turn to persist.

"Maybe"—she glanced back at him, a gleam dancing in her eyes—"because you aren't at all like what I expected a Calder to be."

"What did you expect me to be like?"

"I suppose I thought you'd be pompous and arrogant," she admitted a little self-consciously. "Heartless, too, I guess. But . . . you're nice."

Chase tried to hold back a smile, the corners of his mouth deepening with the effort. "A lot of people expect us to have horns and a tail. They tend to be amazed when they discover we're made of flesh and blood like everyone else."

Maggie laughed, a clear, pure sound. "Hardly like everyone else. Everyone else doesn't own as much land as you do . . . or cattle, or horses, or anything else."

"But we all have the same needs," Chase insisted and held out his hand to her, "even if it's something as simple as someone to walk with."

She looked at him and smiled, then placed her hand in his. The sun was bright and the sky was clear. Out in the deep grasses, a meadowlark sang.

The burly proportions of Bob Tucker filled the saddle seat, leaving no room between the horn and cantle. The size of him dwarfed the bay cow pony he was riding, a picture made more incongruous by the wide brim of the felt Stetson atop his small head, and contrasted by the short, slender rider accompanying him. Tucker stopped his horse close to the grazing cattle and shifted in the stirrups, the saddle groaning under his weight.

"I take back everything I thought, Angus." He studied the rust-colored herd of white faces. "These cattle aren't culls from the Triple C. They're prime stock. How did you manage to persuade Calder to turn loose of them? Or am I looking at stolen cattle?" An indignant look crossed O'Rourke's face. Before Angus could open his mouth to deny the allegation, Tucker laughed. "I guess if you'd stolen them, you wouldn't be going around telling people you had them, would you?"

"I certainly wouldn't," Angus retorted. "They're my cattle and I've got the bill of sale to prove it."

"I'm not doubting your word." Tucker was still smiling. "It doesn't matter to me whether you have a bill of sale or not. It wouldn't be the first stolen beef I've bought if you didn't." Cattle rustling was big business nowadays. Tucker knew a man could make a lot of money at it if he had the right connections. And he was never one to look down his nose at money. "The rancher is the only one who loses in a deal like that."

"Yeah, and the guy who gets caught."

"Do you know what the odds are against that?" Tucker glanced at O'Rourke and smirked. "In order to prove anything, they'd have to catch you in the act, and the chances of that happening are a million to one. Even if they did, the man would probably never go to prison. It's a lucrative business with little risk involved. The days when a rancher would hang a rustler on mere suspicion are long gone."

"That's true enough," Angus conceded and eyed the hulking form of the café owner with curiosity. "I never knew you had so much larceny in your blood, Tucker. I'm going to have to watch you when we start dealing on these cattle so you don't cheat me."

"Basically, I'm an honest person, Angus. I never try to screw the people I do business with—only the other guy," he explained with wry humor. "But I'm just as interested in making money as any other poor devil. If it means doing something a little shady, then a man has to balance the returns against the risks and make up his mind whether it's worth it."

"I suppose." O'Rourke sounded hesitant.

Tucker was slightly contemptuous of the rancher's blindness to the facts. "Crime pays in this day and age. Don't take my word for it. Look around for yourself. This is a big empty stretch of Montana, and all we have in the way of law enforcement are a couple of state police on the highway, and Potter and his excuses for deputies in the County Sheriff's Department. If a rustler wanted to steal some Triple C cattle, there wouldn't be anyone to stop him—or catch him. Even Calder couldn't patrol every inch of his range."

"I guess you're right." Despite the affirmation, Angus continued to sound skeptical.

Tucker glanced around, as if getting his bearings, then turned his horse toward a ridge. "I'll show you what I mean." The cattle scattered as the pair rode through them to climb the rough hill. At the crest, Tucker reined his horse to a stop. Beyond him stretched Calder land. "Do you see that back road over there?" He pointed to a narrow band of dirt in the distance. "All a rustler has to do is have a semi-trailer waiting there while a couple of riders drive the cattle to the fence and load them up. It's a slick operation—in and out in less than an hour. There's no one to see you or hear you. It could be days before anyone knows any cattle are missing."

"If it's so easy, how come no one has tried it yet?" Angus wondered.

"It's usually a hit-and-run operation. They move into an area, work it for a month, come away with three or four loads, and move onto the next. The last time I remember hearing about cattle being stolen around here was about ten years ago," Tucker recalled and stared thoughtfully at the expansive view before him. "Whoever did it got away clean. Around here, though, everybody knows everybody, so they're quicker to notice a strange vehicle or a strange face and not pay any attention to a local—" He stopped abruptly, not completing the sentence. He'd been thinking out loud. Now he wanted to keep those thoughts to himself, on the outside chance something might come of it. With a quick glance at O'Rourke, he changed the subject. "You never did quote me a price on that beef."

Angus was mulling over the unfinished sentence, completing it in his head. He realized it was true; the comings and goings of a local person wouldn't arouse anyone's curiosity—definitely not as quickly as a stranger. He was slow to follow the shift in the conversation.

"You haven't said what you're willing to pay," he finally countered. With a turn of his stout wrist, Tucker started to rein his horse in a half-circle. His meandering gaze noticed movement along the boundary fence between O'Rourke's property and the Triple C and he paused. His interest sharpened when he recognized the couple walking hand in hand.

There was curious speculation in his glance at O'Rourke. "So Chase Calder has come a-courting your daughter. I knew you must have had an inside track. I couldn't imagine Webb selling such high-quality cattle to just anybody."

At his comment, O'Rourke's head jerked around to see the pair. Rage flashed through his expression, but his face was averted from Tucker and the man never saw it. Angus kicked his horse to turn it away from the sight and started down the slope ahead of the heavier rider, leading him away from the couple.

Chapter VIII

Angus brooded over that scene for three days. He didn't confront his daughter with his knowledge of her meeting with Chase Calder; nor did she mention it to him. His darkening thoughts realized that his visit with Webb Calder had accomplished nothing, and to carry another protest to him would be equally futile. There was no justice in the world when a man could take a girl's innocence and go unpunished.

Before he took matters into his own hands, he resolved to give Calder one more chance to stay away from his daughter. If he left her alone, Angus would let the matter drop. If he didn't, Angus would make him pay. He had vowed it to himself.

The emptiness of his stomach told him it was nearly noon, so he left the motor to the well pump, half-reassembled, and started for the house. The cantering approach of a horse and rider caused him to stop. His gaze narrowed in sharp suspicion when he recognized Maggie riding up to the corral. He reversed his direction to walk to the corral, where she was dismounting to unsaddle her horse.

"Sorry I'm late, Pa. It'll only take me a few minutes to fix lunch." Her face was flushed and her eyes were shining when he stopped beside the board fence.

His glance fell to her mouth and noted the swollen soft curve of her lips. He didn't have to be told to know what had caused it. "You've been with Chase Calder again," he accused.

She focused all her attention on loosening the cinch. "I'm not a little girl anymore, Pa." Her low voice was stiff and defensive.

Black anger clenched his jaw, but it wasn't directed at her. To him she was the victim, a helpless female, thus incapable of knowing her own mind. He had no choice but to take matters into his own hands.

"Don't bother to fix any lunch for me. I have to go into town to pick up another part for the pump motor," he lied. It was only half a lie; he was going to town, but not for a motor part.

Maggie caught the note of falsehood in his voice. "Pa, you aren't going to—"

"I'm going into town, I told you!" he snapped and pivoted from the corral. Driven by a barely contained fury, he crossed the littered ranch yard to the pickup.

As Maggie dragged the saddle and blanket into the barn, she heard the slamming of the cab door and the coughing sputter of the truck motor before it started. The truck was bouncing down the rutted lane when she emerged from the barn to walk to the house.

There was still her brother to feed, so Maggie walked to the sink to wash her hands before fixing lunch. She stared at her reflection in the mirror, unable to understand how her father had known she'd been with Chase that morning, or how he had guessed that they had made love.

The pickup's accelerator was pressed to the floor all the way into town, where the truck clattered to a bumping stop in front of the small café. Angus charged out of the cab, slamming the door and stalking into the building. It was lunch hour and the place was half-filled with customers. His glance swept over the occupants in undisguised irritation as he crossed the room to sit on a stool at the far end of the counter. The bullet-headed owner was standing at the grill behind it, a metal spatula in his chubby hand.

"What'll you have, Angus?" Tucker didn't move, except to turn his head and look at his latest customer.

"Coffee."

The owner-cook flipped a pair of hamburgers with the spatula and squashed them flat, then shifted his hulk the two steps needed to reach the coffee urn. After filling a white cup, he traversed the length of the counter to set it in front of Angus.

"Anything else?" Tucker paused to wipe his hands on the stained front of the white bibbed apron.

"Yeah."

"Stick around," Tucker advised. "This place will clear out in another half-hour. Then we'll talk about it." A gleam brightened his small eyes as he added softly, "Partner."

Two weeks later a full moon peeked from behind a cloud, casting its light on a pair of riders walking their horses through tall, Calder grass. The creaking of saddle leather was loud in the stillness. Angus glanced at his son, whose head seemed to be on a swivel, always looking nervously around. He had the same crawly feeling in the pit of his stomach, too, and his throat was dry. Damn, but he wanted a drink. He looked to the front again, gathering courage from his all-consuming hatred.

"That bunch of cattle we spotted should be over that next hillock," he whispered to Culley and pointed.

"Pa, what happens if we get caught?"

"We aren't gonna get caught. Tucker and me have it all figured out. All we have to do is drive the cattle to the road where the truck is waiting."

There were several seconds of silence before Culley asked, "Are you . . . nervous, Pa?"

The choice of that adjective was one Angus could admit to feeling. "Some. But I keep imagining Calder's face when he discovers he has cattle missing. The bastard will be furious." Angus paused to gloat silently over the thought. "No one's had the guts to stand up to him until we came along. No Calder is going to ride roughshod on us little guys and ever get away with it again. I'm going to get even with that son-of-a-bitchin' bastard for all the grief and misery he's caused if it's the last thing I do," Angus vowed. "We'll haul every steer off this place before we're through with our midnight rides. We'll break him, Culley—you and me." A soft, malicious laugh came from his throat. "We'll be rich and he'll be poor. He's going to regret the day he let his son lay a hand on your sister. He's going to regret it real bad."

"And we're going to make sure of it," Culley murmured in fervent agreement.

Removing his hat, Chase combed his fingers through his unruly brown hair and set the felt Stetson back in place. The sun was directly overhead, scorching the metal of the pickup where it wasn't protected by the tree's shade. He scanned the hillside in the direction from which Maggie would be coming. She was already almost a full hour late.

They usually managed to meet twice a week at a pre-arranged location. It wasn't the most satisfactory solution, meeting in the daytime with limited time to spend together. Even if he ignored the fact that her father would never give Maggie permission to openly date him, where would he take a fifteen-year-old girl? The only social gathering place close by was Jake's, and he couldn't take her there.

So they had met when and where they could. A couple of times ranch work had kept Chase away, but this was the first time Maggie hadn't shown up. He felt raw inside, eaten up with a need he couldn't control.

He had waited as long as he could. Abandoning his vigil, Chase turned and grabbed the shirt draped over the side of the pickup bed. As he pushed his arms into the sleeves, he walked to the cab of the truck. He had yanked open the driver's door before he heard the hoofbeats of an approaching horse.

Remaining poised beside the open door, Chase turned toward the sound. Some of the tension eased from him at the sight of the horse's rider, a slim extension of the mount she rode. She cantered the bay toward him, weaving through the stand of trees to reach him. Pleasure swept through him, soft like the stirring warmth of a summer breeze, when she reined to a stop near the truck and kicked her feet out of the stirrups to slide to the ground.

There was a certain knowing look to her smile, an awareness that the rounded shape of her upper body sang to him and excited his male interest. She was a picture of country freshness, framed before his hungry eyes. The pull of her was urgent, but Chase stayed by the truck door, making her walk to him.

"Sorry I'm late, but I had to practically drag Pa and Culley out of bed this morning," she explained with a kind of breathless rush. "Everything ran behind schedule after that. I wasn't sure you'd still be here."

Maggie stopped a foot in front of Chase and tipped her head back to study his face—bony and rugged. Inwardly, she strained toward him, asserting her will on him. It gave her a sense of power to see the glinting darkness of want appear in his eyes. It was there now, but he was resisting it.

"I was just leaving." Irritation flickered through him at being denied the sight of all that black hair tucked under her hat. "Take your hat off. You look like a twelve-year-old when you have your hair hidden in the crown." Chase suffered small spasms of guilt when he was reminded of her youth, but they were never strong enough twinges of conscience to make him stop meeting her.

With a soft laugh, Maggie swept the hat off her head and shook her hair free. She eyed him with a challenge that was unknowingly provocative before her gaze drifted down to brazenly admire his hard-muscled torso where the unbuttoned front of his shirt swung open.

"Do you like what you see?" His dark eyes were three-quarters lidded, and there was a lazy curve to his mouth.

"Yes—what little I see."

Her audacious reply produced a deep chuckle from his throat. "You are turning into a bold little hussy," Chase mocked.

"Considering that you were my teacher, are you bragging or complaining?" Maggie countered.

"Bragging." When she turned to catch the trailing reins of her horse, he frowned and reached out to stop her. "Where do you think you're going?" She didn't resist when he turned her back to face him.

"You said you were leaving when I came. I didn't want to keep you from your work." Her green eyes blinked with too much innocence. Maggie enjoyed exercising the power she'd discovered she had over him, the ability to make him want her despite other prior claims on his attention . . . even from his father.

"You little liar." Chase smiled and pulled the reins from her hand to let them drop while he hooked her hat on the saddle horn. Then his hands were on her shoulders, rubbing the rounded curve of her bones and feeling the soft flesh of her upper arms. "You know . . . now that you are here . . . I'm staying. And to hell with any work."

There was nothing in her hands, and nothing to keep her from touching him. Her fingers felt the flatness of his stomach and the involuntary contraction of his muscles beneath them. Slowly, she let her fingers glide up his rib cage to his hair-roughened chest and shoulders, staying under the shirt. His hands tightened on her shoulders to pull her up on her toes so that she would meet his descending mouth halfway. His hungry kiss did such warm, delicious things to her. Sometimes Maggie felt there was a Fourth of July display going on inside her, with brightly colored stars shooting all through her, spraying their light and heat to every corner of her body.

She pressed closer to him, wrapping her arms around his neck and arching her body against his hard, rangy length, not satisfied until she was molded intimately to him and the heat of his flesh was burning its imprint on her. The crush of his encircling arms echoed the need for absolute closeness. When he began nibbling on the curve of her neck, Maggie couldn't contain the soft animal sound that came from her throat, but she tried to deny that he was equally empowered to devastate her.

"Sometimes"—her voice was a hoarsely disturbed whisper—"I think you're only interested in sex."

His hands moved to cup her firm bottom and fit her hips tightly to the saddle of his so that she would know she was making him hard. "You did this to me deliberately. Now you're saying it's my fault." He was amused, rather than angry.

Maggie lowered her head, wondering if such aggression by a woman was improper, yet unable to feel ashamed of it if it was. She pressed her lips against the nakedness of his chest to taste his skin, liking its smooth texture and salty flavor.

"I can't help it, I guess," she murmured and heard the groan he made deep inside.

"Maggie, haven't you discovered yet that neither one of us can?" he muttered thickly and scooped her up to carry her to a shaded stretch of grass where he put her down.

Once the primitive fires had burned themselves out, there was time to talk. Chase enjoyed Maggie's company as much as he enjoyed her body. She was bright and intelligent, easy to talk to. The responsibility of housework and family at an early age had made her mature beyond her years. Despite the stark difference in their backgrounds—-Maggie coming from a poor family and a home that possessed few creature comforts, and Chase reared in an environment of wealth and power—they had both been raised with hardship: in his case, by his father's decree; and in hers, by reality. Life held few illusions for either of them. Nothing was free; there was a price to be paid for everything. Yet there was something special between them, given freely and without expectation for more than what was received.

With regret, Chase signaled he had to leave. He had allowed himself over an hour to be with her, but he'd used most of it waiting for her to come. The time they had spent together made him more than an hour behind schedule. He walked her to the grazing horse and gathered her into his arms for one last, lingering kiss. The tooting of a truck horn ended it before either of them was satisfied.

Chase straightened and cast an impatient glance over his shoulder. A ranch pickup was bouncing over the uneven terrain toward them, a trio of cowboys laughing and hooting from the cab. The one with the grinning face stuck out the window was Buck. A grimness masked his features when he turned back to Maggie.

"You'd better go," he said, wanting to protect her from any ribald comments that might be made.

He helped her into the saddle and passed her the reins, waiting until she had turned the bay into the trees before swinging around to face the approaching pickup. It slowed long enough to let Buck hop out, then made a wide arc to return the way it had come. The pickup Chase had driven was parked in the open ground between the two. Chase started toward it, and Buck did, also.

"In case you forgot, you were supposed to pick me up an hour ago so we could load that bull up at the Crosstree pasture," Buck reminded him with a wide grin and approached Chase with a swaggering stride. "Clay and Jerry were headed this way. I hitched a ride with them to see if you'd broken down somewhere."

"I hadn't forgotten." Chase replied only to the initial remark.

"I guess I don't need to ask what kept you." His gaze sought out the horse and rider disappearing over the hillside, then returned to sweep over Chase, a knowing gleam dancing in the blueness of Buck's eyes. "Or how you got them grass stains on your knees. That was the O'Rourke girl, wasn't it?"

Chase darkened in anger, his rough features hardening as he ignored his friend's comments and walked past Buck directly to the pickup. "Let's get a move on."

Buck climbed across the open bed of the truck, rather than walk around the tailgate to the passenger's side. Both doors were slammed shut in unison and Chase turned the key in the ignition.

"Now I understand why you bought those rubbers a couple of weeks back." Buck was still grinning, his hat tilted to the back of his head, an arm resting on the frame of the opened window. He loved to tease, especially when he could get a rise out of his victim. "You don't want to get a young thing like that knocked up, but I don't know if I would trust those rubbers if I were you. You don't know how long they've been sitting on the shelf under Lew's counter. They're probably yellow with age now. They're liable to split on you just when you need them the most."

"Lay off it, Buck," Chase warned and shifted the truck into gear. It jumped forward as his foot tromped on the accelerator, then eased back with an effort at control.

"How come you never told me you had some action going on the side?" Buck persisted in a mock complaint. "We never had any secrets from each other before. We're practically brothers. You know I would never try to move in on your territory, so how come you never mentioned this hot little affair you have going with the O'Rourke girl!"

It was true. They rarely kept any information from each other, trading stories and experiences, bragging and joking about the women they'd had.

"Maybe I just didn't want to hear any of your crude remarks." Chase's expression remained stern, his gaze not straying from the bumpy path through the grass.

"Come on, Chase," Buck grumbled. "Where's your sense of humor?"

"I'll find it when you show some sense of decency."

"Man, you're as testy as a bull on the prod." Buck slouched in the seat, pulling his hat forward and low on his forehead, and stared out the side window for a sullen moment. "What you need is a few beers to loosen up," he said finally. "It's Friday and I'm going into town. Why don't you come with me?"

"No, thanks."

"Come on, Chase," Buck urged. "You haven't sampled any of Jake's new entertainment yet. You need a wild night of whoring and drinking to get rid of that chip on your shoulder."

"I'm not interested." He repeated his refusal. A whore's sex didn't interest him, not when he'd just had the satisfaction of the real thing. As for the drinking, that didn't appeal to him, either.

"Then I'll go by myself." Buck shrugged, paused a second, then glanced at Chase. "Loan me twenty dollars till payday."

"Twenty?" He sliced an impatient glance at his buddy. "You already owe me thirty. That would make fifty you've borrowed this month."

"So? I'll pay you back when I get paid."

"Yeah, and then borrow it back the following week."

"Hell, you can afford it," Buck retorted. "I'm not the one next in line to inherit all this. What's the big deal, anyway? All I'm asking for is a lousy twenty-dollar loan from a guy who's supposed to be my best friend."

Chase stretched his right leg stiff and lifted himself slightly off the cab seat to reach deep into the pocket of his jeans for his cash. All he had was four singles and a twenty. He separated the twenty from the dollar bills and handed it to Buck.

"Here." His glance took in the sulky look on the usually grinning face, and a smile eased the stiffness of his own mouth. "Who is being the sorehead now?"

Buck met his glance, then slowly laughed at himself, and took the money, stuffing it into his shirt pocket. "Thanks, Chase. You'll get it back. I wish you'd change your mind about coming with me. We could have a high ole time, you and me."

"I'll go next time." He realized he'd been neglecting his best buddy and felt obligated by friendship to do something about it.

Resting a heel on the running board of the truck, Nate Moore took the makings of a cigarette out of his shirt pocket while he watched the riders gathering cattle into a holding pen. Webb Calder stood beside him, an arm braced against the cab of the truck, his expression grim.

"I went by here about ten days ago and noticed that one steer with the split ear wasn't at the salt block. He's always been there in the mornings. It got to where I looked for him automatically," Nate explained. "At first I thought maybe he'd broken a leg or got bitten by a rattler, so I mentioned to Slim to keep an eye out for him when he checked the herd the first part of the week. A couple of days later he told me he hadn't seen hide nor hair of that steer. That spooked me and I rode out to take a look for myself."

"How many do you think are missing?" Webb watched the riders bringing the cattle to the pen in small bunches.

"A conservative estimate would be forty to fifty head. It could go higher." He returned the cigarette papers and tobacco pouch to his pocket, a rolled cigarette dangling from his lips, and raked a match across his jeans to light it.

"Any guess about when the rustlers hit us?"

"It's hard to say. More than ten days ago." He squinted at the smoke. "Probably backed a semi up to the fence gate and loaded 'em in. That's the way it's usually done."

Webb breathed in deeply and straightened from his leaning stance against the truck. "Right." It was a terse agreement. Nate stepped out of the way as Webb reached for the door handle. "Let me know the final count as soon as you get it."

"Will do."

Driving out of the pasture, Webb took the ranch road back to the headquarters and stopped the pickup in front of The Homestead. He called to one of the ranch hands passing by: "Find Virg Haskell and send him up to the house. I want to see him." A hand was lifted in acknowledgment of the order, and Webb continued on his way to the house.

Twenty minutes later, a slim, brown-haired man entered without bothering to knock. None of the employees observed that formality. A Calder was always accessible to those who worked for him. Virgil Haskell walked directly to the den that doubled as Calder's private office and removed his hat as he entered the room.

"Bevins said you asked to see me."

"That's right." Webb leaned back in his chair to look at the man. He'd never been impressed with Haskell, although he couldn't fault the man's work record. Virg had been Ruth's choice for a husband, and Ruth was a dear friend, closely linked to the family. Yet Webb had always suspected that Haskell trod on that relationship to advance himself at the ranch. There had never been any definite proof of that, and Webb had decided that it was a natural prejudice. No one would ever be good enough for Ruth. Although he'd never admitted it, not even to himself, Webb was half in love with her. After he'd gotten over his wife's death, he probably would have married Ruth if she had been free. But she hadn't been, so he had channeled his affection for her into a brotherly concern, his head ruling his heart with typical Calder discipline.

"We've had some cattle stolen, roughly fifty head from the north pasture," Webb began.

"When?" Haskell frowned in surprise.

"Ten days to two weeks ago, as close as we can tell. The first thing I want you to do is organize a count of the rest of our herds, starting with those pastured close to the main roads. Then I want you to take a couple of men and question everybody in the vicinity of the north range. Someone might have noticed a semi-trailer rig, or something out of the ordinary. Report back anything you find, immediately."

"I'll get on it right away." The hat was pushed onto the brown hair as Virgil Haskell left the den to begin carrying out the instructions he'd been given.

With his own inquiry begun, Webb reached for the telephone to notify the sheriff's department. It was strictly an afterthought that he observed the formality of letting the authorities know about the theft.

Chapter IX

Maggie glanced at the wall clock to check the time. It was almost eleven-thirty. If she hurried, she'd be able to finish the dusting before she had to fix lunch. Lifting an ashtray, she ran the oiled cloth over the top of a magazine stand moved onto the desk. It was an old thing, badly scratched and scarred. The top of it was strewn with papers, mostly advertisements, which Maggie shuffled into a pile. As she lifted the cigar box of bills, she accidentally bumped the decorative stein. It teetered on the edge of the desk and fell to the hard floor—her saving grab missing it. The stein broke into three pieces.

"Damn!" She cursed her clumsiness as she knelt to pick up the pieces.

A section of the handle was broken, and the hinged lid to the stein had snapped off the mug. There was a vee-shaped chip broken from the body of the stein. As Maggie picked up the main body of the stein to see if the chip could be glued into place, she noticed something inside. She reached in, careful to avoid the broken points on the lip, and took out the roll of dark paper.

Only it wasn't paper. It was money. She sat back on her heels in stunned disbelief. She had never seen so much money in all her life. She fingered the bills, all crisp and green. They didn't look like counterfeits; the money looked real. Maggie started to count it with trembling, eager fingers. Too dazed by her find, she didn't hear the footsteps on the porch. She wasn't aware of anything until she heard the screen door slam. Then she looked up to see her father and brother had entered the house.

"Look what I found!" Maggie lifted her hand to show them the money, laughing and excited. "There's hundreds here and more!"

"What are you doing with that?" The angry demand from her father was followed with action as he strode quickly over to take it from her hands.

"It was in the beer stein. When it fell—" Maggie stopped when she realized that neither of them was surprised. Culley looked uncomfortable—worried, almost. The sparkling excitement of discovery faded from her green eyes. A sharp-edged tension claimed her, running tautly through her nerve ends. "Where did you get this money, Pa?"

"It's none of your affair." He avoided her gaze and shoved the roll of money into his pocket."

Maggie pushed to her feet, an unknown fear gnawing at the pit of her stomach. "Yes, it is. I want to know how you got that much money."

Her father glanced at Culley, a secretive gleam dancing in his dark eyes. "We've been doing a little moonlighting," he said, sounding deliberately mysterious. A smile didn't quite make it onto her brother's face, but Maggie could tell they were sharing a private joke. It increased her suspicions.

"Are you trying to tell me you earned that much money working for someone else?" she didn't believe them. "Who? When? You've been here all the time."

"It's night work," Culley said and grinned at his father.

"Night work? Doing what?" Her uneasiness grew as she looked from one to the other.

"Now just what do you think we've been doing, little girl?" her father challenged with a cocky look.

A cold, sinking feeling chilled her. The one thought her mind had been avoiding became the only one left. The clues were all there—night work, a large sum of money, and the widely known fact that someone had been stealing Calder cattle. That was all anyone had talked about for the last two weeks. And her father had smirked with satisfaction each time the subject was discussed in front of him.

"Have you . . . had anything to do with the cattle that have been stolen?" Maggie had to force the question out, her voice flat and hard in its accusation.

A smugness came over her father's face. "You're looking at the brains behind it."

"You fools! You crazy fools!" Maggie stormed. "Do you think you're going to get away with it?"

"We haven't been caught the last three times—and we aren't ever going to be caught!" Her father stretched his short body to attain every inch of his height and pushed out his chest.

"Three?" Maggie frowned. "But I only heard about—"

"Yeah." There was a malicious grin on his face. "Calder hasn't discovered the last one yet. That's the problem with owning so much. It takes a while to find out if something is missing."

"We're just like two pesky mosquitoes," Culley inserted, "buzzing around and stinging him where he ain't expecting it, taking little bites here and little bites there—until pretty soon he's all ate up." He laughed and her father joined in with him.

Maggie stared at them, chilled to the bone and frightened, although she didn't let it show. "What happens when he gets mad, Pa? What happens when you sting him so much that he comes after you?"

"How's he going to know which mosquito to swat at?" he retorted. "He'll go stomping around, swiping at everyone, but he'll never be able to prove nothing."

Maggie shook her head slowly, not believing that. "You've just been lucky."

"Lucky, hell! We've been smart! Tucker and me have worked this thing out to where it's foolproof!" he bragged. "Not even the guy we're selling the beef to knows who we are. We can't be traced. Even the semi changes drivers so the guy making the delivery doesn't know any names on the other end."

"Why are you doing this, Pa?" she demanded. "Because of Chase? Because of—"

"Calder's had everything his way in this part of the country for too long. It's got to the point where he thinks him and his can do anything without being touched—without being made to pay for it. He's squeezed us little guys out, taking the best land and water, controlling the market so we don't get decent prices for our beef, and lording it over us like he was some damned king!" Angus towered in his role as champion of the oppressed, David rising up to smite Goliath. "We're going to get even with Calder for everybody! And we've only started!"

"You have to stop!" Maggie insisted, and she vibrated with an anger that came from an inner fear. "Quit while you're ahead, Pa. You've got all that money. It's more than we've ever had. It's enough. You've showed Calder—now quit while you can."

"We aren't quitting. We're going to keep taking from the rich and giving to the poor until there isn't anything left to take. We're going to break Calder."

"No. If you don't stop stealing cattle, I'll go to Calder and tell him what you're doing," she threatened.

"No, you won't." He shook his head, unalarmed by her threat. "You won't send your father and brother to prison. Right now Chase Calder has you blinded, but the day will come when you'll see what the Calders are really like. They think they are so big and powerful that they can do anything they want and get away with it. But they won't—not as long as there's an O'Rourke around." He studied her, then gave a decisive nod. "You'll keep quiet about what you know."

Her father was right. It had been an empty threat. She wouldn't tell old man Calder or Chase that her father and brother had joined up with Bob Tucker to rustle Triple C cattle. She couldn't turn in her own family.

"You'd better get some lunch on the table," Angus advised now that he had silenced her argument for good. "We've had a full morning's work and we have to meet Tucker in town to start working out the details of which spot we're going to hit next."

In a numbed state, Maggie prepared the noon meal and put it on the table for them. She had no appetite as she picked at the food on her plate. While she listened to the confident voices of her father and brother, there was no question in her mind that her loyalty was to them, but how could she meet Chase again, knowing what she did? If she saw him and didn't mention anything, then wasn't she a party to the rustling? But if she stopped meeting him, wouldn't he become suspicious and wonder shy? She was caught in the middle with no way to turn.

The theft of the cattle had meant a lot of extra work at the Triple C, so it had been a week since she'd seen him for more than a couple of minutes, just long enough for Chase to explain why he couldn't stay. Maybe he wouldn't be able to make it tomorrow afternoon, either, Maggie hoped. Then perhaps she'd have time to decide the best way to handle the situation.

But he was there waiting for her when she arrived the next day. His horse was grazing in the wildflower-strewn meadow in the section they called the Broken Bluff. Chase walked forward to meet her, the white flash of his smile showing against the layered tan of his features. Maggie stopped her horse before she reached him and slipped out of the saddle without giving him a chance to help her down. She let the reins trail the ground and patted her horse's neck, not looking at Chase when he walked up to her, postponing the moment when she had to meet his eyes.

"I thought you might be too busy to come today." She gave him an immediate opening to say he had to leave.

"We're busy, all right, but not *that* busy." A hand was hidden behind his back. He brought it around to offer her a bouquet of wildflowers. "These are for you, Maggie."

Her throat grew tight when she looked at the collection of riotous color held in that large, masculine hand. She reached for them hesitantly, encircling their stems with her fingers and lifting them to her face to inhale their wild fragrance.

"No one's ever given me flowers before." She glanced into the dark intensity of his eyes and ached inside.

There was a faint curve to his mouth. "If any of the boys saw me picking those flowers, they would never let me hear the end of it."

She could well imagine how much he would get ribbed if he had been seen doing something so blatantly romantic. It was difficult for her to imagine this virile and husky man picking flowers. Such sentimentality didn't seem to fit the image of rough, raw manhood.

"Do you like them?" he prompted.

"Yes." Maggie nodded, unable to lift her gaze from the bouquet, her fingertips lightly tracing the satiny petals.

The point of his finger raised her chin. "Then how about thanking me for them?" he suggested.

Her gaze went no higher than his mouth, its strong, firm line coming toward her. She was shaken by a fervent need to know the forgetfulness of his embrace, the heady wildness his kiss could bring. She didn't wait for his lips to complete their descent to claim hers. Instead, she flung herself into his arms, the bouquet slipping from her hands as they wound around the thick column of his neck. Her mouth moved hungrily and desperately over his.

She was seeking and demanding, driving against him with her lips and her body. There was heat. There was fire. There was the wild tingling in her loins. But she didn't find the needed assuagement for that niggling feeling of duplicity. The steel band of his arms and the fierce pressure of his roaming hands tried to absorb her into his body, but the physical impossibility of such a feat soon made itself known. Slowly, crying inside, she turned her face away from him and pushed at his shoulders.

"The flowers. I dropped the flowers." She used them as an excuse to end an embrace that fulfilled every physical and emotional need except one.

Chase was reluctant to let her go because he sensed that he had somehow failed her. He mouthed the sensitive spot on the curve of her neck, knowing how the caress always aroused her and feeling the subsequent shivers of stimulation, but she continued to resist him. Confused by her conflicting signals, he loosened his hold and she quickly moved out of his arms, bending to pick up the scattered flowers. When she straightened, her back was to him. His hands moved to rub the soft points of her shoulders.

"I've missed being with you, Maggie." His voice was husky with meaning. "I've missed *you.*"

"I know." Her head was bent, her expression nidden from him. "I missed you, too." But the tone of her voice sounded deliberately light. In the next second, she was walking away from his hands. "Thank you for the flowers. They're lovely."

A frown plowed a furrow between his brows as he watched her walk to an outcropping of rock and sink to the ground to rest against it. He followed her after a few seconds, his keen gaze studying her smooth, expressionless features. He stopped near her feet, towering above her.

"What's bothering you, Maggie?"

"Nothing," she insisted, then looked up at him with a certain thoughtfulness. "You want to make love to me, don't you?"

This candor wasn't what he had expected, not that she wasn't usually direct in her statements. He could scarcely deny her question, but he guessed it wasn't sex that she wanted from him.

"Yes, I want to make love to you." He lowered himself to the

ground beside her, "but not if it isn't what you want me to do."
With his back against the same rock, he hooked an arm behind her
waist and started to pull her toward him. "Come here."

"No, I don't think I want—"

"I know you don't." Chase guessed what she was going to say.
"And I'm not going to try to persuade you to change your mind
and let me love you. All I want to do is hold you. Okay?"

She searched his face for an instant, then let him turn her
sideways to lie across his chest. Chase took off her hat so her head
could rest against his shoulder and smoothed the tangle of long,
black curls. A hand was doubled near her mouth while the other
rested lightly on his chest. He could feel the tension in her body
and held her loosely, one hand resting on her hipbone and the
other cupping her rib cage below the swell of her breast.

He made no attempt at conversation, simply holding her in his
arms. The sun was warm and a light breeze rustled the grass.
Gradually, he felt her relax against him like a slowly uncoiling
spring. A quiet contentment seemed to claim both of them. Chase
had no idea how long he held her like that; five minutes or twenty.
His muscles were starting to cramp; soon they would be numb if he
didn't move. He shifted slightly, tucking his chin into his chest to
look at her. Her eyes were closed, long curling lashes lying
together.

"Are you sleeping?" he murmured.

"Uh—" It was a negative sound. "Thinking."

"About what?" A strand of black hair laid across her cheek and
Chase gently pushed it back with the others.

She smiled, almost sadly. "I don't think you would understand."

"Try me."

"I was thinking"—her eyes opened slowly as she shifted in his
hold so that she was lying with both shoulders against his chest and
facing the open sky—"that I won't always be cooking and cleaning
and mending worn-out clothes for my father and brother. When I
finish school, I'm leaving the ranch. I'll get a job somewhere and
have a place of my own . . . and new clothes. People won't look at
me and click their tongues, saying the poor girl doesn't have a
decent thing to wear." She mimicked the words with bitter pride.
"I'm going to work and make something of myself. And my hands
won't have callouses. They'll be smooth, like a lady's." She paused
to look at her hands. "I suppose that sounds silly to you."

"No, it doesn't sound silly." Chase smiled against her hair, breathing in the freshly washed smell of it. "Those are the kind of dreams about the future just about everybody has." He hadn't because his future had been all mapped out for him since the day of his birth—taking over the Triple C Ranch. A man couldn't dream much bigger than that. "They rarely come to anything, though. You'll probably marry some cowboy and have three kids before you're twenty."

The words twisted inside him like a sharp knife at the image of Maggie in another man's arms and her belly swollen with someone else's child. This violent feeling of jealousy took him by surprise. He was distracted from the discovery when Maggie twisted angrily out of his arms and bounded to her feet, her green eyes blazing.

"I won't!" She stormed in an unbridled fury that rolled Chase to his feet. "I won't marry some two-bit cowboy and live like this the rest of my life! I won't be like my mother, existing on dreams and broken promises! I won't! Do you hear me?!!" Her clenched fists pounded at his chest to drive home her words. "I'm going to be somebody! And no one can stop me! I won't let them!"

"Hey, I believe you." Chase caught at her hands, amazed by her vehemence. His smile was one of admiration and respect. But Maggie caught the laughing inflection in his voice and glared at him, daring him to laugh at her. "I believe you, Maggie," Chase repeated, this time without it. "As a matter of fact," he added wryly, "I feel sorry for anyone who tries to stand in the way of what you want."

Her anger died, but the determination remained. "I'm not like my father, Chase. I'm not like him at all. And I'm not weak and passive like my mother."

"I'm convinced there isn't anybody like you," he declared and let go of her hands to tunnel his fingers under her hair. Bending his head, he kissed her mouth. With persuasive pressure, he coaxed it open while his hand cupped the thrusting point of her breast in his palm.

After that it seemed a natural progression of events that found them on the ground again, the barrier of their clothes being dismantled with consummate ease. They stroked, caressed, demanded, and aroused each other, then coupled in a passionate union that left no shadows between them, mental or otherwise.

It was harder this time for Chase to leave her, and he couldn't say why. He insisted on riding with her partway. There was a place where he could cut across the sections that would intercept his original route.

"Won't anybody ask where you are?" Maggie wondered as she walked her horse through the grass beside his.

"They might, but Buck will cover for me," he assured her. "We're moving a herd from the adjoining range here onto the Broken Butte."

"Why?" The comment aroused an idle curiosity. At this time of year, the summer pasture was usually established for a herd.

"To get them away from the main road, where it would be too easy for the rustlers to reach them," he replied.

"Oh." She looked straight ahead, realizing she had artlessly garnered an important piece of information. She caught her nether lip between her teeth, her mouth dry. "Do you have any idea who is stealing your cattle?"

"No. If we did, we'd stop them. But they won't find that it's easy pickings anymore," he stated confidently.

"Because you're moving the cattle," Maggie concluded. A sense of guilt made her try to have the O'Rourkes look innocent. "Maybe I should mention something to Pa about moving our herd in case they decide to leave you alone and hit us."

"It might be a smart thing to do. With rustlers working in the area, you should take some precautions," Chase advised.

"You're right," she agreed and hoped he didn't detect the nervous tremor in her voice.

Most of the wildflowers wilted during the long ride home. Maggie put the few fresh ones in a bud vase and set them on the table. Her father noticed them as soon as he sat down for the evening meal. He eyed her curiously when she passed him the platter of meat.

"What's the occasion?"

"No occasion," she responded in a cool, composed voice. She wasn't about to tell him that they were the first flowers any man had given her, not when it was Chase Calder. "I thought they would look nice."

"You were with *him* today," her father guessed.

Maggie knew she hadn't given anything away, yet she could see the knowledge in her father's eyes every time after she'd come back from meeting Chase. What was different about the way she looked after she'd been with Chase?

"Yes."

"What did you say to him?" He passed the meat to Culley.

"Nothing."

Satisfaction curved his mouth. "Did he have anything to say about the cattle that's been stolen?"

"Only that they don't know who is doing it," she admitted and helped herself to the potatoes.

He laughed with exultant glee. "Didn't I tell you!"

"Pa, it isn't going to be so easy from now on," Maggie protested. "They're moving the herds."

He sobered to dart her a sharp look. "Where?"

"I don't know. Chase only mentioned that they were switching one of the herds to the Broken Butte range, away from the main roads," she informed him with a worried frown. "It's going to be too risky for you to try anything."

But he wasn't listening to her. Instead, his attention was on Culley. "Maybe you and me should go into town for a drink tonight. Tucker can join us after he closes up. We might want to rearrange our plans some. I seem to recall a back road that isn't used anymore. It goes right by the Broken Butte."

Her brother's eyes glistened a devil-green. "It sure would be nice if we hit a herd they thought was safe, wouldn't it?"

"It sure would." Her father grinned.

Maggie stared at the pair of them. "You're crazy! Both of you! I don't know why I should care whether you get caught or not!" But she cared because they were her family. Blood ties weren't severed by the right or wrong of a thing.

A dozen men were gathered around the massive desk in the den, their attention centered on Webb Calder, standing in front of the large map on the wall. Chase sat with one hip on the corner of the desk, bending his head to light the thin cheroot in his mouth with a match flame.

"Starting tonight, we're going to patrol every road on this ranch," Webb announced. "That means every main road, back road, and side road. We've divided the ranch into eight sectors and worked out a loop that will cover every road." He assigned a sector to a man and outlined the individual route for each one.

When he was satisfied the routes were clear, he continued with the general instructions. "I want those pickups moving constantly, no stopping for a short snooze—only to gas up. When I say no stopping, that's what I mean. If you think you'll have to relieve yourself, then take along a can. And vary your pattern—counterclockwise one time, clockwise the next. I don't want any semi to be able to predict when you'll pass a given spot and slip in and out while you're gone. Is that understood?"

There was a silent bobbing of heads. Someone from the back of the circle asked, "What happens when we see something? What are we supposed to do?"

"I sure as hell hope you don't go up and kiss them," Webb declared with a half-grin which brought a round of subdued laughter.

"I guess what I meant was how do we let the others know?" The question was clarified.

"Unfortunately, we aren't equipped with radios, although that might come in time," Webb stated. "Bill—Bill Vernon"—he identified the warehouse manager-bookkeeper by his full name—"has already made certain that every one of the trucks has a flare gun in it. If you see anything suspicious, fire it in the air. The rest of us will come."

"And in the meantime?" a different cowboy asked.

"In the meantime . . . you all have rifles." Webb glanced around the half-circle of men. "Stop at the commissary before you head out and Bill Vernon will see that you have a supply of ammunition. Do whatever you have to in order to keep them there until you get some support."

"You mean shoot out the tires?"

"If that's all you have the guts to aim at," Webb retorted and fixed the man who asked the question with a hard stare. Then his gaze swept the rest of them. "Any more questions?"

They looked at one another, the silence stretching. Chase studied their faces. All of them were serious, yet there was a certain glitter in their eyes. It burned through them like contagious fever, because here was something outside of the normal routine of work—something that held an element of danger and excitement, a thing every red-blooded cowboy thrived on.

"All right. Those of you assigned a patrol, get started," Webb, ordered. "You others will stay here with Nate, Virg, and the rest of us," he said, including Chase with a glance. A wry smile slanted his mouth. "We're going to be the calvary, arriving in the nick of time."

With a curt nod, he dismissed them. Chase stayed while the others wandered en masse from the room, talking low among themselves, but there was no trace of disapproval or dissension in their voices. Chase glanced at his father, who had taken a seat behind the desk.

"Do you think it will work?"

Webb raised an eyebrow and shrugged. "Between moving the cattle and the patrols, it should. Thieves are basically a lazy lot. They help themselves to whatever is laying around. If it's risky or hard to get at, they tend to move on to something that's easier. They're allergic to work or they wouldn't be stealing. It's my guess they'll drift to a climate where it isn't so hot for them."

"I hope you're right." Chase straightened from the desk.

"So do I. We can't afford to keep losing beef," he replied grimly.

Chapter X

"Afterward, it will be as easy as pie," her father insisted while Maggie continued to stare at him incredulously, unable to believe what he was asking her. "We'll load the horses up in the horse trailer and take off one way. The semi will head in the other direction with the beef."

"You can't expect me to agree with this wher you know how I feel," she protested.

"The Broken Butte is rough country," he reminded her. "The cattle will be scattered along the base of the butte. It'll take some time bunching them together unless we have a third rider to help. If you come with us, we can get in and get out in a hurry. If you don't, Culley and I could be there too long."

"Then don't go," Maggie argued. "Or make Tucker ride with you and earn the cut he's taking."

"He can't. He has to ride with the driver to show him where to meet us to pick up the cattle," he explained. "It isn't easy to find where you're supposed to be going when you're driving without lights. No, Tucker has to be with the semi so we can keep to the time schedule. Are you coming or not?" Her father paused, then added, "If you don't, we're going to take our chances without you."

She could see the reckless determination in his face, and in Culley's, too. She half-turned from them, rubbing her arms in agitation and uncertainty.

"There's nothing to it," Culley assured her. "You just bunch up

107

some cattle and drive them into the truck. I was nervous the first time, too, but it's easy, Maggie. Honest.''

She wanted to laugh at that, but she couldn't. "When?" She glanced at her father.

"Tonight," he stated, and Maggie stiffened because she wasn't being given a chance to think it over. "We'll leave here around two A.M., which gives us time to have a couple of hours of sleep before we have to pull out.''

"That isn't fair, Pa." She was angry with him. "You deliberately waited until the last minute before asking me to come with you.''

"You're just like any female. If I would have asked you sooner, you would have fretted and stewed over it. Your imagination would have run away with you,'' he reasoned.

"I won't go! There's nothing you can say that will make me change my mind! Ever!" She stalked from the room, refusing to be maneuvered into doing something she knew to be wrong. She was angry because she was afraid—afraid for her brother. Because of Chase, she couldn't share her father's unreasoning hatred for the Calders, but it didn't lessen her fear for the safety of her family. Maggie raced to her bedroom.

There was a knock at her bedroom door and Maggie turned around to face it. Still raw with temper, she guessed it had to be her brother. Her father wasn't likely to come around to calm her down or attempt to make amends for his action, not when she had rebelled against his authority.

"Come in." The permission was abrupt and unwelcoming as she turned her back on the door.

It opened. "It's me—Culley." He entered the small, low-ceilinged room, an addition slapped onto the existing side of the house.

There was barely enough room for a single bed and dresser and the space to walk between them. One wall still consisted of the exterior siding. He came up behind her and hesitated. "Don't be upset about tonight, Maggie. You don't have to be scared for us. Nothing is going to happen."

"I'm angry. I'm mad. I'm upset. But I'm scared, too. What you're doing is stupid. You'll be caught.''

"No, we won't. We've done it before and got away with it. We'll do it again," he promised.

"Oh, Culley." He was trying to reassure her, but it wasn't the kind of reassurance she needed. Maggie turned her head to the side to bring him within her vision. "It's crazy. You know that."

"You only think it is because Chase Calder has your head turned. You aren't looking at it right, or you'd be able to see that we're giving the Calders the grief they deserve."

"You don't know Chase." She couldn't accept this all-encompassing condemnation of the Calders. "He treats me nice, Culley. He picks me flowers. Sometimes we just talk about different things and he holds me. He makes me feel good, Culley." She tried to make him understand. "Like I'm somebody special."

"Nothing is ever going to come of it, Maggie. Can't you see that?" Culley argued. "He's just using you right now, so, sure, he treats you nice. But what about later? What's going to happen if you get pregnant?"

"He's careful." She glanced away.

"And if that's not good enough, who is going to suffer the shame? You can bet it won't be him. He won't even claim to know you." Culley could see he wasn't getting through to her and sighed heavily. "Look, does he ever take you anywhere? Have you ever had a real date with him? No," he answered the questions himself. "Because he doesn't want to be seen with you. So he arranges to meet you, takes what he wants, and sends you home. You say he's nice to you, but is that the way he would treat a girl who he thinks is respectable and good?"

His questions stung already-sensitive emotions. Before she realized what she was doing, her hand arced to slap his face. The contact turned his head, and Culley was slow to turn it back. Maggie stared in dismay at the white mark on his cheek that was gradually turning red. She bit at her lip, unable to apologize.

So Culley did. "I'm sorry. I didn't mean to upset you." He regarded her with sad green eyes. "You'd better get some sleep."

Her eyes smarted with tears she wouldn't shed as he turned and left the room. In angry gestures, she brushed them from her lashes and began jerking off her clothes to go to bed. She knew worry would keep her from sleeping. She wouldn't have a restful minute until Culley and her father came back from their night's escapade—if they came back.

It was pitch-black. Shapes were only distinguishable by varying degrees of darkness. A cloud-covered sky hid the stars. If there was a moon, Culley hadn't seen it. All his senses were honed to razor-edge sharpness, magnifying the combined thud of hooves of trotting horses and cattle to a loud drumbeat. The jangle of bits and spurs and moaning saddle leather competed with the grunting breathing of moving horses and the lowing protests of the cattle. Culley glanced to the side, trying to make out the shape of his father against the night-darkened landscape. He was a shadowy, indistinct form, outlined briefly, then melting into the background.

Some distance ahead of them, a diesel motor idled impatiently where the semi-truck waited to load up the cattle they were driving. He had heard it arrive and maneuver into position not ten minutes before, its roar shattering the night's quiet. Culley was certain they were making enough noise to wake up the whole state.

It seemed they had been here forever, but Culley knew the apparently slow passage of time was another exaggeration of his nerves. When they had arrived, they had fanned out swiftly, flushing whatever cattle they found toward the center until they had gathered this bunch. It was the nervousness of guilt that had tied the sickening knot he felt in his stomach. There wasn't any fear as such, although he could hear the hammering beat of his heart pumping adrenaline through his system.

His constantly roaming gaze saw the black rectangular shape of the semi outlined by the lighter darkness of the road. They were almost there. Relief wavered through him that this ordeal was almost over. He let his guard down for an instant. His horse stumbled, throwing his relaxed body against the saddle horn before he could right himself. His heart catapulted into his throat and stayed there even after his horse regained its stride.

A pair of bright lights bounced into his peripheral vision. An alarm sounded in his head as his gaze jerked around to identify the source of the lights. A cold finger of fear ran down his spine.

"Pa, there's a pickup coming down the road!" His voice rang out strong and clear.

There wasn't time to panic, only to react. His warning had barely been issued when a whistle and a yell came from the direction where Culley believed his father to be. It started the cattle into a run, and his horse leaped into a gallop to follow their headlong flight. They had been less than thirty yards from the semi when the discovery had thrown the operation into wild confusion, and abandoned their plans.

The ground vibrated with the thunder of stampeding hooves and the air was filled with shouts and the bellowing of frightened cattle. Overhead, the sky exploded with light and Culley saw the black opening of the trailer yawn before them. Then his ears were deafened with the resounding report of rifle fire. He whipped his horse with the ends of the reins, his mind void of any conscious thought, operating now on pure instinct. The artificially lighted sky permitted Culley to see his father racing with him across the long stretch of open ground.

"Get the horse trailer out of here!" his father shouted to Tucker and the semi driver. "We'll ride in the truck!"

Culley realized there wasn't time to load the horses if they hoped to get away. He had a glimpse of Tucker's massive form running for their pickup and horse trailer parked on the road, the jackknifed semi hiding it from view. Red bursts of light punctuated the rifle fire being exchanged between the pickup and the semi. One of the pickup's headlights was already out, the other beam illuminating the slatted sides of the long stock trailer.

A few of the cattle veered away from the black opening of the trailer and the downed gate that formed a ramp to it. The rest stampeded into it, cloved hooves clattering on the trailer's floor. His father's horse lunged up the ramp ahead of Culley. He waved him to follow him inside, but the steer running beside Culley balked at the ramp and spun into his horse. It knocked his mount sideways, its flank hitting a fence post, but his wild-eyed horse kept its balance. Culley ignored the scrape of the saddle against the post as he urged his horse after his father's and plunged into the black bedlam inside the trailer.

The cattle were spilling back toward the opening, bawling in panic, the clatter of hooves mixing with the frightened whinny of the horses. Charging animals turned Culley's horse sideways, effectively blocking the way out and turning the cows back. He was conscious of the whine of bullets and rifle shots, but his attention was focused on controlling his plunging and half-rearing mount as it danced in place. Somewhere in the darkness of the trailer, he heard his father cursing. Part of him knew that if either one of them went down, they would be trampled to death.

"Cover me!" a voice shouted beside the opening Culley blocked.

He glanced down as a stranger tossed him a rifle, the metal

barrel gleaming briefly in the headlight. Lightning reflex allowed him to make a one-handed grab on the gun. The man left the protection of the trailer side to raise the tailgate they had used for a ramp, thus exposing himself to the rifle fire from the pickup.

Kicking and pulling, Culley forced his horse to swing around broadside to the trailer wall. Spooked animals battered his legs and he banged a knee painfully against the side of the trailer. Hemmed against the side by the cattle, Culley pushed the rifle muzzle through the openings between the slats and aimed it at the bright headlamp of the pickup. After the first bruising recoil of the rifle butt against his shoulder, he was numb to the pain as he sprayed the hood of the truck with bullets. He could have been shooting at a coyote for all the thought he gave to what he was doing. Self-preservation dictated his actions.

The revving of the diesel engine was followed by a shifting of gears that jerked the trailer. His horse crouched low and Culley had to grab for the saddle horn as the horse shifted frantically beneath him to keep its balance in the moving vehicle. The splat of a bullet ruptured a wood board near his head. Another shot and something collapsed on the truck floor with a heavy thud. Fear raced through his veins. It might have been his father who had fallen.

"Pa?"

"I'm all right." His father's reply contained only a thin echo of its former confidence. "They shot one of their own cows."

The semi was moving swiftly down the road and there weren't any more sounds of gunfire. Culley strained his eyes, but he couldn't see any vehicle pursuing them. They were going to get away, after all. For a while there, he had thought that Maggie was going to be right. Until this minute, he hadn't been sure they would succeed in their escape. The same thought seemed to occur to his father as he laughed.

"We made it, Culley!" Angus declared triumphantly. "They tried to spring a surprise on us with that patrol, but we outsmarted them and got away clean!"

"Yeah." He was hesitant at first in his agreement, then gained confidence with a building sense of victory. "Yeah, we sure did!" He let out a shout that started the cattle milling again.

The elation didn't last long as reaction set in and he began to shake uncontrollably. It was a combination of the closeness of their brush with danger and his own action that aided their escape. What if he had shot somebody? True, he hadn't been aiming at a human target, but a bullet could have ricocheted. It was a very real possibility.

He sat on his horse in a state of shock, barely conscious of the truck's grinding gears and the whooshing of air brakes as it began to slow down. It came to a stop, the diesel motor idling while a cab door slammed. There was a pounding on the tailgate.

"Are you all right in there?" It was Tucker's voice that called to them.

"We're okay!" his father replied, but Culley felt badly shaken.

"Hold on. We're going to get you out of there."

The cattle stirred as his father worked his horse slowly toward the rear of the truck. His own horse pricked its ears and snorted at the noise of the gate being lowered. Bob Tucker's big hulk was in the opening to shoo aside the cows. While his father filed out, Culley waited, then nudged his horse to follow him. He wasn't aware that his hand had retained a death grip on the rifle until the truck driver reached for it.

"I'll take my rifle back now. You did a good job of keeping him pinned down, kid." The man's face was in the shadows, but he glimpsed the white of his teeth when he smiled and took the rifle from his stiff fingers.

"I didn't hit him, did I?" Culley asked hoarsely.

"No." He shook his head, quite definite about that. "He was lying in the ditch beside the road, but you put his pickup out of commission."

"Any damage to the rig?" Tucker questioned the driver.

"He put a hole in two tires, but I can make it," he said and gave the big man a hand in fastening the truck gate.

They had stopped at a fork in the back road, the semi pointed down one and the pickup truck and horse trailer headed down the other. Culley dismounted to help his father load the horses. They finished as the semi pulled away, heading down its road with a night's drive yet to be made. Their job was done and they took the other road that led home.

Unable to sleep, Maggie finally gave up trying. She got up and dressed, went to the kitchen to put on a pot of coffee, even though she didn't need the stimulant to keep her awake during the long vigil.

The pot was almost empty when she heard the rattle of the pickup and horse trailer drive into the ranch yard. A shudder of relief went through her that they had made it back safely. She pushed open the front door and walked outside. She didn't immediately see her father in the darkness of the yard, but Culley was backing the horses out of the trailer.

"Are you all right?" she asked.

"No thanks to you." Her father came around the far side of the trailer to take the reins of the horse. "Why didn't you tell us Calder had put out patrols?"

"Oh, no." It wasn't any comfort to realize she'd had cause to worry. "I didn't know about them." Chase hadn't mentioned it. If he had, she would have tried harder to keep them from going. "What happened?"

"They damned near caught us—that's what happened!" her father retorted.

"Did they see you? Did they recognize you?" Her questions were like more rifle fire as she fell in step with her father and brother as they went to unsaddle the horses and turn them loose in the corral. Her glance kept skittering to Culley, who had not made a single comment, but she couldn't read what was in his shadowed expression.

"No. They never got close enough to us to get a good look, not with all the shooting going on." It was her father again who answered.

"Shooting? Was anybody hurt?" She thought immediately of Chase.

"No. Nobody got a scratch," her father boasted. "They tried to surprise us, but it didn't work. We got away—and with the cattle. Two minutes, if we'd just had two minutes, we could have been loaded up and gone without them even knowing we'd been there. We could have been, too, if you'd come along, Maggie. If anything would have happened to us tonight, it would have been your fault for not coming with us and giving us that edge of having a third rider."

He had already found a justification for the narrowness of their escape. He was blaming Maggie. She resisted the guilt he tried to place on her, recognizing the attempt for what it was—another one of his excuses for failure—but it wasn't easy.

When they reached the corral, Angus handed Maggie the reins to his horse. "Unsaddle him for me," he ordered. "I'm going to unhitch the trailer."

She didn't argue. As her father walked away, she glanced at Culley, who was quietly unsaddling his horse.

"What happens now, Culley?" Maggie deliberately hadn't asked her father that question. Coming from her, he would have regarded it as a challenge. "Is he finally going to call it quits?"

"We'll lie low for a while—until the heat's off."

"You were lucky tonight," she reminded him. "Next time you might be recognized."

"Then, again, maybe we won't." Culley shrugged and lifted the saddle off his horse to set it on the ground.

Once the horses were turned loose in the corral, they carried the saddles and gear into the barn. Maggie was adjusting her father's saddle on the wooden saddle rest when she noticed Culley staring at his saddle.

"What's wrong?" She moved over to see what he was looking at.

"A rosette's missing." He pointed to the round patch of unweathered leather where the ornamental tie had been. "It must have gotten ripped off when my horse scraped up against the fence post. What if they find it, Maggie?"

She knew what he was thinking It was evidence that he'd been on the scene. "I'll get it for you," she promised.

The road in front of the gate to the Broken Butte was crowded with parked vehicles the next morning. All of them belonged to the Triple C, except for the sheriff's car. Out in the fenced range, riders were rounding up the remaining herd to make a tally of the loss. Elsewhere, a chain was being attached to the truck that had been shot up the night before so it could be towed to the ranch garage for repairs. Sheriff Potter, a harried-looking man in a crisply starched uniform, was off to one side talking to Slim Bevins, the man who had surprised the rustlers. The grim trio standing in the shade of one of the horse trailers was made up of Webb Calder, Nate Moore, and Virg Haskell.

"We nearly had them," Virg grumbled. "If Slim could only have held them another fifteen minutes, your plan would have worked."

"Close doesn't count, Virg," Webb replied.

"Whoever these rustlers are, they know this country," Nate observed. "They either did some damned thorough scouting, or they're local. This road isn't on any maps. And it doesn't look like any more than a pair of ruts where it joins the other."

"They're smart," Virg declared.

"They can't be too smart," Webb denied, "or they would have figured out we were patroling the roads and had someone on lookout." He glanced at Nate. "But you are right about one thing, Nate. Only someone who has been on this road before would know it isn't an abandoned one. It's entirely possible we have someone local working with this band. The problem is—who?"

None of the three would speculate. The discussion wasn't continued as Webb noticed Sheriff Potter crossing the road toward him. The short, wide-hipped man walked with small, jerky steps, as if his feet were hurting him. He wasn't a man to exert himself, firmly believing that things had a way of working themselves out if left alone. He was neither incompetent nor dishonest, but somewhere in the shadows of laziness.

"I talked to your man, Webb," he stated as he came to a mincing stop to complete the circle partially formed by the three men. "I can't see where we have any more to go on than we did before. The ground is too churned up to leave any tire tracks that might do us some good. The bullets we got out of the truck are unlikely to tell us anything. They're an ordinary thirty-thirty slug. Every man in the state of Montana has a hunting rifle. With no license number, no description that would do us any good, I'd say we're still on square one. But"—the sheriff brightened, or as much as his tired expression would allow—"I think you scared them good, surprising them like that. I'm sure they won't be back."

"I hope you're right, Potter. Thanks for coming out personally." Webb shook the man's limp hand.

"It's my job, Webb." He shrugged and toddled toward his car.

"And what happens if they do come back?" Nate grumbled to the sheriff's back.

There was a flicker of amusement in Webb's dark eyes before they turned to the tired and drawn face of Slim Bevins, who hadn't yet had any sleep. With the sheriff gone, he wandered across the road to join them. His expression was still apologetic, unable to shake the feeling that he had let his boss down.

"Sorry I couldn't be of any more help," he apologized to Webb, and not for the first time. "It just all happened so fast I never really got a good look at anything or anybody. The riders were crouched so low in the saddles that I couldn't tell if they were tall or short, or fat or thin. All I saw for sure was that there was two of them, plus the driver and another big guy. The trailer was just an ordinary cattle truck, and I couldn't see any lettering on the cab. If there was a license plate, it was all muddied up," he sighed and shook his head. "There for a while there was so much lead flying through the air, I thought I was in the middle of a shootout in a Western movie."

"You did the best you could under the circumstances. I don't ask more from a man than that." But Webb was conscious of the frustration he felt at the lack of information the man had been able to obtain.

"Are you positive there isn't anything, Slim?" Virg Haskell persisted. "None of them called each other by name?"

"Nope." The man shifted uncertainly and gnawed at the inside of his lip. "There was something familiar about one guy's voice."

"Do you mean you had heard it before?" Webb's gaze narrowed on him.

"Well, it kinda sounded like . . . Angus O'Rourke," Slim admitted finally.

"Are you sure?" There was a steel quiet to Webb's voice.

"That's just it," the cowboy sighed. "I'm not sure. That's why I didn't mention it before. Hell, it could have been anybody's voice."

On that negative note, Webb turned to the man at his right. "Take Slim back to the headquarters so he can get some sleep. And, Virg, let Ruth know I probably won't be back for lunch until around one."

"I'll tell her." Virg nodded and moved off toward one of the parked trucks, with Slim Bevins tagging along a step behind.

"Seems to me you could use some sleep yourself." Nate ran a critical eye over the sharply etched lines on Webb's face. "In case you forgot, you've been up all night, too."

"I've gone without sleep before," Webb retorted.

"Yeah, but you weren't pushing fifty when you did it," Nate pointed out.

"What's the matter, Nate?" A wry glance was cast in the foreman's direction. "Do you want me to send you back to the bunkhouse so you can get some sleep? You've been up all night, too, and you're right up there with me, pushing close to that half-a-century mark."

But Nate just grinned. "I'm not the one who's got a son you might be thinking you have to keep up with." He glanced toward the cowboys with the herd where Chase was. "Looks like he wore out a horse already," Nate observed as both Chase and Buck left the herd to ride their sweating horses toward the fence gate to get fresh mounts that were picketed along the fence line. Seeing Chase made Nate wonder, and he did it out loud. "Do you suppose it was O'Rourke?"

Webb flashed him a sharp look but didn't answer as he stepped out of the shade of the trailer to walk to the fence. "How's it going?"

"The herd didn't have a chance to scatter much," Chase replied, already dismounted and tugging the cinch loose on his saddle. "We should have a count somewhere around noon."

"Is there any coffee in that Thermos yet?" Buck wanted to know as he looped his horse's reins around the gate post. "I sure could use some."

"There might be half a cup in the bottom. It's in the cab." Nate motioned over his shoulder to the truck parked behind him.

Buck started to open the gate when something in the grass caught his eye. He bent down to pick it up. "Is this off your saddle, Chase?"

Chase glanced to see what it was, then shook his head. He didn't need to check his saddle to know. "It isn't mine. The leather ties on mine are plain circles. That's scalloped."

"It isn't mine, either." Buck looked at it again. "Maybe it's off Clay's saddle."

"Or it might be off one of the rustler's saddles," Webb suggested striding forward. "Let me see it."

His suggestion prompted both the foreman and Chase to walk over for a closer look. It was a slim lead, but at this point, it could turn out to be the only important clue they had. Nate was the first to hear the canter of a horse on the road and looked up just as the rider came into sight.

"Someone's coming," he told the others, and they turned their attention to the rider.

When Chase recognized the slim, supple rider, his tiredness fell away. Maggie had reined in her horse at the sight of all the vehicles and people. Turning at a right angle to them, her horse danced sideways for several steps before she brought it around to approach them at a trot. A single black braid fell across the front of her shoulder. When she stopped her horse near the gate, he could see the faint tension in her features, the subdued flash of defiance in her green eyes. His father had a way of intimidating people; because of her slight inferiority complex, Maggie was obviously affected by it.

"Hello." It was an all-encompassing greeting, given as she swung out of the saddle in a single fluid motion. "I heard you had some excitement here last night."

"And where did you hear that?" The sharp demand of his father drew Chase's glance. The harshness didn't seem necessary.

But Maggie just smiled, the green flashing a little brighter in her eyes. "Anything that happens to a Calder travels through this area like wildfire. Birdie Johnson called me this morning." Then her glance lighted on the leather rosette with its twin strips of rawhide. "Hey, that's mine. Where did you find it?" She took it from his father's hand before any of them had a chance to react to her startling announcement.

"Buck found it in the grass by the gate," Webb answered.

"I noticed it was gone the other day, but I didn't have any idea where I had lost it." Her mouth had relaxed slightly to smile.

"We thought it might have come off the saddle of one of the rustlers," Webb said, looking at her carefully.

The laugh she made was slightly forced. "I assure you it is off my saddle, and I was in bed asleep last night by nine-thirty."

Webb let his gaze wander around the immediate area before returning to her with pinpoint sharpness. "This is quite a ways from your father's place. What were you doing here when you lost this?"

Chase would have spoken up at that moment, but he held his silence when he saw the bold way she challenged his father. He

had been on the receiving end of one of those daring looks before.
A mixture of pride and amusement surged through him.

"I had arranged to meet your son," she retorted in a very clear
voice.

Beside him, Buck shifted and cleared his throat. His sparkling
blue eyes said he found the situation very entertaining.

"And did you meet him?" his father prompted.

"Yes, she did," Chase answered for her, coming to her support,
but the glance she sent him didn't thank him for it.

"Yes, I met him," Maggie confirmed in a spark of temper. "And
I don't like it when people infer I'm lying, *Mr.* Calder." The
emphasis was arrogantly sarcastic as she pivoted away to mount
her horse.

Chase started to push his way forward to stop her from leaving,
but his father laid a restraining hand on his arm, not taking his eyes
off the girl reining her horse in a circle. When Chase attempted to
shrug aside his father's hand, the grip tightened.

"Let her go, son," was all he said. "We have work to do."

The incident gave Webb something to think about. He was
willing to concede that the O'Rourke girl hadn't been one of the
rustlers, but it was entirely possible she was covering for one of
them. Even if she wasn't and the saddle tie had come off her saddle
when she'd met Chase here, it became highly likely that she knew
the cattle were being moved to this pasture, information the
rustlers had to obtain somewhere. There were several definite
possibilities to keep in mind.

PART III

A sky of challenge,
A sky of right,
This sky that strikes with
A Calder's might.

Chapter XI

Most of the clothes in the little dry-goods store in Blue Moon were work garments, designed for durability rather than fashion. Of the two racks of dresses in the ladies' section of the store, only half of one rack was reserved for dressier clothes. The rest were all housedresses. Whenever Maggie had the extra time, she looked through the dresses on the hangers. It was better than a catalog because she could actually touch the clothes and hold them up against her while she looked in the full-length mirror.

This afternoon she had the time to spare because her father and brother were in Jake's having a beer. She entered the store and made her way slowly toward the ladies' section. Lew Michels, the proprietor, was measuring a length of chambray for a customer when Maggie passed the yard-goods department. He glanced up and smiled in recognition.

"Hello, Maggie. Dorie is out back in the storeroom. Stop in and say hello. It will give her an excuse to take a break," he said.

Doris Michels was his daughter and a classmate of Maggie's at school. They had never been friends, but not because Maggie didn't like her. Dorie was nice, but her best friend was Cindy Schaeffer, who also lived in town. The two of them were inseparable, and there never seemed to be room for a third person to join in their gossipy girls' chatter. Besides, with her parents owning the store, Dorie always had nice clothes to wear, and Cindy's mother could sew anything and not have it look home-made.

"Thanks, Mr. Michels." But Maggie doubted that Dorie would be overjoyed to see her. They usually ran out of conversation after a few minutes. She walked to the back and knocked on the storeroom door. There was a clatter and thump of someone stumbling over boxes before the door was opened. A slightly plump girl with sandy-blonde hair blinked at her in surprise.

"Hi, Maggie. Gee, I haven't seen you since summer vacation started." Then she laughed. "I didn't see much of you during school, either. You were hardly ever there."

"I missed a lot of school helping my father," Maggie admitted. "Your dad said you were back here." She already found herself searching for something to say.

"Yeah. He's put me to work in the afternoons now that school's out for the summer, so I can earn some money. There just isn't any place around here to get a job," the girl explained.

"It is hard," Maggie agreed and started to back away.

"Why don't you come on back?" Dorie Michels invited. "I'll show you the new dresses that just came in. I'm in the middle of unpacking them now. It will give us a chance to talk for a while." Maggie accepted the opportunity to see the dresses before anyone else in town did and followed her classmate into the storeroom. "Did you hear that Cindy Schaeffer's parents might move to Miles City?"

"No, I didn't."

"Well, they might. Isn't that awful?" She made a face at the thought. "Here are the dresses. Aren't they gorgeous?" She picked up a long-sleeved knit dress in a dark green color. "Of course, they're for winter. Isn't it crazy to get winter dresses in the middle of summer? But that's the way the world of fashion works."

"It's nice." Maggie lightly touched the dress, liking the soft feel of the heavy materials.

Dorie pushed it into her hands to reach for another. "Don't worry about wrinkling it. I have to iron them all when they're unpacked. This one is pretty, too." She lifted another one from the pile. "But it has too many ruffles and makes me look fatter than I am. Momma says it's baby fat, but I don't think it's ever going to melt away. Oh! This one would look fabulous on you, Maggie."

It was a bold rust color, the same material and style as the one she was holding. Maggie draped the other one over a box to take the one Dorie held.

"There's a mirror behind you." Dorie pointed, and Maggie turned to see how it looked on her.

She like the contrast of its vivid color with her dark looks and the sophisticated style that made her appear older. "It's lovely," she murmured.

"Why don't you try it on?" her plump blonde classmate urged. "There's a dressing room right over there."

Maggie hesitated only briefly before accepting the invitation. She couldn't resist the chance to see what she looked like with the dress on. Using the dressing room Dorie had indicated, she peeled out of her clothes and boots and slipped the dress over her head, twisting her arms to zip the back.

"It's perfect on you!" Dorie declared the minute Maggie stepped out of the dressing room. "I knew it would be. Come look in the long mirror out front."

When Maggie saw her reflection, all her expectations were exceeded. The transformation from a blue-jeaned tomboy into a young lady was a startling change; the dress showed off her high-breasted figure in a way the ill-fitting male clothes never could. Not even the bareness of her feet detracted from the genteel femininity of her mirror's image.

"Can you imagine if you had your hair up how sophisticated you'd look?" Dorie's suggestion prompted Maggie to sweep the heavy weight of her hair off her neck to hold it atop her head. One glimpse of the possibilities was all the sandy-haired blonde needed. "Wait here, Maggie. I'll see if I can find some pins in the back."

In the men's section of the dry-goods store, Chase waited with diminishing patience while Buck tried on a variety of straw Stetsons in different shapes and styles. When they had driven into Blue Moon twenty minutes ago, Chase had recognized the rusted and dented truck parked in front of Jake's as Angus O'Rourke's. He had used the excuse of buying cigars to stop in the grocery store to find out whether Maggie was in there shopping and lingered until he was certain she wasn't. Then he'd let Buck drag him across the road to the combination dry-goods-and-hardware store. His eyes had already searched the place without finding Maggie here, either. He was trying to hurry Buck into making a choice when he heard a young girl's voice say Maggie's name.

"This one ain't bad." Buck twisted and posed to study the straw Stetson from all angles, then discarded it. "Did you see that hand-tooled saddle Lew has up front? You should buy me that, Chase. It's a beauty."

"Save your money and buy it yourself." Chase was moving away, homing in on the direction of the voice, as if it was a signal beacon.

"Hell, it'd take me a year to save enough," Buck snorted, but Chase wasn't there to hear him.

Crossing the store, he stopped within five feet of a young, dark-haired woman standing in front of a full-length mirror with her back turned to him. When his gaze met the green eyes in the mirror's reflection, Maggie turned, posturing slightly as a model would do. The style of the richly vibrant rust-colored dress was too old for her, but it permitted Chase a glimpse of the woman she would be in a few years. Many reactions stirred within him; hot and disturbing, foremost among them was a desire for sole possession. Chase studied her quietly, but kept his feelings away from his face; he was not at ease with them.

"I'm glad you saw me in this." Her voice was low, lower than a whisper, yet steady and direct. "I wanted you to see that I really can be a lady someday."

The statement prodded his memory, recalling her vehement declaration that one day she would leave to better herself and become a lady. It jabbed him that she would leave. He was filled with the raw urge to crush her composure, that cool certainty of her. His gaze made a raking sweep of her and the dress.

"You'll never make it," he said, his dryness rustling through his voice. "I've never met a lady yet who went around in bare feet."

A green-eyed fury shattered the picture of composure as Maggie reached around for the first thing she could lay her hands on. It was a folded cotton slip that went sailing through the air at him. Chase ducked it and moved forward to catch her hands before they could find a deadlier missile to hurl at him. Maggie struggled, and he laughed softly because this kind of lady he could handle. He pulled her toward him and forced her hands to flatten themselves on his chest.

"I *will* be a lady," she hissed and tried to strain free of his steel hold.

"It doesn't matter." Lazy with satisfaction, he ran his eyes over her animated features. "What man wants a tame, dull lady when he can enjoy the excitement of someone who is all woman? You don't need to change to satisfy me."

The need to impose his will on her ran through him. The rashness of it made him catch her shoulders and pull her against him. His mouth silenced her faint outcry with the domination of his hard kiss. It lasted only seconds. Interrupted by someone's approach, Chase released her and stepped away, trying to get a hold on the turbulence of his emotions.

"Hello, Chase," The slightly timid voice of a young girl announced the intruder.

Indifferent recognition registered on Chase's face. "Hello, Dorie." He ignored the shyly flirtatious look she gave him, mentally dismissing her as too young to warrant more than polite attention.

"Is there anything I can help you with?" the girl offered.

"No, thanks." His gaze had already returned to Maggie, clashing with hers before it suddenly hit him that the two girls were roughly the same age. His mouth twisted in self-mockery as the hard brown of his eyes softened to velvet in a silent apology to Maggie for his actions. Some of her stiffness melted in an equally silent acceptance of his apology. His finger briefly touched the pointed brim of his hat to take his leave from them before he turned to retrace his steps and rejoin Buck.

"Gee," Dorie murmured enviously as she watched him walk away. "I wish Chase Calder would look at me the way he looked at you." With a sigh, she glanced back at Maggie and smiled to show there were no hard feelings. "I found some hairpins. Would you like me to fix your hair?"

"No." This time when Maggie glanced in the mirror, she saw what Chase had noticed. She was too young for this particular style of dress, and a change in hairdos wouldn't alter that. She felt like an adolescent caught wearing lipstick and playing at adulthood. That's what the mirror showed her, regardless of the maturity she felt inside. Yet Chase's remark hadn't shaken her resolve that someday she'd wear a dress like this—with high-heeled shoes, jewelry, and all the accessories that belonged with it. No one was going to say she couldn't be a lady, especially a Calder. Unconsciously, Maggie shared her father's resentment of the Calders' status, power, and prestige.

After one last look at herself in the mirror, Maggie turned from it. "I'd better change back into my own clothes." She started toward the dressing room in the back and her schoolmate tagged along, eyeing her with new interest.

"I heard that you've been seeing a lot of Chase Calder lately," Dorie remarked. "Is that true?"

"Where did you hear that?"

"I don't remember." The girl shrugged, because the source didn't seem important. "You know how it is in the store; half the people come in just to gossip. Have you been meeting him?"

"I've seen him a few times," Maggie admitted and felt herself being elevated to a new position of importance by the association.

"What's it like . . . when he . . . does it to you?" The girl stammered over the question, too embarrassed to be forthright, yet too curious to keep silent.

And Maggie realized what kind of gossip had been circulating. Her lips came together in a straight line as she regarded her supposed friend with a steadiness Dorie couldn't match.

"When he does what?" Maggie challenged. Then she bluntly added, "Do you mean when he makes love to me?"

"I wasn't trying to pry, Maggie. Honest."

The end result was the same, and it hurt Maggie, stinging her temper. "Why don't you go ask Chase to show you? Then you won't have to ask me what it's like. You can find out for yourself."

"I couldn't." The girl drew back in shock.

"Why not? He's very good at deflowering virgins." Maggie closed the dressing room door and began trembling. Her eyes smarted with tears, but she determinedly blinked them away and stripped out of the dress. Dorie had vanished from the back storage area when Maggie came out wearing her blouse and jeans again.

Webb pulled up to the gasoline pumps and stopped the station wagon. As he climbed out, a teen-aged boy came trotting out of the building. "Shall I fill it up for you, Mr. Calder?"

"Yes, and check the oil." Automatically, he glanced at the vehicles parked nearby. The ranch pickup he passed over, but his gaze paused on the truck belonging to O'Rourke. The sight of it aroused the suspicious questions that had been running through his mind for the last week. They were little more than hunches, but Webb often relied on gut feelings, which ultimately proved to be correct.

He walked over to the truck and wandered around it, stopping to poke at the dirt and gravel lodged in the tire treads and pull out the long grass stems caught in the rusted cracks of the chrome bumper. The grass was a common variety, although it grew in abundance on Triple C land, especially around the Broken Butte. The main road bisecting the rarely used track to that section had recently been resurfaced with new gravel. A sharp-edged chip of stone was wedged in the tire treads. Neither item was conclusive evidence that O'Rourke had been in the vicinity, yet they both showed he could have been. Webb strolled thoughtfully back to his car, running this information through his mind.

"Sometimes I wonder how Angus keeps that truck running," the boy at the pumps remarked with a shake of his head. The comment revealed he had observed Webb's close inspection of the pickup. "You were almost a quart low, so I put one in."

"Fine." He nodded, but he was more interested in what else the teen-ager might have noticed. "Trucks take a beating in this country, especially the kind of range land Angus has."

"Yeah, I suppose. Lately, most of his miles have been put on coming back and forth to town. I'll bet he's been here almost as much as he's at home." The pump nozzle automatically shut off and the boy clicked it to manual to fill the gas tank all the way to the top.

"Oh?" It was a prompting sound.

"If he isn't in the café having coffee, then he's at Jake's having a beer with Tucker," the boy explained. "It's no wonder his place always looks like it's about to fall in around his ears."

Tucker. Webb glanced at the café. A "Closed" sign hung on the door. He sifted through the information he knew about the man, ignoring his reputation as a cook. Some years ago, there had been a questionable involvement in the purchase of stolen goods, but there had been no proof that Tucker had known what he was buying. The man kept his hands clean, but Webb was equally certain that Tucker had contacts with dirt on their hands. Tucker could easily act as a middleman for O'Rourke, possibly even a silent partner. He doubted that O'Rourke was in this alone—if he was the one who had stolen the beef.

Coyotes were cowardly thieves. A single coyote would slink away rather than confront an opponent of equal or superior strength, but with others of his kind, he gained courage and exhibited a cunning unequaled by any other, more forthright predator. Webb classified Angus O'Rourke in that category, an essentially spineless man with flashes of brilliance.

Webb was convinced he was being harried by coyotes who struck under the cover of darkness and then stole away into the night. He even hazarded a guess at the cowardly justification for the illegal act—the affair between Chase and O'Rourke's daughter. The fifty head of cattle he'd given O'Rourke hadn't appeased the man. It had merely whetted his appetite. The stolen cattle amounted to involuntary payments of blackmail. The thought burned through Webb like a hot iron. It was an intolerable position, and he reacted to it accordingly.

With a shake of his head, he overruled his emotions. So far his suspicions had uncovered nothing but a workable theory, no matter how much his instincts insisted it was fact.

Even he would not condemn a man on that alone. If he could never prove it beyond the law's doubt, he would prove it beyond his own. In those cases, there were ways range justice could be served while the legal branch of government wore its blindfold.

Webb signed his name to the ticket, charging the purchase to the ranch account. "Thanks, Mr. Calder," the boy said.

An absent smile came and went from Webb's face as he turned away. He recalled the boy had said if O'Rourke wasn't in the café, he was usually at Jake's having a beer. He angled a course for the bar. The interior had the definite flavor of an old-time saloon, complete with hand-carved mahogany bar and its brass footrail. Behind it was the large mirror backing mahogany-carved shelves for liquor bottles and glasses. There was an assortment of round tables and unmatched straight-backed chairs. Dirty spittoons were strategically located for those who chewed or took snuff; an abundance of sawdust was scattered on the plank floor for those who missed. Beside the bar, there was a staircase leading to the second-floor rooms, the steps worn from a thousand footprints. The staircase was conveniently situated by the bar to permit Jake to see who went up and down the stairs with his "nieces." In addition to the private poker room in the back, there was a jukebox and a pool table.

Unlike the old saloons, it lacked swinging doors—the flies were too plentiful in the summer. The walls were dingy, their color long ago lost under layers of nicotine, smoke, spilled drinks, and tobacco juice, not to mention good ole dirt. There wasn't any red brocade wallpaper or wood paneling. There were no chandeliers or wall sconces. The lights were few and scattered, which was just as well, since the dimness hid the dirt. Most of the pictures on the walls were cheap Russell prints, not portraits of voluptuous naked ladies lounging on purple beds. Instead of a fan turning slowly overhead, an air-conditioner whirred in the corner. In truth, Jake's was probably a more accurate representation of the true Western saloon than those depicted in Hollywood movies.

It served its purpose as a gathering place to exchange gossip and bellyache about life, or kill time over a few beers. Usually there was less than a handful of people inside, unless a bunch of cowboys came in to party and raise hell. That's when Blue Moon was as lively as it ever got.

Webb paused inside the screen door while his eyes adjusted from the brightness of the afternoon light to the relative dimness of the saloon. His appearance brought a pause to all conversation, except for an exchange of quick whispers on his left. In his side vision, he noticed the trio sitting at a table and identified the large-built man dwarfing the other two. There was not another man in town that big or that solid—or who possessed a head so small for the size of his body. Without question, it was Bob Tucker. Seconds after Webb entered, Tucker pushed his massive frame out of the chair and spoke in a deliberately loud voice.

"I'd better get the café opened before the supper crowd starts coming. See you around, Angus." It was all very nonchalant, very casual.

The remark permitted Webb to let his gaze stray to that table. He took a step away from the door, but remained in Tucker's path to it. They exchanged nods instead of verbal greetings, and Webb stopped, forcing Tucker to do likewise.

"It's been more than a month since you mentioned to Chase that you'd be out to buy some beef to butcher. We've been wondering what happened to you?" The slight curve of his mouth was challenging.

"Angus gave me a good deal on some cattle he bought from you. So I'm still selling Calder beef at my place, its ownership once removed," Tucker replied without a trace of unease, then shrugged. "I guess I should have let you know, but I'm not what you would call one of your big buyers, so I didn't think it was important."

"It isn't." The mention of O'Rourke gave Webb an opening to shift his attention to the short man still seated at the table with his son. "How are those cattle doing, Angus?"

"Fine. Just fine." Despite the casual tone, O'Rourke was watching him closely, as if trying to detect some other meaning to the question.

"I've gotta move on." Tucker walked around Webb. "Stop in for coffee sometime."

"I'll do that, Tucker," Webb promised with a fixed glance at the big man. He saw Tucker's gaze dart to Angus.

It was a small thing, but in Webb's mind, it added up to a connection between the two men stronger than just an exchange of idle talk over a glass of beer. There was some truth to the old phrase, "thick as thieves," since they usually sought out each other's company in a need for moral support. He didn't attempt to hide the silent speculation in his gaze when it swung back to O'Rourke.

"Why don't you sit down, Webb? Let me buy you a drink." Angus exuded a cocky confidence in both the invitation and familiar use of Webb's first name, when he usually addressed him with more of a show of respect. Webb walked to the chair Tucker had vacated in mute acceptance of the offer. "What will you have? Whiskey? Beer?"

"Beer is fine." Webb sat down and nodded to O'Rourke's son.

"Dolly?" Angus gestured to the gum-cracking blonde perched on a stool at the end of the bar. "Bring Mr. Calder a beer."

The Calder name brought an instant response from the brassy blonde. Sliding off the stool, she ducked behind the bar to tap a glass from the keg. While it was being drawn, she discreetly slipped her gum out of her mouth and fluffed her already-puffy hair. As she crossed the room with his beer, she managed a fairly provocative wiggle, which Webb observed with passing interest. A long time ago, he'd made it a rule to avoid Jake's girls and satisfy his occasional needs during visits to Miles City or Helena. It was inconvenient at times, but it guaranteed that his private life remained private and didn't become a subject of local conversation.

"Have you had any more trouble with those rustlers?" Angus inquired. Webb wondered whether the man was clever, or just a fool for broaching the subject.

"Not in the last few days," he admitted. "Since I put the men out patrolling the roads, it looks like they've decided to lie low for a while."

"Do you think they're still around?" Angus appeared surprised. "All the talk going around town has been guessing that the rustlers skipped the country, headed for greener pastures and fatter cattle."

"They're still here." Webb nodded decisively and held the man's look. "I'd bet on it."

"What makes you say that?" Angus leaned back in his chair.

"Because they outsmarted themselves by knowing too much about this area. These cattle thieves aren't strangers. They're locals." Out of the corner of his eye, Webb noticed the boy shift in his chair, but Angus released a disbelieving laugh.

"You don't really think it's someone we all know?" he scoffed.

"I'm convinced of it."

"Just who do you suspect?" Angus was still pretending it was a joke.

Not once did Webb release him from the iron directness of his gaze. "It could be any number of people, but *you* know who I believe it is." The stress on the pronoun was deliberate, made to put the emphasis on O'Rourke without actually naming him.

There was a significant pause before Angus replied with a challenge. "If you are so positive that you know who it is, why haven't you done something about it? You're just guessing. You don't have any proof. If you did, Potter would have an arrest warrant ready."

"The law is very slow, and not very dependable. Even if Potter had enough evidence to arrest the man, the thief would get out on bail pending trial, which might be months away. There's no guarantee he would be convicted by a jury. And if he was, it's conceivable he could be paroled after serving only a short sentence. What's to stop him from rustling more cattle while he's awaiting trial, or after he's out of prison?" Webb eyed Angus coldly. "Things were a lot different in the old days. Rustlers were hanged on the spot, and a running iron was all the evidence a rancher needed."

"Have you found a running iron?" Inside, Angus was squirming. The challenge was sheer bravado.

"No, but Slim Bevins recognized a voice when he surprised the rustlers at the Broken Butte." Webb watched O'Rourke turn pale under his tan, and knew with absolute certainty that he was the cattle thief.

"So?"

"So . . . I want to make my warning clear to this man. If one more head of Calder beef turns up stolen, I'm coming after him personally." It was stated quietly, a deadliness in its flat tone.

"Why are you telling me?" Angus sat up straighter. "You're just bluffing, Calder."

"All the man has to do is call my bluff." Webb pushed the chair away from the table and stood up, dropping a bill on the table for the beer he hadn't touched.

Chapter XII

When he left Jake's saloon, Webb walked back to the grocery store-gas station. The station wagon was still parked by the gasoline pumps, but he walked past it to enter the store. Behind the counter where the cash register was located, there was a side window which gave him a view of both the front of the saloon and the café. Webb bought a pack of gum and chatted with Helen Kirby, the plump wife of the owner, while he unobtrusively kept watch on the two buildings.

He saw Chase and Buck climb into the pickup and drive away in the direction of the ranch, but it was five minutes before Angus O'Rourke and his son emerged from the saloon to head directly for the café. Webb didn't believe for one minute that it was coffee or food that O'Rourke was seeking, but the courage of the pack. Tucker was involved, without question.

Satisfied with the confirmation he'd seen, he left the store. As he came out, O'Rourke's daughter was approaching the door. He noted the sudden lift of her head when she saw him, the wary defiance that prompted her to squarely meet his gaze. She was not only an unusually attractive girl, but she also had spirit and guts. He experienced a twinge of pity that she had such a worthless father. It was unfortunate that she would suffer because of her father.

An age-old courtesy insisted that he hold the door for this young member of the opposite sex, while a sense of male responsibility made him speak. "Miss O'Rourke." Circumstances made him be formal with her.

"Yes?" She stopped, stiff and defensive, but not intimidated.

"Tell your father that I never warn a man twice," he said. "I want him to understand that—for your sake and your brother's." There was a momentary flash of anxiety in her eyes before it was quickly hidden with a sweep of her lashes. When they lifted, she was once more cool and composed.

"I'll tell him what you said, although I don't think it'll make any more sense to him than it does to me," she replied, and Webb had to admire her calmness, unusual in such a young person.

"I'm sure he'll understand." He touched his hat as she swept smoothly past him to enter the store. Webb closed the door behind her and walked to his station wagon.

Buck entered The Homestead all slicked up in a white Western shirt with pearl snaps and a string tie. The new straw Stetson was atop his curly hair, and his smooth cheeks were tangy with the spicy fragrance of an after-shave. There was an eager impatience about him as he glanced swiftly around the living room. The double doors to the dining room stood open. When a sound came from inside the room, Buck moved with a quick, buoyant stride toward it and stuck his head inside.

Webb was seated at the head of the large walnut table, puffing on a cigar, a cup of coffee in front of him. The blonde-haired woman clearing the table of the night's dishes looked up and paused when she saw her son, a smile coming onto her mouth. His glance shifted from his mother to Webb Calder and back again. More than once he had suspected there was more between them than mere friendship. If his own father was dead, Buck suspected his mother might marry Webb Calder. Sometimes he couldn't resist fantasizing about a role as Webb Calder's stepson, and the increased importance of his place on the ranch, a part of the hierarchy. He fancied owning all this someday.

"Did you want something, Buck?"

He shook his head, smiling quickly. "Just looking for Chase."

"He went upstairs to his room to get ready," Ruth Haskell replied.

"The man is slow," Buck complained with a grin. "I'll go hurry him along. Don't wait up for me, Mom. We might not come back 'til morning." Pure devilment danced in his eyes as he left the dining room doorway and crossed to the staircase, familiar with the way to Chase's room.

There was an unconsciously soft quality to the smiling glance Webb sent to Ruth. "We have waited up many a night for our boys, haven't we, Ruth?" He tapped the ash from his cigar into a crystal ashtray.

"We certainly have," she agreed and let her gaze wander toward the doorway. "I expect we'll stay awake a lot more nights even when they say we shouldn't."

"Leave the dishes for a minute and have a cup of coffee with me," Webb suggested impulsively.

She hesitated, then shook her head in refusal, not looking at him. "Virg is waiting for me at home." Regret flickered in the faintness of her smile. "I hadn't better dawdle over the dishes."

"No, of course not." The gruffness of his answer held under-standing and a vague irritation with himself for making the suggestion. He rose from his chair. "I'll finish my coffee in the den. I have some paperwork to do."

As he crossed the foyer that separated the dining room and den, Chase and Buck descended the stairs to the living room. He glanced at his son, aware that this was the time in Chase's life to be wild and carouse with the boys. Soon enough these days would be behind him and he would have to assume a man's role in the ranch operation.

"Behave yourselves, boys," Webb advised, using the plural, but looking at his son.

"Yes, sir." Buck sketched him a salute while Chase nodded. "Don't you be worryin' about Chase. I'll look after him like he was my little brother."

"If you're looking after me, who is going to keep you out of trouble?" Chase mocked.

"Hell, I am trouble!" Buck bragged with a laugh as he opened the front door and motioned Chase to walk ahead of him to the pickup parked in front.

"Who's driving?" Chase wanted to know.

"I am, since I may not be sober enough to drive home," Buck declared and hopped behind the wheel. "That's going to be your problem. I'll get us there and you can bring us home."

"Okay." That was the way it usually worked out.

"Man, am I glad we didn't pull patrol duty tonight." Buck started the engine and revved it to a roar before shifting into gear, spinning the tires. "I thought it might be exciting riding shotgun on those roads at night, but it is boring as hell! I'll be glad when the Old Man calls it quits. Those rustlers are probably clear into the next damned state by now."

"They could be," Chase conceded.

There were already a dozen Calder riders, as well as a few other local customers, at Jake's when they arrived. A poker game was in progress in the back room. Chase took a beer back to watch, and eventually sat in for a few hands, but he couldn't concentrate on the cards, and luck was against him, so he wandered into the main saloon again.

Through the room's dim, smoky haze, he spotted Buck sitting at one of the tables with his arm around the neck of a sultry brown-haired "niece" named JoBeth. Buck was smiling, nuzzling and whispering things in her ear while his hand wandered inside the plunging neckline to fondle a heavy breast.

Aware that his buddy would not welcome his company at this point, Chase strolled over to watch a couple of Triple C riders playing pool. He dropped some quarters in the jukebox and punched a selection of records to add to the raucous din of cowboys letting loose. Dolly came around with a tray of beers and Chase paid for another.

It was half-gone when he noticed Buck walk to the end of the bar closest to the staircase, the dark-haired girl pressing herself all over him, scarlet lips always upturned. Buck shouted for Jake and slapped his hand on the bar top to gain the man's attention. Jake was a spare, big-boned man with thinning hair bushing into tufts at the sides.

"We need the key to the upstairs room," Buck demanded. There was an exchange of folded money for the key.

"Don't be too long. We're busy tonight," Jake informed his "niece."

Buck laughed and squeezed the girl. "As long as it takes, Jake. Only as long as it takes." Then the two of them were mounting the stairs to the second floor.

Chase watched them go and downed the rest of his beer. His

gaze swung slowly around the dirty, smoky place, taking note of the laughter and bantering voices. Something was wrong with him. Here he was in the middle of a bar and bawdy house, and he was bored.

The beer tasted flat so he walked over to the bar to have a fresh one drawn from the tap. Clay Vargas, a cowboy who had drifted from Colorado to work at the Triple C, was standing at the bar, talking with two other non-native ranch hands. They made room for Chase to join them. It was a silent invitation issued out of deference to his position as heir, a respectful gesture which Chase accepted for the same reason.

Hooking a boot heel over the brass footrail, he ordered a beer and listened to the trio trying to top each other with wild stories of past places of employment. Jake set a glass in front of Chase and took his money, all in the same motion. Although Chase laughed in all the right places, his mood didn't improve with either the beer or the company of tall-tale tellers.

Albert was the drifter with two chipped front teeth, broken when a horse kicked him in the mouth a year ago. He lowered his head to whisper to Clay Vargas. "Do you see the way that Dolly gal is giving me the eye?"

"You? Hell, she's looking at Chase!" Clay laughed.

Albert looked again and considered that he could have been mistaken. "I wish she'd look at me that way."

Chase glanced around as the brassy blonde slowly looked him up and down, and turned away, unaffected by the obvious invitation. "She will . . . for a price."

"Yeah, but you're getting it for nothing," the drifter protested. "Aren't you going to take her up on it?"

"Not interested." He lifted his glass to take a swallow of beer.

"Chase has hisself a little Lolita who gives him all he can handle," Clay Vargas drawled. "This must be his night of rest. What happened, Chase? Wouldn't her daddy let her come out tonight?" Clay slapped him on the shoulder and laughed.

All in one motion, Chase set the glass down, turned to knock the man's hand off his shoulder, and swung his fist into the relaxed midsection. The air whooshed from Vargas' lungs, doubling him up and throwing a look of stunned shock into his expression. Blood sang through his veins. The jarring, violent contact was just what Chase needed. He felt good for the first time all night. As he started to finish off Vargas with an uppercut to the jaw, the drifter on the other side of him grabbed his elbow.

"Hey! What the hell are you doing?!!"

Chase didn't attempt to shake free of the hold. Instead, he rammed his elbow backward into the man's stomach, then pivoted to plant his feet and swing at the next of Vargas' buddies coming to his rescue. His leading punch was blocked; then someone grabbed his arms. A fist exploded against his mouth before Chase could shrug aside the man holding him. He tasted blood and shook his head to stop the ringing in his ears, turning in time to see Vargas coming at him.

He ducked the first swing, but the second bruised his shoulder. Then the two were grappling, heaving and twisting, grunting like animals while they butted and gouged at each other before springing apart. Vargas caught him above the eye with a clumsy swing, but Chase got in three hard, fast blows to the body and clipped the point of his chin with an uppercut. Vargas came at him swinging wildly, one blow glancing off his cheekbone, but Chase stepped in instead of away from the attack and buried a wicked right in the man's belly. A quick left, followed by a feint with his left that had Vargas raising an arm to block it, and Chase went under it with a stiff left to the chest. Vargas landed a wild swing, but Chase hit him with another left and knocked him to the floor with a hard right.

The killing instinct was strong. Chase grabbed Vargas by the shirt collar to lift him from the floor, but a pair of arms circled him to pull him off. Chase pivoted into his new assailant, breaking the hold with an upward sweep of his arms and swinging to knock the man backward before he bothered to see who it was. The two fighters were encircled by a ring of cowboys, one of them supporting an off-balance Buck.

"Dammit, Chase!" Buck cursed him. "What the hell did you hit me for?" He rubbed his jaw, working it as if to make certain it was operational. "You damned near broke my jaw!" Chase glanced back at the man on the floor. "Vargas is out cold. I was trying to keep you from beating him to a pulp."

"Sorry." His breath was coming in hard rushes, labored and aching. He weaved slightly, his fight-numbed body beginning to feel the blows that had landed. He turned to the two drifters who were buddies of Vargas. "Tell him . . . when he comes to . . . to watch the kind of remarks he makes about people."

He moved toward the bar with a lurching stride. Something trickled into his eye. He wiped at it, thinking it was sweat, but there was blood on his hand from the cut above his eye. His lip was split, too. It burned when he took a drink of the whiskey Jake shoved into his hand. He winced and pressed the back of his hand to the cut.

"You'd better wash those cuts." Dolly was at his side, pressing a towel to the cut above his eye. "Why don't you let me do it?"

Chase submitted to her ministrations without protest, yet totally indifferently. It was strange how good the physical hurt made him feel. The tension that had been knotted in him for days was gone.

Looking in the mirror behind the bar, he saw his own bruised reflection and Buck helping the other two Triple C cowboys lift Vargas to his feet and drag him over to a table in the corner. Then Dolly was turning his head to dab the towel on his mouth and someone came to return his hat.

"What started the fight?" Buck draped a limp arm over his shoulder while Albert did the same with Clay's other arm. Together they carried him to the chair at the empty table.

"One minute we were talking about Dolly. Then Clay said something about Chase having a girl friend named Lolita. The next thing I knew, fists were flying." Albert helped to prop up the unconscious man in the chair.

Something fell on the floor and Buck crouched to pick it up. "Clay's hat is out there on the floor. Do you want to get it before someone steps on it, Albert?" he suggested.

The third cowboy had already gone to wet a towel to wash the bloodied face. There wasn't anyone around to see the leather wallet or the folding cash that had slipped from it. Buck hesitated, then picked the two up, slipping the money into his own pocket and the billfold into Clay's hip pocket.

"It ain't right to tempt a man by carrying around a month's pay in your wallet, Clay," Buck scolded the unconscious man in a very low murmur.

Albert came back with the hat and looked anxiously at his friend. "Do you reckon he's hurt bad enough to need a doctor?"

"Now, I don't know." Buck sharply slapped the man's cheek a couple of times and Vargas stirred, his hands coming up heavily. Buck stepped back. "He'll be all right. Probably'll even look human when you get that blood washed off him."

Shifting out of the way so the returning cowboy could do just that, Buck lingered for a minute, then sauntered toward the bar, where Chase was leaning. The cash was a hard lump in his pocket, but he rationalized that Vargas was only a drifter, not one of Calder's own. Besides, it was a proven fact that a fool and his money were soon parted. Vargas was obviously a fool, or he would have known better than to take on a Calder. The Old Man had taught both Buck and Chase every dirty brawling trick in the book. Buck walked up behind Chase and dug his fingers into the shoulder muscle.

"What the hell is the idea of starting a fight while I'm otherwise occupied?" he accused. "A guy can miss out on a lot of excitement that way."

Chase took the towel from the blonde's hand, signaling he had no more need for her assistance. "I'll try to remember that the next time." His injured mouth worked stiffly as he spoke.

"What happened?" Buck eyed his friend, already knowing the answer.

There was a lift of his shoulders in a dismissing shrug. "You know how it goes. Somebody says something that happens to rub you the wrong way—and that's it."

"Sometimes it's just one word," Buck agreed and paused deliberately. "Like Lolita." Chase slashed him a hard look. Buck grinned. "Pretty soon folks are going to realize how touchy you are about her. Somebody might use that against you if you aren't careful."

Chase took a long, slow breath and realized that Buck was right. He had to start learning to control this. He couldn't fight every man who mentioned her name. Glancing in the mirror, Chase saw Vargas leaning on the table and holding his forehead.

"Jake." He pushed away from the support of the counter bar. "Give me a bottle of good whiskey and a couple of glasses."

The instant he started toward the table where Clay Vargas sat, the place became hushed. Albert poked Vargas in the ribs to warn him of Chase's approach. The cowboy looked up, battered and wary. Chase stopped in front of the table and set the empty glasses on top.

"I'd like to buy you a drink, Clay," he said and uncapped the whiskey bottle to wait for an answer.

"You beat me. Hell! You whipped me," the cowboy retorted, but resentment gave way to honest defeat. "I guess maybe I deserved it for that crack I made about your girl."

"No hard feelings," Chase assured him and filled the shot glasses with whiskey, pushing the first toward the cowboy. They shared another drink and talked before Chase went back to the bar.

It was another hour before Chase and Buck left the saloon to return to the ranch, which made it well after midnight. Buck drove.

"I though you weren't going to be sober enough to drive home," Chase reminded him when they started out.

"I changed my mind." Buck shrugged and changed the subject. "The next time we come, you're going to have to reserve yourself some time with JoBeth. She is the sexiest damned thing—and wild! Whooeee! That damned bitch got scarlet lipstick all over my shorts before I could get them off. Can't you just see Mom's face when she finds them in with the dirty clothes?" He laughed and shook his head. "I tell you, Chase, that JoBeth is something else!"

Chase made a murmuring sound of agreement and stared out the window at the midnight-black sky. It was a different dark-haired girl he had on his mind.

The supper dishes were washed, dried, and put away in the cupboards, but Maggie was still in the kitchen, alone, staring at the calendar by the back door. She counted and counted again, unable to believe she was that late. She couldn't be pregnant. She just couldn't be.

What was she going to do? She turned away from the calendar, fighting the waves of panic rushing through her. Forcing herself to think calmly and rationally, she reasoned that being three weeks late did not necessarily mean she was pregnant. There were other factors that could have affected her cycle.

She'd go see Doc Barlow on Thursday and find out for sure. Until then, it was ridiculous to worry herself into a nervous state.

After all, Chase had assured her he was careful. But what if she was pregnant? a frightened part of her mind asked. What then? What would she do? What would Chase say when she told him?

A door slammed; Maggie spun around. There were three different sets of footsteps approaching the kitchen. Two were obviously those of her father and brother, and she realized the third belonged to Bob Tucker when she heard him talking.

". . . . It happened three nights ago, on Friday."

"What started it?" her father asked.

"Jake heard them talking about Dolly; then suddenly they were fighting." The three entered the kitchen as Tucker finished his reply. He took off his hat when he saw Maggie, smiling with his small mouth. "Hello, Maggie. How are you this evening?"

Tucker was always polite to her, respectful and warm. There was never any pity in his eyes, only silent approval. Although there was a certain grotesqueness in his disproportioned shape, the large body and the small head, she liked him, anyway. When he said something, she felt she could believe him.

"I'm fine. I didn't expect to see you around here for quite a while." She thought they had decided to keep away from each other after Calder had seen them together. They were going to let everything cool down for a while, so her father had said. She glanced at her father. "Calder is already suspicious of you," she reminded him and noticed the way he avoided her eyes.

"Put on some coffee, Maggie," he said rather than reply to her comment. "Tucker and me have some things to talk over."

But she wasn't about to be distracted. "What things?" A chill ran down her spine.

"Calder is positive that he's scared us off with his patrols. We figure it's time we hit him again," her father admitted and swaggered cockily to the table. "He can be as suspicious as he wants, but he can't prove nothing. If he could, he would have been all over us already. Tucker and me have decided to call his bluff."

"But the patrols!" Maggie tried to think of something to dissuade them.

"After this much time, they won't be as alert as they were in the beginning," Tucker assured her. "They'll be bored with the routine of it. Don't worry."

"When?"

"That's what we're going to decide. Now, put some coffee on girl, like I told you," her father ordered.

Two nights later, Webb Calder was asleep in his heavy-framed bed when the fire bell outside clanged its alarm. The signal awakened him instantly to full alertness. Throwing back the covers, he stepped into his pants as he rose from the bed. Out his window, he could see the faint glow of an orange flare.

He stared at it for a long minute, standing with his pants fastened but still unzipped. He shook his head sadly, but there was no compromise in him. He'd taken his stand, made his statement; now he had to back it all up.

"Damn you, Angus," he sighed heavily, then reached for his shirt.

The sun was hot overhead. Webb wiped the perspiration from his upper lip with a handkerchief, then rubbed the cloth down his neck. "How many, Nate?" His voice was hard, as unyielding as his granite-brown eyes.

"The plane is making one last sweep to see if we missed spotting any. Right now it looks like twenty-eight."

"It's Angus O'Rourke," Webb stated, and his foreman didn't appear surprised.

"What are we going to do?" Nate took it for granted that they would do something. He only waited for orders to carry them out.

"I warned him I'd come after him personally if any more beef was stolen." To this point, Webb had not taken his gaze from the herd being counted. "I want you, Chase, and three other men to meet me at the north range by ten o'clock tomorrow morning. We'll ride over to O'Rourke's from there." Now he swung his gaze to probe into the foreman's face. "We're taking a rope with us, so keep that in mind when you pick the three men."

"We'll be there at ten." Nate casually crushed a cigarette under his boot, then walked slowly away.

Part of the instructions were understood without being spelled out. The three men would be Calder men, born on the place, rather than drifters, who would travel and talk. They would be given their orders in private—orders that would never be mentioned again, not even in their own bedrooms. All would leave their respective locations on the ranch separately, without telling anyone where they were going. It all went without saying because of the nature of their mission.

Chapter XIII

The six men met in silence and rode together in silence, their faces grim and resolute. At the boundary fence with the Shamrock Ranch, Chase knocked out the rock wedging the sagging post in place, downing the fence for the riders. His father's private explanation of their mission had been brief—a simple statement that O'Rourke was the cattle thief, and they were paying him a visit.

Chase had wondered why he wasn't more surprised by the announcement of O'Rourke's guilt. Perhaps because the man had always been lazy, a weak man. Although O'Rourke was Maggie's father, he didn't link them together in his mind. They were two separate people, entirely different in both character and values.

He had taken one. look at the hand-picked riders and guessed that his role was to observe and learn. His father had not taken him into his confidence or consulted him regarding his decision or plans. That would come later—after the fact, with a step-by-step analysis of all that had transpired.

There were certain things his limited experience could infer from this show of force. They were all close-mouthed men, loyal to the brand. Nothing that happened today would go beyond these six people. It was equally obvious that Angus O'Rourke was to be taught a lesson that wouldn't quickly be forgotten. Chase didn't know what it would be, but it occurred to him that there was a reason his father hadn't told him.

They climbed the slope above the fence line at a canter, slowing to a trot between the scattered trees where the terrain was rough. Chase rode at his father's right side; that was his place. Their route was a direct line to the Shamrock ranch-house.

Maggie ducked her head to avoid a low-hanging branch as she followed her brother on horseback through the trees. They were working their way homeward for lunch with one detour to check a salt block. Ahead of her, Culley abruptly reined his horse to a stop.

"What is —"

He silenced her question with an upraised finger to his mouth and a frowning scowl. Then she head the creak of saddle leather and the muffled hoofbeats of several horses. She looked beyond him, her view partially obscured by the stand of trees they were in. She had a glimpse of the big yellow horse Webb Calder always rode. A cold, sharp fear started her heart thudding against her ribs. She glanced at Culley. He'd barely moved a muscle since that first signal for quiet. The riders were more than a hundred yards away, heading toward the house, but Culley waited until they were out of sight.

"We have to warn Pa," she whispered. "He's there alone."

"I know," Culley snapped impatiently and kicked his horse out of the cover of the trees. "Follow me."

Spurring, they set their horses at a gallop. They circled wide to avoid being spotted by the Calders and to approach the ranch from the barn side, where there was more cover. But it was also longer, which lost them precious time. The Calders were walking their horses into the ranch yard when Maggie and Culley reached the back fence of the corral.

"We're too late," Maggie realized when she saw the riders fan out to block her father from reaching the house, trapping him in the open area in front of the dilapidated barn. Her widened eyes saw the rifles lying across the saddles. She glanced at Culley. "What are they going to do to him?"

"I don't know." He dismounted and tied his horse's reins to the corral railing. Maggie did the same, following him as he crouched low to move closer.

"I warned you, Angus." Webb sat his horse in the middle of the riders who fanned out on either side of him. "You should have believed me."

"You warned me about what? That beef you've had stolen?" O'Rourke blustered, but his face was white. "You haven't got any proof I had anything to do with it."

"I told you before, Angus, that I don't put much stock in the kind of proof you're talking about. You know you've been stealing my beef. And I know it." At a nod from Webb, a mustached rider dismounted and walked toward O'Rourke with a pigging string in his hands. "You should have quit when I gave you the chance, Angus."

"What chance?" O'Rourke stole an anxious glance at the man approaching him, but didn't run. His feet were rooted to the ground. "What chance does a little guy like me have against a big outfit like yours? You buy supplies cheaper than I can. There's no market for my cattle 'cause you've glutted it with yours. You take the best graze and water and watch the rest of us try to scrape out a living on what's left."

His arms were pulled behind his back and O'Rourke staggered a step, but didn't offer any resistance. With two wraps of the string, his wrists were bound and tied, and the cowboy stepped back to stand behind him. Nate reined his horse out of the semi-circle and walked it to the open doors of the barn.

"You think you're some damned king around here." Hatred gave O'Rourke the strength to stand and defy Calder, even though he was quaking with fear inside. "You think you can ride through the country and us peasants are supposed to bow and scrape and take care to please you, even if it means you or yours wants to screw our daughters." His glance flashed to Chase with pure venom. "We're supposed to take it and be grateful for the tips you give."

The claybank stallion moved restlessly beneath Webb and pawed the ground with an impatient hoof, sensitive to the volatile undercurrents ripping the air, but Webb sat calmly in the saddle, listening to the vindictive speech. A man was entitled to his say before he died.

"I stole your cattle, Calder, and I'm glad I did!" O'Rourke drew back his head and jeered Webb with the truth. "It's time someone started taking from you the way you've been taking from us all these years. It sticks in your craw, doesn't it? So the big, brave man comes here with five of his hands to teach one little guy a lesson. What are you going to do?" he demanded. "Have them work me over? Whip me? That ain't gonna stop me. I'm going to take every head of cattle you've got and destroy you. You're going to be nothing, just like the rest of us, before I'm through with you."

"You just put your own neck in a noose, Angus," Webb stated.

Over by the barn, Nate stepped out of the saddle, carrying a coiled rope in his hand. O'Rourke wasn't paying attention to anyone but Webb, but Chase saw the foreman walk into the barn. The wide doors at the opposite ends were open, leaving only the middle of the barn's corridor in shadow. Nate stopped in the middle and tossed one end of the rope over a thick crossbeam. A white noose dangled in the air, tied in nine wraps that made a hangman's knot. Chase shot a questioning glance at his father as his horse moved under him, reacting to the unconsciously applied pressure on the bit. There was nothing in Webb Calder's face to reveal his intentions. There was only an unbroken hardness that covered eyes, mouth, and jaw.

Unaware that Calder's remark was any more than a slang expression, O'Rourke responded to it. "Why? This confession isn't going to do you any good. I'll just deny that I ever made it, and it'll be your word against mine. It doesn't matter how many witnesses you've got. Everyone knows they're your men and they'll say whatever you tell them to say. I stole your cattle, but you'll never prove it."

"I told you before, Angus, I had all the proof I needed." He nodded to the man behind O'Rourke.

The mustached cowboy stepped forward to take O'Rourke by the shoulders and turn him toward the barn. O'Rourke made a show of resistance and contempt by twisting his shoulders out of the grip while making the turn. The cowboy clamped a hand on the bound wrists and marched him forward.

When Angus saw the noose waiting for him, he stumbled and cast a panicked look over his shoulder. Fear ran out from him like a living thing, but it made no impression on Webb Calder. The cowboy continued to push him forward and Angus looked to the front again, mesmerized by the noose swaying in the slight breeze. Nate had pulled up a wooden crate and stood it on end directly under the rope. The riders followed Webb's lead and closed in around the barn doors.

Crouched in a clump of young alders growing along the corral's dirt-walled pond, Maggie and Culley had a clear view of all that was happening through the opposite side of the barn. It was a nightmare scene unfolding before their eyes, while each waited for the other to wake them up. The reality of it finally shook Maggie out of her disbelieving trance and she started to move to her father's aid, but Culley grabbed her and pulled her back into the cover of the young trees.

"We have to help him." She struggled quietly against his grip.

"No. I don't know what they might do to us, and I have to think of you, Maggie," he insisted and held her tighter, even after she stopped trying to pull free of his hands.

Her gaze went back to the barn. "They won't hang him." It was a desperate hope because Chase was there, astride a liver-colored chestnut at his father's right.

Chase wouldn't let them hang her father—not Chase, who had taken her so gently that first time, then washed the stains from her legs; not Chase, who had picked her a bouquet of wildflowers. Her eyes clung to him, but he bore no resemblance to that gentle man. He wasn't Chase. He was a Calder, and an icy band of steel closed around her heart.

One of the riders rode his horse into the barn while the other cowboy helped O'Rourke onto the box. Chase glanced at his father again, uncertain how far this scene was going to be acted out. His own throat was tightening as the tension mounted.

"You aren't going to hang me, Calder." His voice wavered without confidence as the rider stopped his horse beside O'Rourke and looped the noose around his neck, fitting it snug. Nate took up the slack and tied the free end to an upright support. Marble-white, O'Rourke held himself rigid, afraid to struggle in case he knocked the box out from under him. He stared ahead, his eyes wild and fully open. "You won't get away with this, Calder," he warned hoarsely.

"You hanged yourself, Angus. Everyone is going to think so, except your partners in this. The word will spread and it will be a long while before anybody will help themselves to Triple C cattle again.''

Webb Calder did not sadistically draw out the moment and wait until O'Rourke dissolved into a blubbering mass of fear, begging for mercy. He gave the signal while the man was standing straight, with a trace of weak defiance. And the signal was no obvious nod, just a mere blink of an eye.

When the box was kicked out from under O'Rourke, Chase was stunned. He heard the odd whining thump of the rope, strained by the sudden weight pulling it taut, and O'Rourke's startled gasp. The short legs kicked, churning the air in an effort to find something solid beneath them, an action that lasted only seconds but became indelibly imprinted in his mind. O'Rourke's face was turning gray, his eyes and tongue bulging. The kidneys and bowels had released to add to the stench of death.

Chase felt his stomach roll violently. He'd never seen a man die before. He'd never seen a man hanged. It sickened him. Chase hunched his shoulders and started to lower his head, but the claybank stallion sidled against his horse, jostling him.

His father's voice came to him, low and heavy with disgust. "If you heave your guts in front of these men, I swear I'll—" He ground his teeth shut on the rest of the threat, but the contempt in the words stiffened Chase, straightening his shoulders and lifting his chin. He stared at the limp body swaying on the end of the rope, no longer seeing a human being, but just a thing. The rope made a grating sound as it rubbed against the crossbeam under the pendulous weight of its burden.

"He's dead." The voice came from one of the three men inside the barn; Chase wasn't sure which one.

"Untie his hands," his father ordered, and the man on the horse rode over to remove the pigging string.

Culley's hand was still clamped over Maggie's mouth, placed there when the box was kicked away from their father to smother her scream. His arm was crushed around her, holding her hard against him. He had tried to turn her head so she wouldn't see the hanging, but she had refused to look away from the horror of it.

When all the riders were mounted, they left the ranch yard at an unhurried trot, going back the way they'd come, with Calder and his son in the lead. Once they were out of sight, Culley loosened his hold on her and Maggie tore away to race for the barn, not stopping until she reached the rope tied to the upright roof support. Her fingers clawed at the knot, pulled so tight, little animal sounds of frustration coming from her throat. Her wild efforts broke and tore her fingernails all the way to the quick, trickles of blood from the cuts smearing the white rope. She was indifferent to the pain, not pausing until she worked the knot loose. As she tried to slowly lower her father to the barn floor, his dead weight pulled the rope through her hands, burning the palms. She clamped a lip between her teeth and held on, steadily lowering him.

Before his boots touched the floor, Culley had a hold on the body and Maggie let go of the rope. It slithered over the crossbeam like a treacherous white snake, following the body that Culley gently lowered to the floor. When Maggie reached them, her brother had thrown a saddle blanket over the head and shoulders of the body. She sank to her knees beside it and her fingers reached out to grap hold of the blanket.

Culley pulled her away. "Don't look at him, Maggie." His voice was a harsh, anguished sound.

"I want to look at him!" She turned on him, her face deathly pale, but there was a fiercely burning light in her eyes. "I want to remember how the Calders murdered my father!"

His hands framed her face and held it tightly. There were tears streaming down his cheeks and his mouth was drawn back in a grimacing smile to control them. "Don't look, Maggie. You'll remember how they killed him just like I will. You don't need to see him to remember." Then she was enveloped in the crush of his arms. Maggie clung to him, sharing the intense pain that racked his body with shudders, but there were no tears to bring her relief. She envied her brother because he could cry. Her throat was raw and aching and her eyes burned, but no tears fell.

Finally they found the strength to stand apart from each other, brother and sister, sharing the same grief-torn expression. Culley had always been closer to her father than Maggie, had more understanding of his weaknesses, while she had condemned them. She was sorry now that she hadn't been more forgiving of her father's faults. He had been a weak man, not a bad one.

"We'll have to call the sheriff." Maggie made no attempt to turn back to her father's body, respecting her brother's wishes in this.

"Yes," he agreed and rested a hand lightly on her arm to draw her away from the body. "I'll call." They began walking, slowly, leaving the death shadow of the barn for the bright sunlight. "Maggie, listen to me. When I talk to the sheriff, I'm going to tell him that we came back and found him—"

"You aren't going to tell them that—" She interrupted in a blaze of anger, only to have Culley cut across her protest.

"No." He stopped. His cheeks were still wet from the tears, but his face didn't belong to an eighteen-year-old boy anymore. It was a man's face, embittered and hard. "Who is going to believe us, Maggie?" Culley challenged. "Calder has everyone around here in his pocket. What proof do we have except our word? Nobody is going to take it against that of a Calder."

She knew he was right, and she stared to the south, hating. "We can't let them get away with it!"

"I won't. The day will come when they'll pay for this," he vowed. "I swear it."

When they rode away from the ranch yard, there was no doubt in Webb Calder's mind that he had done the right thing. He had weighed the other alternatives and chosen his solution. He did not pretend that another man might not have handled it differently, but neither did he dwell on it. It had been unpleasant business without satisfaction in finishing the task.

He felt a thousand years old as they returned to their point of rendezvous on the north range. He had done what the country demanded of him, the way he'd been reared, nothing more and nothing less. What sorrow that was in his heart was reserved for O'Rourke's son and daughter.

With the horses loaded in the trailer, Webb climbed behind the wheel of the truck and glanced at his son. Not a word had been spoken between them since he had cursed him in the ranch yard, but it had been for the boy's own good. He noticed the flesh stretched white across cheekbone and jaw. Chase had stood up well, never showing himself to be soft or weak. Webb had given him the time to think things through on his own during the return ride. Now was the time to speak, not to defend his action, because Webb never defended a decision. No, he wanted to talk to find out what was in his son's heart.

"There are a lot of hard decisions a man has to have the stomach to make, some more unpleasant than others. Angus was warned and given the chance to leave the Triple C alone, but he came back to take more cattle. If you let one man walk over you, then two will, then three, then four . . . so many that you won't be able to stop them. You have to stop the first man, or they'll all eventually come. Angus made it clear that he wanted to bring the Triple C to its knees."

"It started because I had taken his daughter." Chase spoke in a flat voice, devoid of emotion.

"No." Webb didn't accept that. "The farmer, Anderson, has a son about your age. If O'Rourke's girl had started slipping off to meet him, Angus would have turned a blind eye and shrugged it off as part of being young and impetuous. But you are a Calder, and Angus used you as an excuse. You became his justification for stealing Triple C cattle. If it hadn't been you, he would have found something else. And he would have kept on stealing because it made him feel big. Angus hated being small."

Chase took in a breath and let it out, turning a cynical glance out the window. "I can't say that I feel big right now . . . or proud."

"There was nothing good about what happened today." Webb felt easier in his mind. A man had to face up to things without liking them, which was what his son was doing. "You can't go through this world without being scarred. That's part of life. You aren't living in a paradise. There's always dirty work to be done, but don't ever send someone else to do it for you."

Webb was satisfied with his son's attitude and lapsed into silence to let Chase think over what he'd said. So far the road to manhood had been relatively smooth for his son, but it was going to get rougher and lonelier. Webb had traveled it once himself, so he knew what he had to prepare his son for.

Just before the evening meal, the telephone rang in the den. Webb waved Chase back into his chair. "I'll answer it." He walked to the extension on his desk and picked up the receiver. "Triple C."

"Webb? This is Sheriff Potter," said the slow-talking voice on the other end of the line.

"Yes, Sheriff. What can I do for you?" Webb sat his drink down and moved behind the desk to sit in the swivel chair, leaning back to gaze sightlessly at the ceiling of the den.

"I thought you might like to know that Angus O'Rourke was found dead in his barn today. Hanged," he drawled heavily.

"Committed suicide, did he?"

There was a long pause before the sheriff answered. "That's the way it looks to me."

"That's unfortunate."

"Yeah. Yeah, it is," the sheriff confirmed in a sigh. "Well, I just thought you'd want to know."

"I appreciate the call."

"Any more problems with those rustlers?"

"No. I guess they're going to leave us alone."

"Good. Take care now, Webb."

"You do the same." He replaced the receiver with a thoughtful look, glanced at Chase, but made no comment.

Chapter XIV

The scissors lay beside her on a table, but Maggie bit the dark thread with her teeth and set the spool aside. Moistening the frayed end of the thread to a point, she ran it unerringly through the eye of a needle; then her fingers rolled the end of a thread into a knot. The button didn't exactly match the others on the suit jacket, but it was the closest she had been able to find in her mother's sewing basket. Her mind was empty, blessedly blank, as she held the button in place with a thumb and forefinger and ran the needle through the cloth, its silver point pushing up from the thread hole of the button. It was a simple task to sew on a missing button, requiring little concentration, something that could be done automatically, but it was infinitely better to be occupied. She could drift, feeling no pain, no grief, no bitterness or hatred, just numbness while the silvery needle flashed in and out of the button.

A pickup drove into the yard, breaking the stillness. Her gaze lifted from the suit jacket to the front window. It was probably Culley coming home from town, she thought absently. But it was a tall, loose-striding man who was approaching the porch steps. Her fingers lost their rhythm with the needle, and its sharp point jabbed into a sensitive fingertip. All the tangle of hot emotions returned to burn her into consciousness as she sucked at the red spot of blood on her finger. When Chase Calder knocked on the screen door, it thumped against its frame.

Maggie neither moved from her chair nor looked up. "Come in." There was no trace in her voice of all that seethed inside.

The door was opened, that sound followed by footsteps entering. They hesitated, then came the rest of the way into the room and stopped by her chair. She could see the brown toes of his boots as she knotted the thread and picked up the scissors to snip it in two.

"Hello, Maggie." His voice was quiet.

"There was a button missing on the suit." She poked the needle and thread into the strawberry pincushion and draped the jacket over the arm of the chair. "I had to sew it on because my father is going to be buried in it. It's the only suit he owned." Maggie stood up, her fingers still tightly gripping the handles of the scissors.

Chase had removed his hat and was holding it in front of him. His broad chest lifted as he took a deep breath and brought his gaze up to meet the dark green of hers. "I'm sorry about your father, Maggie," he said grimly. "If there is anything I can do—"

His hypocrisy sent the blood rushing hotly through her veins. "There is nothing you can do now! If you wanted to do something to help, why didn't you stop them from hanging him?!!" she raged. Shock flickered across his carved features. It made her taunt him with what she knew. "I saw you with your father and the others. You didn't think anybody else was here to watch you hang him, did you? But we saw it all!!"

He turned his head aside, showing her a hawk-like profile. A muscle worked along his jawline as he appeared to struggle to control some emotion. Then he swung back to look at her, nothing showing in his expression, neither regret nor sorrow.

"I wish you hadn't." There was no break in his voice, all feeling repressed. She faced him, staring at a stranger, not at a man in whose arms she had lain so many times. Inside, she was coiling like a rattlesnake preparing to strike. His eyes grew narrower, probing in their intensity. "You heard your father admit that he was the one who had been stealing our cattle."

"He didn't do it alone!" Maggie flared. "What about the others? Are you going to hang them, too? I'm part of it. I knew about their raids. I even covered for them. Are you going to hang me, too?"

The admission caught Chase unaware. Until that moment he had believed she knew nothing of her father's involvement in rustling Calder beef. A cold sense of betrayal ran through him.

"Why didn't you tell me before?" he demanded.

"What would you have done? Turned me over to your father?"

She was trembling with the rage that boiled inside. It hammered against her control, seeking an outlet, an escape. "What do you suppose he would have done to me? Strung me up beside my pa?"

Chase bristled. "My father wouldn't have lifted a hand against you. He wouldn't intentionally harm a woman."

"That's where he made his mistake!" She shook with fury, her hand tightening on the scissors. "You should have gotten rid of all of us! All of us! Do you hear?!!"

Something warned him at the last second. Perhaps it was the steel blades of the scissors flashing in the sunlight or the slight movement of her head that signaled her strike. But as her hand arced toward his stomach, Chase hunched away from it and flung up his arm to knock the scissors off target. The blade points ripped into his shirtsleeve and raked a diagonal slash the length of his forearm. It felt as if a hot iron had been laid across his skin, but there was no time to consider his wound.

He grabbed the wrist of the hand holding the scissors and wrenched it backward until he heard her gasp of pain mixed with the animal sounds of cornered rage, and then her fingers unwillingly loosened their grip. A wide band of blood was already staining his shirt red and running onto the back of his hand when he took the scissors from her and pushed her backward, away from him.

A violent swing of his arm threw the scissors to the far side of the room. The action sent a raft of pain shooting up his arm. It produced an involuntary grimace as he clamped a hand over the throbbing wound and felt the blood pulsing from it to seep between his fingers, warm and sticky.

"You crazy little fool!" He glared at Maggie, holding his bloodied arm. In the state she was in, there was no hope of reasoning with her, but he couldn't blame her for the bitter hatred she felt over what they'd done. He scooped his hat off the floor and jammed it onto his head as he turned and walked out, blood dripping from the ends of his fingers.

In the cab of the truck, Chase pulled the handkerchief from his back pocket and wrapped it around his arm just below the elbow. Holding one end in his teeth, he pulled the knot tight in an effort to apply pressure to the wound and stem the flow of blood. His whole arm felt like it was on fire.

When he finally arrived at the Triple C, he was gritting his teeth against the pain. He drove directly to the first-aid dispensary and parked in front of it. The bleeding had practically stopped, but the bottom half of his sleeve was saturated with blood and it had started to cake on his hand and fingers. He climbed out of the truck, gingerly holding his forearm.

"Hey, Chase!" Buck came trotting toward him. "Webb's been looking for you. Where have you been?" Then he noticed Chase's arm and the questioning smile was wiped from his face. "Holy shit! What did you do to your arm?"

Chase ignored the questions and continued on his way to the first-aid office. "Come on inside and help me get it fixed up." Buck hurried forward to open the door and Chase walked directly to the sink, tugging at the knotted handkerchief. When it was loose, he turned to Buck. "Rip the sleeve off at the elbow. The shirt's ruined, anyway." The front of it was all smeared with blood.

The material tore easily at Buck's pull and fell around his wrist. Chase unbuttoned the cuff and tossed the blood-wet sleeve into the wastebasket. Turning on the faucet, he held his arm under the water to wash off the worst of the blood. The force of the water beating against the ragged wound rekindled the fiery pain. Chase was white around the mouth before he was through, and a little shaky in the knees.

Grabbing a chair, he pulled it up to the sink and sat down, resting his arm on the counter. "You can finish it," he told Buck and took off his hat to hook it on the spindled top of another chair. Blood had started to ooze slowly from the jagged slash.

Buck looked at it and shook his head. "What did you do? Get in a knife fight with somebody?" He dabbed at the ugly wound.

"Will you just shut up and take care of it?" He ground out the demand, fighting the waves of weakness that washed through him.

"This looks deep, Chase." There was a worried look of concentration on his friend's face. "Maybe I should take you into the doc and have it stitched."

Chase flexed the fingers in his hand and made a fist. It hurt like hell, but he couldn't feel any damage to the muscles or nerves. "If it has to be sewed, you can do it. You've stitched up enough animals; you should know how it's done."

Buck hesitated, uncertain. "You might need a shot for tetanus."

"No, the scissors were clean." Besides, he'd bled enough to eliminate any risk of infection.

"Scissors?" Buck looked at him with raised eyebrows. "A woman did this?"

"Would you get the damned sutures out of the drawer and sew this up! And stop asking questions!" Chase snapped.

"All right. You don't have to bite my head off." Buck recoiled with mock exaggeration and walked over to a cupboard where the sterilized needles and suture thread were kept. Before he started to sew up the wound, he glanced at Chase. "This is going to hurt. You know that?" At the glaring answer he received from Chase, Buck shrugged to indicate he'd been warned and inserted the needle into the flesh to make the first stitch.

Sweat broke out on his forehead as Chase clamped his teeth shut against the waves of pain. His arm quivered with the effort of trying to remain motionless, aided by the iron grip Buck kept on it. Each breath bordered on a groan.

"Did you hear Angus O'Rourke hanged himself yesterday?" Buck inquired to make conversation.

"Yeah, I heard." Chase wished he'd chosen a different subject. "Damn it, I could use a drink."

"They oughta keep some whiskey in here," Buck mused, then spared a second to grin. " 'Course, these cowboys would come running in here every time they bruised their finger."

"Aren't you finished yet?" Chase asked through his teeth and glanced over to see Buck tie off the last stitch and step back to admire his handiwork.

"I bet I would have made a good surgeon," he declared as he began expertly bandaging the wound.

"Not with your bedside manner," Chase denied. "You get too much pleasure out of other people's pain."

The door opened as Buck applied the last strip of adhesive tape to hold the gauze pad in place. Chase glanced over his shoulder, then let his gaze slide away without meeting his father's.

"I saw the truck outside." Webb Calder wore a frown at the bandage running the length of Chase's forearm. "What happened?"

"I cut myself. Buck overdid it in the bandage department." Chase attempted to make it sound like a minor wound, but he was slow rising to his feet, unsure of their support. "I guess he's practicing to become a doctor."

Buck took the hint and discreetly gathered the instruments

before Webb noticed them, concealing them in the folds of a towel. He carried them to the far side of the room to stash them for the time being. He heard Webb question Chase about where he'd been and strained to catch the low answer.

"I went to see Maggie." Chase picked up his hat and examined the inner sweatband, "She was there—both she and Culley. They saw us—all of us."

Webb breathed in deeply and let it out in a troubled sigh. "I didn't know."

"No." Chase put his hat on, setting it on his forehead first, then pushing it down on the back of his head. "I'm going away for a week or two."

His father let the statement ride for a minute or two, then asked simply, "Where?"

"I thought I'd take a packhorse and head up into the mountains, maybe check some fences." Chase studied the pattern of the floor tile. "I guess it never would have come to anything. Maybe I knew that from the beginning."

It took Buck a minute to realize Chase was referring to Maggie O'Rourke. He pursed his lips in a silent whistle as he guessed she had been the woman with the scissors. The other part about her seeing them, he hadn't figured out yet. At first he had thought Chase meant the girl had seen her father hang himself, but when he'd added that she'd seen them, it hadn't made sense. What would Webb and Chase be doing there? But he'd said "all of us." Webb and Chase had gone somewhere yesterday morning. He'd seen them load up their horses and leave together. Nate had taken off, too—and Stumpy. Buck decided it might be interesting to find out who else had disappeared at the same time.

"If you feel it's necessary to go away, I won't try to stop you." But Webb didn't sound pleased.

"I need some time to think things through." Chase didn't back down.

"When will you leave?"

"Now—this afternoon, as soon as I get some things packed." Cradling his injured arm against his waist, Chase moved past his father and out the door of the dispensary.

By four o'clock that afternoon, he was riding out of the ranch yard on a liver-colored chestnut, a bedroll tied behind his saddle and supplies loaded on the spotted packhorse he was leading. He headed toward the small range of mountains that intruded on the western edge of the Triple C.

The next day was Thursday, the day that Doc Barlow regularly had his clinic opened. When Maggie walked out of his examining room, nobody thought it was odd that she looked so white and strained or that she didn't speak to anyone. The poor child was burying her father the next day. Wasn't it terrible that Angus had committed suicide, leaving two youngsters orphaned? Their tongues wagged in pity.

Culley was waiting for her at Tucker's café. Tucker was the only one who actually knew the truth about the way their father had died. Culley had informed him the day it had happened. Tucker had turned white as a sheet and questioned them to find out if Calder knew he had been involved. Culley had angrily denied the insinuation that his father had given Calder any names. But Tucker had seemed equally worried about what Calder might do to them and agreed that no one would believe their story.

When Maggie slipped into the booth where Culley was sitting, he asked, "Did the doc give you some pills to help you sleep?"

That had been her excuse for seeing the doctor. She wasn't ready yet to tell her brother that she was pregnant, so she let him believe the other reason for a while longer. "Yes."

Tucker brought her a piece of apple pie and a glass of milk without bothering to ask if she wanted anything. "How are you feeling?" He had assumed the role of a distant relative, a kind of Dutch uncle to the pair.

"Fine." She nodded and glanced uncertainly at the pie.

"It's on the house," he assured her, then moved away as another customer entered.

"Tucker and I have been talking," Culley began, leaning forward in a somewhat earnest manner. "And I've been doing a lot of thinking about what we're going to do now that Pa is gone. I found Aunt Cathleen's phone number in an old address book of Mom's. I called her a little while ago to tell her about Pa . . . and to ask her if you could come live with her."

"What?" Maggie wasn't certain that she had understood him correctly.

"You're going away from here and live in California with Aunt Cathleen. After the funeral tomorrow, I'll put you on a bus." He stopped looking at her to fiddle with a paper napkin. "You've always wanted to get away from here and make something of yourself. You're going to have your chance now."

It had always been her dream, yet the present circumstances were all wrong. "But what are you going to do?"

"I'll stay here and try to keep the ranch going."

"You can't do it alone." Her father had failed with the two of them there to help.

"It won't be easy," he admitted with a defensive shrug. "I can use some of Pa's money to hire me a regular hand, and Tucker said he'd help out. But I want you to take most of the money with you." When he saw the protest forming, he quickly inserted, "If anybody asks you where you got it, just tell them Pa had some life insurance."

"I can't go live with Aunt Cathleen," Maggie stated firmly.

"Why not? I don't want you staying here," Culley declared with a trace of anger.

Her mouth thinned in grim resignation. "Culley, I went to see Doc Barlow because I'm pregnant. I'm going to have Chase Calder's baby." Her voice trembled bitterly on his name.

Culley stared at her with bleak eyes before he finally lowered his forehead to his hands, cradling his head as he rocked from side to side. "I knew it. I knew that devil bastard would plant his seed in you." It was a long moment before he raised his head and sighed. "That's all the more reason why you can't stay here, Maggie. Did you tell Doc Barlow who the father is?"

"No. He asked me if it was Chase. He'd already heard talk that I was seeing him." Her fingers dug into her palms as she simmered with the remembered embarrassment. "I made him swear not to tell."

"Everybody's talking because everybody knows—and they'll guess. Don't you see, Maggie?" Culley reasoned earnestly. "It will get worse if you stay here. Besides, Aunt Cathleen really wants you to come."

"But will she when she finds out I'm pregnant?" Maggie questioned.

"Once you're there, how can she turn you away?" he argued. "And if she does, then you can hop on the bus and come back here. But she sounded real nice on the phone, Maggie. A lot like Mom." He looked at her with eyes that were haunted and sad, burned wtih a bitter hatred that would never go away. "I'm trying to do what I think is best. I don't know if I'm right, but staying here will be no good for you. Leave tomorrow, Maggie. Leave before the Calders hurt you again."

"I'll leave, but I'm not running from them," she insisted.

In two days, Chase reached the mountains. For a week he rode the rocky ridges and pine-studded slopes, looked at the vast blue sky, ever-changing, ever-constant, and thought . . . sometimes about nothing more significant than the way the sunlight streaming through the trees dappled the ground.

Camped out under the stars wtih the horses picketed in a grassy clearing, Chase puffed on a thin cigar, stretched out on the ground with his head pillowed on his saddle. On a distant hill, a coyote barked, its call the loneliest, saddest sound in the world. The campfire had died until only its red heart was glowing. A star fell, the light of its million years leaving a white scratch in the black sky that quickly disappeared, as if it had never been.

Life did not always turn out the way a person wanted it to be, or even the way he tried to make it. He had taken a girl and made her into a woman before her time. He had ignored her youth, her background, and her father's resentment toward the Calders, certain these factors could never touch them, that they could be isolated from the world's unpleasantness. Chase realized that their relationship had been without depth because it denied what each of them were. A thing endures when there is commitment, and collapses when there is none.

Chase flexed his arm. He was able to move it more freely now; the soreness was easing from it. In time, it would heal completely, but there would be a scar.

After two weeks in the mountains, Chase rode out. He made a detour to the north range, a farewell ride to the simpler days that would never come again. He had finally accepted that and turned his horse toward The Homestead without looking back.

When the rider and packhorse were first sighted approaching the main quarters of the Triple C, a ranch hand was dispatched to The Homestead with word that Chase was coming in. Everyone carefully avoided noticing Webb Calder as he strolled toward the barns. There was no one within twenty yards of the father and son, meeting after a two-week separation.

"I see you finally made it back," Webb observed with a feigned air of only mild interest. But his eyes were sharp in their study of the rider, a heavy beard growth shadowing the rough features.

Chase's mouth split into a smile, showing white teeth against the dark beard, and there was a glittering brilliance to the deep brown eyes. "I ran out of cigars," he replied and clicked to his horse, walking it past his father and into the barn with the packhorse in tow.

There was pride in the lift of Webb Calder's head. His son was back and he was whole. Nate Moore wandered out of the barn and paused briefly beside Webb. He looked back toward the opening where Chase had disappeared.

"Do you have the feeling that he left a boy and returned a man?" Nate asked and moved on without waiting for an answer.

It was several seconds before Webb followed his son inside and walked to the stall where Chase was unsaddling his horse. "Maggie O'Rourke has left. She's gone to California to live with a relative of her mother's—a sister, I think."

There wasn't a break in the rhythm of the hands unloosening the saddle cinch. "I'm glad for her," Chase stated and lifted the saddle from the horse's back. Pivoting, he swung it onto the top of the stall's partition wall and smoothly met his father's look across the saddle seat. "It's what she always wanted—a chance to get away from here and make something out of her life. It's best."

"Yes," Webb agreed.

PART IV

A sky of parting,
A sky in two,
This sky that carries
A Calder through.

Chapter XV

There was a great deal about her aunt that reminded Maggie of her mother. Their coloring was the same, except that gray strands had begun to silver her aunt's black hair, and her eyes were a darker shade of green. Cathleen was taller than her mother had been, and plumper, but during those last years of her life, her mother had worked herself thin. Most important, though, her aunt had the same, sweet, caring disposition. She had welcomed Maggie into her home with open arms.

Maggie stared at the hands wrapped so warmly around her tightly clasped fingers. It hadn't been easy to inform her aunt that she was going to have a baby. Despite this gesture of affection and understanding, Maggie braced herself for the words of reproach.

But they didn't come. "It's possible that this might be a blessing in disguise," Cathleen Hogan suggested.

Maggie lifted her head, wary and skeptical. "How?" She had glossed over the circumstances of her relationship with Chase Calder, just as she had been uncommunicative about her father's death, relating only that his neck had been broken and he'd died instantly, and letting her aunt assume it had been an accident. She took advantage of the fact Cathleen expected her to be too upset to discuss it.

"I've been worried about leaving Mother and Dad Hogan alone all day while I'm working," Cathleen explained, referring to her late husband's parents, who presently lived with her, too. "There are days when Mother Hogan is so crippled by her arthritis that she can't get around at all. With Dad Hogan's hearing growing worse every day, I worry that if she fell, he might not hear her cry out for help. My neighbor, Mrs. Houston, looks in on them once or twice a day, but I can't afford to hire someone to stay with them all the time. With you here, Mary Frances—" She used Maggie's given name and paused.

"I'll look after them and fix their meals," Maggie volunteered, relieved that she could help her aunt and not be a burden. It was more than her iron streak of independence could have tolerated—to be pregnant and dependent on a relative stranger.

"It would certainly ease my mind if you did." Cathleen smiled warmly. "I was afraid I was going to have to quit my job, and the Gordons have been so good and understanding." She squeezed Maggie's hands in a reassuring manner. "I'll have to ask Dr. Gordon to recommend an obstetrician for you. I want you and your baby to stay healthy."

Since she had arrived in the Chatsworth area of California's San Fernando Valley three days ago, Maggie had learned that her aunt was employed by a family named Gordon. She had been hired as a housekeeper for the brother-sister pair, but her duties had gradually evolved to include taking personal care of the sister, Pamela Gordon, who had been partially paralyzed after a fall from a horse. Naturally, it was Pamela that her aunt mentioned most often. She knew little about the brother.

"What kind of doctor is your employer?" Her curiosity was aroused by the comment.

"He's a plastic surgeon, extremely well known, too." Cathleen seemed to take a personal pride in the fact. "People scarred in fires or accidents are always being recommended to him. He has his office and clinic in Los Angeles which is about a forty-minute drive from his home, so he commutes daily."

Maggie didn't envy him the drive back and forth every day. The streets and highways were clogged with vehicles. She'd heard about the traffic in Los Angeles, but seeing it was quite another thing.

"I'm glad you're here with me, Mary Frances." Her aunt filled the brief silence that followed her remark. "I know it's what your mother would want."

Which prompted Maggie to say, "Momma was always determined that Culley and I were going to have a good education.

Even though I'm going to have a baby, I'm still going to get my diploma."

"That won't be any problem. The schools here have night classes three evenings a week. Also, there are correspondence courses available that enable you to learn at home," her aunt replied. "We'll check into both and see which works best. Everything will be all right. You'll see."

As her aunt left the small bedroom that was Maggie's to return to the living room, where her in-laws were watching television, Maggie was more optimistic about her future than she had been in many days. At least now she had something definite about which she could write to Culley.

Nearly a month went by before she received a letter back from her brother. In the meantime, she had started taking correspondence courses and her life had settled into an undemanding routine of keeping house and looking after Grandma and Grandpa Hogan, as she had begun to call them. Culley's letter arrived just as she was putting lunch on the table. She let her bowl of soup cool while she read it.

September 28

Dear Maggie,

How are you? I am fine. The weather is starting to turn cool here. How is it in California? I am glad you like it there.

Tucker's café burned down last week. Jake saw it from his window when he was closing up and turned in the alarm. The whole building was in flames by the time the county fire truck got there. They let the café burn and pumped all the water on Jake's place to keep the fire from spreading to his building. There's nothing left of Tucker's café but the burned-out shell. He lost everything, even the money he had in a metal box in the back room. The fire was so hot I guess it just turned the bills to ashes. He didn't have any insurance, either.

They said the fire started in the kitchen. They claimed it was caused by grease. But I'll bet it was Calder who started it. Tucker thinks so, too, but he can't say nothing any more than we could.

I had a man hired to help me on the ranch, but he quit yesterday. Nobody will convince me that Calder didn't have something to do with him leaving. He'll never drive me out. I'll get even with them for what they've done. It may take me a while, but I'll do it.

There isn't any more news, so I will close for now. Take care of yourself.

> *Your brother,*
> *Culley*

Maggie read it through again, then slowly folded it and slipped the letter back into its envelope. A moodiness settled over her, raw memories freshened.

"Who is the letter from, Mary Frances?" Grandpa Hogan inquired in a loud voice so he could hear himself. He always used Maggie's given name, as Cathleen did.

"Culley." Her voice was dull and flat.

"Who?" He frowned and cupped a hand to his ear.

"My brother!" This time Maggie answered loud enough for him to hear.

The following Sunday, Cathleen packed a picnic basket and surprised Maggie with a drive to the beach after Mass. It was her first sight of the ocean. The minute Cathleen assured her that she and Mother Hogan could cope with setting out the picnic lunch, Maggie slipped off her sandals and walked barefoot across the sun-warmed sands to the water.

Stopping short of the beach-licking waves, she gazed out over the vast expanse of ocean swells, dark green beneath an enveloping sky of blue. For an instant, she was spun away on a memory of Montana, a sea of grass under a stretching sky.

A fingerlet of sea water curled around her toes, drawing her back to the present. It felt cool after the heat of the sand. Wading a little ways in, she turned and walked parallel with the tide mark as the waves broke gently over her ankles. The air had a tang to it. Suddenly curious, Maggie bent down and scooped up some water in the cup of her hand. She touched the wetness with the tip of her tongue and wrinkled her nose at its salty, fishy taste, shaking the moisture from her hand.

The beach began to fill up with the swimsuited crowd, making Maggie conscious that her summery cotton dress was out of place. It was an old one of her aunt's, made over to fit Maggie's burgeoning figure . . . not that she was actually showing so much yet. It was only when she looked sideways in the mirror that the protrusion of her stomach was noticeable.

Sharing the beach and ocean with others didn't diminish her enjoyment of the experience, but Maggie did retrace her steps to rejoin her aunt and the elderly couple. Cathleen smiled when she saw Maggie approach.

"What do you think of the Pacific?"

"It's wonderful," Maggie admitted, sinking onto her knees on the blanket her aunt had spread on the ground. "I'll have to write Culley tonight and tell him the ocean really does taste salty."

"Are you hungry? We have cold cuts, avocado salad, cheese, and fruit." Cathleen passed her a plate.

"It all looks good." She started filling her plate by taking a little of each.

"What would you like to drink, Mother Hogan?" Cathleen asked her mother-in-law. "I have cold water or lemonade."

"Lemonade." She turned to her husband. "What do you want to drink, John?"

"Hasn't Art come back with the beer?" he asked, referring to Cathleen's late husband, his son.

"John, you are getting old," his wife reproved him sharply. "Your mind is wandering. Our son has been dead for twelve years now." She cast a sad, apologetic glance at Cathleen.

"Don't worry, Mother Hogan. It's all right." She smiled.

Maggie guessed she was more aware than her aunt was about the frequency of these memory lapses by Cathleen's father-in-law. She'd run into it often during the week. As much as she'd grown to like the aging couple, it made conversation difficult. She didn't mention that to her aunt, but she did write about it to Culley in a letter.

A few days after Thanksgiving, there was a letter in the mailbox from him.

November 30

Dear Maggie,

I'm sorry I haven't had time to write to you, but I've been real busy.

What did you do for Thanksgiving? Tucker came over. He brought food to fix dinner. He's working for Calder now as a cook. I couldn't believe it when I heard it in town. He said it

*was the only place he could get a job. I told him he could have
stayed here, but he said he was a cook, not a cowboy. But he
still hates Calder the same as we do.*

*There was a big fight at Jake's last weekend. Some new guy
accused Buck Haskell of stealing money out of his wallet. They
argued and it turned into a free-for-all, with Chase Calder and
the Triple C against the others. The sheriff had to break it up. I
always knew they were a bunch of crooks at the Triple C.*

It's starting to snow. I have to go check the cattle.

> *Your brother,*
> *Culley*

Two weeks before Christmas, Maggie sat cross-legged in the
middle of the living room floor wrapping the shirts she'd bought
for Culley so she could mail them to him. An artificial Christmas
tree stood in front of the picture window, a Nativity scene
displayed at the base of its cotton-swaddled feet. Outside, the
grass and trees were still green, the air warm.

"It's hard to believe it's almost Christmas," Maggie declared
with a glance at her aunt, busy addressing her Christmas cards.
"I'll bet Culley is snowed in."

Cathleen paused in her writing. "You miss him a lot, don't
you?"

"Yes." It was a simple admission, and Maggie didn't attempt to
elaborate on it.

"Why don't you write and ask him to come here for the
holidays?" she suggested.

Maggie shook her head sadly, knowing it wasn't possible. "The
weather is too unpredictable at this time of year, blizzards and ice
storms. He couldn't risk being gone from the ranch." Her answer
was logical and sensible, but it didn't stop her from wishing she
could see him. She needed someone she could talk to, someone
who knew the facts surrounding her father's death, someone who
understood her inner anguish. As wonderful and good as Cathleen
had been to her, Maggie wan't able to confide these secrets to her.
They were all bottled up inside, silenced by pride.

As if sensing that it would be best to change the subject, her
aunt asked, "Have you picked out any possible names for the baby
yet?"

"Yes." Maggie heard the thud of a cane in the hallway and rose automatically to help the arthritically distressed Mother Hogan into the living room, seating her in one of the armchairs. "If the baby is a boy, I'm going to name him Tyrone," she told her aunt. "If it's a girl, I'd like to name her Cathleen, after you."

From the minute she had become aware of the life growing inside her, Maggie had begun to block out the part Chase had played in the baby's conception. She considered the baby solely her own.

"What a lovely thought, Mary Frances!" her aunt declared, genuinely moved by her words. "Thank you."

As Maggie started to sit down to finish wrapping Culley's package, she paused to pull the gray sweatshirt down past her hips. It stretched across her stomach.

"It's going to be a boy," Mother Hogan stated. And she observed, "Look at how low she's carrying the baby."

"That's an old wives' tale." Cathleen smiled away the remark. "It doesn't have a thing to do with the sex of the baby."

Before that moment, Maggie hadn't considered whether she would prefer to have a boy or a girl. Boys certainly had an easier time of it in this world than girls.

"I suppose Dr. Gordon told you that," Mother Hogan replied in a tone that questioned his knowledge.

"Does he have children?" Maggie asked. His sister, Pamela, she recalled, had never married, but she didn't remember her aunt saying anything about the brother.

"No, he and his late wife were childless," Cathleen answered.

"His wife died?" Maggie pressed the last piece of Scotch tape onto Culley's package.

"Yes, some years ago in an automobile accident." Her aunt paused, a sudden smile breaking across her expression. "I wish you could see the way the house is decorated for the holidays, Mary Frances. I swear, Pamela has persuaded the doctor to hang garlands and holly in every room of that house. You have never seen a brother and sister so devoted to each other."

Maggie thought about that as she wrote Culley's name on the package. Maybe they were separated by thousands of miles; maybe they hadn't always agreed on everything; still, they were close.

But Christmas came and went without Maggie hearing a single word from Culley. She worried silently while she listened to weather reports that spoke of the blizzard burying Montana in snow. It was after New Year's when she received his Christmas card with a ten-dollar bill tucked inside and a hastily scribbled note.

January 3

Dear Maggie,
    I'm sorry this is late, but I couldn't get out to mail it. It's been a bad winter so far. One of the horses—the bay with the bad eye—slipped on the ice by the water trough and broke its leg. I had to shoot it.
    Sorry this can't be a longer letter, but I've got a dozen head of cattle missing. I can hear Calder's plane flying over. He's been dropping hay to his cattle. I doubt if he's lost a single cow. He has the luck of the devil.
    Thanks for the Christmas card and the shirts. They are nice. I gotta go now.

Your brother,
Culley

She shivered, remembering those Montana winters—the frigid air pressing an invisible icy band across the forehead and freezing the moisture in the nose; blowing snow clinging to eyebrows and eyelashes; and the cold that numbed the legs until a rider couldn't feel the horse under him.

The baby kicked inside her and Maggie rubbed a hand across her swollen stomach, as if comforting it. The walls of the house seemed to close in on her, confining her. She wanted to get out—go somewhere, anywhere—but she couldn't. It was almost time for lunch and she still had an American history lesson to study, not to mention the two older members of the household, who shouldn't be left alone. She fought down the restless melancholy and waddled to the kitchen.

The last weekend of March Maggie went into labor. Seven hours later, she gave birth to a strapping eight-pound, nine-ounce baby boy. She was allowed to hold the squalling infant, with its prune-red face and mass of wet-black hair. None of it seemed quite real until later, after she was wheeled to her room to rest.

It was the next day when the nurse brought him in for his

morning feeding that Maggie examined his tiny, perfectly formed fingers and toes, and laughed at the little mouth eagerly seeking the bottle's nipple. Then came the surge of maternal love. It was a warm glow that radiated from within and shone from her features when she glanced across the room to her aunt, who had arrived a few minutes earlier.

"Isn't Ty the most beautiful baby you've ever seen?" Maggie insisted.

The remark was an indirect invitation to be a part of the scene, and Cathleen walked closer, stopping beside the bed. Her fingertips made a caressing brush over the baby's thick, down-soft hair.

"He certainly is," Cathleen agreed and laughed softly. "I feel like a grandmother instead of a great-aunt." She paused to admire her nephew again. "He has so much hair. I think his eyes are going to be brown."

"My father had brown eyes." Maggie refused to remember that Chase's eyes were brown. The bottle was emptied of its formula. She set it aside and shifted little Tyrone O'Rourke to her shoulder, patting his back to burp him.

"Mother Hogan sent along a present for the baby." Cathleen handed Maggie a gift-wrapped box.

She managed to balance the baby against her shoulder and slip off the ribbon to open the box's lid. Inside there was a little blue sweater and a matching knitted cap with a small, rounded bill.

"I'm going to dress him in this the day I take him home," she decided. When she looked up, she saw the leather-bound Bible Cathleen was holding, its edges worn.

"This is for you." Her aunt ran a loving hand over the book's surface before she offered it to Maggie. "It's the Bible of the Malloy family, your mother's parents and mine. Since you, little Tyrone, and your brother represent the last remaining descendants, I wanted you to have it. My mother gave it to me, but I have no children of my own. It's right that you should have it."

Maggie gazed at it, not knowing what to say. "Thank you," she murmured at last, a vague tightness in her throat.

The nurse came into the room, bright and cheerful, as all of the nurses on the maternity ward seemed to be. "Has Tyrone finished his bottle?"

"Every bit of it," Maggie confirmed.

"My, he's a hungry boy, isn't he?" the nurse declared with a wide smile of approval, her look gentle as she gazed at the sleepy head resting on Maggie's shoulder. "He's going to grow up to be big and strong to take care of his momma." She glanced apologetically at Maggie. "It's time to take him back to the nursery."

"Yes." She reluctantly surrendered her son to the nurse.

"It looks as if Tyrone received a present today." The nurse paused beside the bed with the baby in her arms to admire the sweater set. When she noticed the Bible on Maggie's lap, her expression became curious. "What's this?"

"The family Bible." She opened the Holy Book to the page that recorded the births, deaths, and marriages of the Malloy family and their children.

"Well, isn't that nice?" the nurse declared and shifted slightly for a closer look. "There's the place where you enter the information for Tyrone's birth, listing the date, time and place, your name, and the father's, if you know it."

It was an innocent remark with absolutely no slight intended against Maggie's character. Yet she stiffened at the implication she didn't know the name of Ty's father. To her, that was a sin worse than giving birth to a baby out of wedlock.

"May I borrow your pen, Aunt Cathleen?" she requested. "I want to enter Ty's birth in the Bible."

The nurse left the room before she saw the clearly legible handwriting spell out the name of Chase Calder. Her aunt wasn't able to stay long because her in-laws were home alone. When she left, Maggie wrote Culley to inform him of his nephew's birth.

April 2

Dear Maggie,

I'm glad you and the baby are okay.

I hope you didn't worry because you hadn't heard from me in a long time. It was a rough winter, but I made it through in pretty good shape. The cows are calving, so I'm real busy. I've lost some weight. I guess I miss your cooking. The way the house looks, it misses you, too.

Buck Haskell has been charged with robbery and assault and battery. Neil Anderson got drunk at Jake's the other night.

Buck followed him out to the truck and hit him over the head
and robbed him. One of Jake's girls saw it all from an upstairs
window. What do you want to bet Calder gets him off?
    Take care of yourself.

                                        Your brother,
                                            Culley

Chapter XVI

Buck pivoted away from the desk in agitation, then turned back to face Webb Calder, his boyish features screwed up in fury. "You aren't going to take a whore's word against mine? I tell you I was nowhere near Anderson! I didn't even see him leave! That bitch is lying through her teeth!"

Webb looked at Ruth, who was standing to one side. She was biting her lip, her eyes blinking, as if holding back tears. "Watch your language, Buck," he cautioned. He didn't hold with swearing in front of women. It showed disrespect. And he especially didn't like the idea of Buck swearing in front of his mother.

"I can't help it!" His fist made a downward stroke through the air. "I never expected that you would doubt—"

"It isn't a question of doubt, or what I believe," Webb interrupted sharply. "These are serious charges that have been leveled against you. I'm not taking them lightly, and neither should you. I have always stood behind my men when they were in trouble. I'll stand behind you. Now, the young lady claims she saw you hit Anderson over the head and rob him. We need to establish where you were and what you were doing at the time."

"Who notices the time when you're drinking?" Buck argued. "I didn't know I was going to need an alibi. I played some poker, drank . . ." He paused, struggling for something more specific. Then his glance fell on Chase, standing by the fireplace, an arm hooked on the mantel. "I was with Chase most of the time. Ask him."

"It's true." Chase nodded, wearing the same grim expression that was on everyone's face in the den—his father's, and Buck's parents, Ruth and Virgil Haskell. Only on Buck, it took on a desperate quality. "Buck and I were together almost the entire evening, but, like him, I didn't pay attention to the time."

"I could have been in the john when Anderson got banged on the head." Buck lifted his hands in a beseeching gesture. "That . . . girl claims she saw me, but maybe she said that because she's the one who really did it. Where's her alibi? Who was upstairs with her when she supposedly saw me? She could just as easily be the one who knocked Anderson out and rolled him. I'll bet that's what really happened. Anderson never saw who hit him. He said so. Why couldn't it have been a woman?"

"I admit it's possible," Webb conceded.

"Why else did she wait until the next day to tell the sheriff? Why didn't she come forward that night when they found him? It sounds fishy to me," Buck insisted. "Wait a minute!" He turned again to Chase, remembering something. "I borrowed five dollars off you last night—*before* they found Anderson outside. Would I be borrowing money off you if I had just robbed somebody?"

"No, it wouldn't make sense," Chase agreed.

"There! You see! That proves it!" Buck declared with a decisive nod of his head.

Webb rubbed his hand across his mouth in a thoughtful manner, then brought it down to the desktop. "I'll see what can be done to get this straightened out. In the meantime, Buck, I advise you to stay away from Jake's until it is."

"I'll make sure he does," Virg stated. "Come on, boy." He motioned to his son to come with him, then glanced at the man rising from the chair behind the desk. "Thanks, Webb, for backing the boy."

"Buck is family." The statement explained it all.

Virg turned to his wife. "Are you coming, Ruth?"

Her gaze darted away from Webb to her husband. "In a minute, Virg." There was a slight hardening of Virg Haskell's expression as he flashed a sharp look at Webb, then turned to escort his son from the room. When the pair had left, Ruth took a hesitant step toward Webb. Her hands were clenched together in a knotted ball. The tightness of her smile revealed how deeply worried she was. "I just wanted to thank you . . . for helping Buck." Her voice was very low, but otherwise steady.

"You know I'll do everything I can, Ruth." He felt a strong urge to reach out and take her in his arms, hold her there and comfort her, but it wasn't his place to offer that kind of comfort.

"Buck is wild sometimes, but he isn't bad," Ruth insisted.

"I know." Webb took her clenched hands and smoothed them out to rest between his rough palms. "Don't worry about it. Okay?"

"Okay." Ruth smiled, but there was a shimmer of tears in her blue eyes. "Thank you." It was a whisper, given as she squeezed his hands and quickly withdrew hers to follow her husband and son.

Webb stood for a long time after the front door had closed, staring in the direction that had given him the last glimpse of Ruth. He hated to admit it even to himself, but he was worried about Buck. The boy was intelligent, maybe too damned smart for his own good. There was a conflict going on inside of Buck, part of the transformation into manhood when the impulses for good and bad remain matched or tip one way or the other. There was larceny in the soul of every man; it was only a question of degree.

He took a deep breath and turned to glance at his son. Webb was bothered, too, by the blind loyalty of near-brotherhood that tied Chase to Buck. There were flaws to be overlooked in friends, but first they must be seen and recognized before they could be ignored. Otherwise, there would be a hard road of disillusionment ahead. If Chase had a blind spot, it was Buck. Webb wanted to open Chase's eyes.

"What do you think? Did Buck do it?" The sharp challenge within the question was hidden by the offhand delivery, so casual, so smooth.

"Buck?" Chase lifted his head to frown at his father. "Of course he didn't do it. A dollar doesn't stay in his pocket for more than ten minutes, but he doesn't steal it from somebody else's." He pushed away from the fireplace, a certain agitation in his action that showed he resented the question even being raised. "Besides, he was with me when it happened."

"I thought you weren't sure about that," Webb reminded him.

"I'm sure. I'll swear to it," Chase stated.

"If you supply an alibi for him, the charges will be dropped."

Webb sought to make it clearly understood the power that a Calder's word carried, a power not to be abused.

"The charges should be dropped, because I know he didn't do it. That girl can't be positive it was Buck she saw from the window. It was too dark outside, too many shadows. She made a mistake."

"As long as you aren't making a mistake," Webb murmured and moved to his desk.

Chapter XVII

A month after Maggie had brought Ty home from the hospital, Dad Hogan suffered a stroke that left him paralyzed. Cathleen was forced to admit him to a nursing home, where there were the proper facilities to care for him. The household routine that had been changed once to accommodate the addition of an infant was changed again to include twice-daily visits to the nursing home by the arthritic Mother Hogan.

Cathleen took her to visit every evening for an hour, while Maggie arranged to accompany the elderly woman to the home every morning after Ty had been given his daily bath. The situation was a strain on everyone, but it was especially hard on Mother Hogan. The couple had never slept apart during their entire married life. For hours, the woman sat in the front room staring into space, lost without the company of her husband of fifty-odd years.

Returning from a morning visit, Maggie sighed dispiritedly and shifted Ty into the crook of one arm so she could unlock the door. They had never locked their door in Montana, but she had quickly learned it was almost a cardinal rule in the city. She pushed the door open, then turned back to assist the elderly woman up the front steps and into the house, and went back outside to get the day's mail from the box.

"The new issue of *Reader's Digest* arrived, Grandma Hogan." She noticed it among the few envelopes as she re-entered the house, closing and locking the door. "Would you like to look at it?"

There was no reply and no indication the woman had even heard her as she used her cane to lower herself into the armchair in the front room. Maggie didn't press for an answer. Ty had begun to show signs that he was hungry, so she carried him into the kitchen to warm a bottle and some baby food. Fortunately, he was a good baby, a healthy baby, hardly ever crying and always sleeping the nights through.

Once she had Ty fed and tucked in his basket to sleep, she put some soup on to warm for herself and Mother Hogan, then glanced through the rest of the mail. One of the envelopes had a Montana postmark. She opened it and read:

May 20

Dear Maggie,

I was sorry to hear about Aunt Cathleen's father-in-law. I hope he's getting better.

I was right. The robbery charges against Buck Haskell were dropped. Chase Calder claimed that Buck was with him when Anderson got robbed. The fools believed the murderer's word. And the sheriff made Jake's girl—the one who saw Buck Haskell—leave town.

That Calder crowd think they can get away with anything. But they won't. Sooner or later I'll find a way to stop them.

I am fine. Will close for now.

Your brother,
Culley

Maggie folded the letter and put it back in the envelope. She could feel her brother's need for vengeance run through her. It was an ever-pervading poison sweeping through her system, hardening her so that she could never forgive.

It worked on her, as did the strain of these last weeks and the natural depression that followed childbirth. Both she and Mother Hogan barely touched the lunch she fixed. Once the kitchen table was cleared, Maggie got out her lessons. Through it all, she hadn't neglected her education, but today she wasn't able to concentrate. She was too restless, too confined. Finally, she gave up trying and wrote a letter to Culley, instead.

When Ty woke up from his afternoon nap, she used the finished letter as an excuse to get out of the house. She asked the next-door neighbor to look in on the elder Mrs. Hogan while she took the baby for a walk and mailed the letter to her brother.

Once Culley's letter was dropped into a corner mailbox, Maggie continued her stroll. It was a considerable distance to the home where her aunt worked for the Gordon family, but she knew she could ride home with Cathleen, so she set a leisurely pace. These outings were too rare for her to rush through them. Carrying the dark-haired, dark-eyed baby in her arms, she walked along the grassy verge of the highway winding through this upper end of the San Fernando Valley.

Being alone without friends was nothing new to her. Neither was the responsibility of keeping a home and taking care of others, even though she wouldn't turn seventeen until this summer. But being confined for long periods of time was unusual. Maggie had adjusted to the warmer climate, the large population of the area, and even having a child to look after, but being restricted to the house and small yard was stifling her.

Her lifelong ambition to get away from Montana had not lived up to her expectations, and she blamed the Calders for it. Because they had killed her father, she had been forced to leave home before she was ready. Even though she loved Ty and wouldn't even consider giving him up for adoption, she was aware that he was a burden for a sixteen-year-old girl. That was Chase Calder's fault, because he had tricked her into believing he wouldn't get her pregnant. All her troubles could be traced back to the Calders.

There wasn't any way to shut out her memories of the past. She was linked to it by her brother's letters and his embittered references to the Calders. At night, she had erotic dreams of Chase making love to her—dreams that always ended in nightmares, with the hanging of her father. And the past lived in the man-child she carried, a boy who already showed the big-boned frame of the Calders, instead of the slender bone structure of the O'Rourkes. Maggie couldn't forget, so it burned in her, making her determined to succeed, despite all the obstacles.

Slowing her steps still more, she gazed at the estates she passed, homes as fine as The Homestead, except they were situated on much smaller parcels of ground—forty to one hundred acres, as opposed to hundreds of thousands. White paddock fences gleamed in the California sun while tree-shaded white mansions marked the lane's end. Within the paddocks, horses grazed, their slick coats polished and shining.

Once Maggie had looked on horses as a necessary means of transportation and associated riding with long, tiring hours in the saddle. Now, she could imagine nothing more enjoyable than having a horse beneath her and the space to ride it . . . to feel the thunder of its hooves on the ground. She missed the smell of horse sweat and saddle leather, all the things familiar, the bellow of cattle and the taste of coffee boiled over a campfire. An aching grew within her and she gritted her teeth because she had turned her back on that life. Her skin would never again feel flannels and denims. It was going to be silks and laces and perfume.

Shifting Ty to a more comfortable position in her arms, Maggie turned down the private lane leading to the Gordon house, a two-story white Colonial with a colonnade front, and the green expanse of a tree-shaded and shrubbed lawn. Her aunt's car was always parked by the garage at the rear of the house, which was where Maggie always waited the few times she'd met her aunt here. Her destination was the same this day, until she was distracted by a commotion at the stables.

There was shouting and the angry, panicked whinnying of a horse. The uproar had the other horses in the paddock moving nervously, ears pricked toward the stable, snorting as they shifted anxiously. Curious, Maggie strayed toward the source of the noise, leaving the private drive to follow a side loop to the stables.

A sleek chestnut had escaped its groom and was loose outside the stables and their fenced paddocks. Three men were trying to catch it by trapping it in a corner formed by an outside stable wall and the white rails of a fence. They had succeeded in confining it to that general area and turning it back whenever the horse attemped to dash for the freedom of the unfenced yard, but the chestnut eluded each attempt to grab its halter, striking out with its front feet. All the shouting and arm-waving was exciting the already-high-strung animal, its dark eyes rolling in panic until the whites showed and its neck darkening with nervous sweat.

A man came around the corner of the stables with a coiled rope in his hand. At his arrival, a tall, lean, gray-haired man withdrew from the participation to direct the capture. Maggie spared him one inspecting glance that took note of the white knit shirt with a rolled neck and the black jodhpurs tucked into knee-high leather boots. His attire set him apart from the other men, clad in shirts and jeans, as did his quiet manner of authority.

Movement drew her attention to the man with the rope. With the first feeble loop he cast, it became apparent to Maggie that he'd never roped anything more than a post in his life. Each try became more pathetic than the last; the stinging slap of the rope on the horse's flank or leg frightened it to a higher state of agitation. The chestnut gelding was shying wildly from anything that moved. Maggie realized that any minute the animal's sheer panic would cause it to injure itself. The ineptitude of its would-be captors was more than she could stand. Disgusted and impatient with what she was witnessing, she strode forward to the tall, gray-haired man. His glance ran down at her in surprise when she pushed the baby into his arms.

"Hold Ty for me," she instructed curtly and didn't wait for his answer, half-aware that she had left him speechless and staring in bemusement. Without the encumbrance of Ty, she ran to the man with the rope and reached to take it from him. "Give me the rope."

"Hey!" He scowled in surprise at the grim-faced girl, with her black hair in a ponytail, and tried to jerk the rope out of her grasp. "What are you doing? Get away from here before you get hurt."

"The only one likely to get hurt is that horse. Now give me that rope. You obviously don't know how to use it." Maggie planted her feet firmly on the ground and used every inch of her five-foot, three-inch frame as a lever to pry the rope out of his fingers. Unprepared for her strength and determination, the man lost his grip and Maggie wound up with the rope, quickly backing out of his reach. She snapped an order to the others. "Everybody just shut up and stand still! All that waving is just scaring the horse."

Shock and the sight of a petite girl taking charge moved them all to obey, and Maggie advanced slowly toward the horse while her fingers absently got the feel of the rope and shook out the noose. The chestnut eyed her for a suspicious second, then bolted for a gap between two men. Maggie's reflexes were just as quick, the pattern of action firmly embedded in her mind, even though it had been months since it had been called into play. With one overhead swing of her arm, she cast out the noose, anticipating which way the horse would shy and leading it. The horse swerved and stuck its head right through the loop.

There was nothing to snub the horse to, and Maggie flanked the end of the rope with her hip, using the entire weight of her body to hold the horse, rather than rely on the dubious strength of her arms. She braced herself for the instant when the chestnut hit the end of the rope and let its impetus carry her forward at a sliding walk. Once the noose tightened around the animal's neck, it ceased to resist the pressure, although it continued to half-rear and prance anxiously. Two of the grooms rushed forward to grab its halter, while the third man, the one who had brought the rope, came forward to assist Maggie. There was grudging admiration in his look, plus a sense of resentment that a mere slip of a girl had succeeded so easily where he had failed.

"I'll take him now," he insisted. Maggie surrendered the rope to him without protest. The exhilaration of success was in her eyes.

A plaintive whimper from Ty made Maggie realize she'd left her baby with a perfect stranger. Tyrone was squirming in the man's arms, his fist waving the air as if he, too, realized he didn't know this man who held him. She rushed to claim him before he started a full-blown protest.

"Thanks for holding him." She barely met the man's warm gray eyes as she reached for Ty, who was screwing up his face to cry when she lifted him into her arms. It took him a second to realize he was on home territory before he relaxed.

"I should be thanking you," the man stated and tipped his head to one side, studying her with interest. "Where did you learn to rope like that?"

"I was raised on a ranch. I learned to rope almost as soon as I learned to ride." Maggie patted Ty's back in a manner that soothed and reassured. After her experience with Chase, she had developed a wariness of men, so when she looked up at the man, she didn't altogether trust the pleasantness of his smiling and handsome face. His hair was a dark iron-gray, but the suntanned vitality of his features made him appear mature and distinguished rather than old.

"I'm glad you did. If Copper's Chance had slipped by us and reached the road . . . with all that traffic, I don't like to think about what might have happened to him. I didn't pay twenty-five thousand for that horse to have him hit by a car, so I am eternally grateful you happened along when you did.''

Maggie stared at him incredulously for an instant, then laughed shortly. "I don't think you know very much about horses. You've just been taken. That horse is a gelding."

His head moved back to release a throaty laugh skyward. "I am well aware Copper's Chance is a gelding. I didn't buy him for breeding purposes, but for the show ring, Miss ———?''

"Maggie. Maggie O'Rourke," she supplied her name absently, still trying to comprehend his explanation. "Do you mean that horse really is worth that much money?"

"Yes. He's a first-class jumper."

Maggie knew about jumping horses, but she had never known they could be that valuable. A stallion of any breed could, conceivably, be worth that much, but a gelding with no reproductive prowess—that took some adjusting to.

"What spooked him?" she asked.

"I don't know," the man admitted. "I just had him flown in from Virginia this morning. We unloaded him from the horse van not twenty minutes ago. Perhaps he was nervous from all the traveling." He shook his head to show he could only guess at the cause.

The last sentence was barely spoken when Maggie felt a strange vibration. It felt as if the ground was moving underneath her. Her eyes grew wide with alarm as the sensation increased.

"What's happening?" She hugged Ty closer to her and looked around to see the limbs of the trees moving, even though there wasn't a breeze.

"Come on." The man's arm was around her, pushing and directing her to a more open area. His hand reached across to protectively include the baby and keep it safely in her arms. By the time they had taken a half-dozen steps, the curious vibration had stopped.

Maggie's rounded gaze lifted to the man, seeking an explanation. "Was that . . . an earthquake?" She'd heard about them before, but she wasn't entirely certain that was what she had just experienced.

"Yes. That must be what spooked the horse. They say animals can sense an earthquake coming." He smiled at her, his arm loosening from around her shoulders to let her stand free. "Your first?" he guessed.

"Yes." Her knees still felt shaky.

"Where are you from?"

"Montana." When Ty gurgled against her shoulder, Maggie quickly glanced at him to see if he was frightened, but he had one of those toothless, baby smiles on his face that indicated delight rather than fear. "It's okay, Ty," she soothed to reassure herself since he didn't need it.

"That's a healthy-looking boy," the man observed. "Is it the Van Doren's baby?"

"No, Ty is mine," Maggie asserted with a quick, proud look that was also defensive. She saw the start of surprise and the questions that leaped into his gray eyes. She answered them without waiting to see if good manners would keep him from asking. "I'm sixteen, and no, I'm not married." She was braced for an expression of disdain to appear on his face, but it didn't come, even though his study of her sharpened.

"Ty." An approving smile began to show as he said her son's name. "It's a nice name."

Maggie lowered her gaze to the baby, not certain the man's reaction was sincere. "Thank you."

There was a pause before the man suggested, "May I offer you a lift somewhere? It's the least I can do after you rescued my horse," he explained, as if guessing she would be sensitive about anything resembling charity or pity.

"No, thank you." Maggie was glad she could refuse. "I'm meeting my aunt. I'll ride home with her. She works for Dr. Gordon and his sister."

"Mrs. Hogan—Cathleen Hogan is your aunt?" His frown was both curious and pleasantly surprised.

"Yes."

"Forgive me for not introducing myself. I'm Dr. Phillip Gordon." He extended a hand to her. She noticed his fingers were long and almost femininely slender. "I recall now that Cathleen mentioned she had a niece living with her. I didn't make the connection that you might be she."

"I don't know who I thought you were, either." Maggie shook hands with him, feeling the strength of his fingers as she tried to remember all that Cathleen had told her about her employers. He had just turned forty, Maggie recalled. Her Aunt Cathleen had said only good things about him. Maggie was more willing to trust her aunt's judgment than her own. She relaxed her defenses slightly.

"Why don't you come to the house?" he invited. "I know my sister, Pamela, would like to meet you and the baby."

Maggie hesitated only an instant before accepting. "All right, and I can let Aunt Cathleen know I'm here."

The house was every bit as grand on the inside as it looked on the outside. All spacious and airy, decorated in bright California colors, it had cool, tile floors and plush furnishings with a scattering of antiques. There was a certain fragility in its look that spoke of a woman's influence.

Maggie's breath was taken away when Dr. Gordon introduced her to his sister. Despite the confinement of the wheelchair, Pamela Gordon personified all that Maggie hoped someday to attain. Her eyes were the warm gray color of her brother's, but heavily fringed with lashes and a trace of lavender shadow on the eyelids. Her features were slender, like his, but beautifully feminine. Instead of iron-gray hair, hers was silver-blonde and elegantly styled. She was wearing a sleeveless Oriental robe with a mandarin collar, her lifeless legs hidden under the long length of the gown. Everything about her seemed the epitome of beauty and grace. If that wasn't enough to earn Maggie's admiration, it was sealed by the blonde woman's entrancement over Ty.

"May I hold him?" Pamela Gordon asked in a voice that was so softly cultured. Maggie surrendered Ty to her arms. He immediately grabbed a handful of silver-blonde hair. Maggie, who had always been surprised by the strength of a baby's grip, quickly rescued the lock of hair and freed it from his grasp before he gave it a yank.

"Maybe I'd better hold him," she apologized.

"Oh, no, please," Pamela protested and held him a little closer, catching the small hand before it could grasp another handful of hair. "He can pull my hair any time he wants." She pressed a perfumed cheek close to the baby's. "He is precious."

"That is one thing Pamela and I have both missed in life," Phillip explained in a quiet aside to Maggie, and watched his sister playing with the baby boy. "The joy of having children around."

When Maggie's aunt came in a few minutes later to say she was ready to leave, Pamela begged them to stay. "Just a little while longer—long enough to have a cold drink," she coaxed.

"We can't," Maggie refused gently, but firmly. "Grandma Hogan is expecting us. I promised we'd come straight home so she could go to the nursing home early to see Grandpa." There was a moment of resistance when she started to lift Ty out of Pamela's arms before the woman reluctantly let him go.

"You will come again?" Pamela turned her eager gray eyes to Maggie, so soft and shining, like rich velvet. "And bring Ty?"

"Yes," Maggie promised.

The next day she wrote Culley another letter while Ty was napping. She described her first earthquake, how she had roped this expensive horse, and how nice Phillip and Pamela Gordon had been to her. It was the first really special thing that had happened to her since coming to California, except giving birth to Ty, of course.

Chapter XVIII

The doorbell rang. Maggie smoothed a hand over the black skirt of her dress. It was the second occasion she'd had reason to wear black in the last two weeks. The first time had been in June to attend Dad Hogan's funeral. The second was to attend the funeral of Mother Hogan, who had willed herself to die a week after her husband.

Maggie hadn't cried when her father died, and she had shed no tears with the passing of this elderly couple. She silently wondered if there was something wrong with her—if Chase had taken away her ability to feel things. The strain of keeping it all bottled up inside showed in the tautness of her features, made whiter by the black dress she wore and the jet-black color of her hair.

When she entered the living room of her aunt's house, Cathleen had already answered the door. Maggie watched with an outward impassivity while her aunt submitted to the compassionate and comforting embrace of Phillip Gordon, then dabbed at her tear-red eyes with a lace handkerchief. Pamela was with him in her wheelchair and hugged Cathleen when the older woman bent to greet her.

Phillip crossed the room, resplendent in a gray suit. He smiled at Maggie in that quiet way of his and took the hands she had unconsciously clasped in front of her. "How are you, Maggie?" he asked and studied the stillness of her features. He knew perfection when he saw it: the balanced contours of bone structure, everything in proper proportion. In no way could his surgical skills improve on the gift of natural beauty.

"I'm fine, thank you," she replied in an emotionless voice.

His gaze ran over her purposely blank expression. He'd seen this wall erected before the few times she had visited his home. Mostly, it came when she was asked an innocent question about her parents, her childhood, or the father of her illegitimate child. The latter he could understand she would be reluctant to discuss. Yet she didn't want to talk about her parents, especially her father, or what her life had been like prior to moving to California.

"This must be difficult for you. It is a lot to deal with for someone as young as you are," Phillip sympathized.

Maggie withdrew her hands, refusing the comfort he offered. "Dying is only hard for those who live." Her wisdom and experience belied her age.

"Pamela and I stopped to offer our condolences and see if there was anything we could do to help." He was aware of her rejection. Phillip could not recall meeting anyone so young who had this much pride and independence. "I have already told Cathleen that she should feel free to consult with my attorney if there are any legal questions regarding the estate of her late husband's parents. As for any medical bills or—"

Maggie stopped him before he could offer any financial assistance. "I believe there was sufficient life insurance to take care of their bills and pay for the funerals. They had no estate, except their personal belongings." Belatedly, she realized she had been cold in denying his overture of assistance. "It's kind of you to offer, though." She smiled somewhat stiffly.

"It isn't a question of kindness, but one of caring," he insisted. "Over the years, Mrs. Hogan—your aunt—has become more than an employee to Pamela and me. This is a difficult time for her . . . and you. We would like to make it as easy as possible."

"Of course." She could think of nothing else to say.

"What will you do now, Maggie?" He disliked that name. It didn't seem to suit the self-possessed young woman standing in front of him.

"I'm going to continue my correspondence course so I can get my diploma," she replied without hesitation. "Meanwhile, I'm going to look for a job and a good nursery to look after Ty while I'm at work."

"Jobs are hard to find," Phillip murmured.

"I'll find one," she stated. "As soon as I have my high school diploma, I'm going on to college."

Admiration glimmered in his eyes at her unwavering determination. She *was* going to find a job, and she *was* going to college. It hadn't been "I *want* to," but "I'm *going* to." She was a remarkable girl, beautiful and determined.

She half-turned to include Pamela. "May I bring you some coffee or tea?"

The consensus was for tea. Cathleen let go of Pamela's hand to rise. "I'll fix it, Mary Frances."

"You stay here and visit with the Gordons," Maggie insisted. "I can manage."

As she left the room, she heard Cathleen say, "God sent that girl to me because He knew I would need her to get through these weeks."

The comment made Maggie feel glad that her presence served a purpose and she wasn't a burden on her aunt. She made the tea properly, the way her aunt had shown her, letting the pot warm while the water was heating. She filled it with the hot, but not boiling, water, and added the loose tea leaves. Setting it aside to steep, she fixed the serving tray as precisely as she had seen it done at Pamela Gordon's home, complete with the fragile china cups and cream and sugar, and wedges of lemon.

When she carried the tray into the living room, she heard Pamela Gordon insisting, "What you really need, Cathleen, is a change of surroundings. Phillip and I have always wanted you to live with us. We never pressed the point because we knew you had your husband's parents to look after. Come live with us now." She was so beautiful, so persuasive that Maggie wondered how anyone could resist, but her aunt glanced at Maggie.

"I couldn't leave Maggie and the baby by themselves." She shook her head sadly, reluctant to refuse her employer anything.

Phillip had been watching Maggie since she had returned to the room with the tea service. She was a magnet, drawing his gaze whenever she was near. The stark simplicity of her black dress revealed its homemade origins, yet it gave her body an understated sexiness. The thrust of ripe breasts filled out the plain bodice before the material was darted and tucked to fit her narrow waist. When she bent over to set the tray on the table, the skirt was drawn tautly across the round cheeks of her bottom. Desire stirred within him, but Phillip angrily pushed it down. My God, he was old enough to be her father, he reminded himself. His interest in her was strictly paternal.

This rationale permitted him to suggest, "Maggie and the baby are welcome to come, too. The apartment over the garage hasn't been used for several years, but I think we could convert it into comfortable living quarters." Forcing his gaze from Maggie's wary look, he addressed himself to her aunt. "With the way property values keep rising, I wouldn't suggest that you sell this house. Rent it and keep it as an investment. Then, if you ever wanted to move back, you could."

"I suppose I could." But Cathleen Hogan was hesitant.

Maggie stayed out of the discussion that ensued. Sitting on the edge of a chair, she poured out the cups of tea and tried to do it as gracefully as she had seen Pamela do it. The prospect of living on the Gordons' ranch estate, where she could observe Pamela and learn more about becoming a lady, seemed like a dream come true, even if it meant living over a garage. It was previous disillusionments that kept her silent. But Phillip and Pamela talked her aunt into making the move.

"You haven't said what you think about it, Maggie," Phillip prompted. "Do you have any objections to the plan?"

"No, but as soon as I find a job, I'll start paying you something every month for rent," she stated.

Phillip knew better than to argue about that. "You mentioned earlier that you would be looking for work, and I've been giving it some thought. You don't need to look any further for a job. I need someone to exercise my horses and help with light work in the stable. I'm convinced you have the experience with horses to handle it. And it will mean you will have more time with Ty."

"Oh, yes!" Pamela enthusiastically endorsed the proposal. "I would adore watching him for you, Maggie. There wouldn't be any need for you to hire a sitter. You could just bring him over to the house." As if realizing he was the subject of conversation, Ty began crying from his crib, squeezed into Maggie's small bedroom. Pamela laughed in delight. "I knew if we stayed long enough, Ty would wake up from his nap."

The move was accomplished much quicker than Maggie had believed possible, her life-style changing so swiftly that she was a little dazed. It was as if she had stepped out of the haunting shadows of her past and into the bright sunlight of a new life.

The letters she wrote to Culley were filled with her enthusiasm for her new home and new job. When Phillip had mentioned an apartment over a garage, she had envisioned something entirely different from the huge living quarters with walls freshly painted and new carpeting on the floors.

There was a nursery for Ty and enough space in Maggie's bedroom to allow her to have not only a bed, dresser, and chest of drawers, but also a chair and desk so she could study her lessons. Pamela had given them some furniture from the main house, insisting she would give it to some charity if they didn't take it.

Her new job entailed getting up early every morning to groom and exercise Phillip's show horses. It turned out to be different from what she had imagined, since she'd never ridden with an English saddle before. She was very awkward at first. Phillip insisted that she had natural hands and a natural seat. When he first suggested that he could teach her the finer points of dressage and show-jumping in the evenings, she had been reluctant, but when he mentioned that most of the female show riders were young ladies from society families, Maggie accepted his offer. If riding English-style rather than Western made her a lady, then that was for her.

August came and went, her seventeenth birthday along with it. When the evening dishes were done, Maggie kissed Ty and left him in her aunt's care so she could meet Phillip at the stable for her riding lesson. He was waiting for her in the tack room when she arrived.

Calling it a tack room was almost a misnomer, although it was where all the riding equipment was kept. It was a combination office and lounge, complete with shower facilities so Phillip could clean up before going to the house. Trophies and ribbons were displayed on the walls, interspersed with photographs of his horses. Besides an antique mahogany desk, there was a leather-covered divan and chairs in a rich shade of California tan to complement the paneled walls.

"Have you been waiting long?" She hoped not, but there was a settled look about him, as if he'd been sitting in the swivel chair behind the desk for some time.

"Hours," he joked dryly.

In her new environment, Maggie found it easier to respond to his warm sense of humor. She had begun to like him—his gentle ways, his comfortable maturity, and quiet authority. "You haven't been waiting *that* long." She slanted him a reproving look that both mocked and laughed with him. When she started to cross the room to gather her riding equipment, he called her back.

"There's a present on the divan for you." He waved a hand in the general direction of the leather-upholstered couch.

"A present?"

"It's in the way of a belated birthday gift . . . from Pamela and me."

Uncertain whether it was proper to accept the gift, Maggie moved slowly to the divan. Laid out neatly on the cushions was a pair of tan jodhpurs, a black hunting jacket, and a white blouse. A pair of tall riding boots sat on the floor in front of the divan. Overwhelmed by his generosity, she could only look at him.

"Do you like them?" He prompted a response from her, his gray eyes smiling.

"Yes." But she was shaking her head.

"We decided that a lady should have the proper riding costume."

"You've done so much all ready."

"Maggie—" He stopped, his mouth quirking. "That name doesn't suit you at all."

"It's a nickname my father gave me." She was almost glad of the change of subject. It gave her time to think. "Aunt Cathleen calls me Mary Frances."

"With all due respects to your aunt's religion, the name sounds like it belongs to a nun—Sister Mary Frances."

"It does," Maggie admitted with a laughing smile.

"Is that your full name? Mary Frances O'Rourke?" Phillip asked.

"Mary Francis *Elizabeth* O'Rourke," she corrected. "Quite a mouthful, isn't it?"

"Elizabeth." He savored the name with satisfaction. "You look like an Elizabeth. It's a queen's name. Would you mind if I called you that?"

Her teeth sank into her lower lip to halt the unqualified permission from rushing out. He made her feel so important that she waited until the bubble of pleasure had been squelched. "It's all right. I answer to just about anything these days," she said with a little shrug that concealed her pleasure.

"All right, *Elizabeth*. Change into your new riding clothes while I saddle your horse." He paused long enough to pick up the saddle and bridle from the rack, then walked out. It was a full second after the door had closed that Maggie realized she hadn't told him she couldn't accept the present. She glanced at the clothes again and reconsidered. Maybe it would be all right to accept it this time.

During the next month, she discovered just how difficult it was to resist the Gordons—both of them. At Phillip's insistence, the huge library in the main house was put at her disposal. And Pamela, who welcomed any reason to look after Ty, showed her the proper use of makeup and took Maggie on shopping trips to give advice on clothes.

When she received a letter from Culley, she experienced a twinge of guilt. Her life had become so much easier, so rich and full, while he continued to struggle to make a living—against the weather, against the land, and against the Calders.

September 23

Dear Maggie,

I was glad to hear that everything is working out so well for you. The Gordons sound like really nice people.

The roundup is over for another year. Two of my cows strayed onto Calder range and I had to go get them and cut them out of their herd. Calder sat there on his yellow horse, just as big as you please, acting as if he owned the whole world. Tucker was there. Offered me a cup of coffee, but I told him I'd rather drink poison than coffee brewed in a Triple C pot. He may have sold out, but I never will.

That bunch will probably be at Jake's tonight, kicking up their heels after three weeks of roundup. I don't go to Jake's anymore. He and Tucker might not mind associating with scum, but I do.

I'm tired and there's hay to cut tomorrow for the winter. I just can't seem to find anybody to work for me.

I'm glad everything is working out all right for you, Maggie. Take care.

Your brother,
Culley

For a fleeting second, she wished Culley would sell the ranch and come to California, but she knew he wouldn't. She didn't even think she wanted him to, because deep down, she wanted her brother to get even with the Calders someday. She didn't know how, and she didn't care. She just wanted to know that someday they would be brought to their knees.

Chapter XIX

Jake's place was wild and raucous. The Triple C was enjoying its first real blowout since the fall roundup. But it wasn't just Triple C riders who were celebrating, although they did outnumber the other small ranchers and townspeople. It seemed everyone had chosen this Saturday night to party before the long winter set in. This night would provide subject matter to talk about during the cold evenings ahead.

As Chase started across the saloon to freshen his drink at the bar, a hand slapped him on the back. "Hey, *Boss!*" Buck mocked his new status at the Triple C. Chase was no longer just a cowboy. He had been promoted to foreman. "It ain't dignified anymore for you to get drunk," Buck warned. "You gotta look after the rest of us and keep us out of trouble, *Boss.*"

Buck had been razzing him since the day his father had made the change. Chase thought the constant teasing was beginning to wear thin, but he let Buck's remark slide off, as he'd let all the others.

"Thought you were in the back room playing poker," he said, instead.

"I decided to quit while I was ahead."

"Buy you a drink?" Chase offered.

"Nope." Buck shook his head and winked broadly. "I'm gonna go rub bellies with Connie Sue while they're playing something my two left feet can dance to."

With that, Buck moved off to the small area by the juke box used as a dance floor. Connie Sue Bingham was a local girl, recently divorced. She'd been somebody's date that night, but Chase had seen her with so many cowboys, he had given up trying to decide who it was. He watched Buck cut in and whirl her away from her previous partner, and smiled as he continued to the bar. There were times when Buck seemed totally irresponsible, yet he was a damned good cowboy.

He shouldered his way up to the bar and signaled Jake to refill his glass. Several cowboys at the bar were embroiled in a discussion about the long-range forecast for the winter ahead. Chase listened in on it, like every other cattleman wanting a way to outguess the weather. Someone wedged a shoulder into the small space beside him, and Chase shifted to make room, turning to see who it was.

"Hello, Fred." Chase greeted the man, a bull-rider on the rodeo circuit with a few acres outside of town where he spent the winters. "How did you do this year?"

"Not bad, not bad," the cowboy drawled. "Broke two ribs at Wolf Point, dislocated a shoulder in Miles City, and cracked my wrist in Butte. All things considered, I had a good year. Wasn't ever injured so bad that I couldn't ride."

"That's not bad," Chase agreed.

Fred popped the top of a beer can and took a swig. "You'd better teach your buddy how to play poker. He lost damned near everything but his shirt."

"You mean Buck Haskell?" Chase frowned. He'd had the impression Buck had come out ahead at the poker table for a change.

"Yeah. I don't think he won a single pot tonight, but he played 'til he was broke. He's either stubborn or stupid." The cowboy pushed away from the bar with the beer in his hand. "Guess I'll call it a night while I'm still able to walk." He lifted his beer in a farewell salute. "See you around, Chase."

"Take care, Fred." Leaning an elbow on the white-ringed bartop, he turned at a right angle to it and watched the rodeo cowboy wend his way to the front door in that peculiar rolling gait that accompanied bowed legs. His glance strayed to Buck, on the dance floor with Connie Sue. He didn't know what it was about Buck and money. He'd never known anyone so anxious to get it and so quick to get rid of it.

With a wry shake of his head, he faced the bar again and leaned both elbows on the countertop. The weather was still the subject of discussion around him, mostly an individual recounting of previous hard winters and debating which was the worst.

As he lifted his glass to take a drink, his gaze automatically went to the long mirror behind the bar. From where he was standing, the mirror reflected a view of the front door. Buck was beside it, looking around in an odd way, as if to see whether anyone was watching him. A frown narrowed Chase's eyes as he watched his friend slip outside. He lowered the glass, the frown deepening while he swirled the melting cubes in the amber liquid. Maybe Buck was meeting Connie Sue outside on the sly, Chase thought and tried to dismiss the incident with a shrug. His gaze absently searched the mirror's reflection until he found her. She was sitting with someone else and showed no signs of having a rendezvous to keep.

Overcome with curiosity about his friend's whereabouts and his reasons, Chase pushed away from the bar. An impulse he didn't quite understand carried him to the rear entrance of the saloon instead of the front door. It was used mainly as a rear access to the second floor, permitting customers to come and go without necessarily being seen by anyone in the bar if they chose.

Before he reached the door, it opened and Buck walked in, rubbing his hands together and blowing on them in an effort to warm them from the exposure to the chill of the November night. He gave a guilty start when he first saw Chase, then recovered quickly to grin.

"What are you doing, Chase? Sneakin' up the back stairs?"

"Where have you been?" A half-smile softened the challenge, but Chase couldn't stop the suspicion running through him concerning Buck's odd behavior.

"Just stepped out for some air," Buck shrugged and continued to grin. "The smoke's so thick in here it burns your eyes."

"Is that why you went out the front door and came in the back?" Chase asked and saw the discomfited look flash in Buck's eyes.

"What're you talking about?" Buck laughed.

There was a shout from the bar area. "Hey! Somebody help! Fred Dickens is outside with his head bashed in! We gotta get him to a hospital!"

Chase shot his gaze at Buck, narrowed in disbelieving accusation. His friend had a look of surprise on his face, too. Chase couldn't tell if it was faked or real. Buck started to push by him.

"Let's go see what the trouble is," he urged, but Chase caught his arm to stop him.

"How much money do you have on you?" he demanded.

Buck pulled back, appearing confused by the question. "What? A few dollars. What's that got to do with anything? Come on. I want to see what's happening."

But Chase wouldn't let him pass. "I thought you hit it good at the poker tables."

"Okay. So maybe I got a couple hundred bucks in my pocket." Buck's temper had a short fuse. It was sputtering now as he angrily shrugged a challenge.

"Fred told me you were busted at the tables tonight."

"I had a run of bad luck," he admitted.

"Then where did you get the money in your pocket?" Chase threw the previous remark back in Buck's face.

"I said, 'maybe' I had it. I didn't say I *did!*"

Chase grabbed him by the shirtfront and slammed his back against the wall, shaking the dust loose from the woodwork. "Goddammit! Don't lie to me!" He tightened his hold on the material and shoved his clenched hand up to Buck's throat. "I saw you sneak out the front door a couple of seconds after Fred left. Now he's laying out there with his head bashed in. I'm willing to bet he's been robbed like the others, too! And I want to know what you had to do with it!"

"Chase! You're crazy!" Buck argued, his anger strictly focused on his own defense. "I didn't have anything to do with it!"

With an effort, Chase relaxed his hold on the shirt and stepped back. "Prove it," he challenged. "Empty your pockets."

Buck licked his lips and looked away from the unwavering stare of Chase's eyes. "It didn't happen the way you think," he murmured, and Chase found himself wishing he had never pushed the issue. A bitter disillusionment was rising in his throat, choking him with its bilious taste. "I just wanted my money back," Buck insisted, but his voice had taken on a wheedling tone. "The game was crooked. Fred had been dealing from the bottom of the deck. I couldn't let him get away with that, could I? I mean, I had to teach him a lesson. All I did was just tap him on the head a little."

"What about Anderson? Jeffers?" Chase named the other two victims and felt the cold hand of betrayal touch him. It hardened him to ice. "Both times you used me. I provided the alibi because you were my friend and I believed you." He turned and walked away, afraid of what he might do to this man, who had been like a brother, if he stayed.

Buck followed him into the main room of the saloon, whispering urgently. "Chase, it won't happen again—I swear it! Let me explain how it was so you'll understand." There was suppressed anger and impatience in his voice as he exhorted Chase to listen.

The saloon was nearly empty. The few customers who remained were clustered together talking about this latest assault and robbery. Before Chase reached the bar, the front door opened to admit Sheriff Potter. His weary eyes scanned the remaining group, immediately bringing silence. His search stopped when he saw Buck and Chase.

"Buck." He walked forward, his boots shuffling on the wood floor, as if it was too much effort to lift them. "You're going to have to take a ride with me."

"You've got no call to take me in," Buck denied and edged closer to Chase. "If anybody says they saw me out there, they are lying."

"It's different this time, Buck," the sheriff said. "Fred Dickens regained consciousness before the boys took him to the hospital. He named you. He recognized you just before you hit him over the head."

"He made a mistake! I was with Chase. Ask him!"

The sheriff pulled his mouth down at the corners as he reluctantly glanced at Chase. "Was he with you?"

Chase didn't have to think about his answer, or look at Buck. "No." His reply was flat and final.

"What are you doing to me, Chase?" Buck protested and tried to prevent him from walking to the bar by getting in front of him, but Chase looked right through him. "You're supposed to be my best friend. We grew up together. My momma raised us both. Tell the sheriff I was with you!"

Chase made no reply and brushed past Buck as if he wasn't there. Buck had lied to him and deceived him. For the sake of the friendship they had shared, Chase would not add his voice to the condemnation. And neither would he offer anything in Buck's behalf, because what he had been was not what he had become. So anything good he might be able to say did not apply.

"You'd better come with me, Buck," the sheriff said again and took him by the arm.

"No!" Buck whipped his arm away to rage at Chase's back. "What kind of a friend are you? You're supposed to be my buddy, my pal! You think you're so damned high and mighty just because you're a Calder! Well, it could have been me instead of you!" He punched a finger against his own chest to emphasize the point. "It could have been me, you bastard!"

Chase glanced down the bar to where Jake was standing. "I'll have a whiskey, straight," he ordered.

"Buck, you're coming with me." This time the sheriff's voice was more decisive. "Don't make me add resisting arrest to the other charges."

Buck continued to yell and curse at Chase until the sheriff led him out of the saloon. The area at the bar around Chase remained clear. Not even the Triple C hands approached him. They left him alone to mourn the loss of his friend in private.

Chapter XX

Presents were heaped under the Christmas tree. It was Ty's first Christmas and most of the packages were for him, mostly from Pamela. She would have bought everything in sight for him if Maggie hadn't finally threatened not to let her take care of him anymore.

Maggie smiled as she watched Ty banging a rattle on the floor and absently opened the Christmas card from Culley. There was a letter inside.

December 19

Dear Maggie,

Remember I told you Fred Dickens, the rodeo guy, went into a coma and died? Well, Buck Haskell was convicted on manslaughter charges. He claimed he was drunk and didn't know what he was doing. I heard Chase Calder wouldn't even testify on Buck's behalf as a character witness. I can believe that. One of their thieves got caught, so they washed their hands of him. I told you they were like that— you get into trouble, and suddenly they don't even know you.

When the judge sentenced Buck to prison, I guess he started

*yelling and making all kinds of threats to get even with Chase. I
heard it took three men to take him out of the courtroom.*
   It's snowing.

                                        Merry Christmas,
                                           Culley

She felt pity for Buck Haskell—pity because he'd been betrayed
by the Calders, specifically by Chase, who had been his friend.
Betrayed just as she had been. Her gaze lifted to the star atop the
tree; she hoped the Calders would never know the peace it
symbolized.

The early spring foal teetered unsteadily on bandy legs, its
whisk-broom of a tail rotating wildly for balance. With legs too
long, a head too large, and eyes too big, it blinked at the bright,
strange world it had been so eager and insistent to enter only
minutes before. It whickered, a sound that needed some practice
before it would resemble a horse's neigh. For a newborn foal, it
was good-sized and obviously healthy. It should have been the
center of attention, with its snow-white blaze running down the
center of its concave forehead.

But everyone's eyes were on the old mare lying in the straw.
Each breath she took was labored. Maggie's fingers dug into the
side rail of the stall; she was mentally willing the mare to move.
Morning Mist was a hunting mare, a sentimental favorite of Dr.
Phillip's. He'd kept her, after her career in the show ring finally
ended, as his sole broodmare. At twenty-one, even that was
becoming too much for her. This time it had been a long and
difficult birth. What strength she had, the foal had taken, and the
mare appeared to have none left.

When the stud colt whickered bewilderedly again, the mare
snorted weakly and tried to lift her head, but she couldn't get it off
the straw. The mare's eyes closed as Maggie looked on, as the
effort had drained the last ounce of energy. With his shirtsleeves
rolled up, Dr. Phillip stood to one side of the stall, next to his
stable hand. A grim look of worry was etched in his tanned and
handsome face.

"Let's try to help her up," he suggested.

While Maggie watched, the two men knelt beside the mare and
tried to lift and push her into a position where she could get her

legs under her, but the horse hadn't the strength to cooperate. After much struggling, the stable hand, Ralph, gently laid the mare's head on the straw-covered floor.

"It's no use," Ralph said, breathing heavily from the exertion.

"I fixed some hot mash." Maggie unlatched the stall gate and stepped inside. "Maybe if we can get her to eat something, she'll get her strength back."

"See if you can, Elizabeth." Phillip agreed with the suggestion, but didn't rely on it as he turned to the groom. "Get some ropes and we'll rig up a sling. If we can just get her on her feet and keep her there, the foal can nurse, and Misty will stand a better chance, too."

Kneeling beside the mare, Maggie set the pail of mash on the floor and pulled a clean rag from her hip pocket. She dipped it in the mash and squeezed it into the mare's mouth. Most of it trickled out. She stroked the mare's throat to help the horse swallow whatever it could, then repeated the process.

Ralph returned. "I've got them, Dr. Phillip. How do you want to work this?"

"We'll use this crossbeam. It should be strong enough to support her."

Busy concentrating on her task, Maggie was only half-aware of what the two men were doing. A soft thump was followed by something white slithering into her side vision. Maggie glanced up to see the white rope dangling from a crossbeam. Her mind clicked in another image of the ranch barn and the rope that had hung from its center beam.

A horrible tightness gripped her throat and Maggie stood up. She saw again the plain rope over the stable's beam. Then another image clicked to replace it. It was the barn again and there was a noose swaying at the end of the rope. She backed up to escape the frightening picture and had a moment's relief when reality surfaced to bring the stable into focus. But her mind wouldn't stop its gruesome recall. The color drained from her face as the last picture came to her mind's eye and stayed—the one of her father's body swinging from the noose.

It wouldn't go away. Her hands were raised close to her face, her fingers spread. Maggie squeezed her eyes shut, trying to block out the mental image. But all the sensation, all the horror and anguish came flooding back to make it as real as if it were happening now. From far, far away, she heard someone screaming—incessantly, endlessly.

She had to get him down! She had to unloosen the rope! She ran to get it down, clawing at the hands holding it. Even when she realized it was just a rope again with no noose on it, it remained imperative that she take it down.

When she had backed away from the horse, she had drawn Phillip's glance. A frown creased his forehead at the look of terror on her whitened face, bewildered by her fixation with the rope. He was about to ask her what was wrong when she started screaming. His groom had stood motionless in stunned shock when she had attacked him to tear the rope from his hands and pull it off the stall's crossbeam. Phillip rushed over and grabbed her shoulders, pulling her off the defenseless man.

"It has something to do with the rope. Take it down," he snapped over his shoulder, prodding the groom into action as he hauled the rope from the crossbeam. "Elizabeth, the rope is gone! Look! It isn't there anymore!" His voice was firm and commanding, pushing at her to obey. "Open your eyes and look. It's gone. It doesn't exist."

She stopped struggling to get free and turned her head to look. For an instant, she was still. The rope was coiled in a harmless heap on the floor. A violent shudder went through her. Dry, hacking sobs began to shake her shoulders as Phillip put his arms around her.

"Come on. Let's get you out of here," he murmured.

"What should I do about the mare and foal?" Ralph asked somewhat helplessly.

Phillip ushered Maggie outside the stall and paused to send him an impatient look. "Try to find someone to come over and give you a hand. Call Simmons at the van Doren ranch."

She stumbled, but his strong arm was around her to support and guide her into the privacy of the tack room. Maggie choked on the sobs she tried to swallow and wiped awkwardly at the few tears that slipped from her lashes. Phillip led her to the divan and set her on the cushions.

"I'm sorry." She tried to get hold of herself. Phillip was sitting on the couch near her, leaning toward her with his elbows resting on his knees and his hands clasped in front of him. His patient gray eyes were watching her closely.

"There's no need to apologize," he assured her. "The rope triggered some traumatic recall that your mind couldn't cope with, so you went a little crazy." His faint smile seemed to say it was all perfectly normal. His quiet understanding was too much for her. She breathed in sharply, wanting to cry. "Would you like to talk to me about it, Elizabeth?" Phillip suggested. "Sometimes that helps."

Tears began to slide down her cheeks. "I wish my brother was here." Maggie turned her head to the side. "I could talk to Culley." A tear crept across her mouth, which she wiped with a trembling hand. "I didn't cry when they buried my father. I didn't even cry when it happened."

"Were you there when the accident happened that killed your father?" He studied every nuance of her expression, guessing that he was close to the truth. Somehow this was tied in to the death of her father.

"It wasn't an accident." Although she knew that was what her aunt, and everyone else here, had been led to believe. "He was murdered."

Before she could stop herself or think about what she was saying, Maggie was pouring out the whole story to him—about the Calders, her affair with Chase, the cattle-rustling, and the hanging of her father. Through it all she cried as she had not been able to do before. At some point, Phillip sat on the edge of the divan and gathered her into his arms while she sobbed out her story.

It was a bizarre tale, farfetched and difficult for him to believe, yet her anguish and pain were very real and genuine. Even if there was an exaggeration of the truth, his questions concerning her reticence to talk about the past were answered. Half of what she had endured would have crushed a girl of average resilience.

His hand smoothed the black hair on her head as he cradled it against his shoulder. "You should have gone to the police and told them," he stated grimly.

"They wouldn't have believed us." She sobbed out a bitter laugh. "They probably would have thought we were crazy. Besides, they take their orders from Calder, anyway. We had no proof except our word. And they would have asked what Calder's motive had been. What would have happened to us if we'd told them Pa was stealing his cattle and about our part in it? Culley could have gone to prison, and they would probably have sent me to a juvenile home."

Phillip could see that they had been forced into silence in order to protect themselves. The one thing he found so difficult to accept was the continued existence of a vigilante style of justice. More objective than she could be, he recognized that both her father and Calder had some justification for the actions, however misguided they might be. Naturally, because of his own interest in her, his sympathy was on her side, but it didn't blind him to the other.

"They ruled his death was a suicide." Her voice continued to waver with the flow of tears. "That's why I let Aunt Cathleen think it was an accident. I couldn't tell her about it—she's a devout Catholic. It wasn't suicide, anyway, although sometimes I think he must have subconsciously had a death wish." She began to tremble violently, vibrating in his arms. "I hate them. I hate the Calders for what they did. I hope somebody destroys them someday."

The depth of her passionate hatred shook Phillip. "Don't hate them, Elizabeth. Hate invariably destroys the one who hates. Put it behind you," he urged. "Don't forget the father of your child is a Calder."

"Ty will never know that," she stated emphatically.

"Someday he'll ask you about his father." Phillip attempted to reason with her.

"I'll never tell him who it is. I'll make up some story," she vowed and began crying again.

He held her closer and pressed his lips against her temple in an attempt to comfort her the way a father would kiss a child to make the hurt go away. That's the way it started—with Phillip pressing light kisses over her forehead and cheekbone and whispering soothing words to her tortured soul. She turned her face toward him, tilting her head back so he could continue this assuagement of her pain and grief.

When his mouth brushed her lips and he felt them yielding softly in response, it all changed. His senses signaled an awareness of firm breasts thrust against his chest and the soft contours of her slender body curved against him. She was wholly desirable and she was in his arms. His mouth came back to seek the sweet taste of her lips beneath their salty covering of tears. Her body warmth ignited the desire that simmered below the surface whenever he was around her. Somewhere he'd lost the reason to control it. Passion flamed through his kiss and she returned it, her lips moving against his in the same spontaneous reaction. He hungrily deepened the kiss and felt her yield to him.

Suddenly her hands were pushing against his chest and she was wildly breaking free from his kiss to stare at him with green eyes that seemed to see a stranger. His hands started to reach for her, but she recoiled from him.

"Don't touch me," she warned and managed to scramble to her feet, backing away from him.

"Elizabeth, I—" He searched for the words to apologize for his behavior—for taking advantage of her when she had been in such a vulnerable state.

She rushed to the open door, pausing just long enough to get her bearings before she sped across the yard to the apartment above the garage. Phillip watched her from the stable doors.

Chapter XXI

Someone was climbing the flight of stairs outside the garage. Maggie could hear the footsteps, but she pretended she didn't and continued to spoon-feed Ty in the high chair. Ty tried to grab the spoon, so she held his hand down and held the spoon to his closed mouth. He regarded her for several seconds with steadfast brown eyes, then shook his head.

"Come on, Ty. Just one more bite," Maggie coaxed at the same instant there was a knock on the apartment door. She glanced at her aunt, who was scraping the plates from the evening meal before washing them.

"I'll answer it." Her aunt smiled at the young mother and child.

While Maggie's attention was distracted, Ty grabbed the spoon with his free hand. Strained apricots squished through his little fingers and dripped onto the high-chair tray. Releasing an exasperated breath, Maggie reached for the damp washcloth kept nearby for just such emergencies. After prying the spoon out of his strong grasp, she wiped his hands and mouth, then her own and the tray. It had been the last spoonful of apricot sauce from the jar, so she untied the stained bib protecting his T-shirt. His legs kicked the chair while he cooed with delight.

"You want to get down to play, do you?" Maggie teased him while part of her listened to Phillip greeting her aunt. She had guessed he would come see her after what happened that afternoon. She wanted to panic, but that was against her nature.

"May I speak to Elizabeth alone?" she heard Phillip ask.

There was a split-second hesitation before her aunt agreed to the request. "Of course. I was just going to take the garbage out, anyway."

Maggie had never known her aunt to ask personal questions, and she hadn't this afternoon when Maggie had dashed to their apartment above the garage. Cathleen hadn't even delved into the reason Maggie had passed out, except to ask if she felt better. That consideration afforded Maggie the privacy she needed.

"Elizabeth, Dr. Phillip is here to see you." The influence of the Gordons had prompted her aunt to stop using her given name of Mary Frances. Maggie was beginning to believe that was the name of another person. She looked up to acknowledge the statement and met the level glance of his gray eyes. Then her aunt was gathering the garbage sack to carry it downstairs and leave them alone.

Ty was becoming impatient with Maggie for being so slow in unlatching his high-chair tray and sliding it back. When she lifted him out of the chair, she didn't put him on the floor as he wanted. Holding him gave her a convenient distraction, an excuse to avoid Phillip's eyes.

"Elizabeth, I came to apologize for my actions this afternoon," Phillip said.

"There's no need," she denied stiffly while Ty squirmed in her arms.

"I'm afraid there is every need," he insisted. "I can't excuse what I did. The only explanation is that I discovered a beautiful woman in my arms and I did what any normal man would do in my place—I kissed her. I never intended to frighten you."

The last statement made her lift her gaze. She finally looked at him and saw all the things she had been trying not to notice these last seven months. He was handsome and lean, suntanned and vigorous. His hair was the color of steel, but his eyes were a warm gray velvet. Where Chase Calder had been composed of all rough, unfinished edges and aggressively male, Phillip Gordon was the smooth, final product of manhood, suave and charming, always immaculately dressed. A true gentleman.

"You didn't frighten me." When Ty started to squeal in anger, she put him on the floor. He crawled hurriedly to his toys in the middle of the living room. Maggie turned to him to finish explaining her answer. "It was me." She stopped trying to hide her feelings. "You see, I wanted you to kiss me. I wanted you to touch me. More than that." She grew bolder with returning confidence. "I wanted you to make love to me. I didn't think a man could make me feel like that again. I didn't think it would ever be like that."

"Elizabeth." He took an involuntary step toward her, desire shining in his eyes. It was there for a fleeting second; then it was gone when he stopped short and shook his head. "You don't know what you're saying."

"Yes, I do, Phillip." Of her own accord, she dropped the professional title that usually preceded his name when she addressed him.

"You are seventeen and I just turned forty-one. I'm old enough to be your father," he explained gently.

"I'm not pretending that it's right to want you to make love to me, but I can't deny that it's the way I feel," she stated, effectively throwing his logic out the window with her counterpoint of the truth.

"It's only because I'm the most likely male around, and you're a naturally loving young girl. I'm not going to let you get involved with me. You have too much going for you, Elizabeth." He stroked a finger across her cheek in a reluctant caress. "You're intelligent, determined, and ambitious. The last thing you need is an affair with an old man."

"You aren't old, Phillip."

"I suppose you think all this gray hair is just a form of camouflage," he mocked.

"It makes you look distinguished," she insisted.

"Which is just another way of saying 'old.'" He shook his head and smiled. "This fall, when you start college, you'll be surrounded with lots of handsome young men. You'll be happier with someone closer to your own age."

"Like Chase Calder!" Maggie hurled the name, her temper surfacing. "I don't remember that experience as a happy one."

"Chase Calder was just one man. You can't judge all other men by your experience with him. You can only learn from it."

"Chase was always teaching me something," she remembered bitterly. "Unfortunately, it was about sex instead of love."

"You have a lot to learn about a lot of things."

"And I'm going to learn about everything I can." From what

she had learned so far, Maggie knew there was a great deal that went into making a lady besides fine clothes and fancy homes. There was the whole cultural world to be absorbed. "I want to know about art and music, the theater and the classics. I want to speak other languages fluently and—" She stopped because her list had become endless the more she became exposed to different things. She looked up to see the benevolent twinkle in Phillip's eyes.

"And you want to travel and see places for yourself." He perceptively added another item from her long list. "There isn't room for an old man in your young life. You have too much growing up to do."

"Phillip—" She attempted a protest.

But he interrupted. "I'm flattered that you find me attractive, Elizabeth. I'm at the age where I would like to kick up my heels and recapture my lost youth with someone like you. Please don't tempt me. I'd like to be spared the indignity of making a fool of myself over you."

"I would never make you look the fool. I know how that hurts."

He cupped her cheek in his hand. "Let's make a pact. When you finish college, we'll see if you still feel the same way toward me or if you've acquired a taste for the young, adventurous type."

She turned her face into his hand, closing her eyes in silent enjoyment for the feel of his smooth hand against her skin. With a clear-eyed certainty, she met his gaze. "We'll see what happens when I finish college," she agreed, because she sensed the wisdom of his suggestion and because she was somehow certain her feelings wouldn't change. They had grown slowly, not flared up suddenly.

"In the meantime, I'll see what I can do about broadening your cultural horizons." This one simple sentence hinted at the things to come.

On a late afternoon early in June, Maggie climbed the steps to the apartment over the garage. She had been with Pamela Gordon, viewing a traveling art exhibit at a local gallery. Each month they visited a different art gallery in the Los Angeles area as a fulfillment of Phillip's promise to educate her in the arts. In addition, Pamela and Phillip—always the two of them together—

had taken Maggie to several symphonies, and to a ballet and the opera.

As she entered the apartment, Maggie called out brightly, "Hello! Anybody home?" A happy squeal came from the kitchen, followed by the sound of running feet. Ty crossed the living room to greet her as fast as his stout little legs could carry him. He was almost a year and a half old—and all boy. Laughing she swung him into her arms. "You never walk anymore, Ty. You always run." She hugged him while he jabbered away an answer. "You're growing so fast," Maggie sighed and drew her head back to look at him. "Have you been a good boy, Ty?" He regarded her silently with eyes that were decidedly brown.

"Of course he has." It was Cathleen who answered, entering the living room. "How was the exhibit?"

Carrying Ty in her arms, Maggie walked over to the blue sofa and sat down. "Fascinating." She tickled the little boy on her lap and watched him giggle while she continued to address her talk to her aunt. "Even when I don't understand some of the paintings, it's fascinating." She laughed, sliding her aunt a rueful glance. "The symphonies, the opera, the ballet, and the art museums— all get confused in my mind sometimes. The terms are so new to me that I get surrealists, impressionists, and cubists all mixed up with counterpoints, fugues, and arias. I have so much to learn."

"You'll learn," Cathleen assured her. Then she said, "There was a letter for you in the mail today."

"From Culley?" Maggie asked hopefully. "He hasn't written since Christmas. I know he's been busy, but I'm beginning to worry about him."

"It wasn't from your brother." The envelope was on a side table. Cathleen brought it to her, a pleased look about her expression.

When Maggie saw the return address that was stamped on the envelope, she set Ty onto the floor and eagerly tore open the flap. "It's my high school diploma!" She proudly showed it off to Cathleen while she continued to stare at it herself. "Now I'll be able to go to college this fall. Did I tell you? Phillip thinks he'll be able to get me a scholarship. Of course, it will mean taking more tests to prove I'm scholastically capable, but I don't mind. Even if the university won't accept me, I can enroll in one of the community colleges."

Maggie won the scholarship and enrolled at the university as a full-fledged student that fall. She received one short letter from Culley that summer, but his letters became less frequent. Mostly, they consisted of notes scribbled in a Christmas card or in the birthday card he mailed each August, with an occasional half-page letter sprinkled in between. Each of them contained some stinging reference to the Calders, a vow of retribution. They never allowed Maggie to push the past totally out of her mind.

She was busy, too. Between carrying a full load of classes at college, taking care of a growing and rambunctious boy, and showing and exercising Phillip's horses, she continued to avail herself of all the cultural entertainments Los Angeles had to offer. Sometimes she was accompanied by Phillip and Pamela, never Phillip alone. Often she was escorted by a classmate. Those were the occasions when she usually dated, which wasn't all that often. She did attempt to follow Phillip's advice and go out with men closer to her own age. Few of them impressed her, but a couple of them had been a lot of fun. She had discovered that passion could be a manufactured emotion.

It was only with Phillip that she felt safe and comfortable. He was a good influence on her, able to turn aside her temper and make her laugh. They usually rode together in the early morning, schooling and exercising his show horses. Sometimes he talked about his work and the built-in rewards that came from taking something scarred and broken and repairing it. It seemed that's what he was doing with her. As a plastic surgeon, his skills were renowned in medical circles. Maggie admired, trusted, and respected this man, and the physical attraction remained, too.

It was the same for him. She knew it because she had frequently observed the way he looked at her when he thought she wasn't watching. When they were in a crowd during a theater intermission, there was always something possessive in the way he touched her and kept her by his side. Maggie was tempted many times to use the feminine wiles she had learned and ignite the desire smoldering under his smooth surface. She didn't because she remembered the kind of talk that had circulated about her and Chase. Phillip was so sensitive about their age difference that she knew it would be the first thing the gossip-mongers picked on. She cared about him too much to have people making cutting remarks behind his back. So she bided her time.

Tears shimmered in her green eyes as she clutched the college diploma in one hand and hugged the dark-haired five year old boy who had wound his arms around her neck, and smacked a wet kiss on her cheek.

"Congratulations, Mommy." Ty struggled over the long word, but he pronounced it correctly. He was big for his age, with a large-boned frame that indicated he would grow much taller. His hair was brown, not black, partially bleached by the California sun, and his eyes were brown, but Maggie shut her mind to the child-softened resemblance to Chase Calder. Ty was *her* son.

"Thank you." She kissed the air near his cheek because he hated it when her lipstick left a red mark on him. Still bending down to his height, she drew back to look at him and smiled. "Who told you to say that?"

"Pip." He had never quite managed to twist his tongue around Phillip when he was learning to talk. It had long ago been shortened.

She glanced up to meet the warm pride in his expression, but when she unwound her son's arms from around her neck and straightened, it was her aunt whom she embraced. This kind, gentle woman who had taken her in, never asking any questions, never offering any recriminations for the illegitimacy of Ty's birth, and always treating Maggie like her own daughter, an uncomplaining woman so very much like her sister—Maggie's mother, who had wanted above all else for Maggie to have a good education. Now it had happened.

"I know your mother is very proud of you, Elizabeth." Cathleen cried softly—as she did everything else.

Her thoughts, too, had taken the direction Maggie's had gone. There was a lump in her throat, which didn't allow more than a lovingly stressed, "Thank *you*, Cathleen."

Her aunt hugged her close once more, then moved back. "I only wish your brother was here to see you. Do you suppose he didn't get the plane ticket you sent him?"

"Culley . . . was probably too busy. There's a lot of work to be done on a ranch at this time of year." She made his excuses for him. She had wanted Culley to be here to share this moment with her, but she also realized that he would feel out of place in these surroundings, uncomfortable. Perhaps he knew that. Or perhaps he was really busy. That was more than likely the reason, but she couldn't help wishing he was here. Turning, she bent down to press her cheek against Pamela's. The lovely blonde was stunning, as usual, dressed in a long pink gown that flowed softly down the front of the wheelchair. Maggie had lost some of her illusions about Pamela. The woman had been so helpful and instructive, but Maggie was accepted by Phillip's sister because of Ty. She doted on Maggie's son. Ty even called her "Aunt" Pam.

"Congratulations, Elizabeth." Her smile was charming, yet no more than pleasant.

"Thank you, Pamela." Her heart was pounding as she glanced at Phillip, standing attentively by his sister's wheelchair. His steel-gray hair had turned to silver at the temples, but he looked vigorously handsome, so tall and lean and suntanned. "You look very *distingué*, Phillip," Maggie said, practicing a little of the French she now spoke fluently. "It seems I've saved the best until last." She held out her left hand to him, which he took to draw her forward. "Thank you, for everything."

"This is a proud day . . . for all of us." He appeared to add the last to cover the intensity of his regard.

She stood quietly before him, letting him look her over while she radiated a sense of serene confidence. She wore her black hair in a shoulder-length cut that was styled to enhance its tendency to wave. Makeup, artfully and subtly applied, heightened all her best features—softening her strong cheekbones and flattering the brilliant green of her eyes with their sooty lashes. Bold red lipstick outlined the soft contours of her lips. Maggie knew she looked chicly adult and carried herself with an air of maturity.

When he bent his head toward her, she was disappointed when he only brushed his mouth against her cheek. "Haven't I earned more than a peck on the cheek?" she chided and leaned up to bring her lips against his.

His hands moved to hold her shoulders and maintain her position while a pleasant fire warmed her blood. Their lips clung together for only a short span of seconds, but the kiss bridged the four years of anticipation and made the long wait worthwhile. A soft glow filled her expression when she leaned away.

"Pip has Mommy's lipstick on his mouth." Ty laughed and pointed.

"It tastes good," Phillip assured him as he removed the linen handkerchief from his suit pocket to wipe the red from his mouth. He accomplished it with a certain panache that indicated a pride in the action, as if he, too, had waited for a reason to wipe off her lipstick.

The reference to taste reminded Ty of something else. "Can we go, Mommy? Aunt Cath'een made cake and candy and everything. It might spoil if we don't go home."

"It certainly might." She laughed in agreement.

"Wait here," Phillip instructed and added with a wry lift of an eyebrow. "I'll see if I can find the car."

In addition to the cake and tea—milk for Ty—there were gifts waiting for her in the Gordons' home. Before Maggie had a chance to open them, a special-delivery telegram arrived from her brother. She signed for it and tore open the envelope.

It read:

MAGGIE—CONGRATULATIONS. SORRY I COULDN'T COME. ALWAYS KNEW YOU COULD DO IT. WE'LL SHOW THEM CALDERS YET.

CULLEY

The Calder name trespassed onto even this special day.

Later that evening, after Maggie had put Ty to bed, she told her aunt she was going out for a walk, explaining there had been too much excitement that day for her to go to sleep. Cathleen agreed that a walk was what she needed.

A light was burning in the tack room window of the stable. Maggie had half-guessed and half-hoped it would be Phillip. When she entered, the aromatic blend of pipe smoke and saddle soap greeted her first. Phillip was staring at a photograph on the wall, one of her riding his black jumper, Sable. He was dressed in gray, a color that suited him so well, a pearl-colored shirt, and charcoal-gray trousers in the hugging, Continental style. He turned to face her as she approached.

"Do you remember the pact we made four years ago?" She stopped in front of him.

"I remember it very well, Elizabeth." There was a husky pitch to his voice, but he was still wearing the mask that concealed his thoughts whenever she was near.

"Nothing has happened to change the way I feel." Before he could say it, Maggie did. "And don't tell me that you're old enough to be my father, because it doesn't make any difference. So what are we going to do about it?"

A suggestion of a smile spread slowly across his expression. "I think a man is entitled to make a fool of himself over a woman at least once in his life. Why don't you come kiss this old fool?"

With a soft, exultant laugh, she glided into his open arms and lifted her mouth to his descending lips. The kiss was firm in its possession, claiming what had been his for a long time. If it lacked spontaneous fire, his experience at arousing a response more than made up for it. Besides, Maggie had been burned by her affair with Chase, an affair sparked by combustible chemistries. She wasn't seeking that sexual volatility with a man. She wanted something safe and solid, a relationship that would be the complete antithesis of the one she'd known with Chase. Phillip's lovemaking offered her that, his kiss arousing her without ever overpowering her.

When he began to trail tantalizing kisses over her face, she closed her eyes in sheer contentment. Her hands lay quietly on the lean wall of his chest, feeling the erratic pattern of his heartbeat. His arms offered her a safe haven. They promised security, comfort, devotion—all the things she was seeking. He was the father she'd never had; the friend she'd never known.

"I love you, Phillip." The words came easily from her lips.

His exploring mouth lingered near the corner of hers, a shudder running through him. "I've waited so long to hear you say that, my darling, so long." He kissed her, confidently, surely.

She wanted no fire or flame, only a heady glow. Her hands caressed no brawny muscle, only trim, lean flesh. She preferred skill to raw passion. She wanted no man in her arms to remind her of Chase Calder—no ghost from the past to confuse her about who she was with in the present, so she was not disappointed. She was overjoyed that she had found the very person she had been seeking, someone she could care about emotionally, and who could provide an outlet for her sexual needs.

Chapter XXII

Her lounge chair was situated in the shade of a tree so Maggie could escape the heat of a July sun and still watch Ty playing cowboys and Indians on the lawn. She glanced at the brief letter on her lap, but her attention was distracted by the heavy diamond ring on her finger, the engagement ring Phillip had given her.

The wedding was to take place in September, which was the earliest Phillip could arrange to take a month off from his surgical schedule so they could have a proper honeymoon. Maggie had suggested that they marry now and go on a honeymoon later, but he had rejected that plan, insisting he wanted to do it the old-fashioned way—the wedding, followed immediately by a honeymoon. Maggie was certain she was correct in suspecting his true motive was to give her these summer months to reconsider, but she had absolutely no doubts about her decision to marry him.

No one had tried to talk her out of marrying Phillip. Her aunt had hesitated only an instant until she observed how happy and contented Maggie looked and had immediately given them her blessing. Pamela was the only one who had misgivings about their marriage, but for an entirely different reason from Phillip's concern for their difference in ages. As Maggie had gradually discovered, Pamela was essentially self-centered, accustomed to a doting brother. While she was overjoyed at the prospect of Ty living in the same house with her, Pamela didn't care for the idea that she might have to compete with another woman for her brother's attention. It had required a bit of tact on Maggie's part to assure her, there was no cause for concern. Now it was her future sister-in-law who was organizing all the details for the wedding, which was to be a simple affair, nothing grand or elaborate.

Naturally, Maggie had informed Culley of her impending marriage and written to him about her fiancé. There were some things she hadn't told him, some things he wouldn't have understood. A large part of the attraction she had for Phillip came from the positive father image he represented. Maggie couldn't explain that to her brother. Their own father had never been someone she could look up to, admire, or respect. Angus O'Rourke had never assumed the responsibility of looking after his daughter; in fact, it had been the other way around. She knew Phillip would always look after her and be concerned about her interests, as well as his own. He would be there to lean on when she needed someone's support, yet at the same time, Phillip would allow her to be independent, her own person, as a father should.

It was a many-faceted relationship. Maggie had written to Culley only that part of it that he would understand. She read through her brother's reply again.

July 12

Dear Maggie,

Congratulations on your engagement. I hope Phillip makes you very happy. From the things you said about him in your letter, it sounds like he will. I wish I could meet him, but right now I don't see how I can make it to your wedding.

Things aren't going too good here. It hasn't rained since April. The ground is all cracked and hard. The one creek has already gone dry and the grass is burning up. If it doesn't rain pretty soon, I'm gonna have to start feeding my winter hay to the cattle so they'll have something to eat. Just about everybody is hauling water—except the Calders, of course. They got plenty of water. They're doling it out to the rest of us like it was candy, giving us just enough to keep us from dying, but not enough to satisfy our thirst.

I'm glad you got away from here, Maggie. There aren't any

*rich doctors around here to marry, just a lotta dust and heat. I
can't be there, but I wish you all the best.*

Your brother,
Culley

She let the paper settle onto her lap once more and remembered
the way the sun could scorch a Montana sky. She heard footsteps
in the grass approaching her lawn chair. Maggie looked up and
smiled a welcome when she saw Phillip walking toward her.

"Hello." He stopped beside her chair and bent to lightly kiss her
mouth. His glance fell on the letter in her lap. "What's this? A
love letter?" He teased her with a smile as he pulled another lawn
chair closer and sat down.

"Yes, from my brother." She folded it along its creases and
returned it to the envelope. "He won't be able to come to the
wedding. September is a busy time on the ranch."

This wasn't the first time Phillip had observed how quiet and
introspective she became after receiving a letter from her brother.
He guessed they often opened old wounds. He glimpsed a trace of
disappointment in her expression.

"I know how much you were hoping your brother would come.
Maybe if we postponed the wedding until October or November—" Phillip wasn't allowed to complete his offer.

"No." Her refusal was firm. "Everything is already arranged.
We're going to be married in September."

He didn't attempt to discuss it with her, lightening his mood,
smiling and saying, "Good." He reached inside his summer-light
suit jacket and removed a half-dozen travel brochures from its
inner pocket. "Because I've just come from my travel agency.
How does a September honeymoon in Paris sound to you?" He
passed her the brochures and reservations. "I thought you might
like to practice your French."

"Paris?! Phillip, it's marvelous!" She leaned over to kiss him,
then began looking eagerly through the brochures. "I've always
dreamed of going there."

"Then I'm twice as glad I chose it."

"So am I." She reached out to slip her hand into his and let it
remain to link them together. With a mother's watchful eye, she
noticed Ty stalking an imaginary foe near the flowerbeds. "Ty,
don't get into the roses!" she called out the warning. The little boy

paused, then began slinking in another direction. "He's getting to the age where I never know what he's going to be doing next. I expect any time for him to start swinging out of the trees, playing Tarzan," she murmured with a slight shake of her head.

"I have been meaning to talk to you about Ty," Phillip said.

"What has he done this time?" She smiled.

"It's nothing he's done, Elizabeth," he assured her. "It's what I want to do. I'd like to adopt him. I've always wanted a son."

There was a husky quality to her voice when she replied to his statement. "Ty couldn't choose a better man to be his father."

"I'll call my lawyers tomorrow and see about putting the adoption procedures into motion. Hopefully by September, the three of us will legally be one family."

"I'd like that very much." Her hand tightened its hold on his.

Ty hollered a greeting to someone and Phillip glanced around to see Cathleen wheeling his sister across the lawn toward them. "You two look like an old married couple, sitting there holding hands like that," Pamela observed. "I hope you don't mind if I join you."

"Of course not." Maggie was diplomatically quick to welcome her.

It was a very small wedding. One of Phillip's associates, a friend, acted as his best man, and Pamela was Maggie's maid of honor. Since Culley wasn't there to give her away, she and Phillip walked to the altar together to exchange vows and receive the marriage sacrament, while Cathleen and Ty looked on.

The reception was held outdoors on the lawn of the Gordon home with about fifty friends in attendance. Pamela had arranged for it to be professionally catered, complete with uniformed staff. There was champagne, an assortment of hors d'oeuvres including caviar, and the traditional wedding cake. It was all on a small but lavish scale, complete with a photographer to record the event.

During a rare moment when they were alone, a little apart from the throng of well-wishers, Phillip sipped at his glass of champagne and quietly studied his young bride. "Are you happy, Elizabeth?"

"Yes." Her answer was soft and positive, re-affirming what his eyes saw. "Only one possible thing could make me happier than I am this minute. I wish Culley was here. It would have been nice if he could have met you."

"I can have our reservations changed to include a stopover in Montana. It wouldn't be at all difficult to arrange."

"No." It was a very definite answer. She slipped her hand inside the crook of his arm. "This is a happy time for us. I don't want anything intruding on it that might change that."

He smiled an acceptance of her decision and wondered if he would ever know the full truth of her past. She had gone through so much in her young life. It had all happened back there in Montana. He was beginning to realize that she needed the stability he could provide. She needed it as desperately as he loved and needed her.

PART V

A sky of growing,
A sky of pain,
This sky that sees a
New Calder reign.

Chapter XXIII

The grass rustled like dry straw under his horse's hooves. The land looked baked and parched from sizzling sun and lack of rain. Chase squinted his eyes against the slanting afternoon sunlight. Overhead there was nothing but a sky full of bright blue. His mouth thinned at the sight of a cow grazing instead of lying in the shade ruminating. He didn't like to see that this late in the day, because it meant there wasn't enough graze.

The water supplies of the hill ranches around the Triple C had already gone dry, their grass burned up. The Triple C had shared as much of its water as it could with its neighbors. It still had water, but the lush Calder range was reaching a critical stage. They were going to have to round up the yearling steers early this fall before they began to lose weight. That was what the small neighboring ranches should have done earlier to save their grass and water, but they had kept holding on, certain it would eventually rain. But it hadn't. And the other ranchers didn't have the resources to hold out as long as the Triple C.

The blare of a truck horn caused Chase to pull up his horse and turn in the saddle. It sounded as though someone was holding his hand on the horn. A pickup bounced into view, racing pell-mell across the wild range land. Chase recognized Stumpy behind the wheel; he was waving to him frantically. Reining his horse around, Chase sent it forward at a lope to intercept the pickup.

"What is it?" His horse swung its rump around as the truck brakes squealed to a stop.

"Get in." Stumpy reached across to open the passenger's door. "The boss is hurt."

Chase wrapped the reins around the saddle horn as he swung out of the saddle and turned his mount loose. He didn't bother to ask any questions until he was inside the cab. Stumpy took off before he had the door shut.

"What happened?" If Chase's father was hurt, that meant badly injured, and his mind was running through all the possibilities.

"The pickup rolled. He was thrown out, but it landed on him." Stumpy Niles had his foot to the floor and both hands on the wheel to keep it from being jerked out of his grip as the truck sped over the rough ground.

Chase snapped his gaze to the driver, shock slicing through him. "How bad is he hurt?"

"His chest was crushed." Stumpy never took his eyes from the land in front of them, but his profile revealed a grim expression. "He was asking for you." There was a pause as he slowed the pickup and shifted gears to stop at the fence gate.

Climbing out of the cab, Chase ran forward to open the gate so Stumpy could drive through. He was swearing under his breath and absently wondered why man always resorted to profanity in situations where he felt helpless and impotent. As soon as the tailgate of the pickup was clear of the gate, Chase closed it and hurried to rejoin Stumpy in the cab.

When they arrived at the scene of good twenty minutes later, a half-dozen mounted riders had pulled the pickup off his father with the help of a handful of men on the ground. They were coiling the white nylon ropes that had been tied to the truck. Chase spied Nate kneeling beside his father's prone figure on the sloping bank of a ditch.

The silence among the men was deafening as Chase climbed out of the cab. Nate straightened and stepped back when he approached, giving Chase his first glimpse of his father's ashen face and his caved-in chest. He fell on his knees beside him, his arms half-reaching, wanting to do something to ease the pain his father had to be suffering. Eyes opened, eyes the same brown color as his own, but the light in them was dimming.

"They found you, son. Thank God." The rasping voice was interrupted by a cough that spilled blood from the corner of his mouth and drained more color from his face.

Chase clenched his teeth to bite off the anguished groan before it could be released. Whipping off his hat, he gently and carefully lifted his father's head and pillowed his hat under it. Then he wiped away the blood with his handkerchief.

"Don't try to talk, Dad." His voice was taut, squeezed out to keep it steady. He glanced up at Nate. "We'll rig up a bed for him in the back of Stumpy's truck. Make sure someone has the plane running at the airstrip." Nate just looked at him sadly for a long second, then turned to walk a few yards away, where the rest of the men had gathered.

"It's no use, son." But the strength in the hand that gripped Chase's arm seemed to refute that statement. No man that strong could die. "I can hear my ribs grating together like a bunch of broken china. I'll drown in my own blood before you can get me to a doctor," his father insisted. There was a terrible rattle with each short, painful breath he took.

"You just hang on, Dad," Chase urged, refusing to give up.

The brown eyes closed in denial, then opened to stare longingly at Chase. "It's all yours now." Webb searched his son's face with profound sorrow. "You're too young, only twenty-seven. You needed a few more years of seasoning." His fingers tightened on his son's arm. "They'll see that and come after you. You know that?"

"Yes, Dad." There was that mysterious "they" again. His arm was being squeezed so hard circulation was being cut off. It was impossible to believe that anything could kill this man. His father had always seemed indestructible.

"You'll have to fight to keep the Triple C intact. You'll have to be ready." There was an urgency to the weak and rasping voice as another spasm of coughing racked him.

"You're not going to die," Chase insisted, even as he wiped at the blood that flowed from his father's mouth.

It seemed a long time before the coughing stopped and the blood was reduced to a trickle seeping from the corner of his mouth. Webb rested a moment, trying to conserve what strength remained, but there was so much he needed to tell Chase.

"A man should live so he won't be afraid to die. I'm not afraid, but I don't want to go. I don't want to leave you yet." Pain twisted his face. "It hurts . . . feels like my chest is on fire . . . burning me up."

Chase half-turned his head to snap an order to the group of cowboys standing silently to one side. "Somebody bring some water."

He didn't notice who brought him the canteen. He just uncapped it and let a little spill into his father's mouth. The pain slowly eased from his features. His mouth relaxed slightly, almost showing a smile.

"That's better," Webb sighed and lifted his gaze to the sky that crowned the Triple C. "It's clouding up," he murmured. "Good. We need the rain."

An icy chill went down Chase's spine. The sky was a solid blue. There wasn't a cloud in sight. The muscles in his throat constricted fiercely to check the protesting sob that rose. His eyes were burning.

"I wish I could stay." His father's voice was little more than a whisper, the rattle growing louder. "Tell Ruth—" He paused to take a breath, but never finished it.

Chase waited, staring in numbed disbelief, his mind refusing to accept that his father was gone. Not his father. Not Webb Calder, the patriarch of the Calder empire. But the gray head had lolled to the side and Chase looked away as he closed the unseeing brown eyes.

A hand was on his shoulder. Chase looked up to find Nate standing beside him. There was no expression in the man's face. Chase wiped any from his as he stood up and turned to let his gaze swing over the other ranch hands. Some shifted; some looked back; but no one spoke. So many of the Calder native sons were there—Stumpy, Nate, Slim Trumbo, Ike Willis. Their hats were in their hands.

No one came to The Homestead that night, holding themselves aloof as their code dictated to give Chase time to reconcile himself to the loss of his father and do his mourning in private. It wasn't Ruth, but one of the other wives who fixed his meal that evening, set it on the dining room table, and silently withdrew.

The table looked huge. Chase stood beside it and stared at the empty chair at the head of the table, where his father had always sat and where the plate of food waited for him. He turned and walked from the room. Entering the den, he closed the door behind him and crossed to the bar. He poured a double shot of whiskey, downed it, and refilled the glass.

The silence of the house beat on him as he walked to the cavernous stone fireplace and rested a foot on the raised hearth. He lifted his gaze from the yawning blackness of its mouth to the sweeping set of longhorns above the stone mantelpiece. Their story was familiar to him, an oft-told tale from his childhood: every trail herd had a lead steer. Captain was the brindle longhorn that had led the herd of his namesake, Chase Benteen Calder, on the long, arduous trek up from Texas. The wily steer had lived to a ripe old age on the lush Montana grass. At its death, its majestic set of horns was mounted and hung above the fireplace for future generations to point to and tell their children the story of the dangerous cattle drive: the men lost at river crossings, and the young rider killed in a stampede—the price that was paid to reach free grass and carve out a new beginning in what was then Montana Territory.

Chase turned his head to look at the yellowed map on the wall behind the desk. A muscle jumped in his jaw as he inwardly recoiled from the size of the ranch. All his life he had been raised with the knowledge that one day it would all be his. Nothing else had ever crossed his mind. Suddenly he wondered if it was what he wanted. His shoulders sagged under the weight of the responsibility it carried—not just in running it successfully, but all the people whose lives now depended on his decisions. It was awesome. He was shaken by a self-doubt that questioned if he could handle it.

"It's all yours now, son." His father's rasping voice spoke to him again. "Keep it intact."

His fingers tightened on the whiskey glass, his knuckles turning white. He'd never felt so all alone in his life. He wanted to cry out for someone to ease this sharp ache. But there was no one. His mother was long dead, not even a memory of her in his mind. Buck, his best friend, had betrayed him. Now his father was gone, the one unshakable force in his life torn away.

He caught himself longing for a woman's softness. Maggie. It was her image that came to his mind. In her arms, he had always felt so alive. Dear God, how he needed her tonight. But she was somewhere in California—far beyond his reach. Part of him knew if she had been in the next room, he wouldn't have gone to her. They had shared nothing but sex, and sex wasn't what he needed tonight. He needed the support and comforting of someone who cared, someone to stand quietly beside him.

There was no one. He stood alone—tomorrow everyone would look to him for direction—to carry on the Calder tradition. With heavy steps, he crossed the room to the desk. Could he follow in his father's footsteps? No, that wasn't the way it was done. A leader had to blaze his own trail.

Seating himself in the chair behind the desk, Chase began going through the correspondence on the desktop. An official-looking letter gave Chase the first inkling of the trouble his father had warned him to expect.

In a Western-cut suit of dark brown, Chase stood beside the minister at the grave side, holding the cream-colored dress Stetson in front of him. A dry wind ruffled his brown hair and stirred the dust. Indifferent to the words of prayer being offered by the minister, Chase studied the large gathering of mourners that had turned out for the services. His gaze rested first on the delegation from the ranch. All their heads were bowed, except Tucker's. Chase still didn't understand why the cook was still working for the Triple C, why he hadn't pulled out after he'd got some money put aside. Tucker met his look and returned it with unwavering intent. Chase mentally filed away the warning that Tucker was going to cause him trouble.

His gaze shifted to Ruth and Virgil Haskell. The man had his arm around his wife, who was silently crying. Chase had never told Ruth that her name was the last word his father had uttered. There had been no message to pass on except that, and, glancing at Virg, he decided he had been right not to tell her. No purpose would have been served, and it might have caused more grief.

When he shifted his attention to the townspeople and neighboring ranchers who had gathered to pay their last respects to his father, a slight shock went through him. He recalled that once, long ago, his father had told him that nobody liked someone who was stronger, richer, or more powerful than they were. They were always looking for a way to cut them down. Chase could see it for himself now. It was in their eyes that they hoped he would fall flat on his face and bring about the collapse of the Triple C.

Lastly his gaze fell on Senator Franklin T. Bulfert, who had flown in to attend the funeral and was flying out directly afterward. He considered the things he knew about the politician that the public didn't. That would be his ammunition—that and his willingness to use it.

The minister's "Amen" was echoed by the soft murmur of the crowd. The services were over. Chase glanced at the coffin and pushed his hat onto his head. He knew his father would forgive him for not lingering at the grave side when there was important Triple C business to be handled. Pausing to shake hands with the minister, he murmured some meaningless response to the sympathy offered and then walked over to meet the senator.

"It's a grim day, Chase, a grim day," the politician stated solemnly. "I wish I could express what the loss of a fine friend like Webb Calder means to me. I regret that I must leave—"

"I know your time is short," Chase interrupted. "I'll drive you to your plane. It will give us a chance to talk privately."

Suspicion flickered in the man's eyes. "That's very kind of you, but I know there are others here who wish to express their sorrow. I wouldn't want to impose."

"But there are none here as important as you, Senator." There was a cynical twist to his smile as Chase disposed of that excuse. He personally escorted the senator to the waiting black limousine and its driver, politely thanking those who waylaid him to offer their condolences. Once inside the spacious rear passenger's section of the limousine, Chase closed the glass partition so the driver wouldn't overhear their conversation. The senator offered him a fat cigar. Chase refused. "No, thanks. I have my own." He took a slim cheroot from his inside jacket pocket and bent a cardboard match, lighting it with a snap of a thumb. He puffed on it, then studied the smoldering tip, the red glow beneath the white ash. "Within the deeded boundaries of the Triple C, there is a ten-thousand-acre parcel that is leased federal graze. The lease expires next year and I've been informed that the government doesn't wish to enter into another long-term lease. Instead, they want to handle it on a year-to-year basis."

"That's unfortunate," the senator murmured, rolling the cigar between his lips, "most unfortunate, but that seems to be the trend the government is following in such matters."

"I'm not interested in a long-term lease, either," Chase stated and felt the sharpness of the senator's glance. "I want to negotiate the purchase of that parcel. It's already surrounded by deeded Calder land. Since the government already owns roughly thirty percent of Montana, they shouldn't miss ten thousand acres."

There was a brief chortle from the senator. "The same could be said for the Triple C. What's ten thousand acres compared to what you already own?"

"The difference is, Senator"—Chase turned his narrowed gaze on the man—"that you are talking about Calder land. I'm going to correct the mistake my predecessors made and buy that chunk of ground. I'm not going to be at the mercy of Uncle Sam's whims."

"I don't think you understand what you're asking." The man shook his head skeptically.

"I'm asking you to arrange the sale of the land to me."

"That's a tall order. I don't know if I can do it," the politician hedged, unwilling to make a firm commitment.

Chase let an interval of silence lapse. "You're up for re-election this November. I understand your opponent has been closing the gap, giving you a real run for your money. Rumor has it he could beat you with sufficient campaign funds. I wonder what would happen if the Triple C decided to back him."

"That man would be of no help to you. He hasn't the connections that I do," the senator protested. "Besides, it would take more than money for him to win against me."

"What would it take? Maybe if someone leaked to the press about your apartment in a Washington suburb where a blonde and a little boy named Frank, Junior, live, would that do it?" Chase suggested.

"That's blackmail." The senator glared. "I have done many favors for your father in the past. I can't help but feel he would not approve of your threats to a loyal friend of his."

"I mentioned it, Senator, only to make it clear that we need each other." Chase flicked the ash from his slender cigar into the metal ashtray located in the car's upholstered armrest. "You need my support to ensure your re-election. And I need your connections to purchase that government land. If you wish to interpret it as a threat of blackmail, that's your problem." The limousine pulled up at the edge of the airstrip. "Your plane is waiting, Senator. I'll expect to hear from you at the end of the week."

There was an expression of reluctant admiration on the senator's face as he shook hands with Chase. "I think we understand one another, Chase."

"I'm certain we do," he agreed dryly.

From the landing strip, Chase returned directly to The Homestead and entered the den. He spent an hour studying the map on the wall before he called down to leave a message with Nate that he wanted him and the other foremen to meet him in the den after the evening meal.

He was seated behind the desk when they arrived. He noticed the startled flicker in their eyes when they saw him; they were too accustomed to his father occupying that chair. It was something he hadn't fully adjusted to himself, so he understood their brief shock and didn't interpret it as a reflection on his leadership.

When the last man appeared, Chase put a question to all of them. "Where is the best grass and water located on the Triple C?"

"The north range," Virgil Haskell replied and frowned. "We've been saving that for winter graze."

"I know." Chase stood up and moved to the map. "On the boundary of the north range, we have the Shamrock ranch, the Circle Six, and Bill MacGruder's outfit. All of them are in bad shape. It's my guess that they are going to decide to move their cattle onto the north range—either individually, or as a group."

"I imagine it's tortured them to see their cattle starving with all that grass and water on the other side of the fence," Stumpy remarked with an agreeing nod of his head.

"My thought exactly." Chase observed the affirmative looks of the others.

"What do you want us to do about it?" Ike Willis asked, watching Chase closely, as were the others. "I hate to see cattle starve."

"All cattlemen do, but they should have done something before now—sold and cut down their herds to a size their range could support in a drought. We save the north range for our cattle, and we're going to need every blade of grass on it if we don't want to end up like them. When they make their move, we're going to be waiting for them to drive their herds back to their own side of the fence."

At dawn the next morning, three parties of riders separated to patrol the long fence line on the northern boundary of the ranch. Chase rode with Nate's group. Every man had a loaded rifle in his scabbard with orders to use it if he had to.

Chase wondered if he'd guessed wrong. Maybe there were other ranchers on his west boundary, or to the south, who were in worse shape. But the Triple C range in those areas had been fairly well grazed over, and water was scarce. Every instinct insisted that if he was going to have trouble with his neighbors, it would be here on the north range, where there was plenty. This was where the trouble would come—if there was going to be any, which he hoped to God there wouldn't be. He wanted to be wrong.

It was mid-morning when they heard the distant bellow of cattle and rode toward the sound. As they came within sight of the combined herds streaming through the gap in the fence where the wires had been cut, Chase reined in his horse. It danced impatiently under him, tossing its head and pulling at the bit.

He reached down and removed his rifle from its scabbard, his action signaling the other riders to do the same.

The riders fanned out behind him, with Nate moving onto his right side. Chase sent his horse forward at an extended trot while the others followed. His gaze skimmed over the gaunt-ribbed cattle, noting the mixed brands. Then he picked out the respective owners of the ranches, grouping together in a trio to confront him—MacGruder, Hensen of the Circle Six, and Culley O'Rourke. He couldn't help noticing how skinny and hollow-eyed Culley was, but the gleam of hatred was in the green eyes—a look that reminded him of Maggie. But he couldn't afford that memory to soften him, so he blocked it out.

He and his riders stopped their horses in front of the cattle, slowing down the flow through the fence and scattering the cows. The animals immediately started tearing hungrily at the grass.

"You're trespassing on private property," Chase stated. "Turn your cattle around and drive them back on your own side of the fence."

"You got plenty of grass here." It was Culley who challenged him. "And water, too. Our cattle are starving. We need this grass and you don't."

There was no use in trying to reason with a cattleman who was watching his herd getting weaker every day. He didn't want to hear about the need the Triple C would soon have for this grass. He didn't care about the Triple C—only about saving his own cows.

"I'll give you one minute to turn the herd," Chase warned.

"Or you'll do what?" Culley taunted and glanced at the drawn rifles. "Start shooting at us?"

"No." Chase felt the curious glance that Nate darted at him. "I don't need to shoot at you. You brought your cattle here to save them. If you want them alive, you'll move them off Calder land."

"Are you threatening to shoot our cattle?" Bill MacGruder sat straighter in his saddle, frowning in disbelief.

"If you don't start turning them in—thirty seconds, I will," he stated and watched the three ranchers look at one another.

Then Culley scoffed, "You're bluffing."

Chase said no more, shifting with his horse as it stomped at a biting fly. Mentally, he counted off the seconds while he watched the uncertainty on the faces of the three men. Finally, he lifted his rifle and sighted it on a white-faced cow. He squeezed the trigger and didn't wait to see it drop as he pumped another shell into the chamber and dropped a second animal. The other cows around the downed pair scattered in a brief panic at the explosion of shots.

"You murdering bastard!"

Out of the corner of his eye, Chase saw the horse and rider charging him and swung his horse in a rearing spin to avoid it. He glimpsed the spilling rage in Culley O'Rourke's expression as he tried to grab for the rifle. Chase reversed the direction of the barrel and clipped his attacker on the jaw with the rifle butt. The blow knocked Culley out of the saddle. Behind him, he heard the lever action of rifles as his men turned their muzzles threateningly onto the remaining two ranchers, whose hands had gone down for the rifles they were carrying in their scabbards.

"Are you going to turn the herd?" he challenged them, aware that Culley was groggily pushing himself to his feet.

"Dammit, Chase! These animals are starving!" MacGruder appealed to him.

"Nate, I want ten more head to join those two on the ground," Chase ordered without looking at the foreman. "And ten more for every minute they wait."

A mixture of shock and outrage entered the expressions of the two ranchers as there was the immediate crack of a rifle, followed by the grunt of a falling animal. Chase counted off the shots in his head while the dazed ranchers watched their cows fall one by one. Even Culley was staring in grief-stricken shock.

"You can't do this!" Hensen protested when silence finally followed the tenth shot.

"Turn them."

The fools continued to hesitate until they heard the click of a rifle bullet being levered into the chamber. "All right!" Bill MacGruder shouted and raised a hand for them to hold their fire. "We'll drive them back. For God's sake, don't shoot anymore!"

Culley glared his hatred as he caught the trailing reins of his horse and remounted to join his partners. They moved quickly to bunch the herd and push it back through the gap in the fence while Chase and his men watched.

Nate eyed the man sitting so tall in the saddle, unyielding in the way of the Calders, and murmured in a voice that no one heard but himself. "The king is dead. Long live the king."

Chapter XXIV

Chase climbed the porch steps of The Homestead and paused to look over his shoulder. Pride unconsciously registered as his gaze swept the headquarters of the Triple C. Running the ranch had become second nature to him in the five years since his father's death. During the first few months, he had been tested at every turn. Concealing whatever self-doubts he had, he had faced every challenge and the Triple C was intact, and operating smoothly and efficiently. This was the job he'd been born and bred to do, and he did it well. If some regarded his pride as arrogance, then it was an earned arrogance.

He squared around and walked to the front door, his measured strides sounding loud on the wooden floor of the porch. Swinging the door closed after he had crossed the threshold, he started directly toward the den.

"Chase?" Ruth Haskell's hesitant voice made him pause and turn to glance in the direction of the dining room. After his father's death, she had begun to show her age. There always seemed to be a haunting sadness lurking in the shadows of her blue eyes.

But it wasn't Ruth his gaze fell on. There was a moment when Chase thought he was seeing a ghost as he stared at the pale-faced man standing beside her. He was holding his cowboy hat nervously in front of him, exposing curly, dark blond hair. There was hardly any light shining in the blue eyes, certainly not the dancing gleam Chase remembered.

"Hello, Chase." The voice was subdued and hesitant, unsure of his welcome.

But it was Buck's voice. For a fleeting moment, Chase was consumed by the urge to cross the space that separated them and clasp the hand of his long-lost friend. Then he remembered the circumstances under which Buck had left the ranch, and he remained where he was.

"Hello, Buck. I didn't know you were out." His voice was as expressionless as his face. His gaze slid to Ruth, noting the way she was biting her lip. She had known, he realized, and simply omitted mentioning it to him.

"They released me yesterday, reduced my sentence on account of 'good behavior,' if you can imagine that!" His laugh rang hollow and Buck lowered his head, nervously fingering his hat. "I know to say 'I'm sorry' probably doesn't mean much, Chase, but I want you to know I am."

The line of his mouth thinned as Chase pressed his lips together. He disliked seeing Buck humble himself and was glad when Ruth slipped out of the room to leave them alone. Since he didn't know what to say, he remained silent while Buck walked awkwardly into the entryway.

"There's nothing I can say that will excuse the way I behaved toward you," Buck continued, "or make you forget the things I said. When it hit me that I was going to jail for what I'd done, I panicked. Have you ever been scared, Chase—I mean really scared, all the way down to your toes? I was like an animal caught in a trap that turns and starts biting himself." He paused and sighed heavily, finally lifting his gaze to meet Chase's unwavering eyes. "I had a lot of time to think about all this in prison. I just wanted you to know how I feel. And I was sorry to hear about your dad. I know it must have been rough on you. The two of you were always close. Well"—he fingered his hat again and smiled stiffly—"I won't keep you. I know you're busy, so . . . I'll be going."

There was a conflict raging inside Chase as he watched Buck start to turn away. Half of him was saying to let him go, but the stronger side was remembering the good times.

"How about a drink?" he asked and smiled for the first time when he saw the old brightness return to Buck's eyes.

"I'd love one," Buck declared. "I haven't tasted good whiskey in almost ten years."

"We'll correct that." His hand rested naturally on his old friend's shoulder as they entered the den together.

"The place hasn't changed much." Buck glanced around the room as Chase walked to the bar to pour each of them a drink. "Everything is the way I remember it."

"What do you plan to do now?" Chase handed him a glass.

"Find me some work. You don't happen to know someone who might be willing to hire a rusty cowboy who's been out of circulation for a few years, do you?" he mocked with some of his old sparkle.

Chase stared at his glass for a minute, the conflict rising again. "I might."

"Hey! I wasn't hitting you up for work," Buck insisted quickly. "I mean—"

Chase slanted him a sideways glance, measuring him. "Do you mean you don't want to work for the Triple C again?"

"I'd be lying if I said I didn't." There was a yearning quality in his sighing answer. Buck swirled the liquor in his glass and watched the changing amber shades. "Coming home is all I've dreamed about for ten years." He shook his head in silent regret. "But it isn't right for me to expect you to give me a second chance."

"I'll decide that, Buck. And if I discover that you don't deserve it, I will personally kick you out on your ear."

"Hey, I'd paint sheds, clean out barns, repair windmills—whatever you say," Buck promised. "You don't even have to put me on a horse until I prove myself again."

"Sorry." Chase shook his head. "I'm only interested in hiring Buck Haskell, the cowboy."

"I'll work longer and harder than anybody you ever saw. I promise you that, Chase."

By the end of the second month, Chase believed him. Buck was the first one out every morning and the last one in at night. There were times when he did the work of two people. He didn't go into Jake's and rarely drank, except for a cold beer or a glass of whiskey with Chase if he happened to be at The Homestead in the evenings, which wasn't often. From all Chase had been able to gather, he didn't spend his money wildly, but saved some of each paycheck. And he didn't try to pick up their friendship where it had left off, either, as if he knew he had to earn Chase's trust before the old bonds could be established once more.

Elizabeth toyed with her appetizer, broiled grapefruit sweetened with a mixture of sugar and Galliano liqueur, usually something she enjoyed very much. Phillip studied her quietly from the opposite end of the table and recognized the introspective mood, guessing its cause.

"You heard from your brother today."

She looked up in startled confusion. "How did you know?"

"I can tell," he murmured and laid down his serrated grapefruit spoon. "What did he have to say?"

"Just the usual things." Maggie shrugged and explained no further. Phillip had read enough of Culley's letters to know he had ranted on about Chase Calder. It worried her sometimes at how obsessive her brother's hatred had become. Her own had dulled with time and Phillip's loving influence, which had healed much of her pain.

"Have I ever met my uncle?" Ty asked with a deep frown.

At ten, nearly eleven years old, he was acquiring an even more striking resemblance to Chase. Maggie was more conscious of it at certain times than others, like now, when Culley's letter had freshened all her memories of the man.

"No, you haven't." She quickly changed the subject. "Where are you and Jeff going tonight?" Jeff Broadstreet was a friend of Ty's. Both boys attended the same private school. Jeff's parents were taking the two out for the evening.

"To a movie, a Western. Jeff said the previews really looked good," he enthused. "Doesn't Uncle Culley own a ranch?"

"Yes," Phillip answered when Maggie failed to respond to the question.

"How come we never go visit him? That would really be neat to stay on a real ranch. Can we go sometime, Mom?"

"We'll see," she said crisply. She knew they never would, but she didn't tell Ty that because it would require an explanation.

"How about this summer?" he suggested.

"We are going to London this summer," she reminded him.

"London is nothing but a bunch of old buildings and stuffy museums," Ty complained. "I'd rather go to the ranch."

"We are going to London," Maggie stated. "All our reservations have been made and it's too late to cancel them." She realized how sharp her voice had become, so she softened it. "London is a fascinating city. You'll enjoy it. Your father and I had a wonderful time there on our honeymoon."

"I thought you went to Paris for your honeymoon."

"We did, but we spent a few days in London, as well," she explained.

"I'd still rather go to my uncle's ranch in Montana," Ty grumbled.

"That's enough discussion for now, Ty," Phillip advised and changed the subject to one less painful to his wife. But the whole subject needed to be straightened out. Phillip waited until dinner was finished and Ty had excused himself from the table before bringing it up again. "Ty should meet your brother, Elizabeth. After all, Culley is the only uncle he has."

"I'll invite Culley to come to California."

"He won't come. He didn't come to your graduation or our wedding. He's always too busy," Phillip reminded her. "Besides, it's the ranch Ty really wants to see."

"It's just a phase he's going through. He'll outgrow it," she stated.

"I seriously doubt it, Elizabeth. Ty is a natural horseman. That isn't something he is going to outgrow," he reasoned.

"I don't care. He isn't going to Montana—now, or ever." She resented that Phillip was taking Ty's side in this.

"What happens when he's older? When you can't tell him anymore what he can and can't do?" He studied her close-mouthed expression and sighed. "Elizabeth, Ty has the right to be told he's adopted. I've said it before." That was one of the few points in their life on which he disagreed with his wife.

"What would it change? What would it accomplish, except to

confuse him? Ty believes you're his father. You *are* his father," she insisted.

"And if he finds out someday?"

"He won't. He won't ever find out."

With a heavy sigh, Phillip let the subject drop. Maggie simply refused to see the trouble that lay ahead. It worried him, but, as in all things, he gave in to her wishes and held his silence.

PART VI

A sky of union,
A sky complete,
This sky that watches
Two Calders meet.

Chapter XXV

Her fingertips lovingly caressed the photograph of the lean, gray-haired man while her eyes misted over with tears. "My darling Phillip," Maggie whispered, "we had ten wonderful years of marriage. I shall always treasure that." It was still so hard to accept that he was gone, taken from her so quickly, without warning, the victim of a massive cornary two months before.

She looked around the room they had shared, scattered with boxes packed with his clothes slated for donation to a local charity. She had postponed this task for so long, knowing how empty the room would seem without his things. Her glance fell on the family Bible on the bedside table. It had been tucked away on a closet shelf. Everything seemed so final now that she had entered the date of Phillip's death in the record.

A car roared up the private lane, its unmuffled motor shattering the night's stillness. From the paddocks, a horse trumpeted its alarm. Maggie glanced at the luminous dial of the clock on the bed's nightstand. Ty was supposed to have been home over an hour ago. The combination of his fifteenth birthday and his father's death had convinced him that as the man of the family, he could take liberties with the rules. To make matters worse, Jeff had just turned sixteen and obtained his driver's license, so there was always transportation available for Ty.

Reaching for her satin robe lying at the foot of the bed, Maggie pulled it on as she hurried out of the master bedroom, where she now slept alone. She was halfway down the white staircase when she heard the front door slam and the car revving its motor as it reversed out of the drive. A light was already on in the living room. The reason for it became apparent when Pamela wheeled her chair into the foyer.

"Hello, Ty. Did you have a good time tonight?"

The question irritated Maggie. Pamela virtually encouraged Ty with her attitude that anything he did was perfectly all right. It was undermining what authority Maggie did exercise over her son.

"You should have come with us, Pamela. It was great!" At fifteen, his voice was changing, cracking out of its low octave to the high squeak. "Have you ever been to a rodeo? Man, it's exciting!"

"Ty, do you realize what time it is?" Maggie came the rest of the way down the stairs, more upset than she might have been because of Pamela.

"I'm sorry, Mom." He wasn't very successful at looking contrite. An inch short of six feet, he was starting to fill out in the shoulders and chest. His height and his heavy-boned features made him look older than he was. There was just enough fuzz on his cheeks that he had to shave, which really made him feel like a man. He had naturally respected Phillip's authority because he had been a man, but he regarded Maggie's orders with a kind of indulgence, as if he had to humor her because she was a woman. "But the bull-riding was the last event. Jeff and I didn't want to miss it."

"Am I supposed to ignore the fact that you are more than a hour late coming home?"

"Oh, Elizabeth," Pamela rebuked her sternness. "It isn't as though Ty had been to some wild party and come home drunk. It was all very innocent."

"If you don't mind, Pamela, I will handle this," she retorted, fed up with the woman's constant interference. It was difficult to believe she had once regarded her as a model of what she wanted to be. It had only been superficial. She often pitied Pamela because of the emptiness of her life, but it was empty because Pamela was essentially empty. It was something she had been slow to discover. It was only after Maggie had joined the executive staff of an international charity organization, where her facility with languages was so useful, and she had tried to interest Pamela in some volunteer work, that she realized Phillip's sister was a very shallow person, unable to help herself or anyone else. It was more than her body that was crippled.

"You are much too strict with him, Elizabeth," Pamela criticized.

Controlling her temper with an effort, Maggie turned calmly to her son. "Ty, will you please go upstairs and wait for me in *my* room?" She waited silently while he climbed the stairs and she heard the door to the master bedroom close. Then she faced her sister-in-law. "Don't ever interrupt again when I am reprimanding my son, Pamela. I won't stand for it anymore."

"What have I done?" She looked properly astounded.

"You encourage Ty to disregard what I say. I will not tolerate any more interference from you on matters that are strictly between me and my son."

"I will not be told by you how I shall conduct myself in my own house!" Pamela flared. "In case you have forgotten, this is my house! *You* are merely a guest."

"Yes, this is your house. Phillip left it to you, and I'm glad he did. But, in case you have forgotten, Ty is my son. If I leave, he will go with me." She considered that thought a moment. "Maybe it would be for the best, because it seems certain that you and I are not going to be able to get along."

"You can't be serious!" The possibility frightened Pamela.

"If you and I can't come to an understanding about Ty, I don't see where I have an alternative." Maggie pivoted with a swirl of her satin robe and ascended the stairs to the second floor. She didn't want to leave this house, where she and Phillip had lived so happily. It was filled with so many fond memories. Perhaps threatening to leave would be sufficient.

As she entered the master bedroom, she automatically glanced around the room to locate her son. He was seated on the side of the king-sized bed, his back turned to her, his wide shoulders slightly hunched. There was a dazed, pained look to his expression that brought a frown to Maggie's face.

"Who is Chase Calder?" he asked hoarsely.

Shock wiped the frown from her forehead and drained the color out of her cheeks. "Where did you hear that name?" she accused in a whisper.

"I read it. Here." He straightened from the bed and turned to show her the book in his hand.

Maggie recognized the Malloy family Bible. "No." It was little more than a breath.

"It says he's my father. Is that true?" He was tortured by confusion. "Who was Dad? You always told me he was my father, that the two of you just waited until you were older before you were married."

"Phillip . . . was your father in every way that counts."

"But who is Chase Calder?" Ty persisted, his voice breaking. "And why is he named here as my father?"

"Because . . ."—Maggie realized it was useless to try to keep up the lie; she deeply regretted the impulse that had made her write Chase's name in the Bible—". . . he is your biological father. But Phillip is the one who raised you, who loved you as only a father can love his son."

"What you're saying is that he adopted me and Chase Calder is my real father."

"Chase was your *natural* father, but Phillip was your *real* father," she reasoned. "He did all the things with you that a real father does."

He stared at the Bible, opened in his hands. "I remember when we were studying genetics in biology class and I asked you why I had brown eyes when you had green eyes and Dad's were gray. You said it was because I took after my grandfather. But it's from my father, isn't it?"

"Yes."

He turned away, abruptly closing the pages. "I can't believe this!"

"Ty, it doesn't make any difference." Maggie crossed the room seeking to reassure him and ease his confusion and pain, but he turned on her when she approached, his hard gaze boring into her in a way that sharply reminded her of Chase.

"I want to know about him."

"No." She drew back.

"He's my father!" he insisted.

"He was just somebody who lived on the ranch next to ours." What an understatement! "He didn't want us, Ty. Phillip did."

"I was born in California. He's never even seen me. How do you know he doesn't want me?"

"Ty, stop it. Stop imagining things. Stop building up a lot of romantic ideas in your head," she argued out of fear.

"But I have a father out there I've never even seen. He is alive, isn't he?" Although it was in a question form, it was a statement of conviction.

Maggie hesitated a fraction of a second, then lied: "I don't know."

"He is," Ty stated. "That's why you've never wanted to visit your brother—because you don't want to see *him* again."

"That isn't true." But it was.

He passed a hand over his face, as if the action would wipe away the confusion and enable him to understand what was happening. "Why didn't you tell me about him before? Why did you let me find out about him like this?"

"Ty, I'm sorry." Sorry that he had found out at all. "I know it's difficult for you, but what would it have accomplished if I had told you about him?"

"You don't understand! He's my father," he groaned and pushed past her, but not before she had seen the glimmer of tears in his eyes. Long strides carried him out of the room before he did something unmanly, like crying in front of her. She felt his pain, but doubted if he knew hers. He was at that difficult age where he was convinced no one could understand.

For days afterward, he was silent and brooding, shutting himself in his room or going off somewhere alone without telling her where he was going or when he'd be back. She was being punished, Maggie realized, yet she clung to the hope that sooner or later he would listen to her and forget about the man who had fathered him.

The jingle of the morning alarm awakened her and she rolled tiredly over to silence it. Her hand brushed a piece of paper, knocking it to the floor. She reached over the side of the bed to pick it up. The familiar penmanship scrawled across the paper chased the sleep from her eyes as she sat up to read the note.

Dear Mom,
I'm sorry that I couldn't tell you good-bye in person, but I knew you'd try to stop me. Don't worry about me. I can

take care of myself. Please try to understand. I had to do this.

I love you,
Ty

She flung aside the bedcovers and raced to his room down the hall, but he wasn't there. His shaving equipment, toothbrush, and comb were all gone from the bathroom. She searched his closet and drawers, trying to determine what clothes he had taken, but she was too overwrought to remember accurately what he had. He had run away. She began imagining all sorts of terrible things, from Ty being hit by a car while hitchhiking along the highway to some psychotic motorist murdering him. When she called the police, they explained he had to be missing for a minimum of twenty-four hours before they could enter the case. Although Maggie could only guess that he'd left sometime in the night, she got dressed, phoned her office to tell them she wouldn't be in, and went out looking for him herself, driving up and down every street, highway, and interstate looking for him.

Chapter XXVI

Chase wrapped both hands around the steaming mug of black coffee to warm them. It was a nippy spring day that turned his breath to a white vapor. The sheepskin collar of his jacket was turned up against the chill, and his Stetson was pulled down low and snug to keep his head warm. He watched the herd of horses come sweeping over the rise, a sea of chestnuts, bays, buckskins, and sorrels, their shaggy winter coats hiding their smooth, muscled lines. The ground vibrated with the thunder of their galloping hooves and Chase felt that old excitement flare.

It was always like this when the horses were rounded up and brought in from their winter range. Their arrival signaled the start of another season; the spring roundup wasn't far away. A wild and raucous time was ahead as the cowboys picked out their horse strings and threw saddles on horses that had run wild through the long winter. There were some out there that would buck as wild as any rodeo bronc, but their riders wouldn't have the benefit of a timer. No, they had to ride all the kinks and humps out of their horses. There would be plenty of excitement around here for a few days until the crews were selected and sent out on the spring roundup.

The ocean of horses swirled through the open gates of a big pen. For all their wild snortings and carryings-on, they knew the ranch buildings meant hay and grain, so they needed no real urging to enter the fenced enclosure. As the gate was closed behind the last horse, a rider separated himself from the others and trotted his horse toward Chase.

"They look fat and sassy." Buck grinned and swung out of the saddle. He sniffed appreciatively at the coffee. "Boy, that smells good."

Chase took a swallow of the scalding liquid and then handed the mug to Buck. There was no more trace of prison pallor and the smile was back, but there were changes in him—changes for the better, in Chase's opinion. Buck was steady, hard-working, and reliable, never shirking any chores or responsibilities. Buck had become one of the Triple C's top foremen. He and Chase were now the kind of working combination that Chase had always thought they could become. It was a good feeling to have his best friend back.

Shoving his hands into the lined jacket pockets where his gloves were, Chase walked to the fence for a closer look at the horses. Buck accompanied him, leading his horse. He agreed with Buck's earlier assessment.

"They wintered well."

"Uh-huh." Buck made an affirmative sound as he gulped down a swallow of hot coffee and crooked an elbow on the top rail. "When I was in town the other day, I got to talking to Lew."

"Talking, or gossiping?" Chase mocked his friend.

"With him, it's one and the same thing." He grinned. "Anyway, he was telling me that old man Anderson didn't have a will when he died in that farm accident last fall. It seems he was married before and had two children by his first wife. They hired themselves some lawyers and claimed a share of his estate. It looks like Anderson's widow is going to have to sell the farm so his first two kids can get their share of the settlement from the estate."

"I hadn't heard that. It's rough," Chase mused and ran a practiced eye over the horses scattering to graze.

"That started me wondering about what would happen to the Triple C if something happened to you. You do have a will, don't you?" Buck frowned.

The question made Chase pause, hunching his shoulders slightly. "No. I've never got around to it."

"Do you have any relatives? Cousins or anything?"

"Not that I know of. Why?"

Buck moved his head in a sideways gesture. "I hate to think about this ranch getting broken up and sold, and all the money going into the state treasury. It wouldn't be right. Nate, Ike, my folks, and all the rest of us—we'd be out in the cold. If you haven't got anybody you can leave it to, maybe you should think about leaving the company shares to all of us so we could keep the Triple C operating intact," he suggested.

"Not a bad idea." It sounded both logical and fair.

"Talk to a lawyer. He'll probably have some ideas." Buck offered to return the mug to Chase, half-full of coffee. "Want the rest?" The change of subject indicated that he had said what was on his mind; the rest was up to Chase.

"No. You finish it." His gaze narrowed on the herd of horses, but his mind was on another subject. "I suppose I should be thinking about getting married and raising a family."

"You show me some wife material anywhere in the vicinity; then move out of my way," Buck warned with a wry shake of his head. "I'm not getting any younger, and I want a brood of little ones before I die. Trouble is finding a woman who isn't hankering to live in town." He took a sip of coffee and glanced at Chase over the rim of the mug. "What about Sally Brogan?"

Chase lowered his gaze to the ground to consider the red-haired widow he'd been seeing regularly for some time now. Shortly after Buck had returned, she and her husband, an ex-rodeo cowboy, had shown up at the ranch driving an old pickup with a camper. Although they had been short of help at the time, Chase had been reluctant to hire him because he had seemed the type to be more interested in drinking and carousing than working, but he hadn't been able to ignore the redhead's pleading look. Against his better judgment, he'd hired her husband. A month and a half later her husband was killed outright when he crashed his truck into a bridge abutment at two in the morning.

At about the same time, Jake had closed his doors. Another bar had opened up in town. Since there wasn't enough business for two, Jake decided it was time he moved south. Sally had bought the place from him with money from her husband's life insurance. Chase had thought she was crazy, but she had calmly explained that she was tired of moving. She wanted to wake up in the morning, look out the window, and see the same thing every day for the rest of her life. After much scrubbing, cleaning, and remodeling, she turned the saloon into a restaurant and lived in the rooms upstairs.

In the beginning, Chase stopped in to make sure she was managing all right on her own. Then his reason became that she was a very good cook. Finally, one night, she asked him to stay while she finished closing and checking her receipts. The next thing he knew he was kissing her and carrying her up the stairs—only to have her run back down to lock the front door. He smiled at the memory.

"You've been seeing her regularly for what—three years now?" Buck arched a questioning eyebrow and took another drink of coffee.

"You know how it is, Buck." There was a trace of self-mockery in the twist of Chase's mouth. "A man doesn't want to rush into these things."

Buck breathed out a laugh and shook his head. "Sally is a nice, gentle woman. She must be just about thirty-five. She hasn't got many child-bearing years left. How come you haven't married her?"

Chase didn't know the answer to that himself. They got along well together—had a nice comfortable relationship. She would make a good wife and a good mother. He frowned when he realized he had always shied away from the subject of marriage in connection with Sally. He had never considered himself to be a confirmed bachelor. He wanted a son and heir.

He shrugged his shoulders and passed the question off lightly. "Maybe I'm waiting for the bells to ring."

"Listen, fella, if they haven't rung in three years, they aren't going to ring," Buck declared. After draining the last of the coffee, he handed the empty mug to Chase and gathered up the reins of his horse to mount. "I gotta get back to work." Looping the reins over the horse's head, he stepped a toe into the stirrup and continued the motion to swing into the saddle. "See you later." He sketched a salute and rode off.

Chase realized he'd been left with a variety of subjects to think about, but they all had one central theme—the future of the Triple C.

Before the week was out, Chase had a preliminary will drawn up by his firm of attorneys. Of necessity, it was complicated because the structure of the Calder Cattle Company was complicated to obtain the most favorable tax treatment. Essentially, it contained provisions so that if he died without an heir or living spouse, the stock would be distributed among that loyal corps of Triple C native sons and daughters. There were some minor revisions required, but after a long afternoon's meeting with the lawyers, Chase was satisfied they were on the right track.

Since Ruth wasn't expecting him for dinner that evening, he stopped at Sally's to eat in her restaurant and spend the balance of the evening with her. Because of the business appointment in the city, Chase had abandoned his ranch garb of denim and chambray in favor of the tapered but Western-style pair of brown dress pants, pale cream-colored shirt, and a tailored jacket of buckskin suede. As he climbed out of the car, he put on his natural suede, dress Stetson with its brown-feathered hatband and walked to the steps of the saloon-turned-restaurant. The wood building had all been repainted a sparkling white, trimmed with blue, a small hint of the changes inside.

As he mounted the steps, somewhere nearby there was the grating rub of a rope drawn over wood. The measured rhythm of his stride was thrown off tempo by the sound that shivered down his back, a sound he'd never managed to forget. He glanced at the wooden swing, suspended from the porch roof with nylon ropes, and walked inside.

All the paneled walls were painted white and squares of speckled white tile gleamed on the floor. The tables and chairs were painted white with a variety of colorful gingham tablecloths covering the tops. Ruffled curtains were at the windows, the glass panes now minus a thick yellow veil of nicotine. Where the bar had been, there was a counter with stools and pie cases and food coolers on the wall behind.

The supper-hour business was just beginning to taper off. A half-dozen tables and three stools at the counter were occupied. Sally was pouring more coffee at one of the tables when Chase entered. She sent him one of her quiet smiles that was more an expression with her eyes and a faint lift of the corners of her mouth. Her hair was the color of a shiny copper penny, curling loose below her ears. For all her red hair, she was calm and quiet-natured with serene blue eyes.

Chase took a chair at a table that put his back to the counter, yet enabled him to see the front door and the swinging door into the rear kitchen. DeeDee Rains, a Blackfoot woman, helped Sally with the cooking and dishwashing so she would be free to wait tables, work the cash drawer, clear the tables, and help with the cooking, as well. Chase claimed she worked too hard, but Sally insisted that she liked being independent—and hard work was good for the soul.

"What will you have tonight, Chase?" She came to his table and filled his amber waterglass from a pitcher of iced water.

Glancing at her, he realized she was always very straightforward and he never responded to her with suggestive innuendos. He wondered why.

"Steak and fries," he ordered. Coffee later."

The screaming hiss of air brakes coincided with the down shifting of the truck's gears as the semi edged to a stop on the shoulder of the highway. The driver's white T-shirt was stained with brown spots of spilled coffee. He turned his unshaven face to his passenger and didn't bother to remove the cigarette dangling from his mouth.

"This is it, kid," he announced.

Ty stared at the loose collection of buildings. The sky was deepening to a plum twilight that cast the town in shadows, giving the impression that someone had put it here, then forgotten it. It was miles from anywhere, yet everything seemed to be miles from anywhere. He'd never seen so much emptiness in his life. He continued to stare, finding it hard to believe that these few buildings comprised a town.

"You did say you wanted to get out at Blue Moon, didn't you, kid?" The driver frowned impatiently.

"Yeah." Ty noticed the sign painted on the building with the gasoline pumps out front, identifying the place as Blue Moon and giving the zip code. This was it. He grabbed his backpack from the seat beside him and pushed the door open, telling the driver, "Thanks," as he swung down from the cab.

The revving of the diesel motor sent blue smoke into the darkening night. Ty had to close his eyes to shut out the dust churned up by the eighteen wheels as they rolled the huge semi onto the highway once more. When it settled, he blinked the particles from his eyes, wiping them with his hand, and looked around again.

There were pickups parked in front of the next building. The lights were on inside and a sign on the porch overhang that said SALLY'S RESTAURANT. He brushed the dust from his crisp blue jeans and reached inside his pocket to check how much money he had left. He hadn't dreamed it would take almost a week to get here, hitching rides. It had been easy in California, but then he'd hit those empty stretches in Nevada and Utah. Then he'd walked about as much as he'd ridden. In the beginning he hadn't paid attention to how much he was spending, eating three big meals a day and snacking in between, until now he was almost broke.

An uneasy feeling crept over him. What if his mother was right? What if he'd come all this way and his father didn't want to see him? He shook away the thought. After coming this far, he couldn't quit. He had enough money for a hamburger. If no one knew where Chase Calder lived, then he could find his uncle. He'd gotten his address from his mother's address book. If all else failed, he could call her collect and ask her to send him some money so he could come home.

Taking a deep breath, he slung his backpack over one shoulder and hitched it into position, then started for the restaurant. Two cowboys were coming out, so he stood to one side until they were through the door, then entered. His stomach rolled hungrily at the smell of food. There was a sign next to the staircase that said REST ROOMS, and Ty walked straight to it.

Chase had hooked his hat over the spindled back of a chair and was smoking a cheroot while waiting for his meal. He noticed the youth walk in—the thick brown hair waving almost to his collar, the yellow windbreaker, the backpack, the running shoes, and the blue jeans that were stiff and new and made noise when he walked. Mentally, he dismissed him as one of those hippie types or whatever the latest terminology for them was.

Lew, from the dry-goods store across the street, left the counter and brought his coffee cup over to sit with Chase. His wife was visiting their daughter, and Lew was playing bachelor for a few days. When the boy came out from the rest room and sat at a table near Chase, he paid scant attention to him.

With his backpack pushed under the table, Ty scooted his chair up. A red-haired woman in a blue dress and white apron stopped to fill his waterglass. She had a pleasant face that reminded him of one of his grade-school teachers.

"Would you like a menu?"

"Yes, please." For once, his voice didn't crack.

The menu she brought was one of those black vinyl things with the word MENU on front and clear plastic pockets inside so restaurants could insert their own typed fare. He started to look down the list, then realized here was his chance to ask if she knew Chase Calder. Why wait?

"Ma'am?" He called her back to the table and glanced quickly at the price of a hamburger to be sure he could afford it. "I'll have a hamburger with everything on it and a glass of milk." He waited until she had it written on her little pad, then nervously licked his lips. "Ma'am, do you happen to know a man named Chase Calder?"

He saw a flicker of surprise in her eyes; then the corners of her mouth were tilted upward in a faint smile. "Yes."

The first person he asked! He couldn't believe his luck. "Do you know where I could find him?"

She studied him closely for a second, then replied, "He's sitting at the next table—he's the one with the suede suit jacket." She nodded to indicate which table.

Ty looked over his shoulder, a shiver of apprehension running down his back. He was suddenly and unexpectedly nervous and scared. He could feel his palms start to sweat. "Thanks," he added quickly to the waitress and stared at the man long after she left the table.

That was his father, the man he had come to find, the one with the carved and rugged features that the sun had tanned to the color of finely grained leather. He had wide shoulders, and brown hair and eyes. Ty had tried to envision him before, but there he was in the flesh!

The waitress brought a plate with a huge steak covering it and a side of fries to the table where his father was sitting. "One charred steak and fries," she announced as she set them in front of him.

"Looks good, Sally."

Ty heard the rich timbre of Chase's voice and saw the smile he flashed the redhead. It changed him. He didn't look quite so hard and aloof; he could be fun. Then the waitress lifted her gaze, curiously glancing his way before she went back to the kitchen.

What was he waiting for? Ty asked himself. Had he come all this way just to look at him? Why didn't he go over and meet him?

His knees felt shaky when he pushed his chair away from the table, and his heart was pounding when he stood up, but he managed to walk the few steps to the table. His father was cutting his steak and didn't notice him standing there. Ty nervously cleared his throat and he looked up.

"Excuse me." Suddenly Ty couldn't think what he wanted to say. He had rehearsed it all so carefully, and now he couldn't think of the words. He watched his father rest the knife and fork against the plate and study him with cool brown eyes.

"Did you want something?" he prompted.

"I'm Ty Gordon." The name wouldn't mean anything to him, but maybe he would notice a resemblance. Ty could see it. Oh, it wasn't real obvious, but . . . the coloring was the same, and they were both tall.

"Yes?" Chase's expression didn't change.

"I wanted to talk to you, sir." Ty faltered because he didn't know what to call him.

"What about?"

He glanced nervously at the older man sitting at the table with his father and the other customers in the restaurant. "It's personal business, sir."

"In that case"—he ran a lazy, considering glance over him—"why don't we leave this discussion until later? I wouldn't want to ruin my enjoyment of this steak with business talk. I believe you have some food waiting, too." He gestured with the point of his knife.

Ty glanced behind him to see the waitress setting his hamburger and milk at his table. "We'll talk after we've eaten." He reconfirmed and his father nodded.

His gaze narrowed thoughtfully as he watched the tall boy return to his table. Well educated, good clothes, fairly well composed, although he had been nervous about something. Chase began cutting into his steak again.

"What 'personal' business do you suppose he has?" Lew wondered aloud.

Chase let his glance stray from the steak to the boy. "Probably wants a job. Hitchhiked out here to learn to be a cowboy." It seemed obvious. "We're always having some fresh-faced kid apply for a job. Half the time he's never seen a horse in his life."

Forking a bite of steak into his mouth, he began chewing the flavorful, well-done beef. A rancher just didn't have time to train every eager greenhorn who came long. It took too much time, energy, and patience.

Chapter XXVII

Chase finished his meal, had another cheroot with his coffee, and kept an absent eye on the boy. He was sitting slump-shouldered, a little dejected, and refused dessert. Chase watched him carefully count out the money to pay for his meal and noticed only loose change was returned to his pocket. He had already pegged the boy as a runaway, too young to be out on his own, now obviously out of money. He liked the boy's patience; he didn't attempt to resume their "discussion" until Chase indicated that he was ready. The best thing he could do for the kid would be to send him back home.

"You'll have to excuse me, Lew." Chase pushed his chair back and rose to his feet. "I have to attend to some business." He reached for his hat and set it on the back of his head. He passed the boy's table as he walked to the cash register. Behind him there was a hurried scrape of a chair leg. An instant later the boy was beside him, almost as tall as he was. When Sally had counted out the change he had coming, Chase asked, "Is it all right if we use your office, Sally, for a private talk?"

"Go ahead. It isn't locked." Her gaze ran curiously between them, but she didn't ask any questions.

Her office was the old poker room. Chase led the boy through the door marked PRIVATE and wandered to the uncluttered desk, leaning one hip on it and hooking a knee over the corner. The boy stared at him so intently that Chase wondered if there were crumbs on his face.

"What is this personal matter?"

Ty swallowed hard, all his nervousness returning. There wasn't any easy way to say it, so he just blurted it out. "I'm your son." He waited for the expression to change to surprise, confusion, or angry denial, but it didn't.

"I think you've made a mistake," Chase said calmly. "I don't have a son."

"You didn't *know* you had a son," Ty corrected him. "My mother never told you about me."

"What's your mother's name?"

"Elizabeth."

"I don't know any woman by that name." He reached into his pocket and pulled out a narrow cigar, lighting it. "If this is some kind of a joke, I'm not laughing. Or is this some new way to get money from strangers by walking up to them and claiming to be their son?"

"No." Ty felt a red flush creep into his face. "It's the truth. I am your son. My mother told me so."

"Then she has me confused with somebody else."

"No. She told me that my real father was Chase Calder. I didn't know it, either, until a few weeks ago. I didn't know that Dad . . . Phillip . . . had adopted me. I thought he was my real father until I found your name listed in the family Bible." His urgent voice insisted Chase believe him.

"She made a mistake. I don't know any woman named Elizabeth," he repeated.

"Her full name is Mary Frances Elizabeth." Ty waited for a sign that the name meant something.

Chase shook his head. "I don't know her."

"But I came all the way out here to find you!" He was hurting inside, angry and hurt that his claim was being denied. "All the way from California! You are my father!"

"I'm sorry you came on a wild-goose chase. I am not your father." Chase saw the tears of frustration gathering in the boy's eyes. It was going to be embarrassing for both of them if he started crying. He pretended not to notice as he straightened from the desk and stubbed his cigar out in the ashtray.

"My mother wouldn't lie to me about that! She wouldn't!"

"I'm not saying your mother lied. Maybe some man just told her that he was me and she believed him. I'm sorry, kid, but I don't know your mother. I've never heard of her." He walked to the door and opened it.

"Well, she knew you!" the boy raged. "She lived here! That's how I knew where to find you!"

Chase stopped, holding the door open with one hand while he turned to frown at the boy. "Where did she live?"

The boy's teeth were clenched together to hold back the sobs. "She said you wouldn't want me, but I didn't believe her. Why didn't you just come right out and say it instead of pretending you'd never heard of her?" he challenged hoarsely. "I don't suppose you've heard of the Shamrock Ranch, either! Or my Uncle Culley O'Rourke!"

Shock went through Chase like a cold knife blade. He was too stunned to react when the boy pushed past him to bolt out the door. But it was just the jolt he needed. In two strides, he caught-up with him, grabbing his arm and jerking the boy around. Chase was angry, because if this was a joke, it was a cruel one.

"Maggie is your mother?" He demanded an answer. "Maggie O'Rourke is your mother?"

The boy's anger matched his own, despite the tear that slid down his cheek. "I told you! Her name is Mary Frances Elizabeth O'Rourke Gordon! Nobody calls her Maggie!"

"My God." It was a whispered sound, as something like pain contorted his frown. "How old are you? Ty . . . is it?"

"Yes." Ty eyed him warily. "I'm fifteen."

Some grim, faraway look came to his eyes. "Has it been that long ago?" he mused.

"You did know my mother." Ty realized Chase was admitting it.

"I knew Maggie O'Rourke, yes." Chase relaxed his talon-hard hold on the boy and drew in a deep breath. "It's late. You'd better come home with me."

The moon was out and there were huge clusters of stars in the sky, a canopy of lights over the speeding car. For the first thirty miles, they drove in silence. Chase was staring at the road, driving as if there was no one in the car at all, except himself. Night air spilled in from the opened windows. Chase was resting his left elbow on the curved windowframe and rubbing his hand across his mouth in an absent fashion.

"Does your mother know you're here?"

The question came so suddenly out of the silence that Ty nearly jumped. "No. I think she's probably guessed, though."

"You ran away?"

"Yes."

"You mentioned you had been adopted. I guess your mother is married now."

"She was. My . . . Phillip had a heart attack six months ago and died. He hadn't been sick at all. It was a shock . . . for everybody." He still felt sick and empty inside when he thought about it.

"What did he do?"

"He was a doctor, a plastic surgeon, and a real good one, too, not some quack."

"I'm sure he was an excellent physician. Where do you live?"

"In Malibu. We've got about a hundred acres. We keep horses and show them." Ty looked out the window. There was nothing for miles—no lights, no sign of life. "Where are we going?"

"To the Triple C." There was a slight hesitation. "That stands for the Calder Cattle Company." Chase glanced out the window, as if to get his bearings. "We crossed the east boundary roughly ten miles back."

"How far do we have to go?"

"Another twenty-five or thirty miles." He heard the boy's low whistle at the implied size of the ranch, something he obviously hadn't known. "What did your mother tell you about me?"

"Nothing, except you lived on the next ranch."

In the dim light from the dashboard, Chase let his gaze slide to the boy who was his son. The shock of the discovery had worn off and acceptance had settled in. Ty was a fine-looking boy, obviously brave; otherwise, he wouldn't have had the courage to come all this way by himself and confront a father he'd never seen. There was a lot of potential in him. Chase felt a swelling surge of pride. He had a son. A boy of his own flesh and blood. He wanted to shout it. He couldn't help wondering if every father felt such dazed pride.

"I don't know you and you don't know me. I guess we're starting out equal, son." Just saying the word brought a slow smile to his mouth.

Ty felt a funny choking sensation in his throat and the sting of welling tears in his eyes. He didn't understand what prompted this rush of emotion. He fought it down because he didn't want his father to think he was a blubbering fool.

"I want to get to know you." His voice was husky but steady. "That's why I came all the way up here. I'd like to stay for a while?" There was a lilting inflection on the last, changing the statement to a question. Maybe it would be awkward for his father to have him around.

"I want you to stay." It was a very definite response which left no room for doubt about whether Ty was wanted or not.

"Are you married? Do you have any more children?" Ty asked.

"If you had asked me when I walked into the restaurant tonight, I would have said I had no children. Now I respectfully decline to answer that question." Wry amusement glinted in the brief glance he sent his son. "As to your first question—no, I have never married."

"Are you still in love with my mother?" It seemed a logical question to Ty.

Chase breathed in, held it, then let it out. "I don't think it's fair to use the word 'love' to describe what was between Maggie and me. We were both lonely. We each had a physical need . . . a desire for something we could enjoy that—for once—would make no demands on us. If any feelings had started to grow, they were torn out by the roots by circumstances neither of us could control." He looked at Ty. "I doubt if any of this makes sense to you."

Ty was frowning. "Not a lot, no."

"I didn't think so." His mouth quirked in a hard way. "Tell me about school," he prompted, changing the subject, and listened quietly while Ty talked about his school, his friends, and his life in general.

In the distance, there was a very faint glow in the sky that grew steadily brighter as they approached it—the well-lit headquarters of the Triple C. When the main buildings came into sight, illuminated by yard lights, with a sprinkling of smaller lights shining from the windows of houses, Ty stared in vague bewilderment.

"Is this a town?"

"Almost." Chase smiled faintly and made a wide turn with the car to stop in front of the porch steps of The Homestead. "This is the headquarters of the Triple C," he said, switching off the engine and opening his door.

While Ty hauled his backpack out of the rear seat, Chase walked around the car to the porch steps. Ty lagged behind to stare at the sprawling cluster of ranch buildings. Chase waited for him at the top of the porch steps. When Ty realized it, he hurried guiltily to catch up. Once the boy was level with him, Chase swung his gaze to the buildings that comprised the Triple C headquarters, aware that Ty was staring, too.

"Take a good look, son." Chase advised. "It's all going to be yours someday." When he felt the quick glance, he turned his head to meet the look, pride gentling his brown eyes. His mouth twitched in a faint smile as he clamped a hand on the boy's shoulder. "'Course, you've got a lot to learn between now and then—a helluva lot to learn."

Applying pressure to Ty's shoulder, Chase turned him toward the front door and led the way into the house. The lights had been left on in the living room and entryway, but Chase could have found his way if it had been pitch-black. Not a stick of furniture had been changed since his childhood; some of it had been reupholstered, but it was old, solid furniture that would last for centuries with the right care. He noticed the way Ty looked around, taking everything in. Remembering the lone hamburger Ty had eaten, Chase realized it probably hadn't satisfied a growing boy's appetite. When he'd been Ty's age, there had never been enough to eat.

"Hungry?" he questioned.

"Yeah, kinda," Ty admitted a little self-consciously.

"I'll see if I can't rustle up a snack from the kitchen. Look around. Make yourself at home." He left the boy free to explore the house on his own.

There was cold roast beef in the refrigerator. Chase sliced it and mounded a plate with sandwiches. There was half of a chocolate layer cake left, so he added it to the tray along with a couple glasses and a pitcher of milk. When he returned to the living room, Ty was just wandering into the den. He started to retreat, but Chase nodded for him to continue into the room.

"We'll eat in there." He carried the tray in and set it on the coffee table.

"Are those real horns?" Ty was studying the mounted set above the fireplace mantel.

With a strange feeling of *déjà vu*, Chase told him the story of Captain, the brindle steer, and the long cattle drive that had brought the first Calder to this land. Listening with rapt attention, Ty managed to devour the plateful of sandwiches and three glasses of milk, while Chase had only one. When Chase got up to show him the old map on the wall, Ty cut himself a wedge of cake.

"Where did my mother live?" Ty kept one hand cupped under the cake to catch the crumbs.

Chase pointed out the location of the Shamrock Ranch in relationship to the Triple C headquarters. "It sits here."

"It's a lot smaller than the Triple C, isn't it?" he questioned.

"Yes." Chase was reluctant to discuss the O'Rourkes, and the impression was transmitted to Ty in the shortness of his answer.

"Are there . . . bad feelings between you and Mom?"

"I doubt if she likes me very much," Chase admitted.

"How do you feel?" Ty frowned at him anxiously, trapped somewhere in the middle.

"I . . ."—Chase turned away to walk back to his leather chair—". . . have no ill feelings toward her." Absently, he rubbed his left forearm where his shirtsleeve covered the long, diagonal scar.

Ty sensed there was more. "What happened to break you and Mom up?" He remembered his father had said earlier that it had been beyond their control. His father's closed expression made him uneasy—that, and the long, measuring look he was receiving.

"That"—a lazy veil seemed to fall over his father's features, dispelling the impression as he rose from the chair—"is another long story, and it's getting late. I'll show you which room will be yours. You must be tired."

"Yeah," Ty admitted. "I haven't slept in a bed for two days. Mostly, I slept bouncing around in a truck cab."

"You'll sleep tonight, then."

Chase paused in the living room while Ty retrieved his backpack, then led him up the stairs to the bedroom that had been his father's. All the rooms were kept in readiness for guests, so there were plenty of towels in the bathroom and clean sheets on the bed. When he was satisfied that Ty was settled in, Chase took a notepad and pencil from his jacket pocket and handed it to him.

"Write down your mother's telephone number," he instructed.

"You aren't going to call her?" Ty protested with an anxious frown. "Not for a few days yet, please?"

"You know she's worried about you." The statement held a subtle criticism.

"Yeah, but—" He pressed his mouth together grimly. "She'll just want me to come home. And I don't want to go home."

"I'll handle that," Chase stated. "You just give me her phone number and I'll talk to her."

"Okay." Ty wrote down the number and handed the pad and pencil back to him. "Be sure to tell her I'm all right."

"I will." Chase moved to the door, opened it, and paused. "Some advice for you to sleep on. City life breeds weakness into a man. Out here we don't have any traffic lights telling you when to stop and when to go, when to walk or when to wait. There aren't any streets with arrows telling you that you have to go one way. In the city, everything is orderly—soft—governed by a woman's idea of the way it should be. Out here, it's still a man's country, where you're expected to keep your word and never ask for favors. It will be harder on you, not just because you are new to our ways. People are going to expect more from you because you're my son, so"—Chase smiled faintly because the next words were so familiar to him—"you're going to have to work harder, be smarter, and fight rougher than any man in the state. If you haven't got what it takes, then you're better off to go back to California and be with your mother, because otherwise this land will break you. You might want to think on that these next few days."

"Yes, sir." It was a sobered sound, tinged with just a hint of skepticism.

Chase smiled, bemused, because he'd always believed his father had exaggerated a lot, too. "Good night, Ty."

"Good night."

Returning to the den, Chase sat down in the chair behind the desk and reached for the phone, dialing the number Ty had given him. It was answered on the third ring.

"Gordon residence." It was a woman's voice, stiff and haughty, not Maggie's.

"I want to speak to Elizabeth Gordon," Chase requested.

"I believe she has retired for the evening. This is her sister-in-law, Pamela Gordon. May I help you?"

"Would you check to see if she has? Tell her I'm calling in regard to her son."

"Ty? Have you found him? Is he all right?" The woman threw a flurry of anxious questions at him.

"Tell Mrs. Gordon that I want to speak to *her*." He stressed the last word to make it clear he would speak to no one else.

"Just a moment." There was a clunk of the telephone receiver being laid down. In the background, he could hear the woman calling to "Elizabeth." Chase waited, fingering the slip of paper with the phone number on it.

The sleeping pill Maggie had taken in an effort to get some rest after so many sleepless nights worrying about Ty made her uncoordinated. She felt groggy when she came to the phone and pressed a hand to her forehead to eliminate the dullness.

"This is Elizabeth Gordon."

Her voice had changed slightly, a variation in the accent, but it stirred his memory. For an instant, the years rushed away and he could see her green eyes, green as the lush Calder grass, and her hair black as midnight. His hand tightened on the phone, as if to bring her closer to him.

"Hello, Maggie."

No one ever called her that anymore except Culley. It didn't sound like him, yet telephones sometimes distorted people's voices. Maggie clutched the receiver with both hands. "Culley? Thank God, you called. I tried to call you, but the operator said your phone had been disconnected and I— Ty has run away. I think he's—"

"Maggie, this is Chase," he interrupted. "Ty is here with me. He wanted you to know he was all right."

She recognized his voice the minute he started speaking again. The floor seemed to rock under her feet. There was that same gentle persuasive quality in it. She was thrown into confusion, and the drugging effect of the sleeping pill didn't help her to sort through it quickly.

"I want him home . . . with me." On that point, Maggie wasn't confused. "Put Ty on the next plane home. I'll pay the fare."

"No."

"Chase, I want my son." Her voice trembled on a warning note.

"If you want him, you'll have to come get him."

"No." She wouldn't go back there. "Ty is a minor—a runaway. If you don't send him back, I'll notify the authorities and they'll come get him and bring him home to me."

"You've been away a long time, Maggie. I think you've forgotten how much territory this Calder sky covers. I am the authority here. If you want him, you'll have to come yourself. You know where to find us."

Chase hung up the receiver, fully aware he had lived up to her bad image of him, but this had to be sorted out. And he preferred to do it face to face. He leaned heavily back in his chair and stared at the phone, wondering how much she had changed in the last fifteen years. Was she still as beautiful as she had been as a young girl? Had she kept her figure? Or lost it carrying their son? Wearily, he rubbed his eyes.

By dawn the next morning, Chase had showered, shaved, and dressed. Before going downstairs, he stopped at Ty's room and opened the door. The boy was sprawled across the bed on his stomach, his mouth lolling open. The newness of knowing he had a son continued to amaze and delight him.

He knocked loudly on the opened door. "Time to get up, Ty!" Chase watched the teen-ager push himself groggily up on his elbows and frown as he looked around, trying to remember where he was.

"What time is it?" Ty combed a sleepy hand through his hair, trying to shake himself awake.

"Five o'clock."

"In the morning!!" With a groan, he collapsed face down on the bed.

"We get up early around here." Chase moved out of the doorway to the stairs. There weren't any lights, either, to *make* a boy get out of bed. He had to learn to do it himself.

Ruth had just set his plate of steak, eggs, and hashed browns on the dining room table when a sleepy-eyed Ty stumbled into the room. Chase introduced them. Ruth made an embarrassing fuss over him, her eyes misting over with tears when she murmured that she wished Webb had lived to see his grandson. Then she hurried off to the kitchen, dabbing her eyes with the corner of her apron.

"What did my Mom say when you called her last night?" he asked when they were alone.

Chase deftly avoided making a direct answer. "She'll be flying up today or tomorrow. It will depend on how soon she can get reservations."

"She'll want me to go back with her," Ty said glumly.

"I'll handle it." Chase repeated the calm response he had made the night before.

When Ruth brought Ty his plate of steak, eggs, and hashed browns, he stared at it. "I don't know if I can eat all that this early in the morning."

Chase lifted a shoulder in an expressive shrug that said it was up to him, but he said, "It's a long time until lunch."

Ty was making a good dent in it when Buck walked in. Chase was finished and had leaned back to enjoy his third cup of coffee. He saw the puzzled look Buck gave the boy.

"Ty, I want you to meet Buck Haskell, one of my top foremen and a good friend." He introduced Buck and watched Ty lay down his silverware to stand courteously to shake hands. "Buck, this is my son."

"Your . . . *what?*" Buck shot him a look that was sharply incredulous. "But where . . . who . . ."

"Maggie is his mother."

"Maggie O'Rourke?" At Chase's nod, Buck dragged in a deep breath and blew it out. "Well, if that don't beat all!" His face was oddly blank, a hint of exasperation in his voice. Then he was looking at Chase and grinning. "It seems a little foolish to say congratulations at this late date."

Chapter XXVIII

It was nearly noon on the following day when Maggie arrived, driving a rented car. Since no one else knocked before entering The Homestead, Chase knew it was her before he opened the door. He met her cool, green eyes, then skimmed her slender figure, clad in a flattering black suit trimmed in white. Certain things he remembered about her, like her pride and strong will, were in evidence in her stiff carriage.

He glanced beyond her, his gaze settling on a ranch hand passing the house. "Charley, bring Mrs. Gordon's luggage in from the car."

"There's no need." She turned to countermand his order. "I'm not staying."

"Bring them in, Charley," he repeated evenly.

She faced him again with cool composure. "I'll only be here long enough to get Ty. Then I'm leaving."

"Fine." He inclined his head in implied acceptance and stepped aside, inviting her into the house. Leaving the door open for Charley, Chase moved toward the den, listening to the tap-tapping of Maggie's heels on the tiled floor as she followed him. He let her walk past him into the room while he closed the double doors to ensure their privacy. "There is hot coffee in the service on the coffee table."

After her gaze had made a sweeping search of the room without finding Ty, Maggie turned back to confront Chase. "Where is my son?"

"He went with Nate this morning for his first glimpse of an actual roundup." Chase poured two cups of coffee from the silver service. "Cream or sugar?"

"You know I was coming for him." Irritation emanated from her like an electric force field, charging the air around her. Chase felt it without having to look at her.

"But I didn't know when," he reminded her.

She half-pivoted, showing him her profile. There was a filled-out completeness to her body that reached out to him and stirred all his male desires. She had to know she was a picture for his hungry glance, arousing memories of when he'd seen more of those shapely legs than the black skirt slit at the knee revealed. He leaned back in the armchair, holding his cup.

"How soon will Ty be back?"

"Tonight." He sipped his coffee and avoided meeting her accusing eyes.

"You did this deliberately. Why?" She looked at him, taking in the hard vitality that stamped his features. He had matured into a powerful figure of a man, character lines adding to, rather than detracting from, his looks. His mouth quirked in that hard, familiar way she remembered.

"To give us time to talk in private. Why else?"

"We have nothing to discuss," she insisted coldly.

"Why didn't you tell me you were going to have my child?" Chase finally addressed the issue that they had been avoiding.

"Ty is my child. Your part in his conception was purely incidental." Her gaze was averted, her voice stiff and her head held high.

"Do you still hate me, Maggie?" He watched her glance come around to him.

"Hate is a passionate word. Despise or loathe would be more suitable." That was one thing her marriage to Phillip had done for her. It had removed that poisonous seed of hate that could have twisted her. "My husband was a loving, compassionate man. He taught me to forget what I couldn't forgive."

"The day I came to you—the last time I saw you, it was to tell you that I was truly sorry about your father. At the time, I wasn't aware that you knew the entire story." He could see she was closing her mind to him, not wanting to recall anything. "I know you don't want to talk about it, but it must be said."

"Why? My father is dead and buried."

"And we have a son, so you will listen whether you want to or not," Chase replied with no break in his voice. "I understand what my father's reasons were for his actions, but I had no knowledge of his intentions when we rode into the yard that day. Right up to the point where they put the rope around Angus' neck, I thought he planned only to scare him. When they—" His mouth closed for a moment before he continued. "I couldn't have saved him, Maggie. His neck was already broken." He paused again. "Even after all this time, I can't say that my father was wrong. Your father's hatred of us was an obsession. You know that, Maggie, probably better than I do. In a sense, it was a mercy killing, because eventually your father would have destroyed not only himself, but you and Culley, too."

"Are you finished?" She looked at him and Chase couldn't tell if she had understood anything he'd said.

"With that subject, yes." He glanced at his watch. "Ruth will be putting lunch on the table."

"I'm not hungry."

Setting his cup down, he stood and walked over to take her arm in a firm grip. "Make an effort," he said dryly. He could feel the high tension flowing from her, but she didn't resist the pressure of his guiding hand.

He didn't attempt to make conversation during lunch, but let a silence lay over the table, instead. At first, Maggie picked at the food on her plate until the quiet atmosphere aroused her appetite, reminding her she hadn't eaten in twenty-four hours. Relaxed and replete from the meal, she leaned back in her chair and sipped her coffee.

"Do you mind if I smoke?" Chase held a slim cigar halfway to his mouth.

"No, not at all. I enjoy the aroma of a good cigar," she replied diffidently.

"It's a rare breed of woman who likes the smell of cigars." He held a match to the tip and puffed on the tapered end.

"Phillip often smoked a cigar after dinner." Unconsciously, her voice softened in fondness so she didn't understand the suddenly tightened line of his mouth.

"You do realize that Ty wants to stay here."

Maggie was off guard, unprepared for this statement, so she

reacted sharply. "It doesn't matter what he wants. He's coming home with me."

There was something lazy and dangerous about the way he looked at her. "Do you honestly think I'm going to let you take him?"

The coffee cup was shoved onto the table as Maggie rose. It was the very thing she had been afraid of—that if Chase ever knew he had a son, he would try to take him from her. She crossed her arms, rubbing them, as if fighting off a chill.

"I'll fight you before I'll ever let you take him from me, Chase Calder," she warned. "I'm not Maggie O'Rourke anymore, a nobody. I'm Elizabeth Gordon, a wealthy widow whose husband had a lot of influential friends. We're on equal terms now, so you can't just brush me aside."

"Is that what you want, Maggie? An ugly custody battle?" he challenged in a voice that held the ragged edge of anger. "Shall we fight over which of us would be the better parent? Which has more to offer him? Do you want to play a cruel game of tug-of-war with Ty?"

"No, it isn't what I want, but I have very little choice in the matter if you choose to make an issue of it!"

"I'm not making an issue of it. You are, by insisting that he return home with you," Chase replied, once again in control.

"You don't think I'm going to let him stay?"

"He'll run away again if you take him back," he warned her quite calmly. "Eventually you'll alienate him. In three more years, he'll be eighteen—free to live where he wants."

"You surely don't think I'll give him up? Just walk away and let you have him?"

"No."

"Then what do you want from me?"

"Marry me."

Maggie stared at him in open-mouthed shock. "You can't be serious!" She finally managed to laugh at the idea.

"But I am. Don't worry." His mouth quirked dryly. "I'm not nursing any grand passion for you. My interest in marrying you is solely based on Ty. First, it will legitimize his birth. I want no son of mine being called a bastard."

"It's a little late for that," Maggie suggested sarcastically.

"Since I wasn't informed of his existence—or even his expected existence—it is as timely as I can make it," Chase countered. "Secondly, I want to ensure that Ty is legally recognized as my heir. The Triple C is his birthright, and I intend to take whatever steps are necessary to see that he gets it."

"You haven't given me one reason why I should agree to this preposterous marriage." She was motionless and strained, still listening to the run of his voice, and its repressed feelings.

"You want your son, don't you? If we fight over him, Maggie, we'll both lose. And Ty will be the biggest loser of all, because he will be confused, torn between the two of us. By marrying me, you will maintain your role as his mother, live here in this house with him, and be an integral part of his life. In addition, you will be the mistress of this house and have all the attached importance of the name Calder."

"I'm not interested in your name, or your bed." She didn't argue about the part concerning Ty.

"I don't care whether or not you share my bed. That's entirely up to you. I would suggest that you live here without the benefit of marriage, except for the first two reasons I gave you, and . . . the gossip it would create. And you know people would talk if you came back to live in the area, let alone in this house. It wouldn't matter whether there was any truth to the stories; the talk would get back to Ty. I don't think you'd like that. The marriage is a formality. As soon as it has accomplished its objective of establishing Ty as my legitimate heir, you can file for a divorce. I only make one stipulation—Ty stays with me."

"That isn't fair," she said shortly.

"Sooner or later, you'd have to let him go, anyway . . . when he marries or goes off to see the world. You can stay here as long as you like—until he's eighteen, twenty-one—or you can divide your time between here and California. Or stay in California and come here to visit. It's immaterial to me. If you have a better solution, I'll gladly listen."

His statement mocked her. There was no other solution that would meet his terms. And if his terms weren't met, he'd take her to court to get Ty. It didn't matter if she eventually won the case. He made that clear. She could well imagine Ty's reaction to this ranch. It would seem the fulfillment of any boy's romantic dreams about the West, complete with a hero figure as a father. She could never win against a boy's dreams, even if she could win legal custody.

"Ty has a natural affinity for the land, a feeling for this country," Chase went on when she failed to fill the silence. "You couldn't repress it, although I know you tried. It's something he inherited from both of us, Maggie. I'm appealing to your maternal instinct. We are both interested in the same thing—Ty. At least our marriage can start out with that as a common ground." He studied her quietly. "I don't expect you to give me an answer now. You'll want to talk to Ty. Tomorrow will be soon enough."

Tomorrow? She was stung. "How generous of you to give me so much time!"

"Enough time has already been wasted." He pushed out of his chair. "I'll take your luggage to your room."

"I haven't said I'll stay," Maggie reminded him.

He looked at her, running an unamused glance over her face. "You'll stay."

"No." She was not going to bend to his will. "If I must stay overnight, I prefer to do it in my brother's house."

He frowned. "From what I've heard, a rat wouldn't sleep there. The place has deteriorated badly since you left. So has your brother."

Maggie left the dining room and made directly for the front door, her steps quickening in haste. Chase made no attempt to stop her as she left the house and descended the steps to the rental car. Maggie made the long drive to her brother's in a numbed state, not sure what she'd find when she got there.

But Chase's description hadn't prepared her for the sight of the dilapidated buildings that looked ready to collapse with the first strong wind. It didn't look as if there had been an attempt to repair anything in years. The house, her childhood home, looked abandoned.

It had never been much to begin with, but now windows were broken, half of the steps were gone, and the porch floor was rotted and partially caved in. Maggie gingerly picked her way to the door, standing open. The smell that greeted her was nauseatingly rotten. Covering her mouth, she took a cautious step inside. It was dark and dirty. She reached for the light switch by the door, but nothing happened. Cautiously, she moved sideways, feeling her way until she found a lamp. No light came on when she pulled its chain. There was no electricity in the house. Something scurried in the shadows and Maggie recoiled from the sound. This wasn't a home; it was a pest-hole. She shuddered and retreated to the door, sickened because her brother lived in this.

Outside, she inhaled the blessed freshness of the air and looked around. The high heels she wore made an investigation of the other buildings impractical unless she wanted to risk twisting an ankle on the rough ground. She called her brother's name, but didn't expect an answer. She waited in the car for over an hour before she finally gave up. She didn't want to be here when it got dark.

As she drove away, Maggie was appalled by the state of the house. First her mother, then she, had slaved to make it habitable, although neither her father nor brother had ever seemed to appreciate the effort. There were a few home truths to be faced about her family, but she wasn't prepared to face them head-on just yet.

Out of the corner of her eye, she glimpsed the cemetery and stopped the car to reverse it to the turn-in. Getting out of the car, Maggie climbed the grassy knoll and paused beside her mother's grave. No conscious thought crossed her mind. A cold wind finally stirred her awareness of the lengthening shadow cast by the headstone. It was late and Ty would be returning soon.

Moving stiffly, she began descending the narrow pathway between the graves. The ground was fairly smooth, but she watched where she was walking until an inner sense warned her that she was being watched. Maggie paused, lifting her gaze.

A pickup was parked beside her car. Chase was leaning against the bed of the truck, smoking a slim cigarillo. Something told her that he had been waiting there a long time. Pushing away from the truck, he crushed the smoke under his heel and came forward to meet her. Without saying a word, he turned to walk beside her, curving a large hand under her elbow to support and guide her. Numb and somewhat robot-like, Maggie let him escort her to the truck.

The touch of his hand on her hip when he helped her inside the cab burned away her apathy. She turned her head to look at him. He stood in the doorway, one hand on the truck frame and the other holding the door. His look was quietly assessing and astute.

"It hasn't been much of a homecoming for you, has it?" he murmured.

Gazing into that hard, virile face, Maggie was swept away by the memory of their days of joyful abandonment. She wanted to reach out and grab a piece of that careless joy she had once known, recapture the brilliant sunshine that had lightened her world. Something flickered in his eyes, as if he could read the thoughts in her expression. It brought her back to reality.

"Leave me alone." Her voice was flat, dead.

With an indifferent lift of his shoulders, he closed the passenger's door and walked around to climb behind the wheel. As he started the motor and began to turn onto the highway, Maggie noticed the rental car parked beside them.

"The car—" she began.

"I'll send one of the boys to get it."

As they drove through town, Maggie noticed the restaurant sign at the refurbished Jake's Place. "When did Jake open a restaurant?"

"Jake sold the place four years ago. The new owner remodeled it into a restaurant."

"Who owns it?" When there wasn't an immediate answer to her question, she glanced at him, wondering if there was some significance to his hesitation.

"A woman named Sally Brogan." He sounded preoccupied with other matters.

Maggie let the silence ride for a few miles. "What were you doing at the cemetery, waiting for me?"

"I saw your car parked there, so I stopped. I was on my way to your brother's to get you. It crossed my mind that you just might be stubborn enough to stay there, and it isn't a fit place for a lady." He let his gaze stray from the highway to briefly rest on her, skimming over her. "Yes, you did achieve your ambition of becoming a lady: elegant, sophisticated, contained, hardly a hair out of place."

"You don't sound impressed." His tone had almost been insulting.

"Maybe I'm wondering if there's anything left of the girl I knew, or whether she's been polished out of existence." He stared down the road, his head tipped to the side. "I remember one time when I got carried away while I was making love to you and got a little rough. You started nipping me—hard. When I complained, you tole me that if I wanted to play rough, so would you." Cynicism curled the corners of his mouth. "I wonder what you would do today. Yawn?"

Maggie turned away. For the rest of the drive she stared out the passenger's window, her elbow resting on the windowframe and her fist pressed against her mouth.

That night at the dinner table, Maggie faced Chase across the length of the table, while Ty sat, symbolically, halfway between them on the right side. At the moment he was wearing a clean white shirt and dark dress pants, and looked like her son. But when he'd walked in the door that evening, he had seemed almost a stranger, outfitted in dusty Western garb. Initially, Ty had been ill at ease with her, aware that he had hurt her when he ran away, but when she failed to mention anything about it, he began to eagerly relate his adventures of the last two days. Chase sat complacently at the head of the table while Ty proved all his points, letting the boy's enthusiasm beat at her.

Gradually, Maggie worked their California home into the conversation, mentioning Ty's friends and the jumping horses he showed. His replies became briefer until he wasn't talking at all. That's when she began asking him directly if he was prepared to give up his friends, his home, his life in California.

"I'll miss all that for a while," Ty admitted and shifted uncomfortably in his chair before he continued. "Mom, I don't want to hurt you. I know you want me to come back, but . . . I want to stay here."

"You don't want to hurt me, but you would, wouldn't you?" Maggie realized. "If I insisted that you—"

"Don't do it, Mom?" Ty requested tightly, his voice cracking with stress.

If her battle had been only with Chase, she would have fought tooth and nail for her son, but she couldn't fight Ty, too. She knew when she was defeated. She began pushing the peas around on her plate with a fork.

"What would you say, Ty, if I told you that Chase and I have talked about getting married?" she asked, lifting her eyes as she felt the probing thrust of Chase's gaze.

"Have you?" Ty asked warily, not committing himself until he knew if it was true.

"Yes," she admitted and held the level gaze of the man at the head of the table, a mature Chase Calder, laconic and hard to fathom.

"Then we'd live here? Both of us?"

"Yes." She nodded, continuing to return the steady regard of the brown eyes.

"Is that your answer, Maggie?" Chase asked coolly.

"It's what my son wants," she replied. "Yes, that is my answer."

"I'll get the marriage license and the minister. We'll be married here at the house—with no fuss," he said.

Chapter XXIX

The decision to stay and marry Chase left a multitude of loose ends in California. There was her resignation to be submitted as an executive of the charity organization. Arrangements had to be made to sell the show horses. Naturally, there were all her clothes and Ty's, and their personal belongings, which had to be packed and shipped to the Triple C. That part was handled with a telephone call to her Aunt Cathleen. Her aunt was an incurable romantic, so she was delighted that Maggie was finally marrying the man who had fathered her child.

Pamela was another matter. First she was angrily incredulous when Maggie relayed her decision. Then she cried and pleaded with Maggie to reconsider and bring Ty back. Maggie was not about to confide in her sister-in-law and explain why she had no choice. Before the conversation ended, Pamela was livid, accusing Maggie of being unfaithful to Phillip's memory—of never having loved him—marrying him only for his money, and threatening to go to court to have his will reversed, striking both Maggie and Ty from the list of beneficiaries. The vindictiveness of her sister-in-law was enough to convince her that she never wanted to go back.

After that conversation, Maggie had gone outside to walk off her anger. Chase was nowhere around, but then, he rarely was. With the spring roundup in full swing, he was usually gone from daybreak to dusk. She was past the barns and halfway to the bunkhouse before her steps finally slowed and she took the time to look around.

Her eye was caught by a clumsy-looking vehicle parked in front of one of the buildings ahead. It took a minute for her to recognize the motorized chuckwagon for what it was. She strolled closer to look inside the mobile kitchen, complete with a butane cookstove, refrigerator, and water tank. It had returned to the ranch head-quarters to load up on supplies and fuel.

When a hulking figure emerged from a building, a bullet-shaped head was nearly hidden behind the fifty-pound potato sack carried on his shoulder. Maggie blinked at the man incredulously as a smile broke out across her face.

"Tucker!" she cried in delight. The cook swiveled his torso to see who had called his name. He stared at her blankly and she laughed. "It's me! Maggie!"

He swung the sack to the ground as if it were a feather. "I heard you was back, but I wouldn't have recognized you." There was pride in the way he looked her over, taking in the chic hairstyle, the silver-gray designer blouse, and the slim-fitting black slacks. "Welcome home, Maggie."

There was a crazy lump in her throat as she laughed again, this time softly. "Do you know you are the first person who has told me that?"

"I'm glad. I thought about ya and how ya were getting along," he said. "I've seen your boy. Is he Chase's son?"

"Yes." She watched his reaction, remembering the respect he'd always shown her and wondering if this would change that.

"The boys say you're going to marry him."

"Yes." He didn't appear to pass judgment on her behavior those long years ago. Yet she felt obligated to explain to this man her reason for marrying Chase after what the Calders had done to her father. "I don't have any choice. Ty is under his spell. If I don't want to lose my son, I have to marry him so I can stay close to Ty." She drew in a shaky breath and glanced toward the far horizon. "Have you seen Culley lately? I've been over to the ranch a couple of times, but he hasn't been there and I—" She couldn't finish the sentence, unable to express her reactions to the changes there.

"I know." Tucker's comment said she didn't have to tell him. "Culley isn't around there very much. It's haunted for him. He should have left with you and not tried to keep the place. It was too much for a man, let alone a boy. I tried to talk to him, but he wouldn't listen—said the Calders had got to me."

"He wrote to me that you were here, but I thought you would have left by now." She looked at him, trying to understand why he had stayed. "They burned your place down. I would have thought you'd get out of this place as quickly as you could."

"I thought Calder burned it. Maybe it was a grease fire, like they said." He shrugged. "I've been treated fair here. And I'm my own boss. I guess Webb Calder put the fear of God in me. Chase still keeps a wary eye on me."

"Then you have forgiven both of them for what they did to my father?" It seemed another betrayal.

"Haven't you?" Tucker countered, with a slanting look of his small eyes.

"No."

"Do you believe a son has to pay for the sins of his father?" When she started to answer, he interrupted her. "Be careful what you say, because if you're going to make Chase pay for what his father did, don't forget that your son's father is Chase Calder."

A tiny shockwave went through her, his words reverberating in her mind—pay for the sins of his father. She was trembling inside, not certain why. There was a sudden confusion in her head that she couldn't sort through. Her thoughts were all whirling too fast.

"Well—" Tucker hefted the potato sack onto his shoulder. "I gotta get to work. The boys will be hungry soon." Then he paused. "I'll get word to Culley that you want to see him."

"Thanks, Tucker." It was an almost absent reply as she turned to walk slowly toward The Homestead.

The wedding ceremony was quick and painless, held in the evening so it wouldn't interfere with Chase's work schedule. Ruth and Virgil Haskell acted as their witnesses. Ty was the only other one in attendance. There had been only one awkward moment, which occurred when it was time to exchange the plain gold wedding bands. Maggie had forgotten to remove the interlocking diamond solitaire wedding set that Phillip had given her. Looking back, she couldn't be sure whether it was an oversight or subconscious design. Either way, when Chase saw them, his mouth had tightened as he deftly removed them and slipped them into his pocket, returning Phillip's wedding band and ring to her afer the ceremony. Later, his kiss had been cool and impersonal, hardly a kiss at all.

Afterward, Chase had fixed drinks in the den while the license was signed and witnessed. The minister had offered a toast to their future happiness together before leaving. The Haskells hadn't lingered, and even Ty discreetly slipped away to leave them alone. Chase had promptly excused himself to finish some paperwork, leaving Maggie with the feeling that it had all been a farce.

What had she expected? Lying in the bed of the master suite, she stared at the moon patterns on the ceiling. Her ego was suffering. She had wanted to be the one who did the ignoring. She was disgusted with her childish reaction. What did it matter which of them set the mood of quiet civility?

She listened to his footsteps climbing the stairs to the top and the unhurried stride that carried him past her door without any hesitation. His bedroom was located in the northwest corner of the second floor. He had dryly pointed it out to her when he'd given her the master suite her first night. The door to his room opened and closed. Then there was silence.

She rolled onto her side, sliding her hands under the pillow beneath her head. The wide gold band felt strangely heavy on her finger. She wasn't accustomed to the feel of it; she was used to the diamond crown of Phillip's ring. She had barely closed her eyes when the loudest clanging and banging broke out all around her. The deafening racket drove Maggie out of bed. She grabbed for the matching robe to her satin gown and bolted into the outer hall, nearly running into Chase.

"What is that?" There wasn't any letup in the clamorous din.

"I don't know." His shirt was unbuttoned and hanging free. He was just starting to tuck it inside the waistband of his pants when he stopped and drew in a sharp breath of recognition. "Oh, no." It came out in an exasperated sigh.

"What?" She looked at him, puzzled and vaguely alarmed.

He slanted her a wry, downward look. "They are giving us a shivaree. I have no doubt it was Buck's idea." A laugh broke from her throat, short and relieved, then interrupted by the opening of the front door downstairs and the invasion of tramping boots and the clanging of metal pots.

"We want the bride and groom!" A chorus of rowdy voices shouted.

Maggie started to tie the tasseled sash of her robe. Chase raked her with a look that took special note of the way the satin material shaped itself to her breasts and hips. Very little was left to the imagination.

"You can't go downstairs wearing that," he snapped in a low undertone.

For a stunned second, she could only look at him. "I have half a dozen evening gowns more revealing than this!" she retorted. "Phillip never considered I was dressed indecently."

"Well, I'm not Phillip, and this isn't California. Our women don't go around showing their bodies in front of other men." His voice was a sharp reminder that he belonged to a breed of men who judged women by standards different from those of the outside world. Rebellion licked through her veins, either sparked by his rebuke or the possessive ring in his tone when he had grouped her into the category of "our women."

"Hey! Are you coming down, or do we have to come up?" a voice challenged from the foot of the stairs.

"Give us a couple of minutes to get decent!" Chase lifted his voice to reply, then gathered Maggie by the shoulders and marched her into the master suite amidst hoots and hollers from below.

If it wasn't for the very real possibility that Ty was a member of the party downstairs, and Maggie didn't want to embarrass him, she would have refused to change clothes. Chase had already snapped the light on and was going through her meager wardrobe, since the rest of her clothes hadn't arrived. Maggie was irritated further by the implication that he didn't trust her to choose something suitable. Angrily, she shrugged out of her robe and tossed it onto the rumpled bedcovers.

She had just peeled the nightslip over her head and was reaching for her underclothes when Chase said, "Here. Wear this."

"What?" When she turned to see what he had chosen, she was held motionless by the look in his eyes.

They traveled over her nakedness, lingering on the tawny points of her breasts, the flatness of her stomach, and the black vee of curling hair. Then they slowly traveled upward over the same route. Maggie was shaken by the sensation he was making love to her with his eyes, and she felt the heat rushing through her body, the heat of desire. She had to defend herself against this most intimate of invasions.

"Stop gawking like a cowboy, Chase." She spoke curtly because she was quivering inside. "You've seen me naked before."

The taunt broke the spell, and Maggie moved quickly to slip on her bra and panties. Chase had chosen a sleeveless daytime dress of ice-blue, made out of the shimmering terry-cloth-like material. When she reached out to take it from his hand, he held it for an instant, forcing her to meet his eyes, gleaming hard like polished stone.

"But when I saw you naked before, Maggie, I always looked," he reminded her simply and let go of the dress to turn away.

A chanting began downstairs. "We want the bride and groom! We want the bride and groom!" Chase waited at the door with barely disguised impatience while Maggie buttoned the front of the dress and slipped her bare feet into a pair of backless heels. His gaze made a cursory inspection of her when she joined him. She simmered, feeling raw, as if the wall she had so carefully erected to keep out unwanted sensations was being eaten away, and she needed the protection against his vibrant animal attraction.

She was stiff under his guiding hand as they went downstairs, where they were immediately engulfed in the noisy tide of ranch workers and their families, laughing, boisterous, teasing in their congratulations. They may have been denied a big wedding, but they weren't going to be denied the opportunity to celebrate the marriage of their boss. In the crush of well-wishers, Chase curved an arm possessively and protectively around Maggie's waist, molding her tightly to his left side so they couldn't be separated. His hard-muscled frame was like a living rock, generating heat to burn its way into her flesh. She was conscious of his rough virility that didn't rely on sexual charm. It was simpler, more basic than that, an earthiness bred into him by the land. She resisted it, concentrating her attention on the stream of cowboys.

They were caught and swept into the current of bodies that carried them out of the house to the larger crowd waiting outside. A team of horses, skittish from all the noise, was hitched to an old carriage. She and Chase were pressed into its seat while a pair of riders flanked the fractious team and paraded the carriage and its occupants around the ranch yard to the delight of the crowd. Maggie managed to match Chase's calm and smiling acceptance of it all.

Finally, the riders delivered the couple to the front steps of The Homestead. As Chase lifted Maggie out of the carriage, Ruth Haskell emerged from the crowd to murmur to them. "I have refreshments ready for everybody inside." She was keeping the custom of treating the revelers.

Chase and Maggie stood at the door, greeting the individuals as they filed in and accepting the congratulations. A few of them Maggie knew, and others looked familiar. Chase introduced them all, never faltering over a name. Every now and then a cowboy would claim the right to kiss the bride, but it was always a very respectful and contained action. No one took advantage of the privilege, not with Chase standing beside her.

As a cowboy moved on to shake hands with the groom, Maggie turned to the next person in line. There was an air of quietness about the red-haired woman who came next, a quality that stood out amidst all the noise. She felt Chase stiffen and quickly looked at him to determine the cause, yet there was nothing in his expression to indicate anything was wrong. He made the introduction, as he had all night.

"This is Sally Brogan, a friend of mine. She owns the restaurant in town."

"Congratulations, Mrs. Calder." As the quietly attractive woman shook hands with Maggie, she noticed the faint strain in her features. Behind those placid blue eyes, there lurked pain. "You are a very lucky woman."

Lucky? Maggie supposed there were many women who would gladly trade places with her. The knowledge came instantly that this woman was one of them. She was suddenly aware of a certain stillness around them, as if the others were watching the exchange. When the redhead moved on to congratulate Chase, someone stepped forward to immediately claim Maggie's attention.

It was Buck Haskell, grinning and talking loud. "You make a beautiful bride, but you always were a beauty."

She hardly heard a word he said. Next to her, she was conscious of the woman murmuring to Chase. "I wish you both every happiness." And she stretched up to kiss him. It was clear to Maggie there had been more than friendship between them. She was even more convinced when she heard Buck say, in a voice she wasn't supposed to hear, "Sorry, Chase, but Sally asked to come so you would know she wasn't angry or upset."

Then there were more faces and more introductions to be made before Maggie and Chase joined those in the house to taste the refreshments Ruth had fixed. It was an hour before the ranch hands and their families filed out of the house, more quietly than they had arrived.

While Chase began turning out the downstairs lights, Maggie started up the steps. She stopped on the landing where the stairs made an abrupt left turn. "Where's Ty?"

After turning off the hall light to the kitchen, Chase paused to answer her, a dry lift to the corner of his mouth. "He seemed to think it was necessary that he sleep in the bunkhouse tonight so we could have the house to ourselves on our wedding night."

Her fingers curved around the smooth banister of the staircase. The mention of their wedding night and its accompanying intimacies had caused an odd coiling sensation inside her stomach.

"The red-haired woman, Sally Brogan?" Maggie began, not certain why she was bringing up the subject, except that she wanted to see Chase's reaction.

He stopped casually beside a burning lamp and turned his head. "What about her?" His challenge was summer-soft.

"You have been seeing her, haven't you?"

There was no denial. Nor did Chase appear uncomfortable that she had guessed. "I never made her any promises," was all he said.

His reply opened up an old wound, because he had made no promises to her, either, sixteen years ago. He had simply enjoyed the pleasures she had to offer, taking what came his way.

"You never make promises, do you?"

"Your memory is short." There was a sudden harshness in the set of his features. "Earlier tonight I believe I promised 'to honor and keep you until death do us part.'" He moved toward the light glowing from the dining room.

Maggie was shaken by the conviction in his voice as she remained on the staircase landing. In this country, a man kept his word or he wasn't a man. A promise was not something given lightly. The vows she had spoken tonight had been meaningless words to her, an expedient way to keep Ty. Regardless of how lightly she had regarded them, Chase's code would not permit him to dismiss them. He was bound by the promises he'd made, whether or not she believed that she was.

She felt vaguely ashamed. In the eyes of God and man, he was her husband. Was she right to be less than a wife to him? Yet she had been coerced into this marriage. What kind of man would threaten to take a son from his mother? But another, quieter voice asked: what kind of woman denied a father the right to know his son? She was suddenly assailed by a storm of doubts.

When she heard his footsteps approaching the living room, she started up the stairs. All this confusion had brought pain to pound between her eyebrows. She paid no attention to the sound of tires crunching in the gravel outside the house, assuming it was a late-departing member of the shivaree crowd. Chase didn't give it a thought, either. She was almost to the top of the stairs when a rifle shot exploded into the night's quiet, startling a cry from her throat.

The reverberation had barely ended when a voice from outside yelled, "Calder! I want my sister!"

"Culley!" She recognized her brother's voice and sped down the stairs. In the semi-darkness of the living room, she collided with Chase. When she tried to move by him, his arms were steel-strong. She pushed at his chest, tipping her head back to glare at him. "I want to see my brother."

"Not yet." His voice was as hard and unyielding as his grip.

The next shot shattered a dining room window and Maggie was hauled against his chest, crushed against the length of his body while his wide shoulders hunched protectively forward, as if to shield her. Stunned by this selfless action, she stopped struggling. Beneath her head, she could hear his strong heartbeat. When there was no second shot, he moved, pushing her toward the stairwell.

"Calder! Do you hear me?" Culley shouted.

"I hear you!" he answered. And he said to Maggie in a low voice, "Stay here and stay down."

"He just wants to see me," she argued.

"Then he shouldn't have come with a rifle," he snapped.

"Calder! I know Maggie's in there! You let her go, or I'll shoot out every window in the house!" her brother threatened.

Chase moved quietly away from Maggie into the shadows of the darkened living room. He didn't reply until he was on the other side of the room. "If you know she's in here, put down the rifle before you hurt her."

"All you gotta do is let her go and she won't be hurt—because

I'm not going to let you hurt her this time!" Culley lifted his cheek from the rifle to answer as he crouched behind the hood of his pickup.

There was a faint scuffle in the gravel behind him, a whisper of warning. He pivoted sharply, swinging the rifle around to respond to the threat from his unguarded rear. An arm knocked the barrel upward and the bullet was fired harmlessly into the air as he was rushed by three men. He tried to fight them off, but he was outnumbered, and more were coming. Something rammed his stomach, doubling him over with pain, and a fist split his lip open and spun him into the truck. Groggily, he tried to shake the blackness away from his eyes, but they pulled him around, slamming his shoulders and back against the pickup's side. There was a crack of pain along his jaw. Then he was sinking into a dark oblivion and didnt hear the snapped order, "That's enough."

When Maggie heard the scuffling sounds of a fight outside, she ignored Chase's order to stay and followed him out of the house. Culley was on the ground, unconscious, slumped against the truck when she arrived on the scene. She paid little attention to the men standing around as she hurried to her brother.

"What do you want us to do with him, boss?" one asked.

Chase didn't get a chance to answer as Maggie took one look at the bruised face and wickedly cut lip. "Bring him in the house," she ordered. No one moved to obey her, and she looked over her shoulder at Chase with ice in her glance. "He's my brother and he's hurt."

The pause was no more than a heartbeat long. "You heard my wife," Chase said. "Buck, you and Dave carry him into the house." Then he was stepping forward and reaching down to draw Maggie away from her brother. He muttered near her ear, anger vibrating through the low tone. "What did you think I was going to have them do? Dump him in a ditch?"

"How was I to know?" she hissed, equally low. "You let them beat him up."

"He also had a rifle which he was using. What did you expect them to do—tap him on the shoulder and ask him nicely to put it away?" he growled under his breath, not looking at her as his hard-gripping hand propelled her after the two men carrying her brother into the house.

Chapter XXX

In the full light of the living room, the cuts and bruises looked minor. It was her brother's overall physical condition that alarmed Maggie. His black hair was lank and straggly and he was rib-thin. There were dark hollows under his eyes, as if his eyes had sunk into their sockets. His behavior seemed understandable. He was a tightly coiled wire that had sprung and become erratic.

Chase handed her a shot of whiskey to revive Culley and motioned to Ty to clear away the first-aid equipment. Cupping the back of his head in her hand, Maggie poured a little of the whiskey into Culley's mouth. He choked and started coughing, his eyelids dragging open as he attempted to push her away. Out of the corner of her eye, she was conscious of Chase taking a step toward them, ready to intervene if Culley became violent.

"Culley, it's Maggie," she said quickly to calm him down. It idly registered that after sixteen years of being Elizabeth, she was Maggie again.

She watched Culley focus on her and frown, his eyes raw and red, showing the strain of too much work and not enough rest that marked the rest of him. "Maggie?"

"Yes." She smiled. "How do you feel?"

His hands gripped her arms, his fingers digging into her flesh like steel talons, betraying a need to make sure she was real and not a mirage. "It really is you." A smile flashed, the action drawing on his cut lip and bringing an immediate wince of pain. He crushed her against his chest and hugged her tightly. Burying his face in her clean-scented hair, he closed his eyes to hide the tears, because a man wasn't supposed to cry. "I've missed you." His voice was muffled and low.

"I missed you, too, Culley." Emotion choked her voice, as well, and she blinked to keep her own tears at bay. She saw Chase watching them with a tight-lipped grimness and slowly untangled herself from Culley's clinging hold.

"You did it." Culley ran wondering fingers along the side of her face, touching her in a kind of adoring awe. "You are a beautiful lady." She caught his thin hand and kissed it, pity and guilt cutting into her for the misery he'd known while she had been surrounded by everything a woman could desire. Then his fingers closed fiercely around her hand. "I got Tucker's message that you were here and that Calder was making you stay." He looked up, a wildness possessing him when he saw Chase and, off to one side, Buck Haskell and two other cowboys stationed in the room in case there was trouble. "Come on. I'm taking you with me, Maggie, and they can't stop me." He started to rise from the couch, gripping her hand to pull her with him.

"Culley, no." Her resistance baffled him, and it showed. "Listen to me, please. There is something I have to explain." She was already searching for the words to make him understand, knowing there weren't any.

"What?" He eyed her narrowly.

"This is where I live now. We are married." She spoke calmly and concisely, trying not to let the words carry too much import, but she saw the shock and anger registering in his features. "Chase is my husband."

There was a wild, unstable light in his eyes. "Have you forgotten what he did?"

She laid her fingers against his mouth to silence him, her eyes quietly pleading with him to say no more. "There's someone I want you to meet." She sought to distract him and turned to motion for Ty. Rising from her seat on the very edge of the couch, she moved to reach out for her son's hand and draw him closer. He was wearing a wary and bewildered frown, made uncomfortable by the peculiar attitude and behavior of the man who was his uncle. Culley swung uncertainly to his feet, his gaze suspicious of the boy with his sister. "This is my son, Ty." She introduced Ty and prodded him with a speaking smile. "This is your Uncle Culley."

"How do you do, sir." Ty stiffly extended his hand, but Culley didn't notice it as he inspected him with a probing stare that increased her son's unease—and Maggie's.

"Culley?" She nervously prompted him to say something, a little frightened of his long silence.

"Come away from him, Maggie," Culley ordered and held out his hand to take hers, not letting his gaze leave the tall boy. She hesitated, then placed her hand in his to let him pull her away. "Look at him," her brother insisted with burning eyes. "Can't you see it? He's a Calder!"

She felt the rapid beating of her pulse and tried to sway Culley from his condemnation with the cool, reasonable tone of her voice. "He is my son."

He pulled her around and grabbed her by the shoulders to hold her still. "It's *his* son! Can't you see it?" The words carried him on. "Why did you bring him back? Why didn't you get rid of him? Don't you see, Maggie? Now there are two of them! They are just as strong as they were before! You've got to come away with me tonight, Maggie! You've got to help me get back at them for what they did! You finally came back to help me, didn't you? We've got to get even with them for what they did!"

Her eyes stung with tears as she saw how hatred had destroyed her brother, blinding him to everything but his obsession for getting revenge on the Calders. He fed on it instead of food, slept with it instead of rest, breathed it like poisoned air. He had never let the wound heal, and now it had infected his soul.

"Oh, Culley," she whispered brokenly. "Why didn't you come to California with me?"

Maggie was unaware that behind her, Chase had nodded to one of his men, indicating he wanted Ty escorted from the house before his presence precipitated a violent incident. She gazed at the fine glimmer of sweat on Culley's forehead, a glimpse of the hell living inside him.

"I had to stay!" His voice lifted to a breaking pitch in answer to her question. "You've got to come with me, Maggie! I need help!"

She groaned, because he did. His hands squeezed her shoulders together. The pain it caused gave her a hint of the forces pressing and pulling at him. She sank her teeth into her lower lip to keep from crying out a protest at the way he was hurting her. Then it wasn't needed, as Buck and the other cowboy came up behind him, taking him firmly by the arms and forcing him to release her. It was a second before Culley realized what was happening and began struggling to get loose. She took an instinctive step toward him, wanting to help him in some way, but a pair of hands closed on the curved points of her shoulders. Chase was behind her.

As his image appeared to stand beside Maggie, Culley began shouting. "You let her go! You aren't going to keep her here! I'll get her away from you and send her far away from here, like I did before! You can't keep her! Do you hear me, Calder?!!"

"No. You hear me, Culley." His hard voice was clear and strong. "I can't stop Maggie from visiting her brother, but don't you ever set foot on Calder land again." There was an ominous ring to the cold warning. Then Chase was addressing his friend and foreman. "Buck, escort him off the property and don't leave him until he's off the Triple C."

Twisting Culley's arms high in the middle of his back, the two men frog-marched him out of the house to his truck. "I'll ride with O'Rourke and make sure he doesn't get any funny ideas between here and the main gate," Buck said. "You follow us, Dave."

"Right."

Maggie didn't resist the pressure from the hands that turned her away from the front door. She looked up to the grim male countenance.

"I meant it. I don't ever want him on Calder land again," Chase repeated.

"He's my brother."

"That's why he *walked* out of here." His hands tightened, as if he wanted to shake her into realizing the restraint that had been exercised. Control came to the front again, running a muscle along his jawline. "I can't stop you from seeing him outside this ranch. I don't think he'd ever hurt you, but I saw the way he looked at Ty."

Fear choked her for an instant because she had seen it, too, and it had frightened her. "He needs help."

The mute appeal in her green eyes reached out to Chase. "I know." He gathered her gently into his arms, letting her head rest against his chest. His jaw brushed the sleek curls along the side of her hair. "But there is nothing you can do for him, Maggie. It's professional help he needs." He rubbed his hand over her back. His intent was to comfort and reassure her, but he was also feeling the womanly contours of her slender shape. It stirred the desires that had slept within him. As if she sensed the change, she moved out of his arms, and Chase let her go. "I'll go see Doc Barlow tomorrow and ask him to stop out one evening to talk to Culley. Maybe your brother will listen to him," he suggested, noticing that she was avoiding his eyes.

"Yes." It was a level agreement, without feeling or speculation. She moved toward the staircase. "Good night." That was flat, too, drained of emotion.

"Maggie?" The low urgency of his voice brought her head up sharply. She looked fragile and breakable. "Are you all right?"

She wavered, then nodded coolly, "Yes."

When she had disappeared up the staircase, Chase let himself silently out of the house and stood on the porch, where the coolness of the night air washed over him.

It was mid-morning before Chase was able to squeeze some free time out of his schedule. The honking of a truck horn stopped him near the commissary. He turned, impatient with the delay, and saw Nate behind the wheel of a pickup, his head sticking out the window.

"The kid is cleaning out the stud barns this morning!" he called.

A smile slanted his mouth as he sketched the old foreman a salute. That old man had a way of reading his mind. He altered his course for the isolated stable where the ranch stallions were kept separate from the other horses. Ty was leaning against a sturdy fence, a boot resting on the lowest board and his arms crossed on the top rail. A wheelbarrow full of manure and straw was beside him. Chase slowed his steps to study the confused and faintly dejected profile of his son. When he came up beside him, he deliberately fixed his gaze on the claybank horse inside the corral, as if it really was the object of Ty's thoughts.

"The stallion is quite an animal, isn't he?" Chase remarked, aware of Ty's guilty start at being caught loafing on the job.

"Yes, sir."

"Cougar was my father's personal mount, and probably the best cutting horse we have on the place. He passes that cow sense onto his get. That's what makes him such a good breeding stallion." He studied the whitening muzzle of the heavy-jawed stallion.

"Does anybody ever ride him anymore?" Ty asked with only an idle interest.

"No. I retired him to stud when my father died and left the ranch to me." Chase paused and continued in the same conversational tone. "It's natural to be upset and confused about what happened last night, Ty."

The boy looked surprised, then scuffed the toe of his boot in the dirt. "Why does he hate me?"

"He doesn't know you, so it isn't you he hates—it's what you represent." It had been difficult for him to accept when he was young. It wouldn't be easier for Ty. "You are a Calder."

"Why should he hate a Calder?" The answer didn't make sense to him. His frown deepened as he watched his father lean down and pick up a handful of gravel, sifting through it.

"If a man is walking along and falls down, he automatically looks to see what caused him to fall." Chase reached down again and picked up a large chunk of gravel. "Will he blame this big rock—or this small pebble?" He showed his son the two different-sized stones in the leather-covered palm of his hand.

"The rock." It was obvious.

"Because it's the biggest. So it always gets blamed. But who is to say that this small pebble wasn't under the rock, and when it moved, it forced the rock to move?"

"I guess it could," Ty admitted.

"When things go wrong for some men in this area of the state, they look around for someone to blame. There sit all those square miles of the Triple C, so much bigger than anything else around it. We get blamed. Maybe cattle prices go down. All the other little ranchers point at us because we glutted the market, they claim." He observed his son's frown turn to thoughtfulness. "When you are big and prosperous, there are always some who want to cut you down. They move . . . and the rock moves. Sometimes, the rock falls on the pebble. That's when resentment can turn to hate."

"What happened to make my uncle hate us?" Ty looked up from the stones Chase held and searched his face.

"It's a collection of things, Ty. Some of it goes back to his father and mine, and to your mother. After I took over the ranch, Culley and I had a run-in. It's a very long story, but he believes that he has a good reason to hate the Calders. And there are some who would agree with him," Chase added with a slight lift of one shoulder. "The thing for you to remember, Ty, is that when somebody hates you, don't take it personally. It isn't a condemnation of you as an individual, so don't go around thinking there is something wrong with you. Just do what you believe is right and fair, and let the others look at it as they will."

"Yeah," he sighed, a grim resignation stealing across his expression. Chase closed his gloved hand around the two stones, then tossed them to the ground.

"Don't you think you'd better get to work?" he suggested.

"Right." Ty pulled a grin across his mouth and turned to the wheelbarrow. Chase watched him for a second before his own duties called him.

Maggie was surprised at how quickly she settled back into the routine of ranch life. Within two short weeks, it was as if she had been away only a few short months, instead of sixteen years. She rose with the sun and had breakfast on the table when Ty and Chase came down. Ruth had gladly relinquished the kitchen chores to Maggie, although she still helped with the housecleaning.

But it was more than just cooking meals and keeping house, something that had been Pamela's responsibility to supervise when Maggie had been married to Phillip. The ranch terminology and Western lingo all came back to her, slipping naturally into her talk. Within two afternoon rides, she had adjusted from English riding to the less-structured Western style. There were brief moments when she was out riding that she actually forgot she hadn't always lived amidst this vast openness.. During her rides, she gradually noticed less of the raw beauty and paid more attention to down-to-earth matters like the condition of the grass or fences, and the amount of water around. These observations she would absently pass along to Chase in the course of a meal's conversation.

Three times she had ridden to her brother's without finding him home. These, she didn't mention to Chase. It was difficult to describe her relationship with Chase. She rarely saw him, except at mealtimes. He spent the evenings in the den with an endless array of paperwork that couldn't be handled by his accounting help, since it required his personal attention. On the whole, they were civilized, with brief moments when they actually relaxed in each other's company, and other times when their conversations were stilted and forced. The latter occurred when Maggie couldn't pretend that he didn't exist and she wasn't wearing his wedding band. Invariably, it coincided with the times when she yearned to be held and touched—and the natural, biological urges of her body were going unsatisfied. It wasn't easy to look at him then and not remember other days when he had taken care of those needs so thoroughly. To make matters worse, Chase was so damned attractive in that raw, range-toughened way of a Calder.

Seeing him every day and watching him with Ty, it was getting harder and harder to summon her old dislike and have it come with the fierce intensity of before. On the nights she couldn't sleep, she would lie in bed and deliberately compare Chase to Phillip: Phillip, with his fine manners, impeccable dress, and courtly charm, versus Chase, with his blunt authority, rough clothes, and raw earthiness. With Phillip, she had been emotionally safe. With Chase, she wasn't.

The long horseback rides in the afternoons functioned to fill time and get away from the Calder influence of the house. She never admitted it was hard exercise she sought so she would be tired enough in the evenings to fall asleep. Dressing every night for dinner was an attempt to keep alive the link to her past marriage, when it was the custom, not a desire to impress Chase.

Rain threatened off and on all day, keeping her in the house. So Maggie concentrated her efforts on fixing a special dinner that evening. She had sought out Tucker at the cook-shack and asked him to slice a prime-rib roast from one of the carcasses kept in the big cooler for ranch consumption. All the accompanying dishes she chose had been favorites of Phillip's—from the broiled grapefruit appetizer to the baby peas and pearl onions in a light cream sauce. Even the dress she wore had been one he had particularly liked, a silk dress of a bold peacock-blue with a green-colored design.

At the end of a day's work, Chase always showered before sitting down to dinner. As a concession to her habit of dressing for the evening meal, he usually wore a white shirt, but it was open at the throat and the cuffs were rolled back to reveal flat, wide wrists and hair-roughened forearms. Ty copied him.

It was the same that evening when the pair entered the dining room. Chase barely glanced at her as he noticed the table, set with good china, wine goblets, and the heavy silver candleholders. He moved to the chair at the head of the table, raising a questioning eyebrow in her direction.

"What's the occasion?" he asked.

"No occasion," she insisted cooly, then went to the kitchen to bring out the grapefruit appetizer.

Maggie was fully aware that while Ruth Haskell had been a very good cook, she was unimaginative. Her meals had always been variations of the same thing: soup, beef, potatoes, vegetables, and dessert. So when Maggie set the broiled grapefruit half in front of Chase, she observed the faint surprised lift of his eyebrow, but he made no comment about the change in fare. He didn't even say whether he liked it or not, which vaguely irritated her. Nor did he remark on the salad, made with fresh spinach she had picked from Ruth's garden. The dressing was made from a recipe Maggie had gotten from Phillip's cook. No appreciation was expressed for the variety she had managed to inject into their diet, or her cooking skills.

The prime rib had turned out perfectly—juicy, rare, and tender. When she served Chase his main course, he stared at it. "This meat isn't done."

"Of course it is. Prime rib is supposed to be served rare." She glanced at her son. "Would you pass the horseradish sauce, please?"

As Ty started to reach for the silver sauceboat, Chase stated, "I prefer my meat well done. Would you take it back into the kitchen and finish cooking it?" The question was an order.

"I will not!" She refused sharply because she had gone to such effort to have everything turn out perfectly, including the prime rib.

Folding his napkin beside his plate, Chase pushed his chair away from the table and stood. Maggie frowned at him. "What are you doing?"

"If you won't cook it, I will," he said, then walked toward the kitchen, carrying his plate.

She stared after him for a stunned instant. Then she was on her feet, angrily hurrying after him. She reached the kitchen as he forked his prime rib onto the broiler pan and put it in the oven.

"Do you realize how much trouble I went to tonight?" Her voice trembled with her effort to control her temper. "I worked so hard to make everything come out just right, and you're ruining it!"

"You should have remembered I like my beef well done."

"You like? You have absolutely no taste?" Her jaw was clenched tight. "You would have been happy with steak and potatoes."

His hands were on his hips as he regarded her. "I had a feeling all this was leading up to something. Why else would there be this display of gourmet skills?"

"As if you have ever tasted anything but burned steaks," she taunted.

His gaze narrowed. "For you information, I've had better broiled grapefruit in Dallas, and the dressing for the salad had too much vinegar." His criticism stopped her short. "I don't object to variety. And I don't object to the unusual. But the next time you want to show off, don't do it with your nose in the air, thinking you are the only one who knows what is good. And don't forget—I like my meat well done!"

She whirled away from him, stinging from his remarks because they were true. She had wanted to prove he knew nothing about fine cuisine. She had wanted the chance to be condescending, patronizing. She had wanted to be better than he was, so he would be less worthy of her notice. She had wanted him to be the country bumpkin, while she was the lady. But now she was the one coming away from the encounter smarting.

As she entered the dining room, she met Ty on his way out, the plate with his slice of prime rib in his hand. "Where are you going with that?"

He shrugged uncomfortably. "I've never eaten prime rib when it was well done. I thought I'd try it."

"But you always like it rare," she protested. This seemed the final defection.

"I've never had it any other way, so how do I know it's the only way I like it?" he reasoned.

And Maggie was helpless to argue against that. She ate her rare beef alone, while her husband and son waited in the kitchen for their meat to cook to well done.

Chapter XXXI

The bay gelding pulled at the bit, dancing sideways in its eagerness to reach the barns, but Maggie held it down to a fast walk as they entered the ranch yard. She saw Tucker wave to her from the back door of the cookhouse and motion that he wanted to speak to her. She reined the protesting horse toward him, the bay unwilling to be turned away from the bars and the waiting grain.

"Hi." She stopped the horse and swung out of the saddle when she reached Tucker. A brisk ride had brought color to her cheeks and rumpled the black hair curling out from under her hat.

"Culley sent word that he wanted to meet you at four o'clock by the east gate of the north range." Tucker wasted no time passing on the message. "Take the keys to my truck. It's the green one. You'll just have time to make it. I'll take care of your horse."

A quick glance at her watch confirmed his statement, and she handed him the reins to her horse and took the keys he offered. The full impact of the message didn't hit her until she had turned onto the ranch road that branched to the north. Culley asked to meet her on the north range—where she and Chase used to meet, Calder property. And Chase had warned him not to set foot on his land.

Her toe pressed the accelerator down and the speedometer needle swung to fifty-five. She was suddenly frightened by the risk her brother was taking, deliberately defying Chase . . . as her father had defied his father's warning. A dust cloud plumed behind the speeding truck as she raced along the road.

When she approached the north range, the sight of a horse and rider cantering across an open stretch slowed her down. For an instant, Maggie thought the slender rider was her brother, and she knew another moment of fear that he was riding so openly across Calder land. Then she recognized Buck Haskell. Thankfully, he was riding in the opposite direction from the east gate. She breathed a sigh of relief.

There was no sign of Culley when she reached the designated meeting place. She climbed out of the truck and glanced at her watch. She was five minutes late. Had he left when she didn't show up on time? She hoped so.

Tall poles flanked both ends of the gate, standing high to mark where the fence gate was located so a rider could aim for it while he was still some distance away. Maggie climbed to the second highest rail to see if Culley was still in sight and used the tall pole at one end to keep her balance.

A shrill whistle came from the trees near the winding river. Maggie looked to her right and saw the horse and rider standing in the shadows. Culley waved his hat to her. She swung a leg across the top rail, finding a toehold on the same board from the opposite side. Quickly she brought the other leg over and hopped to the ground. She hurried quickly across the open ground to the trees.

"What are you doing here, Culley? I saw Buck Haskell riding south of here. If he finds you—"

"Don't worry about him." He brushed aside her concern. "He's long gone, headed for the ranch." There was a rashness about him; she could see it in his eyes. "I knew you'd come."

"You sent for me. Of course, I came." She tried to calm down her own jittery nerves before she attempted to reason with him and convince him to leave before somebody discovered them.

"You may be married to Calder, but your family is still important to you." He said it fiercely, as if needing the reassurance of her loyalty.

"You are important to me. Except for Ty, you're the only family I have."

He grabbed her shoulders again, as he had done that night at the house, and looked deep into her eyes. "Why do you stay there? Why don't you come home where you belong?"

"I can't leave my son. Ty is only fifteen. Culley, he needs me."

"But he's no good. He's a Calder. Leave him, Maggie. Leave

him before it's too late. You've got to get away from there. I don't want you getting mixed up with this."

"Mixed up with what? What are you talking about?" She frowned, worried by the intensity of his voice.

There was an impatient shake of his head at the interruption of her questions. "You've got to trust me, Maggie. Didn't I do the right thing when I sent you away from here before?"

"Yes, but—"

"Then trust me now," he urged. "I know Calder married you, but he doesn't care about you. He only did it because he wanted his son. He already has a mistress in town, so what does he want with you? I tried to tell Sally that he would hurt her, but she wouldn't listen to me—just like you wouldn't listen to me a long time ago. But I was right. You've got to listen to me now, Maggie. He'll hurt you. When all this starts, he'll turn on you."

Everything about her brother was quick and restless, his mood swinging from angry demand to lame pleas in the span of a few seconds. This wild fluctuation alarmed Maggie, although she tried not to show it.

"I'm listening to you," she assured him. "But why don't you trust me, Culley? You keep telling me I'll get hurt when all this starts, but you won't tell me what's going to happen. How come you won't trust me?"

"I can't tell you, don't you see?" A vein stood out sharply on his forehead as he continued urgently. "Until you're off his ranch for good, I can't take the chance that Calder might find a way to make you talk. You've got soft living in the city, Maggie. You're used to being wrapped in cotton wool and treated like a lady. You've forgotten how to be a woman out here."

"I may have forgotten a few things"—like the binding promise inherent in a man's word, or how strong the basic needs are between a man and woman—"but I'm not soft, Culley."

The hard lines loosened around his mouth, permitting a fleeting smile. "Maybe not. But you've got to leave this place. We're finally going to get even with the Calders for hanging our pa. We've got a plan."

"We? Is Tucker in on this?" There was surprise in her voice, because she had believed Tucker had put all that away.

He gave her a bright glance, turning sly. "There's no way to get to Calder from the outside. But from the inside, his belly is exposed. We'll get him this time. But you've got to leave before it all starts happening. There isn't much time."

"When will it start?" she asked.

"Soon," was all he would say. "You have to leave, Maggie. I want you away, where you'll be safe. You think because he married you that everything will be all right, but it won't be. It never will be until Calder is in his grave."

"Culley—" She was suddenly very frightened—frightened for him and frightened for Chase. Yet, in her heart, she couldn't believe that her brother intended to kill Chase. It had only been a figure of speech. Not even in his wildest moment would he be capable of such a violent act. "Culley"—she started again in a more controlled voice, veering away from the subject—"I saw Doc Barlow in town the other day." She lied, because it was Chase who talked to him. "He mentioned that he planned to stop out and see you some evening. Did he come by?"

"Yeah." He released her. Maggie's shoulders tingled where he had gripped them so hard. "He stopped by last week, said I looked tired and overworked and wanted me to come to his office so he could examine me. He claimed there were pills he could give me to help me rest better at night."

"There are," Maggie insisted.

"I thought you'd understand." He looked at her grimly. "I don't want to rest until I've settled the score with Calder." He walked to his horse and stepped into the saddle. "Don't stay there, Maggie. I can't look out for you the way I should when you're there." He turned his horse and rode into the trees, ducking a low-hanging branch.

That night, she barely had time to change for dinner before Chase arrived home. She said very little during the meal and ate even less. The urge was strong to tell Chase of her meeting with Culley, to warn him, but there was her brother to consider. Maybe he hadn't meant anything he said. Maybe he'd just been talking. Outwardly, she looked very calm and quiet, but inside she was a mass of uncertainty. How could she stop her brother when she didn't know what he was going to do, or even if he was going to do anything?

Chase walked onto the porch, dusting off his clothes with his hat. A series of minor irritations that day had left him in a foul mood. Not that he had been in the best of moods this last week. Maggie had been giving him the silent treatment, barely talking at all.

Inside the house he paused, listening, but no sound greeted him. It was early. Maggie was probably still out riding. He'd like to know where she went on her rides . . . and who she met—if it was her brother, or someone else. She had stopped mentioning what the conditions were in the particular section of range she had ridden, which is what made him suspect she had something else on her mind while she was out there.

The unanswered questions, the half-formed suspicions sat in his mind, working on him, until every other thought he had was about her. He had told her from the beginning that she was free—that she could come and go as she pleased; the marriage was a mere formality to ensure his claim on Ty, so he had no grounds to demand an accounting of her activities when she was away from him. The possibility that she was meeting a man other than her brother awakened feelings in him that were akin to jealousy.

With telephone calls to make, he entered the den, but he walked to the bar instead of the desk and poured a straight shot of whiskey. He bolted half of it down, starting a backfire that he hoped would burn out the smoldering coals of his jealousy. He sprawled in a leather chair, leaning his head back to stare at the stone fireplace. He lit a long cheroot and nursed it between his lips. Had any of his ancestors endured marriages with separate bedrooms? If a man couldn't keep his wife home, he wasn't much of a man. But he'd given his permission.

All taut energy lay inside him, with no release, all the frustrations of wanting without the right to possess, because he'd given it away. He downed the rest of his drink and rolled to his feet with an animal-like tension. After taking one step toward the bar, Chase stopped. Getting drunk wasn't the answer. He shoved the glass onto a tabletop and pivoted. Work. Fill his mind with other thoughts. Exhaust his body until it was unaware of any physical need but sleep.

He walked to the desk to make those phone calls and stopped short with his hand on the back of the swivel chair. All the color drained from his face. Lying in the middle of the desk was a miniature noose made from white string. It was exact in detail, right down to the nine wraps that formed the hangman's knot.

How had it gotten there? Who had put it there? Who would know the significance? Only a handful, and most of that number Chase could dismiss. That left only three—Maggie, Culley and Tucker. Maggie was his wife, but she couldn't be eliminated from the list. A cold rage filled him. Once he had believed her innocent of the rustling, but she had known about it—taken part in one raid.

The front door closed, and he turned his head toward the sound. He heard the footsteps—light, even-paced strides. It was Maggie. He'd listened to her walk often enough during his evenings working in the den. He walked to the open double doors.

"Maggie?" His peremptory tone stopped her midway across the living room, her Stetson swinging in her hand. She looked tired and flushed from her ride. When she turned, he noticed the way her high breasts pushed out the front of the cotton blouse. "Would you come in here a minute? I want to talk to you."

She agreed in that quiet, concise manner that provoked him with its aloofness. "Of course." She came toward him, combing a hand through her hair that curled nearly to her shoulders.

He waited until she was at the door before he turned to escort her to the desk. Out of the corner of his eye, he saw the first tremor of shock and turned to observe her reaction. She had halted, her widened gaze locked on the miniature noose while her face turned ghostly pale. That was a reaction no actress could fake. She hadn't known it was there, he realized, or she would have been better prepared. What anger remained in him was directed toward himself for doing this to her.

"Maggie." His voice was sharp to break the morbid spell of the noose.

Her gaze jerked to him, tears welling in her eyes. "Is this your idea of some cruel practical joke?" She choked on the bitter words.

"I had to find out if you knew about it." He walked to the bar to pour her a drink and she followed him partway.

"If *I* knew about it?" Her fingers were pressed to her breastbone, emphasizing her words as she demanded an explanation.

"Yes. That was left on the desk for *me* to find—not you. Drink this." He extended a shot glass of whiskey to her.

She waved it aside with an impatient gesture. "I don't want it.

You mean someone—" She frowned and didn't complete the sentence.

"Yes."

"But who could have—" She stopped again.

"The list of possibilities is very short." Chase studied the shot glass still in his hand, lifting his gaze to catch hers. "Have you seen your brother lately?"

She moved to a window, staring out of it and clasping her hands in front of her. "Yes, I've seen him."

"Do you remember anything he said?"

"He said a lot of wild things, but he's always talked about getting even. Even in his letters, he was always mentioning it. He never did anything, though—not in all this time."

"That hangman's rope is more than just talk."

"I know." She looked down at her hands. "He's my brother, Chase. I'm worried about him."

"His scare tactics—or whatever he wants to call them—won't work. You can tell him that for me," he said grimly.

She turned her head to look at him, a certain desperation in her otherwise calm expression. "I don't want anything to happen to him."

His nostrils flared in contained anger. "Do you give a damn what happens to me?"

"Of course I do!" The blazing fires in her eyes burned him. For a minute Chase thought he had gotten through to the old Maggie. Then they were contained with cool control. "I care about any human being."

"Do you?" he mocked as she looked out the window again. "Sometimes I wonder." He caught the movement of her hands and glanced down to see her turning her wedding band around and around on her finger. "Is the ring too loose?" His symbolic thought was to make it tighter and cut off all circulation.

"No." She glanced down, as if not previously realizing what she was doing. "I'm just used to my husband's ring."

"I am your husband." His mouth was a tight white line.

A stillness settled over her. "Yes." It was a quiet affirmation. Then she was lifting her head, so cool and poised that he wanted to shake her. "Excuse me. I need to shower and change before I fix your dinner." She moved away without looking at him and left the room.

Chase listened to the footsteps carrying her away from him. As Maggie climbed the stairs, he drank down the shot of whiskey he'd poured for her and gripped the empty glass. In a surge of anger, he hurled it at the fireplace, where it crashed and splintered in the blackened hearth.

The next morning, Maggie was dusting the furniture in the living room while Ruth ran the dustmop over the tiled floor. She heard Chase come in but didn't look around, presuming he would go to the den. It was several seconds before she felt the touch of his gaze on her and realized he was watching her. She turned suddenly, surprising him and catching the hard-biting hunger in his look before he wiped it away. There was a swift, hot rise of her pulse, disturbed by that glimpse of his needs.

"I'll be away from the ranch today, so I won't be here for lunch," he said. "I may be late coming home. If I'm not here by seven, don't hold up dinner for me."

"All right." She kept her voice even. Instead of the regular ranch clothes, he was dressed in a Western-cut suit and white shirt, tailored to fit his long, muscled frame. The effect was one of power and authority—and an ease in shouldering it.

He seemed on the verge of saying something else, then changed his mind as he looked at Ruth. Donning a cream-colored Stetson, he turned and walked to the door. As it closed behind him, Maggie released the breath she had unconsciously been holding and bent to finish dusting an end table.

"Have you quarreled?" The question from Ruth stiffened Maggie.

"No, of course not," she denied, deliberately casual.

The small silence that followed revealed that Ruth Haskell did not fully believe the marriage was without problems. "Try to be understanding, Maggie," she said finally. "Running the Triple C is a lonely job, with an enormous amount of pressure and responsibility. I recall that Lillie—Webb's wife—used to tell me it demanded that Webb be more than a man. And the only time he could be 'just a man' was when they closed the bedroom door at night."

The intimacies—the confidences that a man and wife shared— were something that made Maggie uncomfortable. Chase was her husband. Despite her slip yesterday, that was the way she thought of him. It was this that compounded her fear about what Culley might be planning.

"Chase is the heart of the Triple C. He pumps life to the farthest reaches of the ranch, ties it all together, and keeps it healthy," Ruth continued quietly. "The heart has to be strong and good. A Calder is a special breed of man, Maggie. And it takes a special breed of woman to stand at his side. I wasn't sure at first, but you are that kind." There was a gentle curve to her mouth. "I know you know about Sally Brogan. A woman always knows about the other woman in her husband's life. She is a gentle, loving person who served a need in his life—gave him a quiet place to go and an undemanding affection. But she is like me, a shadow destined to remain in the background. You are like Chase, able to stand in the sunlight, letting it glare on your flaws and shine on your assets. You belong in this house the same way Lillie did." She suddenly realized how much she had talked while Maggie remained silent. Her expression became rueful and apologetic. "I'm sorry. I probably shouldn't be saying all this, but Chase is like my own son. I raised him and . . . I want him to be happy. I know you have what it takes to make him very happy."

Maggie murmured a suitable response and tried not to think about what the woman had said, but the words lingered as she continued with the housework, instilling her with an unconscious pride of possession that hadn't existed before. She found herself rearranging furniture, letting her personality assert its influence on the house. It didn't occur to her that, in effect, she was allowing her role as mistress to assume certain permanence. Too many of her conscious thoughts were spent worrying about the miniature noose and what kind of threat it might signify. That afternoon she rode the hills of the Shamrock Ranch searching for her brother without success, her hope to dissuade him from carrying out his unknown plans unrealized.

Chase wasn't home by seven that evening. When Ty came downstairs after showering and changing clothes, he noticed the table was set for only two, and the place at the head of the table was bare.

"Where's Dad?"

"He said not—" Maggie faltered, realizing how automatically Ty had referred to Chase as his father—and how automatically she had known to whom he was referring. "He said not to wait for him for dinner. He had business away from the ranch today, so he could be late."

"He'll probably eat at Sally's," Ty decided and pulled out his chair to sit down.

The mention of the other woman hit a raw nerve. Maggie suddenly remembered the desire that had been in Chase's eyes that morning before he'd left. He had needs that she, as his wife, hadn't fulfilled. She was suddenly tormented with images of Chase in the arms of the red-haired widow. It was crazy, but it was true, nevertheless. She was jealous.

Chapter XXXII

It was nearly ten o'clock in the evening when she went upstairs to her bedroom. She wasn't tired, but Chase hadn't returned yet and she didn't want to give him the impression that she was waiting up for him. So she tossed and turned sleeplessly in her bed, watching the luminous hands of the clock on the bedside table tick off the minutes.

A little before eleven, Maggie heard the car drive into the ranch yard. She knew it was Chase—just as she knew where he had been all this time and who he'd been with. The hurt that caused her was disguised as the anger of disgust.

Tired from the long session with the attorneys and the long drive, Chase was rankled by the sight of the darkened house; not a single light shone. Maggie could have at least left a light on for him. There was a flatness to him as he climbed the porch steps and crossed to the door. He hadn't eaten, but the prospect of raiding the refrigerator and eating alone in the kitchen didn't appeal to him.

He entered the house and didn't bother to turn on a light. He could find his way to the stairs in the dark. Two steps into the living room, he crashed into a table, cracking his kneecap on the corner of a leg and tipping the table over. Whatever was on top of it clattered to the floor. Grabbing his knee and cursing, Chase lurched sideways and bumped into a chair that had no business being where it was, either.

The racket from below brought Maggie out of bed. It sounded like someone was down there knocking things over. Grabbing her robe in alarm, she rushed out of the bedroom and paused at the head of the stairs to flip the wall switch that turned on the light above the staircase. She heard the muffled swearing, but she didn't see Chase crouched over in the living room shadows until she reached the landing. Her first thought was that he was drunk. Then he looked up and saw her, poised on the landing.

"What's going on down here?" she demanded in icy anger, viewing the table and broken vase in front of him.

"I ran into that damned table!" He released his knee long enough to gesture at the fallen table.

"Why didn't you turn on a light so you could see where you were going instead of crashing into things and waking up the whole house?" she snapped.

"I didn't think I needed a light!" His voice was just as tight and just as angry. "What the hell was the table doing in the middle of the floor?"

"I re-arranged the furniture—that's what it's doing there!" Maggie retorted.

"There was nothing wrong with the way the furniture was arranged! That table and chair had been sitting in that corner for more than thirty years!"

Her hand moved to her hip in challenge. "Then it's time it was moved!" The robe whirled about her ankles as she pivoted to climb the steps.

"Come back here!" he ordered, but Maggie just went up the stairs more quickly. "Don't you walk away from me!" He started after her, tripping over the table leg and swearing savagely.

Maggie had never seen him so angry before. She was suddenly alarmed at what he might do if he caught up with her. She heard him coming after her and ran the last few steps to her bedroom door, hurrying inside and turning the lock. Then she stepped away from it and held her breath. She didn't want him near her. She didn't want to smell another woman's perfume on his skin or know that his hands had touched someone else earlier that night. Every part of her rebelled at the thought.

There was no thought in his mind beyond catching her and putting down this insurrection in his home. He grabbed the doorknob, but it wouldn't yield to the pressure of his hand. The realization that she had locked the door ran through him like a white-hot knife. There were enough barriers between them without a locked door added to them.

His fist pounded on it. "Maggie! Open this door!" The command was a low roar.

"Go away!"

"You unlock this door, or I swear I'll break it in!" he warned and rattled the knob again.

This time there was no reply, only silence from within. He leaned a shoulder against it and pushed, but nothing happened and he cursed the solidness of the door. Once he'd made his intention clear, he couldn't back down. Stepping back, he kicked at the center of the door near the lock. It shook and held. With the second kick, Chase heard the faint splintering of wood. Putting all his force behind the blow, he kicked at the door again and felt the sickening give of the wood. When his boot hit the same weakened area again, there was a ripping sound as the metal lock was torn out of the frame and door whipped open.

Breathing heavily from the exertion, he saw Maggie standing well back from the door holding onto the bedpost that was behind her back. A wariness blazed from her. The satin gown was molded to her figure, outlining the taut nipples of her breast, the little hollow of her belly button, and the exciting vee where her legs came together. She was his wife. The knowledge rose hot within him, arousing him beyond the point of remembering any promise.

Maggie read it in his eyes, but, however much his look aroused the same sweeping passion, her pride wouldn't let her accept him when he'd come here from the arms of another woman.

"Don't you come near me," she warned. "This is my room, and you have no right to be in it unless I invite you. And I don't want you to touch me!"

Her icy rejection was a slap at his manhood. Chase retaliated in kind, his lip curling in disdain. "What makes you think I would be interested?" He had the satisfaction of seeing her wince at his contemptuous reply. It soothed his bruised ego. "Just remember, there are no locked doors in this house." His warning had a figurative meaning, as well as a literal one. Maggie might "shut" him out of her life, but he would never permit her to "lock" him out.

Turning on his heel, he started toward his own room and

stopped when he saw Ty staring at him from the end of the hall. The bewildered look of alarm in his son's face washed away his rage. Chase shuddered inwardly when he realized how close he had come to raping Maggie—unaware that Ty was looking on. Tiredness swept through him, slumping his shoulders.

"Go to bed, son," he said in a voice weary with regret for the apprehension he'd caused. "It's all over." He saw Ty cast an anxious look toward Maggie's open, now unclosable, door. "I won't hurt her," Chase added. "I won't go near her tonight, so you can rest easy."

There was a glimmer of uncertainty in Ty's look, as if he had caught what Chase had not—he had said that he wouldn't go near her "tonight." But Ty accepted his father's word and retraced the steps to his bedroom. Chase continued slowly to his own room.

Dawn came in changing sheets of color. As the sun peered over a hill at the new day, Chase shaved and dressed. Ty was walking down the hall when he left his room. They nodded a good morning and continued toward the staircase. As they passed Maggie's room, where the broken door sagged open, Ty glanced inside and paused.

"Mom isn't up." He darted a questioning look at Chase.

His stride didn't falter as he passed the door, briefly glimpsing black hair against a white pillow. "Let her sleep. We'll fix our own breakfast."

After the meal, Ty left the house to do his morning chores, and Chase went to the ranch office to check the previous day's reports and make any last-minute adjustment's in the day's schedule for the crews. An hour later he returned to The Homestead. It was silent, nothing and no one stirring. He climbed the stairs to Maggie's room.

Crossing the threshold that he had not stepped past the night before, he walked to the bed to wake her up. Uncovered, she was lying on her stomach, her face turned toward the center of the bed. Chase looked at her sleeping form, the slim, white shoulders bare, except for the narrow straps of her nightgown. His gaze followed the smooth line of her spine, the satin material tracing its path past her slender waist to its culmination point. There, he became distracted by the heart-shaped roundness of her bottom, so arousingly defined by the clinging fabric.

He knew it was either slap it or kiss it. He slapped it, bringing the flat of his hand down sharply on a soft cheek. She woke up with a gasping cry of shock and rolled onto her side, facing him and protecting her vulnerable backside with her hand. Confusion, shock, anger, and sleep were all mixed in her expression as she pushed the weight of her rumpled hair away from her face.

"It's time to get up," he said, his gaze drifting to the front of her nightgown as it gaped open to show the curved slope of a breast.

She turned her head to see the morning sun shining in the window. Irritation set a frown on her features as she hurriedly swung her feet out of the bed. "Why didn't you wake me up earlier?"

"There's no need to rush. Ty and I have already had breakfast. We fixed our own."

"Why did you wait until now? You could have gotten me up before." She stood beside the bed, still slightly disoriented.

Chase was totally unnerved by the scene—Maggie standing there, all soft and rumpled from sleep, the turned-down covers of the bed behind her, and the emptiness of the house. He started out of the room while he still had the willpower to walk away.

"I thought you needed the rest," he said as his strides carried him toward the hallway. "I would have let you sleep longer, except one of my men will be over shortly to repair your door and I didn't think you'd want to be in bed when he came."

"What?" Her bare feet made little sound as she followed him into the hall, hurrying to keep up with him, an incredulous expression on her face. "What did you say?" she demanded.

Chase paused for only a second at the head of the stairs to glance over his shoulder. "George is a carpenter. He's going to fix your door." He was halfway down the first flight of stairs when her temper exploded over him.

"When he comes, you can just send him somewhere else on some other job!" she stormed.

He stopped and looked up. She was standing in the hallway above him, her hands gripping the protective railing around the stairwell. "The door has to be repaired."

"You broke it. You can fix it," she retorted.

"I have more important things to do." He started down the stairs again.

"Damn you, Chase Calder!" She rushed down the steps after him. "Did you tell that man how the door was broken?"

"No." He rounded the landing.

"You know what he's going to think when he sees it, don't you?" she demanded in hot anger.

When he reached the base of the stairs, he stopped to confront her and Maggie paused on the landing. "He'll guess that you locked your door and I kicked it in. That's what happened, Maggie." He eyed her with a cool challenge. "And that's all that happened."

"But his imagination won't stop there!" She was trembling, on the verge of losing control.

"I have no control over what else he might imagine," he replied.

"Don't you realize how embarrassing—how humiliating—it is for me to have some cowboy thinking that you broke my door down to get into my room last night?!" she stormed, then came down two more steps to where she was eye-level with the top of his head.

"It never occurred to you last night that I might find it humiliating to be locked out of my wife's room," Chase reminded her harshly. "It isn't so amusing when the tables are turned, is it? Too bad you didn't consider the possible consequences before you locked the door last night."

His gibe stung and her hand lashed out to strike his tanned cheek, the contact with his hard flesh jarring her arm. She had little time to enjoy the satisfaction of hitting him before her wrist was seized and she was jerked off balance, stumbling down to the bottom step, where the solid wall of his body checked her fall. A large hand was on her waist to hold and support her. The shock of being brought so abruptly and so firmly in contact with his muscled frame stunned her for an instant. The rough laugh that came from his throat lifted her head sharply to find him regarding her with a smoldering satisfaction that was lazy, yet hard.

"That fiery-tempered girl still lives behind all that polished sophistication, doesn't she?" He half-drawled the sentence. She started to struggle, but he held her easily, his hand spreading over her spine to press her closer. She stopped trying to fight free of his arms, because when she moved against him like that, it made her sharply aware of his male build and incited all her mating instincts. She stared at the shoulder seam of his shirt and tried to block from her mind all the disturbing sensations that attempted to crowd in. She felt his breath on her hair, and the palm of his hand rubbed the back of her shoulder while her own hands lay motionless on his chest.

"I had forgotten how little you are," he mused. "Strange." There was a trace of irony in his voice. "I remember so many things, yet I forgot that." His mouth moved against her hair, wandering downward toward her ear. Maggie lifted a shoulder, tucking the side of her face against it to prevent him from reaching his objective. His warm, male lips brushed her forehead while his hands roamed leisurely over her back and hips, testing the feel of her in his arms. The satin material of her nightgown was no barrier, able to shield her sensitive nerve ends from the force of his caressing hands. It was a second skin against her body, letting her feel every imprint of his fingers.

"Chase, please don't." But she knew he would pay no attention to her whispered protest. It was only her pride that wanted him to stop. All the rest of her wanted him to go on.

"We were so young, Maggie." His mouth grazed her cheekbone as he spoke. "So young and foolish. We didn't know the first thing about living. It was all sunshine and green grass for us—all smiles and kisses, with no tears or pain." Her eyes were shut as his mouth covered her lips in a sampling kiss, then left, taking a little of her breath.

"We can't go back, Chase. We can't find what we lost," she murmured.

"I don't want what we had in the past." He rubbed his mouth along her lips as he talked, stimulating her with its warmth and moistness. "I want to build on what we have today so there will be a tomorrow. We're married; we have a son; and I want you, Maggie." His voice was rough with longing. "Others have started a life together with less."

"There's so much against us," she reminded him huskily, even while her lips moved in invitation against his.

"Be my wife, Maggie. Let me touch you, hold you, sleep with you," he urged and let his mouth close slowly and surely on her lips.

He kissed her with experience, but he didn't rely on technique to arouse her. There was an element in the kiss that moved to a much more basic instinct—that primitive core that exists in all humans, the need to have a mate, a need that is both physical and emotional, a need Maggie had never had fulfilled. Her hands slid around the muscled column of his neck as she strained against him, trying to absorb and, in turn, be absorbed.

Chase dragged his mouth from hers, reluctantly, a disturbed heaviness to his breathing and a thick-lidded passion in his dark brown eyes. "That had better mean 'yes,' Maggie," he warned. "I can't keep breaking down locked doors. You've got to open one for me."

"Yes." She couldn't fight her instinctive feelings for him any longer. Right or wrong, a part of her had always belonged to him, so why hold back the rest now?

He kissed her hard and long, claiming what she was giving him and crushing her within his hold. When he finally moved to roughly nuzzle her throat, she was dazed and breathless, and trembling with the powerful force of her feelings. A distant part of her mind registered the sound of the front door opening, but its significance didn't click until she heard Buck Haskell's voice.

"Chase . . . uh . . . excuse me," he interrupted with a mocking insistence. "Are you ready to go yet?"

Chase almost turned to look at him, but once his head had lifted, he seemed unable to drag his gaze from her face. Maggie felt a similar fascination with his face, its expression so incredibly warm, melting features that were usually all hard bone and flesh, and the light in his dark eyes glittered so.

"I'm not going today, Buck," he said. "Tell George I won't be needing him." A half-smile lifted the corners of his mouth as her fingertip lightly traced the strong line of his jaw. "And pass the word that Mr. and Mrs. Calder are indisposed today—and aren't to be disturbed."

There was a slight pause before Buck replied with a slightly stiff and formal, "Yes, sir."

With the click of the closing door, Chase moved, bending slightly to slip an arm under the back of her legs and pick her up. She linked her hands around his neck and started nibbling on his neck, tasting his skin and the tangy after-shave lotion while he started up the stairs.

"Do you have any idea how many times I've wanted to carry you up these stairs in these past weeks?" he asked softly. "Or how hard it's been to walk past your door every night?"

She made an agreeing sound while her lips feathered the shell of his ear, her teeth taking a playful nip of the lobe. She was floating on a new emotional high that was languorous and lasting. When her half-closed eyes noticed they were entering her bedroom, she drew back slightly to lazily study his compelling profile.

"We can't shut the door," she reminded him.

"I know." He stopped, looking at her possessively. "I've had my fill of closed doors. Besides, I gave my word that I wouldn't expect you to share my bed—so I thought it would be best if we shared yours."

She laughed softly because he was keeping to the letter of his promise to her. Reaching up, she took off his hat and gave it a little toss. It landed on a chair.

"Be my guest," she murmured and curved her hand along his jaw to turn his head and draw his mouth toward hers.

The kiss was gentle and deep, more ravishing and seductive than hard passion. It was a slow-burning flame that melted them together as Chase let her feet slide to the floor and turned her against his length. His hands moved to slip the straps of her nightgown off her shoulders and slide them down her arms. Then they were against her flesh, pushing the clinging material down past her waist and over her hips. She gave a little twist of her hips to help shed the garment and heard his half-smothered groan at the movement. While his hands wandered over her naked curves in a sensual rediscovery, her fingers began working on the buttons of his shirt, unfastening them and tugging the tails free of his waistband. She helped him shrug out of the shirt to bare his chest to her touch. His flesh was hard and vital beneath her hands as she felt the raw energy rippling through his muscles. Abandoning her lips, his mouth traveled slowly to the curve of her neck, investigating the hollow of her shoulder. She arched closer, the dark cloud of his chest hairs brushing the sloping mounds of her breasts. The buckle of his belt scraped her tender flesh, causing her to flinch briefly before her hands moved to get rid of it.

As she unfastened the snap of his Levi's, he murmured against her throat. "It's easier if we get rid of the boots first. Where's the bootjack?"

"I don't have one." The fevered tremor in her voice brought his mouth to her lips in a hungry kiss before he slowly lifted his head. "I'll be your bootjack."

Her hands spread across his chest to push him backward and sit him on the edge of the bed. The small distance and new perspective gave him an overall view of her nude body, a sight his gaze admired openly. Under the stimulation of his look, her breasts seemed to swell, the nipples growing button-hard with desire. She almost forgot the purpose of the separation.

"Give me your foot," she said, and Chase leaned back on his hands, raising one leg.

She cupped the leather heel in her hand and turned, swinging a leg across his to straddle it and presenting him with a delectable view of her backside. She grasped the back of his boot with both hands, ready to pull when he pushed—only he didn't push. She glanced over her shoulder and saw him staring at her bottom.

"Ready?" she prompted him, flushing a little with embarrassed pleasure.

His mouth quirked slightly when he realized he had been caught looking. He lifted his other foot with a show of reluctance and placed it gently and carefully against one cheek. "It seems almost a crime to put a boot on something so round and shapely, but if a man had a bootjack like this, he'd be putting his boots on and taking them off all day long, just for the chance to enjoy the scenery."

She felt the hard imprint of his boot on her soft flesh as he pushed and she tugged at the boot in her hand, slipping it off. Then she repeated the procedure with the other boot, this time with a stockinged foot against her rump. As Maggie bent to set the boot beside its mate, a pair of hands caught hold of her hips and pulled her backward. Her gasping cry of surprise was a mixture of alarm and laughter as Chase planted a kiss on each rounded cheek of her bottom before he let her wiggle around to face him.

"Why haven't I ever noticed before what a beautiful bottom you have?" he demanded with mock gruffness and tilted his head back to meet her gaze. "Do you suppose I was too busy looking at your beautiful face?"

"Possibly," she conceded with a sharply twinkling look. "I noticed what a nice bottom you had that first time at the river." It was crazy how careless and carefree she had begun to feel. The intimacy was natural, spirited. Maggie didn't feel obliged to flirt or tease or be sexily provocative, which had all been a part of the foreplay with Phillip to manufacture passion through skill and technique.

"You noticed my bottom, did you?" Chase mocked and started to pull her closer, but she slipped out of his hold with a twist of her hips and knelt to pull off his socks.

As she stepped away to tuck them inside his boots, Chase stripped out of his jeans and shorts and half-turned on the bed to drape the Levi's over the far corner so nothing would fall out of his pockets. When she walked back toward the bed, he reached out to take her hand. She slipped her fingers into his large palm and let him pull her forward to stand between his legs. There was so much written in his eyes that she grew dizzy reading the sensual messages and swayed toward him.

A sun-browned hand slid up to hold the weight of a pure white breast and carry it to his mouth, where his tongue and teeth licked and played with the rosy crest. A heady weakness trembled through Maggie. Her fingers curled into the springing thickness of his hair, cupping the back of his head and pressing him more tightly to her breast. Then he was moving, the moist inside of his mouth seeking her other breast. Her limbs were weakening, forcing Maggie to brace her knees against the bed while she leaned more of her weight on Chase. Even that only helped for a short time; then she began sinking.

His arms caught her, twisting her and drawing her down to the bed. As she lay flat on her back, he shifted his position to bring his face level with hers. Lying on his side, he raised himself up on an elbow and looked at her while his stroking hand caressed her. She spread her fingers through the rough hairs on his chest.

"The other day Culley told me I had forgotten how to be a woman," she said softly and slanted him a glance through her lashes. "You were the first one to teach me how to be a woman, Chase. Will you show me again?"

His mouth lowered onto hers and kissed her with drugging insistence. He pulled her closer and levered himself onto her. She felt the stiffening muscle rising from his loins, hard and virile. She had a second to marvel at the physical differences of a man and a woman as his hands slid under her hips to lift them—and how perfectly God had made them to fit together and the awesome pleasure each could find in the enjoyment of the other, an enjoyment all the more beautiful and natural because it was born of emotional commitment to the other.

They were joined in a sweeping rush of sensation that engulfed them both. It bound them together with a wondrous urgency, a sexual brilliance that radiated between them. In the long-ago past, they had glimpsed this closeness, this raw demand, this insistence, little knowing that it could always be that way. That it could never be an end, because they could never know enough of it. Even now, all they could know was that they couldn't get enough of each other.

Chapter XXXIII

Snuggled against his chest, Maggie trailed her fingertips across Chase's flat stomach. The earthy warm smell of him was all around her, and she felt utter contentment.

"Are you asleep?" she murmured. The hand on her waist had stopped moving a couple of minutes ago. The rise and fall of his chest was steady.

A thumb and forefinger pinched the skin over her ribs. A faint yelp escaped her throat as she jerked from the fleeting pain. "Does that feel like I'm asleep?" His voice was low and deep, rumbling through his body beneath her ear.

"No," she admitted.

His right hand moved to stroke the back of her head, his fingers gliding into the dark curls to grab a handful and tug gently to force her head back. He looked down at her face, studying the features, as if memorizing the way they looked. With his left hand, he thoughtfully traced the curve of her chin.

"Will you believe me when I say that I experienced something that I never felt with any other woman when I made love to you just now?"

"Yes. It was different—special," she corrected, and she lowered her head when Chase eased the pressure on her hair. "For me, too. I never felt like this with Phillip."

There was a dismissing rush of breath. "Phillip was old enough to be your father."

In retaliation for that remark, Maggie pulled at the hair on his chest. He breathed in sharply and grabbed her hand. "Be careful when you imply that Phillip was too old to be a good lover. When I married him, he was only a few years older than you are now."

His hands gripped her shoulders and waist to lift her so that her head was lying on the pillow near his. The rawness of possession burned in his expression. "I would rather forget that you have had any lover other than me."

"Perhaps you would, but that isn't the case." She wouldn't let him attempt to erase Phillip from her memory. "He was good to me, Chase, when I needed someone very badly. Phillip was a good husband and a good father to Ty.

"Yes." Reluctantly, he smiled in grim resignation. Finding her left hand between them, he lifted it and kissed the gold band around her finger. "I am your husband now and Ty is our son. The papers will be ready next week to petition the court to legally change his name to Calder—with your permission, of course."

"When did you find that out?" she asked while he continued to keep her hand folded in his.

"Yesterday—at the attorney's."

"Is that where you were?" Part of the time, anyway, she thought, and studied his work-roughened hand.

"Yes." He rubbed his thumb across her fingers. "I seem to spend more time in offices and behind a desk than I do on a horse anymore, but I guess that goes with the territory. After being penned in with those attorneys all those hours, I wasn't in a very good mood when I came home last night. When I discovered you hadn't waited up for me or even left a light on, that didn't improve my disposition. And I hadn't had anything to eat since lunch, so—"

Her gaze lifted in surprise. His face was so close to hers, it was almost a blur. "Didn't you have dinner last night?"

"No."

"But I thought . . . even Ty said you'd probably stop at—" Maggie didn't say it because she didn't want him to know that she had been even briefly jealous. "There was food in the refrigerator. You should have fixed yourself something." She recentered her gaze on his hand.

"Where did you . . . and Ty . . . think I had dinner?" He was already guessing the answer. "You thought I ate at Sally's."

"It was a logical place," she admitted with a show of indifference. "I've heard she's a good cook."

His low chuckle held the hint of satisfaction. "You didn't like the idea, did you? So you re-arranged the furniture to set a trap for me."

"No." Maggie denied that. "I just thought it would look better if a few things were shifted around."

"But it bothered you just a little that I might have been with Sally last night," he said in a mocking tone that insisted she admit it.

"It was possible." She flashed him a look that dared him to deny it. "After all, it had been a long time since you'd had sex with anyone. I mean, you were here every night."

"So you thought I went to her because I wasn't getting it at home." There were lines slashed in his lean cheeks as he smiled at her. "I admit I was frustrated as hell, Maggie. When I told you I didn't care whether or not you shared my bed after we were married, I meant it. I wanted Ty, and I would have married the devil's own daughter to get him. But seeing you every day, the mother of my son, started me wanting. I seem to have an itch that only you know how to scratch. That's the way it was sixteen years ago, and that's the way it is now."

As he moved, she was pulled under him. He was heavy on her, the heat of his body burning her skin. "Scratch me, Maggie." It was a half-growl against her lips before his mouth crushed them. Her arms went around his broad, muscled back as the bedcovers were kicked aside.

It was nearly noon before either of them was inclined to get out of bed. Chase was the first to get up. Maggie stayed under the sheet and admired the hard, lean flanks of his backside as he pulled on his pants. He glanced over his shoulder. "Hungry?"

"A little." She swung out of bed on the opposite side and walked to the closet. "Are you?"

"Yes."

"I thought so." She slanted him a provocative look over her shoulder. "You have the hungriest eyes."

A knowing smile touched his mouth at her double meaning, a dark light dancing in his eyes. "Then fix me some food first, woman."

There was an easy intimacy between them all day, spiced with a running undercurrent of excitement. After lunch, Chase helped her clean up, warning her to take due note of his action, because she may never see him with a dish towel in his hands again. While she moved his clothes to her room, he began repairing the broken door, whistling as he worked.

When the job was finished and the mess cleaned up, he took a shower to freshen up. While he was in the bathroom, Maggie changed the sheets and made the bed.

She heard the shower stop and called, "Would you fill the tub with water for me, Chase? I want to take a bath."

His muffled response was affirmative, and seconds later she heard water running in the tub. She laid out clothes for each of them on the bed and slipped out of the short, cotton houserobe. When she entered the bathroom, the tub was billowing with scented bubbles and Chase was standing at the sink lathering his face with shaving cream, a towel wrapped around his waist.

His gaze met hers in the mirror. "Do you mind if I shave while you bathe?"

"Of course not." She tied the mass of black curls atop her head with a strand of red yarn. "I like company." Turning off the faucets, she immersed herself into the tub, filled with luxuriant bubbles and warm, scented water. "And thanks for drawing my bath—complete with perfumed bubbles."

Chase paused with the straight-edged razor in his hand and studied the reflection she cast in the mirror as she reclined in the tub. "I remember when I saw you bathing in the river. I don't know which way is sexier—bathing in style, or bathing in the raw."

Maggie relaxed in the tub, letting her hands idly play with the mounds of bubbles while she watched Chase shave. It was either a very slow process, or he was deliberately taking his time. She studied the flatly roped muscles of his back and shoulders and the bulging strength of his upper arms. His hair was damp, nearly black. He rinsed the razor in the water running from the sink faucet and stroked the blade down his cheek, exposing the darkly tanned skin beneath the lather.

"An electric razor is a lot quicker," she said for conversation.

"Maybe quicker, but I prefer the blade."

She let her expression tease him. "I suppose an electric razor isn't 'he-man' enough for you."

"Careful," he warned with amusement, and she laughed. "A blade shaves closer. I thought I might need a smooth face tonight."

"You might." There was faint color in her cheeks as she dipped the bath sponge into the water. "Would you wash my back when you're through?"

There were traces of shaving lather on his face when he crossed over to the tub. Kneeling beside it, he took the sponge from her hand and scrubbed her back. Maggie closed her eyes, relaxing under the rough, massaging action.

"You can keep that up all day," she murmured.

"If I hadn't already taken a shower, I'd climb in there with you." He stopped and tossed the sponge in the bubbly water in front of her.

As he started to push to his feet, her glance fell on his left arm. A coldness ran through her when she saw the white scar that slashed crookedly across his forearm, and she remembered that it had been caused when she had stabbed at him. She reached out to cover the mark with her hand and block out the unpleasant reminder.

"What's going to happen to us, Chase?" Her voice was low, flatly questioning.

He knew precisely what she was thinking. He caught hold of her hand, gripping it hard. "This isn't paradise. There are scars and flaws in all of us. God knows we're going to have our share of trouble, so don't go looking for it, Maggie. All we can do is hold on tight to what we've got—and pray to God it's enough. We just have to hold on," he repeated, his voice hard with conviction, "and take it as it comes."

She lifted her gaze, meeting his with a quiet sureness. The chill remained, but she could face it. "Yes."

His mouth curved in approval and he dropped a kiss on her lips. "Hurry up and get out of that tub. Ty will be coming, expecting dinner to be on the table."

Ty noticed the change almost immediately. One of the first things he said was: "You look beautiful tonight, Mom." Chase caught her glance and smiled. "Our son has an eye for beauty."

Ty's gaze darted between his parents, sensing the closeness and the warmth—the secret looks that left him out. He had been aware of the strain between them before and had kept hoping they would start getting along with each other. Now that it had happened, he wasn't altogether comfortable with the change.

That night Maggie was lying in bed when Chase came out of the bathroom and turned off the light. She turned back the bedcovers to let him slide in beside her and snuggled under the arm he wrapped around her.

"Did Ty seem quiet to you tonight?" she asked.

"Yes." His hand rubbed her arm in a semi-absent caress. "Our son is a little jealous, I'm afraid, and a little uncomfortable with us."

"But why?" She turned her head, trying to see him in the dark.

"Children—adolescents—have a hard time accepting the fact that their parents—especially their mother—have sexual desires. It's as if once they have been conceived, their parents aren't supposed to do it again. Don't worry," he murmured, grazing his mouth over her cheekbone. "He'll get over it. Right now, he's just uncomfortable with his own sexual needs."

"I hope so." She rubbed her cheek against his mouth, her hands seeking the hardness of his body under the covers.

"If he doesn't straighten out soon, I'll line him up with a girl. It'll take his mind off us." He had reached the corner of her lips.

But Maggie drew back at his suggestion. "Chase, you wouldn't. He's only fifteen."

"I wouldn't? You were fifteen, as I recall." He reached out and pulled her back, threading his fingers in her hair to hold her head still. "Do you know that I've never made love to you at night? Do you suppose I'll know how?"

His mouth covered hers and she forgot all about Ty.

The world seemed brighter to Chase. The grass was greener, the sky was bluer, and the sun was shinier. These last few days he'd walked with new strength, new purpose. Even the weight of running the Triple C rested more lightly on his shoulders.

As he drove into the headquarters, he saw Nate leaving the office where all the records for the breeding stock were kept. The old cowboy wouldn't tell his age, but Chase guessed he was in his sixties. Age had finally caught up with Nate. He couldn't spend long hours in the saddle anymore without coming away all stoved up. But his eye for cattle was unfailing, so Chase had put him in charge of the breeding program to continually improve their range stock. Chase honked the horn to attract Nate's attention, then pulled the pickup around to park it in the shade of a building. The cowboy was angling in his direction as Chase climbed out of the cab.

"Just came back from checking on the south branch to see how Ike was doing." Chase explained where he'd been. "I saw some of the calves out of your new bull. They must be twenty pounds heavier than the others."

"When we find out what kind of mothers those heifers turn out to be, then we'll know if we've got something." Nate reserved judgment on the worth of the new bull he had advised Chase to buy, but he stood a little straighter at the implied praise.

"Where are you heading?"

"Ownie was going to top off that grulla today. It's one of old Cougar's four-year-old colts. I've had my eye on that horse since he was two. That mouse-colored horse has cow savvy. I see it every time I look at him." There is nothing a cowboy appreciates more than a good cow pony. "I wanted to check and see how he acted with a rider. I'll bet he tears holes in the sky."

"Let's go see." Chase walked with his old teacher and foreman to the corrals where the young horses were kept.

Each spring, the young horses were brought in off the range to be haltered and handled and get accustomed to saddles and bits between their teeth. No rider climbed on them until they were four years old. They arrived at the corral in time to see the horse wrangler take a spill in the dirt, and Chase got his first good look at the horse that had captured an old cowman's eye. The dark gray horse was a well-muscled animal, but with a lean and rangy build, like its sire. Its legs, mane, and tail were black, with a white blaze on its face. Chase saw all that as the riderless horse circled the corral at a lope while its rider picked himself off the ground. A helper rode alongside the grulla and reached down to catch the trailing rope rein. Farther down the corral fence, he also saw Ty sitting on the rail. His mouth thinned in a grim line of displeasure.

"I thought he was supposed to be cleaning the stables." He glanced at Nate to confirm that Ty had been assigned to that task. Since he'd been at the ranch, his work had all been on the ground, from cleaning barns to the windmill crews, to painting, wherever unskilled labor was needed. The only time he'd been on a horse was when Chase had sent him out to see a roundup the day Maggie had arrived.

"He's all finished for the day." Nate looked down the way with a half-smile on his weathered face. "That boy works like somebody set a fire under him so he can get done early and come down here to watch them break the young horses. He's no slacker. He gets his work done before he sits on that fence."

Assured that Ty wasn't loafing, Chase moved down the corral fence to where his son was watching. "That's a good-looking four-year-old," he said.

"Yeah, it's one of Cougar's," Ty replied automatically. Then he realized it was his father and hastened to explain, "I'm all through for today."

"I know," Chase said in a tone that sounded all-knowing.

Ty looked back to the corral, his expression growing wistful. "I sure wish I could ride that horse. You know I'm a good rider, Dad. And I've helped break in green horses before when we lived in California."

"Do you want me to ask Ownie if you can ride him?"

Everything in Ty's eager gaze said "yes," but he sighed a dejected, "No."

Chase turned and called out to the horse wrangler, walking to the center of the corral, where the horse had been led. "Hey, Ownie! There's a boy here who thinks he can ride that horse. Do you want to give him a try?"

The short, wiry man glanced at Ty, who had been a steady spectator for days. He knew Chase was leaving the decision to his judgment, based on the horse and Ty's inexperience.

"Sure. Why not?" he shrugged, and Ty leaped off the fence.

Chase was quick to notice that Nate had crawled into the corral. It was the old cowboy who was standing at the gelding's head to ear him while Ty climbed into the saddle. The wrangler, Ownie Timms, ambled over to the fence where Chase was standing and watched Ty settle deep into the saddle and get a good grip on the rope reins.

"The Mouse is a good honest horse, bucks straight with no meanness," the wrangler told Chase. "But he's young and strong, got a way of twisting and jumping out from under ya sideways."

"We might as well see what he can do," Chase said, and both knew he wasn't talking about the horse.

At a nod from Ty, Nate let go of the horse's ear and stepped aside. The grulla went straight up in the air and down with a jar, then went sun-fishing across the corral, turning its belly to the sky. When the horse lunged sideways, Ty lost a stirrup, and horse and rider parted company on the next jump. Chase watched Ty hit the ground and roll automatically, then looked away.

Shaken and bruised, but unhurt, Ty lay on the ground for a minute, shaking his head and waiting for someone to ask if he was okay, but when he looked around, no one was paying any attention to him, not even his father. He got up, brushing himself off, and looked up to see Nate leading the horse to him. Nothing was said. It was presumed he would get back on, so he did. The second time he was bucked off, it was harder to get back on. The third time he didn't think he could make it. Badly bruised, his knee throbbing, Ty glanced at his father, but Buck Haskell had just ridden up and his father was talking to him. Gritting his teeth, Ty limped to the horse Nate was petting and soothing. He waited until Nate had a hold of an ear, then hauled himself into the saddle, every muscle screaming. He caught a glint of admiration in the old cowboy's eye. Suddenly all the pain seemed worthwhile. Then all hell was breaking loose again as Nate let go.

Nate trotted stiffly out of the way and angled for the fence where Chase watched. "The boy's got try." That was the highest compliment that could be given.

Chase smiled. "Maybe we could put him on a horse for the rest of the year and teach him about cows." He glanced up at Buck, who was sitting in a relaxed slouch over the saddle horn, his hat tipped to the back of his curly blond head. "Have you got somebody in your crew who can keep an eye on him and show him the ropes?" All the while he kept one eye on Ty. This time he seemed to be glued in the saddle, ready for every one of the grulla's tricks.

"Dave is good with kids. I'll keep an eye on him, too," Buck promised.

"We'll start him next week." Chase noticed the mouse-colored horse was only crow-hopping now. "How's everything going?" It was a general question addressed to Buck.

"Fine. Had a kind of freak accident the other day. Lost a calf out on the butte. Got tangled up in a strand of barbed wire." Buck straightened in the saddle, adjusting his hat onto his forehead. "The boy's got a good seat. Talk to you later, Chase."

"Right."

"I heard about that calf," Nate said after Buck had ridden away. "Burt found it four days ago. Calf hadn't even stiffened up yet."

"Oh?" There was a point to this information; Chase could tell by the tone of the man's voice. He remembered he had planned to ride out to the butte with Buck four days ago.

"Yeah. It was kind of funny business," Nate said. "That strand of barbed wire was wrapped around the calf's neck. The theory is it got tangled in it, and when it tried to get loose, it twisted the wire tighter."

"Is that right?" But the words gave Chase an eerie chill for all his outward show of calm. He was almost prepared for Nate's next statement.

"It's kinda hard to figure how the calf got tangled in the first place, and how there wasn't much sign of struggle in the grass. And it's a really strange coincidence that the end of the wire got wrapped nine times."

The hangman's knot. Another message that had been meant for him, but he hadn't gone to get it. The noose on the desktop had been the first warning. The strangled calf was the second. His blood ran cold as a solitary cloud passed in front of the sun. These warnings had to be the product of a twisted mind. There was no way he could outguess what Culley O'Rourke might do next. Even if he could, how could he go against Maggie's brother? Either way, he would be damned. It boiled down to which risk was he willing to take—the chance that the next time Culley might use something other than a dumb animal in his attempt to terrorize Chase, or the chance of losing Maggie. She would never forgive him if he caused something to happen to her brother. How far would Culley go? Was he just trying to scare him, or was there true vengeance planned? Or—was this a clever ploy to cause trouble between him and Maggie so she would leave him and go to Culley?

All he said to Nate was, "That's quite a coincidence. If a man had a guilty conscience, he might make something out of it."

"He might," Nate agreed and moved away from the fence to

saunter bowlegged to the mouse-colored horse standing passively in the middle of the corral while Ty dismounted.

That evening, Ty was already sitting at the table when Maggie saw him for the first time since morning. It wasn't until dinner was finished and he excused himself to leave the table that she noticed how stiff and awkwardly he moved, favoring his right leg.

"Ty, are you hurt?"

"Naw." He shrugged away his aches, but not very convincingly. "I banged my knee a little. Nate gave me some linament for it. It'll be all right."

She watched him limp out of the room, then started clearing the dinner dishes from the table while Chase finished his coffee. When she returned from the kitchen, Chase was staring at his cup with a hard frown. She suddenly realized how quiet he had been throughout dinner, his thoughts apparently elsewhere.

"Is something bothering you?" She paused beside his chair.

He looked up, seeming to bring himself back to the present with an effort. He smiled, but the frown never completely left his face. "Yes. You." He caught her hand and pulled her onto his lap. He kissed her soundly, then lifted his head, his lazy eyes regarding her possessively. "That's what I wanted for dessert." His hand stroked her thigh and hip.

"What were you thinking about before I came in?" she persisted, caressing the angular planes of his cheek.

"You would have been proud of our son today. He rode one of the green four-year-olds we're breaking. He was bucked off four times, but got back on each time and rode the horse to a standstill."

"Chase, he could have been hurt," Maggie protested with a quick frown. "He doesn't know the first thing about riding an unbroken horse. He's been on some young, untrained horses, but never one fresh off the range."

"He has to learn how it's done sometime."

"But—" His mouth was on hers to silence her argument. When she made a half-hearted attempt to elude his kiss, he caught her lip between his teeth and chewed it gently. Her hands wound into his hair to force his mouth fully onto her lips.

Chase didn't tell her about the calf that had been strangled and left with the hangman's message around its neck. He knew better than she did how fragile the feelings she had for him were. Too much outside pressure might snap them before they had a chance to grow strong. Every minute, every hour, every day he could gain just altered the odds a little more in his favor.

He already knew she was his. He could never let her go again.

Chapter XXXIV

Maggie reined in her horse and maneuvered it to open the gate to the Broken Butte range. She was to meet Chase out here somewhere. He'd suggested this morning that she come out this way on her afternoon ride. In these miles of wild country, there were only three places where they would be working a herd. She rode through the gate and closed it behind her, trying to decide which of the three to try first. Then she saw a rider cantering down a slope to meet her.

"Hello, Maggie." Buck Haskell touched the rolled point of his hat and reined his horse, swinging it around beside hers. "Chase asked me to meet you and guide you back."

"I wondered where I was going to find him," she admitted, smiling briefly at the gregarious cowboy Chase counted as his friend.

They started out at a trot. "You're looking beautiful today, Maggie. I think marriage agrees with you."

"It does." Chase had warned her that Buck was prone to flattery. He did have a boyish charm that was irresistible, his wide, appreciative grin prompting her smile to be more natural and less polite.

"I have to tell you that when Chase told me you two were getting married, I didn't think you had a Chinaman's chance after what happened to your pa." He shook his head wryly. "But I should have known that Chase always gets what he wants."

The breeze seemed to take on a chill at the reference to her father. It was better if she didn't let her thoughts dwell too much in the past and open old wounds. She could almost hear Chase saying, "Hold on tight to what we have, Maggie." No, she wouldn't look back, not that far back.

"In this case, it's what we both want," she said.

"I can see that." Buck grinned at her. "Chase thinks the sun rises and sets on that boy of yours. You want to talk about a proud papa—that Chase, he's one. That boy means everything to him. 'Course, that's natural for a father to feel that way about his son."

"Yes." Maggie listened to the praise and felt uneasy.

"I guess there isn't anything Chase wouldn't do for him," Buck said thoughtfully. "Once he sinks his teeth into an idea, he won't let it go. It was just a matter of time before he got you around to his way of thinking. Chase knew what it was like growing up without a mother, and he didn't want that for the kid. My mother was kind of a second mother to him, but it isn't like having your own. I guess that's the way you thought—wanting the boy to have his own father."

"Yes." Maggie didn't dissuade him from that belief. There was no reason to tell him Chase had initially blackmailed her into this marriage with threats of winning Ty away from her.

"Chase and me were practically raised as brothers. I have pretty strong feelings about him. I guess you know the story. There aren't many people that would give an ex-con another chance. I owe him a lot, but I guess I don't have to convince you what kind of a man he is." A short laugh came from him. "Here I am, riding beside a beautiful woman, and what am I doing? Raving on about her husband! I'm really slipping. I'd better deliver you to Chase before I lose my reputation." He spurred his horse into a canter and Maggie followed suit.

The lowing of cattle greeted them as they crested a rise and a meadow spread out before them. The holding pens were in the center of it. Maggie easily spotted Chase among the riders. Mounted on a blood bay gelding, he was positioned near the main gate of the holding pens, watching the action. Buck stayed beside her, not leaving until she was delivered into Chase's hands.

"Here she is, safe and sound," he said with a wide grin.

"Thanks, Buck." Chase was too busy looking at her to notice Buck tip his hat respectfully toward Maggie before reining away.

"You look like a young girl again with your hair tucked under your hat like that."

But he already knew the maturity of the curves beneath the long-sleeved designer blouse of yellow chamois cloth, and his gaze was now lingering on her mouth. She smoothed an escaping tendril of hair under her hat, enjoying the warm disturbance his look caused.

"It's getting too long," she said to explain why she was wearing her hair the old way, then broke contact with his eyes to survey the scene. "Where's Ty?"

"He's out with Dave finishing the gather. We should start moving the herd within the hour." There had been a delay in driving this herd to summer graze due to a breakdown of a windmill pump, and a creek unexpectedly went dry, making the water supply on the range temporarily insufficient. Now the pump was fixed and a beaver dam high upstream had been destroyed to allow water to flow in the creek bed again. He challenged Maggie with a glittering look. "Want to cowboy this afternoon?"

"Sure." It had been a long time since she'd actually worked on a ranch. It sounded like fun.

When the last of the stragglers were brought in and the count was confirmed, the gates to the holding pens were opened and the herd was driven out. While Maggie rode the left flank beside Chase and two other riders, Ty was stationed back on drag. Not wanting to be pegged a "momma's boy," he had barely nodded to her when he'd ridden in with his teacher-partner, Dave. Amused, but understanding, Maggie had been careful not to watch her son too closely.

A cow and calf broke from the herd directly in front of Chase and Maggie. His blood bay gelding made a lunge after them, but Chase reined it short and nodded to her. "They're yours."

Maggie relaxed the pressure on the bit and, quick as a cat, her bay gelding was streaking after the fleeing pair. The old exhilaration of pursuit returned. The cow was turned and trotting toward the herd, the calf at its side. In that wild moment, racing over rough ground, it became sharply clear how much she had missed this life. That was why she had adjusted to it so quickly and so easily. There was a flash of guilt that her education and all the things Phillip had taught her might go to waste out here. Her concentration was broken. She wasn't prepared for the sudden swerve of her horse as it checked a half-hearted attempt by the cow to make another escape to freedom. The gelding jumped out from under her and Maggie tumbled to the ground, rolling and coming to a stop, sitting up, unhurt. For an instant, all she could do was sit there, surprised, stunned. When she saw the black legs of Chase's red bay gelding beside her, she looked up. He could see she was unhurt and amusement glimmered in his eyes. Suddenly a smile broke across her face and she laughed at herself.

"I got caught sitting loose. I guess I'm a bit rusty." She rolled to her feet, brushing off the seat of her pants, and picked her hat up off the ground.

"You'll have plenty of opportunity to practice." Reaching down, he clasped her forearm and swung her into the saddle behind him. She wrapped her arms around his middle, holding on tighter than was necessary as Chase turned his horse toward the herd.

One of the riders had caught her loose horse and was waiting midway to the herd. When they reached him, Maggie loosened her hold to swing down, but the saddle creaked as Chase half-turned to hook an arm around her waist. Instead of lowering her to the ground, he curved her against his side, pressing her hips against his thigh. She saw the dark fire in his look and felt the responding lift of her pulse as his gaze lingered on her mouth.

"They can see us." She reminded him of their audience of cowhands.

"They'll look the other way," Chase assured her and tipped his head to cover her lips in a hard, hungry kiss. Then he reluctantly lowered her to the ground. There was a disturbed rhythm to her pulse as she swung into the saddle of her own mount. Joy filled her when she reined her horse alongside his, their legs brushing, a joy that was both fierce and fragile. They rode forward at a shuffling trot, not in a great hurry to catch up with the herd that had passed them.

Ty had been assigned the position of riding drag with a veteran cowboy. The position at the rear of the herd was the least desirable, since the rider was subjected to the collective stench, heat, and dust of the herd. It was frustrating to be constantly assigned to the lowliest tasks. When he'd ridden that green-broke gelding to a walk, he thought he had proven himself, but he soon discovered he hadn't. True, he was out on the range working cattle, but his remuda string consisted of the worst horses on the ranch, those with either nasty habits or purely mean streaks. The other cowboys made him the butt of innumerable practical jokes, and his ignorance of ranch work and cattle made him gullible to almost any tall tale a cowboy chose to tell him. There were times when Ty was convinced everyone hated him, and other times he was certain he would never be accepted by them. He vacillated between a grim determination to prove himself and a bitter desire to tell them all to go to hell.

What made it worse, he had no one to whom he could confide his frustrations. His father had made it plain from the beginning not to come complaining to him, that he had to sort out his own difficulties. And his mother . . . In the first place, the way she acted around his father, Ty knew she would side with Chase. Besides, he had been so determined to live here, and there was the matter of his pride if he went to her and told her he couldn't take it. And if she did try to intervene on his behalf, then the cowboys would probably start calling him a "momma's boy."

A shallow creek intersected the path of the herd. The first cows were pushed across it and the rest followed. Ty started to follow the stragglers across the stream, but his glass-eyed horse pricked its ears nervously at the glistening sheen of the sun on the water's surface and began mincing along the smooth graveled bank. The water was no more than ankle-deep, and Ty became impatient with his mount and jabbed his heels into the animal's belly to force it into the shallow water. The horse leaped sideways, avoiding the glistening water and nearly unseating him.

With his free right hand, he grabbed for the saddle horn to pull himself back into the seat. He had barely regained the off stirrup when his fellow drag-rider came alongside and brought the end of his nylon rope down sharply on the hand clutching the saddle horn. Even through the tough cowhide leather of his glove, Ty felt the smarting sting of the rope. Still trying to control his unruly horse, he shot a furious look at the cowboy.

"Hey, cut that out!" he shouted. "Are you trying to get me thrown?"

The tobacco-cheeked cowboy just grinned and slapped his hand again. It was harder the second time, the ensuing pain forcing Ty to let go of the saddle horn. Ty was burning-mad, but his hands were full trying to control the iron-jawed horse that had started bucking. Although he was determined not to be bucked off, he hadn't fully regained his balance, so he had to keep grabbing for leather to avoid being thrown. Each time he did, the rope lashed out to slap the offending hand.

Maggie had seen Ty's horse balk at the creek crossing. At first she thought the other rider was staying close to help him. It was only after the third or fourth time that she realized the rider was slapping Ty's hand away from the saddle horn. All her maternal instincts surged as she called Chase's attention to what was happening.

"Do you see what he's doing to Ty?"

Chase barely glanced in the direction of all the commotion, exhibiting little interest in his son's situation. "It's just some harmless hazing, Maggie." He dismissed it as unimportant and angled his horse toward another section of the stream.

"You aren't going to let them do that, are you? He's your son!"

"Just ignore it." The directive was firm and final.

"You can ignore it, but I won't," she snapped and started to rein her horse away from him, but he grabbed the reins, stopping her horse.

His brown eyes were hard as they bored into her. "Stay out of it, Maggie. I mean it. If you intervene, Ty will look like a fool in front of the men."

"Then you do something!" she demanded.

"It may look cruel to you. You're a woman. But the boys and their hazing are teaching him some lessons he needs to learn."

"They don't have to be taught that way." She rejected the code of toughness, a code she had forgotten in the intervening years she had been away. She no longer saw the value of it, especially not when her son was the object of the hazing.

"If he can't take the hazing, he won't be any good running this ranch. He has to have the respect of the men. Without that, he'll fail. This is nothing compared to some of the things he'll have to face when he's older. Believe me, Maggie, I know what I'm talking about. I've been through it."

The argument became moot as Ty regained control of his horse, bringing the bucking to a stop and riding it across the stream. His success brought an end to the hazing, but the incident had created a rift between Maggie and Chase.

That evening Maggie saw the red welts on Ty's right hand and seethed again that Chase had permitted him to be treated in such a manner. When she had finished the evening dishes and returned to the living room, Chase was in the den and Ty was on his way upstairs for an early night. She cornered her son on the landing, determined to find out his feelings.

"What is it, Mom?" he asked impatiently. "I'm really tired. Can't it wait?"

"I—" She studied his listless, exhausted look, the leanness of his chest and shoulders that physical labor had turned into hard muscles. "I just wanted to know if you are happy here." She offered him the chance to confide in her.

Indecision and uncertainty raced through his expression as he returned her searching look. Suddenly her manly fifteen-year-old son appeared no older than eight and confused by the adult world. Just as suddenly, the impression was gone as his features hardened in a way that reminded her of Chase.

"Yes, I am." He turned to ascend the stairs.

That glimpse of another contradicting feeling made her persist. "Then you want to stay here?"

"More than ever," Ty stated and climbed the steps. "Good night, Mom."

"Good night," she echoed, aware that Ty had denounced his need for her moral support, intending to fight his battle alone. He was growing up fast, just as she had at fifteen. It wasn't what she had wanted for him.

When Chase finished his paperwork a little after ten o'clock, the rest of the downstairs was dark. Only the stairwell light had been left on. He hesitated, then started up the steps.

Sitting at the vanity table, Maggie heard him climbing the stairs and picked up the hairbrush to begin running it through her dark hair again. She didn't look up when he entered the room. Her hair crackled with static electricity. She listened to the sounds of Chase undressing and heard the bedsprings squeak under his weight.

"Are you coming to bed?"

His question snapped her silence. "Men always think that will solve everything," Maggie retorted and ran the brush more briskly through her hair.

"What can you solve sitting there brushing your hair?" he countered.

Her hand returned the brush to the vanity top with a quick thud as Maggie rose and hugged her arms in front of her chest. She crossed the room, avoiding the bed where he was sitting in his undershorts.

"It isn't going to work," she announced, then realized it was a statement that required explaining, and she continued in a quick, hard rush. "For you, everything revolves around this ranch. You don't care that a whole world exists outside of it. It isn't the same for me—or Ty. I've become used to a different life—attending the theater or a symphony or going to a museum. I haven't missed those things yet, but I will."

"When you do, then we'll fly to New York or Dallas or Denver, spend a weekend." Chase watched her, aware that she was skirting the real issue of Ty and the incident this afternoon. "This ranch isn't a prison, Maggie. I usually take several trips a year. Granted, it's usually ranch business that takes me away, but we can combine business with pleasure. You're taking a steer and trying to make a bull out of it. There is no validity in that argument, so you might as well say what is really on your mind."

She turned to meet his calm, challenging look. "Very well." She faced him without backing down. "When Ty finishes school, I want him to go on to college."

His mouth thinned. "This ranch will give him a better education than any university—with majors in animal husbandry, agriculture, accounting, land management, and human psychology. Four years on the Triple C will make him better equipped for the future than any college graduate would be."

"I want him to have a college degree," she stated, unmoved by his argument. "I don't want him to be like you when he grows up—callous and caring more about this ranch than anything else." Chase was hurt that she could actually think that was true. Yet that wasn't the point to be debated.

"You know it will only make things harder for him, don't you?" But he could see that she didn't. He sighed heavily. "All right, we'll compromise. *If* Ty wants to go to college, I won't try to stop him or change his mind." When he saw her hesitation, Chase added, "You don't expect to agree when I believe college would be wrong for him. But I promise, I will stand aside and let it be his own decision. We'll work it out, you and I."

She knew he was referring to their marriage in general, and she felt the sudden pull of his love, softening all her resolve. "Sometimes I really believe we can," she murmured.

"Now, are you coming to bed?" His gaze roamed over her nightgown-clad form, conscious of the mature shape it revealed, but more interested in what it concealed.

There was lightness in her challenging response. "What do you think that will solve?"

"Come here and I'll show you." Chase reached out for her hand and pulled her to the bed. Before they sprawled together across the mattress, the nightgown came off, as well as his shorts. While his roaming hands were awakening her flesh, his hungry mouth was seeking her lips.

"The light." She reminded him it was still on.

"All the better to see you, my love," he insisted, drawing back to view her nakedness, eager to discover all her mysteries. "You have a body any man would enjoy making love to, but it doubles my pleasure to watch you."

"Yes." She understood the added sensation as she observed the play of his muscles along his shoulder and arm when his hand cupped one of her breasts. "Love me, Chase." She was shaken by the greatness of her need.

"Always." Then his kiss was filling her mouth as his weight settled heavily onto her slight figure.

Two mornings later, Chase and Ty had just sat down to eat the breakfast Maggie had fixed when the meal was interrupted by Nate. He paused in the doorway of the dining room to remove his hat. Outside, dawn was turning the sky orange and pink.

"Sit down and have some coffee, Nate," Chase invited, but an uncomfortable feeling threaded through him at the old cowboy's still expression. The sensation entered places where primal instincts dwelled. He sensed trouble, the way a dog bristles at a silent shadow.

"Yes, sit down, Nate." Maggie seconded the invitation. "I'll bring you a cup." She started to rise from her chair, but the foreman refused with a single shake of his head.

"No, thank you, ma'am." He didn't enter the room, but remained in the doorway. "Can I speak to you privately, Chase?"

Chase pushed his chair away from the table and moved with the swiftness of a man accustomed to action as he joined the retreating cowboy in the foyer. Maggie knew something was wrong, but she didn't understand what it was. She could hear the low murmur of their voices, the conversation very brief. After she heard the front door open and close, it was a full second before she realized there were two sets of footsteps leaving the house. She rushed to the door, yanking it open to see Chase striding away from the porch with Nate.

"Chase, where are you going? You haven't had breakfast." Her demand for an explanation was cloaked in a wifely excuse.

When he turned, his face told her nothing, his thoughts hidden behind the mask Western men wear. "I'll grab a bite at the cookhouse."

"Has something happened?" She started to cross the porch to follow him.

"Nothing I can't handle. You stay at the house." It was an emphatic order.

Maggie's mouth opened to protest, but Chase was already moving away, taking her obedience for granted. The command made her unease stronger as she watched him crossing the ranch yard, until it finally drove her off the porch after him. She didn't know what it was that he was attempting to keep from her, but she intended to find out.

When he disappeared inside the stud barn, she quickened her steps. She noticed there were others hurrying to the same place, yet no sounds were coming from inside—nothing to indicate a stallion fight. Maggie paused inside the open barn door to let her eyes adjust to the interior darkness. Chase was standing near an open stall, a steely tension about him. She moved closer to look inside, anticipating the sight of an ailing stallion.

Soft morning sunlight streamed through a stall window, glistening over the tawny coat of the buckskin stallion, Cougar. Her eyes widened as she realized the silent animal was frozen in a rearing posture. How? The she saw how and her horrified gasp was audible, despite the hand that she clamped over her mouth. A knotted rope was around its neck, tied to an overhead barn beam. The horse had been hanged.

The sight of it was blocked by a pair of wide shoulders. A pair of hands clasped the soft flesh of her arms as she swayed in shocked revulsion. Her horrified gaze met Chase's. He was visibly gritting his teeth at her pinched-white face.

"I told you to stay at the house," he reminded her in groaning regret that she hadn't.

"Did Culley—" A sob choked her voice, cutting off the question.

Then Chase was turning her away, giving her into someone else's care. "Take Maggie up to the house, Buck, and see that she stays there. Ty, go get Ruth. I don't want your mother to be left alone."

Maggie caught a glimpse of her son inside the open barn door as Buck led her out. Her mind was racing with too many resurrected fears and memories and she barely heard any of the murmured words Buck offered. She wasn't interested in talking to him about the stallion being hanged. She didn't want to talk to anyone about it or make any speculations aloud until she had spoken to Chase, alone.

She saw him at lunch, but Ty's presence didn't give her a chance to speak freely. In front of their son, they pretended ignorance of any motive that would lead someone to hang the stallion. The morning scene in the barn preyed on her mind all day.

In the middle of the afternoon, Chase walked into the cook-house. Tucker's large bulk was leaning against a counter, an elbow leaning on the worktop. A bibbed apron was around his protruding middle. He didn't appear surprised to find Chase entering his kitchen domain.

"There's coffee in the pot." There always was, but Tucker waved toward the metal urn, just the same. "I've been expecting you."

Chase helped himself to a cup, using one of the mugs off the shelf. "I suppose you heard about that old buckskin stud of my father's."

"I heard it was hanged." Tucker nodded, his small eyes observing Chase as he lit a long, thin cigar. "Heard about the calf, too. I figured sooner or later you'd be coming 'round to talk to me. I tell you right now that I didn't have anything to do with it, and I don't know anything about it."

"If you did, you wouldn't tell me," Chase guessed, sliding the man a glance through the smoke trail of his cigar.

"No, I don't suppose I would," he admitted. Then he asked, "How's Maggie? I heard she saw it."

But his question was ignored. "When was the last time you saw Culley?"

"It's been a while." His eyes narrowed, appearing even smaller.

Chase sipped at the murky black coffee, hot and strong. It left a bitter taste in his mouth. "You and the O'Rourkes used to be as thick as thieves." He used the phrase deliberately.

"Yeah." It was a growling agreement. "You can think what you like about me, Calder, and the kind of man I am, but I'd never do anything that might cause Maggie pain. It wasn't a pretty sight she saw. Knowing what you're thinking, she's gotta be hurting inside."

"If you know anything about this, Tucker, and I find out you do, you're through," Chase warned, but he half-believed what the man said. The hardest cases were often easy pushovers where women were concerned, able to bash a man's brains out without blinking an eye, yet helpless as a newborn kitten when confronted with a woman's tears.

"I told you what I know."

Chase took another swallow of coffee and emptied the mug in the sink, flicking the cigar ash down the drain. "Thanks for the coffee."

"You just treat Maggie right, or the next time your cup will be laced with arsenic. I always keep some handy in case a rat turns up."

"I'll remember that." Chase was half-smiling to himself when he walked out. It seemed Maggie had no lack of knight errants eager to save her from him. Didn't any of them realize how much he loved that woman?

The thought of her directed his footsteps to The Homestead. The house was silent when he entered it, except for the sound of an electric mixer running in the kitchen. He walked through, expecting to find Maggie busy with preparations for the evening meal, but Ruth was there alone.

"Where's Maggie?"

"She's upstairs lying down for a while. A headache."

Chase didn't wait to hear more, leaving the kitchen and crossing the living room to climb the steps two at a time. At first glance, the bedroom appeared empty; then he saw her standing at the far window. She had turned when he entered, and the strain of the day's events showed in her green eyes.

"Ruth said you were lying down." He paused a moment to close the door before walking toward her.

"I told her I had a headache. I wanted to get away by myself so I could think." Her glance was pulled to the window, then rushed back to him. "You believe Culley did it, don't you?"

He stopped, searching her eyes. "Don't you?"

She turned away from him to stare out the window and rub her elbows in the palms of her hands. "I can't imagine Culley doing it. I can't believe my brother would hang . . . anything. Culley isn't like that."

"Maybe he *wasn't* like that." He walked up behind her, his hands caressing the soft points of her shoulders. "You were gone a long time, Maggie. You don't know what kind of a man he's become."

"He's still my brother." A chill ran down her spine. "Chase, what are you going to do?"

He turned her around, his hands sliding down her back to fold her into his arms. "I'm going to hold onto you, Maggie. I'm going to hold onto what we've got."

That wasn't what she meant, but it ceased to matter. As long as his arms were around her and his mouth was covering hers, she could forget the rest for now.

Chapter XXXV

In her sleep, Maggie reached out for Chase, but her hand encountered empty space where he should have been lying. She was instantly awake, her eyes searching the night-darkened bed. It was empty. Then she caught the pungent aroma of cigar smoke. Her head turned on the pillow.

The cinnamon armchair had been turned to face the window. Chase was lounging in it, his bare feet propped up on the windowsill. He was partially in the shadows, but the glow of his cigar laid its dark yellow light along his face. In this faint light, his cheeks were flat and ridged beneath the covering of tanned skin.

She was content just to look at him. She had never felt so close to him, so much a part of him than she had that evening. Instead of undermining their love, the incident with the stallion had brought them closer together. Yes, their bodies had joined in lovemaking, but it had gone beyond that, their silences joining, each of their voices speaking the other's thoughts.

Yet he had not slept. She sensed he was pulling away from her. His mind was tracking through their problems alone without her. He was leaving her out, not letting her be a part of it. She couldn't allow it.

"Chase, what are you thinking about?"

"Nothing important," he replied. "Go back to sleep. I'll be coming to bed shortly."

Instead, Maggie pushed back the covers and slipped out of bed. The moonlight cast a satin sheen over the whiteness of her naked

THIS CALDER SKY 359

skin as she crossed to his chair. "You're thinking about the stallion."

There was an indulgent curve to his mouth as he cupped his palm over her hipbone and applied pressure to sit her on the armrest of his chair. "You don't obey orders very well," he mocked and stubbed out his cigar. "I told you to go back to sleep."

"Why didn't you want me to find out about the stallion getting hanged? You weren't going to tell me," Maggie accused. "That's why you ordered me to stay at the house this morning."

"Is it wrong to want to spare you that unpleasantness?" His arm curved into a hook to pull her onto his lap. The hard flesh of his body was warm against her bare skin. His hands wandered over her ripe curves, deliberately attempting to distract her.

"You didn't want to spare me—not as much as you wanted to keep me from finding out about it," she guessed and sensed his hesitation. It increased her suspicions. "What else have you tried to spare me, Chase? I know about the replica of the noose, now the stallion. There's been something else, hasn't there? And you didn't tell me."

His finger absently traced a circle on her throat as his gaze darkened. For a moment, she thought he was going to continue to deny it. "A calf was found strangled almost two weeks ago," he admitted. "Now, are you glad I told you?"

She had wanted to be wrong—she had hoped there had been no other incident like this morning's. "No." Her voice was husky with regret. "What are you going to do?"

"I have to stop him." There was a grim impatience within his words, a reluctance to voice the answer.

"By 'him,' you mean my brother." She said it stiffly.

"Yes, I mean your brother." Chase didn't hedge. His tone was firm and decisive. "So far his victims have been animals, but he's sick. I'm not going to wait to find out what his next move will be. I won't risk it."

That part she wouldn't argue with, since she understood the potential for danger, but that wasn't the source of her uncertainty. She lifted her gaze to search his eyes. "How do you intend to stop him, Chase?" She knew the power he wielded. He had taken his father's place.

He weighed her words, holding her look. "I'll handle it *my* way, Maggie." The slight emphasis excluded her from his action.

Bending his head, he moved to nuzzle the lobe of her ear. "You'll have to trust me."

But she wouldn't be distracted and cupped his face in her hands to hold it away. "No, Chase, that isn't good enough. I'm not some dutiful Western wife who is willing to leave such matters to the menfolk. I'm not the kind to putter around the kitchen while you decide the important things without consulting me. If that's what you wanted, you shouldn't have married me. This problem involves me. I'm your wife and his sister. That gives me the right to know your plans. Don't shut me out."

"It isn't my intention to shut you out." He took the hand cupping his cheek and pressed a kiss into its palm. She ran her fingers lightly over his lips, tracing their masculine outline.

"He's my brother, Chase. I know something has to be done, but I don't want him hurt." The ache of frustration surfaced. "Culley won't listen to reason. I know. I've tried."

He saw the memory that was in her eyes, the range justice his father had imposed to bring an end to the cattle-rustling. He kissed the gold band on her finger. "I would never do anything that might turn you against me. You have my word on that, Maggie." But he wasn't going to involve her in his plans for Culley. Chase knew her well enough to know she would insist on accompanying him, and he could not be sure her presence would not have an inhibiting effect. Men tended to be more reserved, restrained, when a woman was present, expressing themselves less freely.

A slow smile spread across his mouth. "Now that I've satisfied your mind on that score, let's turn our attention to something else. Because it's becoming very difficult to concentrate with a naked woman on my lap." He bent his head to roll a rose-crested nipple in his mouth and felt it harden.

"But you haven't told me what you intend to do," she said in a vague protest as a response trembled through her.

"I intend"—his hand slid between her thighs—"to make love to you for the rest of my life." Then his mouth was on hers, smothering her moan of pleasure.

The next morning, Chase shut the door to the den while he made his phone calls, then left The Homestead in search of Nate Moore. He found him at the commissary, gasing up his truck.

"I want you, Ike, and Slim to meet me at the north gate at two o'clock this afternoon." His choice of men had been deliberate. All had accompanied his father when he'd paid a visit to the O'Rourke ranch.

"What's up?" The shrewd pair of blue eyes showed he had already guessed.

"We're going to return the rope to the person who left it around the buckskin's neck," Chase stated. "I don't want word getting back to Maggie about where I am this afternoon, so keep it quiet."

Uncertainty flickered in the old cowboy's expression. "Chase, I stood by your pa, but—"

There was no warmth in the smile that curved his mouth. It was cold and grim. "I know what I'm doing, Nate. Are you coming with me?"

"Hell, I wet-nursed you since you were old enough to rope your first calf. Of course I'm coming with you." Nate was offended that Chase would suggest he wasn't going to back up his play. "I was just wondering what you had up your sleeve."

"You'll find out. Just don't be surprised by anything I say."

"You can count on me—on all of us," Nate promised.

"I know." Chase clamped a hand on the man's shoulder, then moved away.

At lunch, Chase idly inquired about Maggie's plans for the afternoon and suggested that she might want to explore the southern end of the ranch on horseback, maneuvering her away from the north side, where he would be meeting the men. Part of him knew it wasn't fair to keep her ignorant of his plans, but it went against his grain to involve her in this. Chase saw it as his problem and his responsibility; therefore, he had to handle it. He couldn't allow someone else to do it for him, let alone a woman, even if she was his wife.

When he slid behind the wheel of a ranch pickup, en route to meet Nate and the others, he saw Buck drive into the ranch yard with a horse trailer in tow. It stopped in front of the first-aid dispensary and veterinary-supply office. He would have probably paid no more attention if he hadn't noticed Ty was a passenger in the pickup. He drove over to find out what was wrong. When he called out to them, Buck altered his course away from the dispensary door and ambled toward the idling truck with a sauntering gait.

With a glance at Ty, who remained by the parked truck, Chase asked, "Is something wrong? Is he hurt?"

"The kid? No." Buck shook his head and pushed his hat back on his forehead. "We just came by to pick up some medicine. There's a cancer-eyed cow on the north range that needs some doctoring. I thought I'd show the kid how it was done. That's kind of rough, broken country, so I decided I'd let him get a feel of the lay of the land. He's not familiar with the north section. It'd be terrible if the boss's kid got lost." Buck grinned.

"That's true," he agreed with a wry twist to his mouth. "Just make sure he doesn't cross any boundary fences. Keep him on Calder land." Especially today, he thought, but he kept that to himself.

"Will do." Buck nodded.

Dismissing him with a one-fingered salute, Chase shifted the truck into forward gear and drove out of the ranch yard.

When the ramshackle buildings of the Shamrock came into view, Chase studied them. He'd heard the place was falling down, but he hadn't expected it to look so ruined and deserted, a place for ghosts to live. Nate edged his horse closer to Chase's mount, indicating with a nod of his head the car parked in the yard overgrown with weeds.

"O'Rourke's got company." He seemed to expect Chase to stop, half-checking his horse in anticipation.

"Looks that way." He didn't slow his horse, and the trio of Triple C riders followed him uncertainly, unaware that all was going according to his plan.

When they rode into the yard, Culley stepped out boldly to meet them. He was pathetically thin, his clothes hanging loosely on his skeletal frame. Green eyes gleamed out of dark sockets, alive with hatred and its accompanying madness. Chase eyed his opponent and knew that he couldn't allow this twisted, malevolent man to be on the loose another day.

"You're trespassing on private property, Calder!" Culley snarled. "I got witnesses." He indicated the two men standing in the shadows with a sideways gesture of his head, his gaze never leaving Chase. "Turn around and get out."

Chase looked at the two men. "Sheriff. Doc Barlow." He

acknowledged the presence of the two men by name, without letting it show that he expected to find them there. His stony gaze returned to Culley. Reaching down, he untied the coiled rope with its hangman's noose and held it loosely in his hand for an instant. "I just came by to return something of yours." He tossed the rope to Culley with a flick of his wrist. It landed in the dust at his feet. "You left it around the neck of a stallion. That was careless of you, Culley. You should take better care of your property."

"What makes you think that rope is mine?" Culley scoffed. "I never left anything at your place. The only thing you got that belongs to me is my sister. And I don't know nothing about any stallion."

"Liar."

The soft, one-word taunt made Culley bristle. For one second, Chase thought the scarecrow figure was going to spring at him and tear him apart with his bare hands. But his entire mood changed with a lightning flash. Culley silently laughed at him with a wide grin.

"No, Calder, you aren't going to trick me like you did my pa. You can't goad me into admitting anything," he jeered softly. "That ain't my rope . . . and you can't prove otherwise."

"That's where you're wrong, Culley." The saddle leather groaned as Chase shifted his weight, leaning forward to cross his arms on the saddle horn. "I not only *can* prove it, but I have. We matched that nylon rope we found around the neck of the stallion you hanged with the rope off a spool in town—rope from the same spool that Michels sold you a length from just a month ago. Isn't that right, Nate?" He directed the question to the aging foreman positioned at his left rear side.

"That's a fact." Nate nodded as if he knew what Chase was talking about.

Culley's gaze darted frantically from Chase to the cowboy. "That's a lie!"

"Who's lying?" Chase challenged him. "You shouldn't have left the evidence behind. Didn't you have the stomach to wait around while the horse strangled to death so you could retrieve your rope?"

"I tell you it isn't my rope!" he insisted wildly. "I took it out of the tack room! You don't think I'm dumb enough to use my own rope to hang that stallion, do you?"

"I admit you showed a lot more brains when you wrapped the barbed wire around that calf's neck. It looked like an accident to someone who wouldn't know any better," Chase said.

Culley let out a silent laugh of malicious delight. "I knew you'd get the message I left—nine little twists of the wire."

Chase's jaw was clenched in a rock-hard line. "A fella has to be sick to go around hanging animals." The two men on the ground had silently moved closer to the thin, black-haired man while Chase was talking. "Wouldn't you agree, Doc?" The sudden inclusion of the two spectators in the conversation took Culley by surprise. In his hatred for Chase, he'd overlooked them, forgetting that they, too, were listening to what was said. After the first sharp glance at the flanking pair, a mottled rage crept up Culley's neck to turn his face red.

"You set me up, you bastard!" The snarling denunciation came the instant Culley realized a confession had been tricked out of him. "You always think you're so damned smart."

"No, you do. That was your mistake, Culley," Chase replied.

"You'll be sorry for this." His hatred, so consistent and unwavering, began to shake him even as a smugness entered his expression. "What can they hold me on? Destruction of Calder property?" he taunted. "So maybe I'll have to pay a fine and spend a couple of days in jail. So what?"

"So . . . while you're in jail for those couple of days, the sheriff is going to arrange for a psychiatric examination. You're too dangerous to be walking around free. I'm going to see that you're put away, Culley," Chase said, "before that warped mind of yours gets somebody hurt."

"I ain't crazy. They can't keep me."

"They can, and they will." He looked into those mad green eyes. "Personally, I wouldn't care if they threw away the key and you rotted in hell. So just be damned glad you're Maggie's brother."

The sheriff moved forward to take Culley's arm and lead him away. "Let's go, Culley." Culley made a brief attempt to shake away the hand on his arm, but Doc Barlow came up on his other side, his benign influence quieting the rebellion.

"You need help, some time to rest," Doc said. "We'll see that you get it."

Culley stood his ground for a minute, not resisting, but not yielding to be led away. His half-crazed laugh ran up the scale as he eyed Chase. "I really had you running scared, didn't I? Now you think that by getting rid of me it will be all over." Again came the laugh. "I'll make you a bet that before this week is out your son will be dead. Maybe he's dying right now while you're here. I'd like that."

An icy fire burned within Chase as all mercy went out of him, crowding the restraining image of Maggie from his mind. With cold determination, he walked his horse to the man, turning his mouth until he was looking straight down into the face of his taunter.

"Who's in this with you?" There was a ruthless quality to the harsh glare of his look, and the demand soft enough to be dangerous. A threat had been made against his son's life. It would not go unanswered.

"Wouldn't you like to know?" Culley replied with a jeering smugness. "Wouldn't you like to know who put that hangman's noose on your desk? I think he hates you almost as much as I do."

"Is it Tucker? Who?" His horse sidestepped closer, tossing its head at the tension of its rider.

"That gutless traitor? Keep guessing." Culley was enjoying the angry fear his remark had aroused. "Maybe I'll tell you when you get it right."

His lips disappeared into the thinning line of his mouth. "By God, I'll have his name from you if I have to reach inside your throat and tear it out!" A gleam of satisfaction came into Culley's eyes and Chase realized he would not get his answer by using force. With an effort, he took hold of his temper and drew back, changing his tactics. "It's all a lie, isn't it? You don't have a partner in this. Nobody would be fool enough to team up with a man who's mentally deranged. I don't know why I'm wasting my time listening to a raving lunatic like you."

As she closed the east gate to the north range, Maggie glanced again at the pickup truck and empty horse trailer parked along the ranch road. Turning in the saddle, she scanned the rolling terrain for a sign of the truck's occupants. This far from The Homestead, her presence was bound to raise questions if she was seen by any Triple C riders. She preferred that Chase not find out that she was making one last appeal to Culley to bring an end to this attempt to terrorize them.

The endless sky stretched over the wild plains, empty of any rider, save herself. She sent her horse forward at a canter, angling north toward the Shamrock boundary. She sat in the saddle with a born sureness, a slim extension of her horse. There was a firm line to her lips and a self-assurance in the way she held her head, a driving directness in her attitude.

For so long she had lived with uncertainty, filled with question for what tomorrow held and holding on to Chase's strength. That wasn't her nature. With the morning's decision to face her brother and take a stand against him, her old self-reliance returned. It was a relief not to shy away from the looming shadows of reality. She and Chase would survive this—or they wouldn't, but her resolve to bring the situation to a climax didn't waver. She was cool and strong; the land had bred this into her, as it had bred it into Chase. There was trouble ahead, and she had to face it squarely without leaning on Chase.

The gate to the fenced range was lost from sight. Off to her left, a cow bellowed as Maggie skirted the crown of a hill. She glanced toward the sound, automatically checking her horse to a trot. Motion caught her eye first as a range cow bolted away from a clump of willows to race over the grassy meadows with a calf at its side. Her glance sought the cause for the cow's hasty retreat, and Maggie noticed the two saddled horses standing in the shade of the trees. It was another second before she saw the two riders on the ground and recognized Ty as one of them. On its own, her horse slowed to a walk as she watched her son stow something in the rear pouch of one of his saddlebags. The second rider walked up behind him and raised his arm, bringing it down suddenly. In what seemed to be slow motion, Ty pitched forward against his horse; then his legs slowly buckled and he crumpled to the ground. Gradually it dawned on her that he'd been hit over the head and knocked unconscious.

Maggie's reaction was instantaneous. She spurred her horse and changed its course toward the small clump of trees. She gave full rein to her temper. The thunder of her horse's hooves turned the cowboy's head in her direction. He had grabbed Ty's feet and started to drag him around; then he saw her and stopped, to stand erect. He stepped forward to catch the bridle of her horse as it slid to a stop and Maggie bailed out of the saddle.

"You got here just at the right moment, Maggie. Ty fell and hit his head," Buck Haskell explained with an anxious look of concern. "I was trying to lift him into the saddle. You can give me a hand."

"He didn't fall! You hit him over the head!" she accused in a fiery burst of anger. "I saw you!" She started to push her way by him to attend to her son, but he caught her arms to stop her. Her green eyes flashed him a killing glance. "Take your hands off me! This stupidity has gone too far! And I don't give a damn what the reasons for it might be!"

She attempted to shrug out of his hold with an angry twist of her shoulders, but his grip tightened. The easygoing expression that usually masked his face fell away. In its stead, Maggie saw deadly cunning in his blue eyes. Her primitive instincts recognized the presence of danger.

"So you saw me hit him." His cold smile chilled her and she stopped struggling. "In that case, I guess I'll just have to speed up my timetable and get rid of both of you at the same time."

"What are you talking about?" Until that moment, she had been ready to dismiss this as another hazing incident. A cold chill danced through her blood as she realized differently.

"Why, I was going to wait a couple of weeks before I arranged for your disappearance. You were going to be so overwrought over the death of your son that you just took off for parts unknown." His grin became menacing, cold and calculating.

Her glance flashed to her unconscious son. "Ty—" she began, then felt a tremor of relief when she saw the rise and fall of his chest. He was alive.

"No, he isn't dead yet." Buck followed her thoughts. "The greenhorn kid is going to get his foot caught in the stirrup when his horse spooks at a rattlesnake. I'm going to do my darnedest to help him, but he'll get dragged to death before I can catch his horse." He adopted a look of mock regret and anguish. "I'll tell Chase how it was all my fault, and blame myself for not being able to save him. I'll cry and beg him to forgive me, tell him how terrible I feel."

Maggie felt the curdling of fear in her stomach. She could almost see the scene he was describing. No matter how great his grief, Chase would never blame Buck—would never guess.

"You won't get away with it now. I know about it, so it won't work."

"It will work," he insisted confidently. "I admit it might look suspicious for you to disappear the same day your son is killed in a ranch accident. But even if they suspect foul play, Chase is going to blame your crazy brother. You should never have come back, Maggie."

"Why? Why do you want to kill us?" She strained against the grip of his hands, pulling back as she searched his face for a reason.

"Because the Triple C is going to be mine. If you hadn't come back, Chase would have made me his heir, left me control of the ranch—just the way it should have been from the beginning. I had him convinced of it until you showed up with that bastard of yours." His upper lip trembled on the edge of a snarling hatred. With a rough shove, he pushed her toward his tethered horse. A coiled rope was looped around his saddle horn. Before Maggie could fully recover her balance and elude him, he had grabbed the rope and slipped the noose around her wrist, pulled it snug to tie her hands together. The impulse to fight him rose and was immediately squelched by the glimpse of Ty stirring behind him. Her priority changed and she submitted without a struggle in order to keep Buck distracted while Ty regained consciousness.

"You're responsible for the death of the stallion and that calf, aren't you?" she accused to keep him talking and cover any sound Ty might make as he came to.

"No." He grinned at her, snugging the rope until it bit into her flesh. "Your brother's visit on your wedding night proved to be opportune. We discovered that we both wanted the same thing when I was 'escorting' him off the ranch. We decided to team up."

"That's a lie," she denied. "Culley isn't interested in owning the Triple C."

"Let's say that we both want to see Chase dead and in his grave. We just have different reasons for wanting it. Your brother wants to see every Calder wiped off the face of the earth, and I want the ranch. We just want to have some fun with him first, give him some misery," he taunted. "It really shook him up when he saw that stallion of his old man's hanging from that stable beam. Your brother is really looking forward to the day when he can hang

Chase and call it suicide. Culley told me about your pa and how he died. It's poetic justice for Chase to go the same way."

"I don't believe you." She saw Ty's arm move jerkily, half-lifting it to his head as he started coming around. She talked louder, trying to give her son a warning. "You plan to kill Ty and me. And you expect me to believe that my brother approves of this?"

"Your brother doesn't know about my plans for you. He'll think you disappeared, just like everyone else will. Or else he'll figure that Chase killed you. Nobody will find your body. You're just going to vanish without a trace. It doesn't matter to Culley that the kid is his nephew. He's a Calder first."

She didn't dare look at Ty and possibly draw Buck's attention to him. Out of the corner of her eye, she was aware that he was pushing carefully and quietly to his feet, making very little noise. Her pulse was racing. She was afraid he was going to try something foolish, like attempting to overpower Buck and rescue her. She tried to subtly send Ty a message.

"You won't get away with this, Buck. Chase will find out somehow. Somebody will tell him, get word to him somehow," she insisted, and Ty hesitated, poised beside his saddled horse.

Buck frowned at her. "Who would tell him? Nobody knows. You're as loony as your brother."

"You're the one who's crazy if you think you won't get caught." As Ty put his weight into the stirrup, the saddle leather creaked. An instantly alert Buck spun toward the sound. For an indecisive second, Ty sat motionless in the saddle. Maggie threw herself at Buck, tangling her legs with his to trip them both to the ground. "Go, Ty! Ride for help!" she yelled, and had a glimpse of him spurring his horse away from them before Buck kicked her out of his way. With a grunt of pain, she was sent rolling off him as he scrambled to his feet. He took one step after the fleeing horse and rider, already in full stride and lengthening the distance, then raced to his saddled horse to tug his rifle free of its leather scabbard. Buck looked toward his target but didn't bother to bring the rifle to his shoulder.

He gave Maggie a grimly mocking look as she staggered to her feet, hampered by her wrists, tied in front of her. "It was a nice try, Maggie, but you only postponed the inevitable. The kid isn't going to find any help," he jeered, "not in that direction." With a sinking heart, Maggie realized that the horse and rider were streaking north. "In ten minutes he'll be lost. I won't have any trouble finding him. This just re-arranges things. A fella's gotta stay flexible. I'll work it the other way around—dispose of you now, then hunt down the kid. The result's the same."

Chapter XXXVI

Less than three miles from the scene, the sight of a cottonwood and willow barrier forced Ty to rein his puffing horse to a halt. Through the thick-leaved limbs, he had a glimpse of sunshine glittering on the smooth surface of water and realized he was lost. They had crossed no river.

It was three o'clock and his shadow lay on the grass to his right. The discovery that he'd incorrectly ridden north brought a groan of despair. The pickup was to the east—the pickup, with its citizen's-band radio and the rifle in the rear window rack. He reined his horse to the right to put the sun at his back and kicked it into a reluctant gallop.

Water splashed, followed by the grunts of horses laboring up a bank and the groan of saddle leather and jangle of bridle chains. Ty almost cried aloud with relief when he saw the quartet of riders gallop into view with his father at the head. His hoarse shout pulled them to a halt, their horses plunging excitedly when he approached.

"Where's Buck?" His father's question was urgent and demanding.

Ty waved a hand to the south. "He's got Mom. He's going to kill her, I think." And he breathlessly explained the little he'd overheard and noticed how white his father seemed beneath the layers of tan. Yet none of the information appeared to startle him.

"Show us where you left them," Chase ordered. He loosened

371

the flap securing his rifle in the scabbard and pulled it free. The
trio of riders followed suit.

Her heart was pounding in her chest, but she was thinking
clearly. The more time she gave Ty to get away, the longer it
would take for Buck to find him, which strengthened the chance
that someone from the ranch would stumble across them. The
galloping hooves of Ty's horse faded from her hearing as she lifted
her gaze from the rifle muzzle in Buck's hands. She had to keep
him talking.

"You aren't going to get away with this. Somewhere you'll slip
up. Look at what already has gone wrong. Nothing is going the
way you planned." She tried to puncture his confidence, make him
hesitate.

"I've gone too far to turn back now." He shrugged and the rifle
barrel swung away from her. "I know how to cover my tracks."

"When Chase finds out I'm missing, he'll turn this place upside
down looking for me. How can you be sure there isn't something
of mine here that would be incriminating evidence?" Her hat was
on the ground, knocked off when she fell while tripping Buck.
"Are you positive that you can wipe out all traces?"

With the rifle cradled in the crook of his arm, the muzzle
pointed down, he scooped the hat off the ground and walked over
to push it on top of her head. "It'd be like trying to find a needle in
a haystack."

"How are you going to get rid of my body so no one will find it?"
She spoke matter-of-factly, not letting her imagination dwell on
the subject. "You're running out of time, Buck. If you dig a
shallow grave, you run the risk of a coyote uncovering it. My
bones will be found sooner or later, and people will start putting
two and two together and coming up with your name."

But he just smiled. "I'm not going to dig any grave for you. I'll
just dump your body in the river." He cocked his head to one side,
his attitude smug and mocking. "Gas makes a corpse float. Did
you know that? The insides bloat all up, making it buoyant. When
I was in prison, my cellmate was a half-breed Arapaho. He told me
about it and said you could keep a dead man from floating if you
disemboweled him and filled him with rocks." He paused, then
observed, "You're looking a little pale, Maggie. I admit it's a grisly
thought, but it is effective, very effective."

"You're crazy." She took a step backward, recoiling in a wary move and fighting the tremors that shook her.

His look became ugly. "You may think I'm crazy, but I'm not going to be cheated out of this ranch. It should have been mine from the beginning. I'm a better cowman, a better rider and roper. I'm better than Chase any day of the week. My mother, my grandparents—all the way back, it was their sweat and blood that built this ranch. I deserve to be in charge. It's my right as much as it is anyone's!" He walked over to grab the trailing reins of Maggie's grazing horse. His gesture was impatient as he motioned her over. "Get on your horse."

"No." She backed up another step. "I'm not going with you peaceably. And if you kill me here, then you'll have to carry me to the river. How would you explain the blood on the saddle?"

"Listen, you little bitch—" Buck took a step toward her just as her horse lifted its head and sent out a searching whicker to the right.

Maggie turned. "Chase!" She cried out his name as he crowned the jagged ridge of a hill and started down the slope at the head of a band of riders. She broke into a clumsy run, her coordination made awkward by the hands bound in front of her.

She had barely gone four feet when she was grabbed by the hair and jerked to a stop. An arm hooked around her neck, half-choking her, the toes of her boots barely scraping the ground. Her body acted as a shield for Buck, the barrel of the rifle lying diagonally across her front, the muzzle pointed up toward her head.

"Pull up, Chase!" Buck shouted the order. "That's close enough!"

Chase slid his horse to a plunging stop, the other riders spreading out behind him. "Let her go, Buck. You don't stand a chance against all of us."

Her fingers dug into Buck's arm, straining to ease the strangling pressure on her throat. There were too many. It was impossible for Buck to salvage any remnant of his plan now. She could feel his desperation hover on panic.

"Throw away that rifle!" Buck called. The blood bay shifted nervously under Chase as he tightened his one-handed grip on his rifle and debated his chances, but the risk was too great for

Maggie. He flung it into the tall grass. "Tell Nate and the others to ditch theirs."

"Do what he says," Chase growled under his breath and swung out of the saddle on the right side, stepping to the ground and facing Buck every minute. Behind him, he heard the thud of the rifles being dropped to the ground. "It's me you want, Buck, so let her go."

"If I let her go, I'm finished. We both know that. She's my ticket now."

Chase walked steadily toward them, each long stride shortening the distance. The blue of his chambray shirt was showing patches of sweat. The corners of his mouth were turned inward. There was a stillness about him, a containment, a cold fury held in check.

"What do you want, Buck?" Chase demanded in an unemotional tone. "Me? Money? A free ticket out of here? Name your price for Maggie's release."

"Stop right there!" It was a nervous bark that halted Chase ten feet away. "I'm no fool, Chase. You wouldn't live up to any bargain once I turn Maggie loose."

"I give you my word that I'll meet any of your terms." Then his voice rumbled from some deep, dark place inside. "But so help me God, if you harm her, you'll never be able to run far enough to get away from me. And I give you my word on that, too."

The arm relaxed around her throat, her feet coming fully to the ground again. Buck was breathing hard, an animal trapped with nowhere to hide. Out of the corner of her eye, Maggie saw him lick his lips nervously, thinking—all the time, thinking.

"What if I said you could have Maggie, if you signed the Triple C over to me? Is she worth that much to you?" Buck wanted to know. "Would you give me the ranch for her?"

"Yes." Chase stood completely motionless, his muscles coiled in readiness for an opening—any opening.

Buck unwrapped his arm from her neck and Maggie tried to take a step away from him, bring an end to her use as a shield. His hand closed around the underside of her arm, keeping her at his side.

"You're going to stay right here with me," he ordered. Then he added, in a menacing tone, "You make a move to leave and I'll shoot him. So I wouldn't do anything to upset me, because I'd just as soon kill him."

She believed him. At this point, he had nothing to lose. He'd kill them all if he thought he could get away with it. She stood rigidly beside him, her heart going out to Chase, so close, yet so far.

"I'll sign the ranch over to you the minute you turn Maggie loose, Buck," Chase repeated.

"You want her that bad, huh?" Buck taunted. "You really think she's worth that much, or are you just leading me on?"

"I give you my word." The promise was drawn through his teeth.

"I don't trust you, Chase." He backed off the conditions he'd set, doubting that they would be carried through. There were too many snags, too many repercussions. Chase would never let him get away with what he'd attempted. But he couldn't help wondering how far Chase would go, how far he could push him. "If you want Maggie, you'll have to beg me. Get down on your knees, Chase."

Maggie's lips parted in a silent outcry at the demand. Buck wanted Chase to grovel at his feet, strip his pride, and humiliate him in front of his wife and son, and the Triple C veterans. She looked at Chase, her mind flashing back to a time when she had wanted to see him on his knees begging for mercy.

A violent rage swept across Chase's face and vibrated through him. A searing rawness burned his insides, scraping at his throat. There was a loud roaring in his ears. Silhouetted against the sharply blue sky, he was the power on this chunk of earth, but he was utterly helpless.

"On your knees, Calder!" Buck spoke each word clearly and with taunting precision. "You want Maggie, then beg me!"

Anguish was in his brown eyes. He swayed and sank to one knee, his teeth bared against the effort. In that shocked instant, Maggie knew she couldn't stand it if Chase laid down everything for her. This abandoning of power and strength would live always in their memory. No matter how much he loved her, Chase would hate himself for the rest of his life for surrendering his self-respect. It was an ugly sacrifice that would ultimately split them.

"Chase! No! Don't!" She screamed the protest to stop him from going down on both knees before Buck.

Instinctively, she leaned forward. Buck roughly yanked her back, cursing her as he struck her across the mouth with the back of his hand. The blow sent her reeling backward to land heavily on the ground. There was a roaring sound like a charging range bull, followed by Buck's startled shout. When Maggie looked back, Chase was lunging for Buck. The explosion of the rifle shot deafened her ears and she cried out when Chase jerked. But he kept coming, right over the top of the rifle, knocking it aside and swinging at Buck. As she struggled to rise, she saw Buck fall. Then Chase was there, pulling her to her feet, half-carrying her and half-shielding her while he pushed her to safety amidst a shower of bullets that kicked up plumes of dust. Dazed by the confusion of muffled shouts and gunfire, it was a second before she realized the men had recovered their rifles and were peppering the area with gunshots to cover their escape.

An empty wash, eroded out of the rough land by centuries of rain, offered them shelter. They entered it, half-sliding and half-falling into the shallow ravine, and paused to rest against the bulwark of its bank. At Chase's muffled grunt of pain, Maggie turned her head to look at him. His features were contorted in a grimace as he wadded up the red kerchief from his pocket and pressed it to the spreading red stain on his right side.

"You've been shot!" She moved to investigate the seriousness of the wound.

"It's okay," he insisted tightly. "The bullet glanced off the ribs, probably broke a couple. He didn't have time to aim, but it would have taken more than a bullet to stop me from getting to you." He winced as he applied pressure to the wound to stem the flow of blood.

"Buck, is he—" A scattering of gunshots continued to punctuate the afternoon air.

"He made it to the trees. I saw him. The boys will take care of him." Chase glanced around to get his bearings. "Right now I just want to get you out of harm's way. This gully twists around the hill. We'll come out somewhere behind the boys."

"Ty—" she remembered.

"Don't worry. Nate will look after him."

"How did he find you?" Her heart was beginning to beat more normally. She tugged her blouse free from the waistband of her jeans and tore off a strip of the tail to make a bandage to take the place of the handkerchief.

"Your brother had just told us Buck was in on this with him. We were riding back from his place." He read the sharp question in her glance and smiled wanly. "Doc Barlow is taking Culley to a private mental institution where he can be treated."

"Thank you," she murmured and looked down, unable to express her gratitude that he had not only spared her brother, but was also seeing to it that he got help.

"Maggie." The soft urgency of his voice forestalled the hand carrying the folded square of blouse material to his wound. His left hand cupped her face, lifting her gaze. The deep gratitude in his eyes defied expression and she understood its cause.

"I never could have faced you again, Chase, if you had been brought to your knees because of me. It would have destroyed us. You shouldn't have let him bring you down—"

"Only on one knee, Maggie," he reminded her and held her look; a hunger for all the inexpressible things life had to offer them was in their eyes. She pressed a burning kiss to his mouth, appeasing that need for the time being. She straightened and busily lifted his bloodied hand away from the wound to lay the makeshift bandage against it. "We've been here long enough." He took it away from her and struggled to his feet. "Let's move out."

With Maggie leading the way, they crouched low to take full advantage of the ravine's protection and followed the twisting path of its gravel-strewn course. Occasionally they heard sounds to indicate the riders were still seeking out their quarry. The ground above the wash became rougher, a tangle of rock and brush.

A rustle of grass on the bank behind them was the only advance warning they had. They both turned as Buck vaulted down to the bed of the wash. His startled look told them he had no knowledge they were there. He tried to bring the barrel of his rifle around, but Chase reacted more quickly. With a swing of his arm, he knocked the rifle out of Buck's hand and hit him in the chest with his shoulder, pulling him to the ground with the weight of his body. Buck recovered instantly, bringing up his knees and driving them into Chase's ribs. Pain exploded, rolling Chase aside while Maggie scrambled for the rifle.

Reaching it, she immediately levered a bullet into the firing chamber and raised it to her shoulder. As she took aim on her target, she looked down the sights at Buck's shocked and motionless face, frozen by this glimpse of death, ever the coyote slinking through the dark shadows of life.

A hand thrust the rifle barrel skyward and twisted it from her grip. "No, Maggie." Chase stood in front of her. Before Buck could attempt to flee, two riders halted their horses on the ravine's rim, covering him with their guns. She looked at Chase, half-puzzled that he had stopped her. Within the grimness of his expression, there was the ache of sadness. "He's the closest I've ever come to having a brother," he explained quietly.

He had spared her brother, whom she loved despite everything, and was asking the same for himself. With a muted cry, she went into his arms, wrapping her own around his shoulders and pressing herself close to his side. Her face was buried against his shirt as his hand moved to once again apply pressure to his wound. She felt the brush of his lips against her hair and shuddered in relieved longing.

"Is Mom all right?" She heard Ty ask.

"She's fine. We're both fine," Chase answered.

> *A sky of promise,*
> *A sky so grand,*
> *This sky that carries*
> *The Calder brand.*

Discover the writer women everywhere are talking about—

Janet Dailey

whose contemporary romances win millions of new readers every day.

- _____ 43668 TOUCH THE WIND $2.95
- _____ 43665 THE ROGUE $2.95
- _____ 43667 RIDE THE THUNDER $2.95
- _____ 43666 NIGHTWAY $2.95
- _____ 97634 JANET DAILEY BOX SET $11.80

Janet Dailey—
She'll make you
believe in love again.

POCKET BOOKS
Department JDT
1230 Avenue of the Americas
New York, N.Y. 10020

Please send me the books I have checked above. I am enclosing $_____ (please add 50¢ to cover postage and handling, N.Y.S. and N.Y.C. residents please add appropriate sales tax). Send check or money order—no cash or C.O.D.s please. Allow six weeks for delivery.

NAME_____

ADDRESS_____

CITY_____STATE/ZIP_____